ALSO BY AMALIE HOWARD

DARING DUKES
The Princess Stakes
Rules for Heiresses
The Duke in Question

Any Duke in a Storm

Amalie Howard

Cover design by Alan Ayers

Published by Sourcebooks Casablanca, an imprint of Sourcebooks
P.O. Box 4410, Naperville, Illinois 60567–4410
(630) 961-3900
sourcebooks.com

Printed and bound in the United States of America.
OPM 10 9 8 7 6 5 4 3 2 1

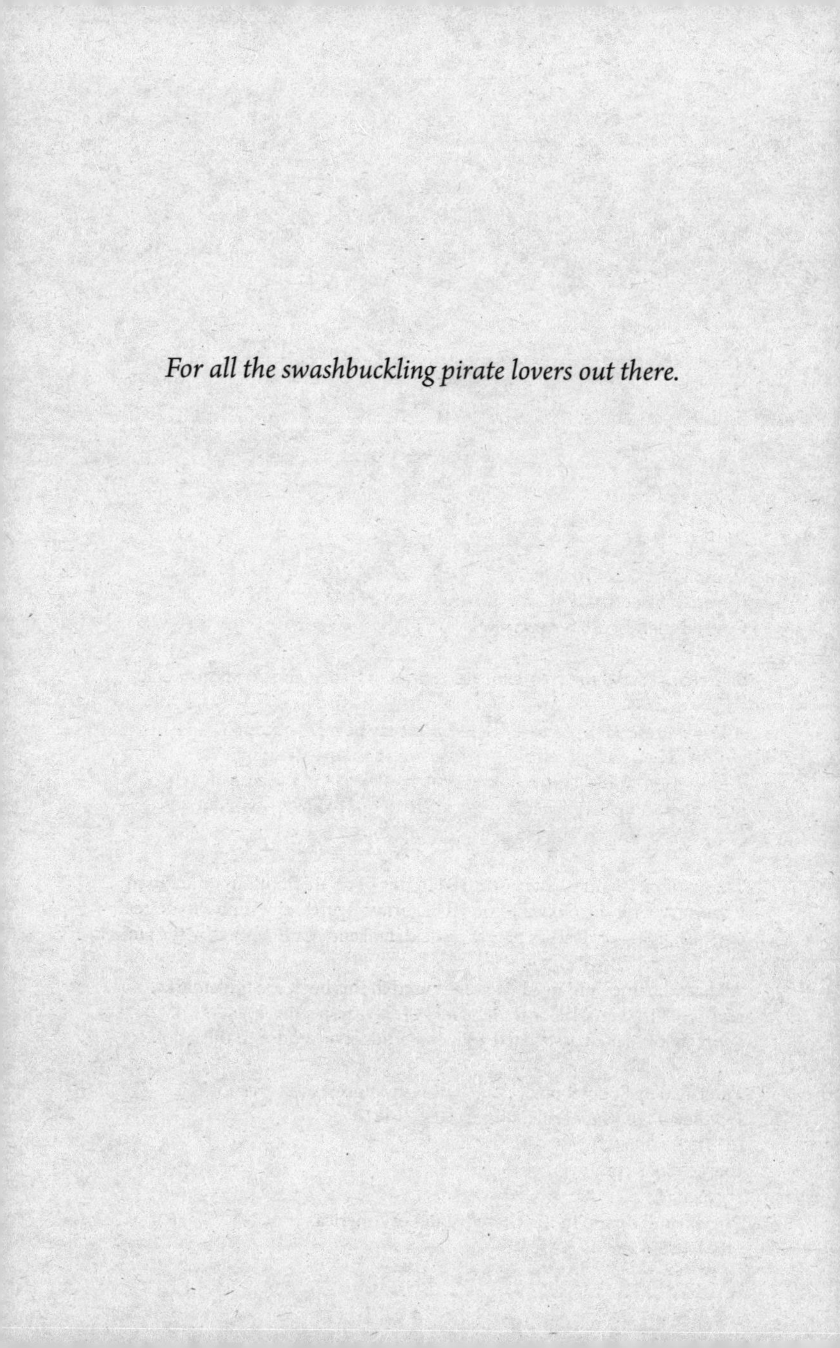

For all the swashbuckling pirate lovers out there.

One

British West Indies
1868

Raphael Saint snarled through the bars of the run-down prison, slamming his abraded hands into the rusted metal pipes. Five weeks and counting since he'd been betrayed and locked in this hellhole...his own shipmates turning on him for the promise of coin. He'd expected to be quietly dispatched within the first days, but time had stretched on from one week to the next.

He knew what they were waiting for—Captain Prince's arrival. Raphael knew without a doubt that the rather *un*-princely rat bastard, also known as his loathsome uncle, was behind all of this.

Charles Dubois was a two-faced turncoat.

Raphael had to escape...before Dubois arrived to gloat and make his death a personal vendetta.

Each day that passed made escape seem a more impossible task, but Raphael wasn't a man to stand idly by and wait for death. He bit his thumb at Death each time he sailed out of the path of a hurricane or took on the lawless cutthroats of the high seas who were intent on anarchy.

Men were always ready to stab him in the back. He had the scars to show for it, but he wasn't a man who gave up at the first sign of trouble. In fact, he welcomed it.

Though he was weak from the lack of food, Raphael kept his muscles strong with daily exercise in the cramped cell. Even when they were burning and quivering, he pushed himself more. Made himself eat the thin gruel his keepers shoved into his cell twice daily. Bided his time. The opportunity would present itself, and when it did, he would be ready.

Raphael ran through his exercises again, running in place to get his heart pumping. When he was through the repetitions and coated in sweat, he sat on the edge of his thin straw-filled pallet and peered upward. The sliver of a window near the high, bricked ceiling let in some golden and red light that told him it was nearly late evening. He had no idea what day it was as the hours had started to converge after enough time had passed, but keeping track was necessary. He slept when it was dark and kept his body and mind honed when it was daylight.

"Time for your bath, yer lordship," a nasal voice called out.

Raphael bristled with irritation, but stood and stripped. Grime and grease were caked onto his skin and his scalp itched. He was lucky if his "baths" came once a week, but at least they kept him feeling somewhat human.

"Top of the mornin' to ya, Monsieur le Duc," Jimmy went on, butchering the pronunciation as he always did, the last part of that sounding like *monshoe lah dook*.

Raphael exhaled a derisive snort at the address. Yes,

it was his title—a disgraced title. Louis-Napoléon himself had granted it to his father as a victory title and then stripped away his lands on the words of a liar—but the men in his line of work used it like an insult. Raphael supposed it was.

Then again, he didn't give a shit about being a duke. If it wasn't a matter of his family's honor, he'd stay far away from Paris. He wouldn't think twice about returning and attempting to clear his father's name. But vengeance boiled in his blood and his uncle had to pay.

Jimmy screwed up his ugly countenance and tutted. "All of it now," he said, when Raphael stood in his filthy smallclothes that used to be white linen but were now dingy and gray.

"Get on with it, Jimmy," he snarled back, irritated at being treated like a dog.

The man laughed, baring rotted teeth. "Got a treat for ya today, since you'll have a visitor soon and he wants ya nice and sparklin'-like."

Raphael blinked at that news as the narrowest sliver of soap was thrown through the bars. That could only mean one thing: his time was running out. If Dubois was on his way here, then his window of opportunity was closing.

Think, you big bastard!

He'd gone through every inch of his cell, but the walls were brick and the floor packed dirt. The ditch in the corner that served as a latrine was a narrow hole in the ground. His pallet was nothing but woven twill and straw. All outer layers and his boots had been taken, and all he had were the soiled shirt and trousers in a pile. He'd even tried to use the bowls that his gruel came in to fashion a pick for the ancient lock, but the brittle clay shattered each time. Jimmy had burst into laughter when he'd seen the broken dishes.

His eyes narrowed on the old guard. Jimmy had to have something on him that Raphael could use! The trick would be to get him close enough to the bars, but the man wisely never came within reach.

"Ready?" Jimmy said. "Come to the edge, *Dook*."

Obeying, Raphael shivered as the first bucket of cold water doused him from head to toe, and blinked the streams out of his eyes as the second came on the heels of the first. Knowing that he had to be quick, he made short work of running the harsh soap through his wet hair first, and wincing at the sight of the gray suds dripping down his bare chest. Forgoing his pride, he turned and stripped out of the smalls. It was a small price to pay for being clean.

He scrubbed lower when he heard Jimmy shuffle out, presumably to get more buckets of water for the rinsing. When he was done, he used the edge of his tattered shirt to scrub his teeth, grimacing at the bitter taste of the soap. Thankfully, his warden returned with refilled buckets and repeated the process of dousing him from head to toe, before shoving a thin strip of toweling and a pile of fancy clothing through the bars.

Raphael frowned at the clothes: trousers, a frilled shirt, and even a finely milled coat with pewter buttons.

"Time to look pretty," Jimmy crowed. "I've a special surprise for yer last supper."

Last supper? Well, of course it might very well be. His luck had been on borrowed time for days now. He wondered what Dubois's game was. Did he mean to turn him over to the American Treasury Department and not kill him? Show him up in front of his crew? Spin a yarn of lies about his supposed sins and betrayal of their smugglers' code? Commit him to an asylum as Dubois had his own brother?

Raphael had too much support from his men—ones loyal to him—for any accusations to truly stick. But many of those men weren't here. The ones here were only loyal to deep pockets and the promise of pay. Raphael did not blame them. One had to feed one's family, and times were thin.

In silence, he dried himself and dressed in the ill-fitting but tasteful clothes. He was a big man, and most of his apparel had to be cut to his frame, but anything was better than the filthy rags he'd worn before.

Jimmy returned with a steaming dish in his hand and sketched a ridiculous bow before shunting the bowl in under the bars. It wasn't the usual fare of colorless, lumpy gruel. Whole pieces of cooked fowl sat in a fragrant broth over thick dumplings. Raphael's mouth watered and his belly yowled with hunger, but he forced himself not to descend on the meal like a rabid beast.

Jimmy wasn't stupid enough to give him a fork, but this was a windfall he'd not lose.

Raphael waited until the man left before filling his belly, savoring each bite, and then carefully pulling the meat from the bones of the chicken leg and wing. His fingers shook. He might not have any metal on hand to fashion a picklock, but a shard of bone could do just as well. When he was finished and the bones were stripped clean, he had three somewhat sturdy pieces. He took one and ground it against the brick until it was flat and curved, painstakingly working so it didn't split or snap.

When he was ready, he approached the warded lock of the gate. The latch was old, just like this place, and probably would not take much. Then again, it was old iron and might shatter his makeshift key. Raphael inhaled a deep breath and exhaled it slowly.

"Now or never," he mumbled.

Using the curved piece, he stuck it in the top part of the keyhole and wiggled it around until he could feel the slight pressure of the internal ward. *There.* Without losing his grip, he took the second piece and inserted it just below. Jiggling it up and down, he tried to engage the simple locking mechanism. Almost there… Suddenly, the bone bowed in his hands and he froze, but it was too late. It snapped in half.

"Merde!"

Discarding the broken piece while still holding on to the curved shard, he reached for the third and final spindle of bone he'd fashioned and repeated the process. As slow as molasses this time. His hands went numb with strain, sweat beading along his spine, when he inserted the shard and gently turned clockwise.

Don't break, don't break, don't break.

The sound of grating iron filled his ears as the lock

disengaged and the cell door whined open a sliver of a crack. Raphael didn't stop to celebrate his victory. He exited, grabbed his boots and hat from where they'd been tossed in a corner, and ran toward a low window. The front and back entrances would be guarded, and he had no intention of being caught. He grabbed the bottle of rum on the desk and took a healthy swig, letting a good amount splash his clean coat with a wince.

Better to be seen as a drunk than an escaped convict.

Since he couldn't get to his own ships in the harbor, which would be empty of crew, he'd have to find a way off this island somewhere else. He was almost seen twice as he skulked through the back-alley streets and crept toward the wharves. The late-evening shadows helped keep him hidden. Skirting the main street where the most bustling taverns were, he kept his head down and stumbled every few steps like a sot. When he reached the docks, he slowed his pace and tried not to seem as though he were a fugitive.

Instead, Raphael squared his shoulders and strolled with the confidence of a king toward a sleek-looking frigate that was loading provisions and supplies. That one would likely be his best bet, since its crew was preparing to leave port. He pasted on a smile, reached for his long-forgotten charm, and swaggered to the gangway. He noticed a passing boatswain loaded down with crates and purposefully blocked his way. "Oh, sorry, mate. Need help?"

A muffled voice that sounded female came through the boxes. "No thanks. If you're here for the sailing master position, Estelle's on the foredeck."

Raphael couldn't help his grin. Apparently, the Fates hadn't abandoned him after all.

Now he just needed to put on a convincing show.

Lady Lisbeth Medford, Countess of Waterstone and current espionage agent of the American Treasury, hoped she wasn't going to get blown to pieces. The fuses were fairly long, thank goodness. A short fuse was an accident waiting to happen, and she'd heard enough horror stories with the chemical she was using. As a blasting agent, nitroglycerin wasn't the most stable. Two years ago, an explosion of the leaking liquid chemical had leveled a building and killed fifteen Wells Fargo workers in San Francisco. While black powder was undoubtedly safer, nitroglycerin worked when wet, which was critical for her current purposes.

Her fingers trembled as she moved to ignite the twined length of the fuses that connected the two ships moored next to each other in the harbor. She'd planted explosives on each ship's hull, which would hopefully generate a blast big enough to take down both. This wasn't one of her smarter decisions, but she'd been found out anyway, and she couldn't leave the ships fit enough to chase after her when she left port. And she certainly wasn't going to let ships of smuggled cargo fill the coffers of a bunch of lawless criminals.

They aren't all lawless.

Lisbeth shook her head hard. Most of them were,

however, and this wasn't the time to grow a bleeding heart. Smuggling was a delicate business, with powers shifting as easily as fortunes did. If one didn't want a knife lodged in one's back, one had to be ruthless. This was a hard world and she was not a soft miss... At least her current identity, Bonnie Bess, wasn't.

No, Bonnie Bess was made of salt, vinegar, and bloodthirsty, jagged edges. Known for having a blade on her at all times, the cutthroat captain wasn't a woman to be trifled with, as many had learned through painful, if not deadly lessons. But now...Bonnie Bess was in real trouble. The kind of trouble that would tell no tales because they'd be rotting at the bottom of the sea. Her identity had been compromised.

Damn and blast that meddling, skulking boy!

Lisbeth let out an angry huff. There was no time to wallow and curse Davy. It was her own fault. She'd blow up the ships, run, and figure out her next steps. A disguise of some kind and another way back into the smuggling ring she'd been infiltrating. Damn her eyes, she'd been *so* close to breaching the inner circle of the notorious smuggler known as Captain Prince. She gritted her teeth in frustration and quelled her spiking nerves.

Was she doing the right thing by destroying Prince's ships? The combined worth of the cargo in each hold had to be tens of thousands of dollars. Lisbeth frowned, thinking of all the stuffed crates she'd spied in the hull. Maybe more. Criminals shouldn't get off scot-free, and she knew for a fact these were smuggled goods and not honest trade.

Besides, she *had* to do this to save her own neck.

Not that she was any different, considering the contraband on her own ship, but that was sanctioned. Smuggling was the price of the mission and it was *necessary* for her to play the part. Then again, some of the men and women who worked on these vessels were only trying to feed their families and eke out a living. Disquiet roiled in her gut.

Stop it!

Lisbeth closed her eyes and wiped her sweaty palms on her trousers. The longer she took, the greater the risk of being discovered trying to sink the ships. Now *that* would warrant an immediate watery execution by the cold-blooded seadogs gambling in the nearby tavern.

Nearly two years' work to infiltrate a shipping group that she knew was part of a larger illegal ring, and she'd been a heartbeat away from working her way into the inner echelons, instead of being held to the outskirts. *Damn it!* She had no idea how Davy had found the papers from the American Treasury Department buried deep in the straw of her mattress. She'd received new instructions from the New York Customs Office and hadn't had time to destroy them.

Lisbeth should have disposed of the damned things the minute she'd read them, but she hadn't and that mistake was on her. The young boatswain couldn't read, she knew, but he also wasn't stupid. Those documents with their crests and stamps looked official. The connection wasn't much, but it was definitely enough to cause suspicion. Because why would *she*—a merchant's daughter and petty thief, and someone known as the vicious Bonnie Bess—be receiving orders from the American government?

Stupid, stupid, *stupid*!

Lisbeth had underestimated the boy's fascination with her. At first, she'd tolerated it, using him to get information on the movements of the men on the island—and thanks to Davy, she'd known that the mysterious captain who called himself the Prince was en route here—but lately, the boy seemed to be everywhere. Even in her room, apparently, snooping through her private belongings.

"Bess! Where are you?" came the familiar high-pitched voice from the end of the dock.

"God damn my hide," Lisbeth snarled under her breath. If that infatuated goosecap died in the explosion because of her, she wouldn't be able to live with herself. He might be a pain in her arse, but he was just a child. The fuse would give her a handful of seconds to run down the wharf to safety, but if he remained close, he would be hurt. Clearly, the besotted fool had followed her. *Again.*

"What do you want, Davy?" she replied, though not loudly. The two ships were unoccupied as far as she knew, but she didn't want to attract attention. Destroying illicit cargo and thwarting pursuit were one thing; killing people in cold blood was another.

"Cap'n Delaney is looking for you," he called back.

Could mean anything, she told herself, though a slither snaked down her spine.

"Very well. Tell him I'll be along shortly."

She strained to hear any footsteps but none came. "Cap'n said now," the boy insisted. "He wants to talk."

Christ up a ship pole. That could mean anything, but an urgent summons was ominous. *Think, Lisbeth!*

"Yes, I know, Davy. I'm just getting a surprise for you. A special treasure for a good friend. Wait for me near my quarters, will you? I want you to be surprised. I won't be long, just a couple of minutes for me to get it ready." She could practically hear his brain ticking over. "I promise it will be worth it and then we can both go to the tavern."

"A treasure for me?"

"You bet. A splendid one." Lisbeth swallowed the knot of guilt in her throat. Playing on his fixation was a shitty thing to do, but she had no choice, not if she hoped to make it back to her ship and save his life in the process. "You're going to love it."

She crossed two of her fingers and held her breath.

"I'll wait there."

Thumping footsteps faded away and she exhaled a sigh of relief. She counted to a hundred silently in her head, giving the boatswain enough time to get out of range. She truly didn't want any harm to come to him. He was barely seventeen—a grown man by many standards, but green just the same.

It was now or never. Lisbeth lit the fuses, threw up a hasty prayer to the heavens, and took off running. Her muscles burned, her lungs ached in her chest, but she had to get as far away as possible before they ignited.

Explosives weren't her favorite, especially since another agent and friend had lost an entire hand with a similar concoction some time ago.

Breathing hard, she raced to the other end of the dock, counting the seconds. She grabbed the stuffed rucksack she'd left in a hollow at the end of the dock with her clothes, notes she'd compiled, and a stash of maps she'd drawn. The rest of her belongings were on her ship… which hopefully Estelle had ready to depart. Her quartermaster was unfailingly precise with orders.

A small trickle of unease made Lisbeth frown as the seconds mounted with each stride. The chemical in the small vials should have exploded by now, unless somehow the fuse went out. No, they were long and maybe they were damp from the sea air. She'd miscounted the time, that was it. But the further away she got, the more her stomach dropped.

Curse her miserable luck!

It didn't matter. She still had time to get away. They'd come after her once they realized her ship was gone, but that could not be helped. She'd lose any pursuers on the sea. She'd done it before and she could do it again.

Her eyes darted to the far end of the dock where her ship, the *Syren,* was a sight for sore eyes. At the very least, she'd get back to New York and convince the Treasury Department to give her another chance. Time was running out and she would be extracted from her current post if she didn't have something tangible to show for her efforts. Twenty-three months was a long time, but she was in deep.

Too deep with too much to lose.

Her reputation. Her career. Everything she valued.

The whole point of this assignment was to capture one of the most disreputable smugglers in American history—Charles Dubois, the Prince of Smugglers—and bring him to justice. She was *so* close, and now she could feel nearly two years of toil slipping away like sand through her fingers.

Maybe she should stay and brazen her way through it.

Lisbeth gnawed her lip. It would be Davy's word against hers. And besides, the documents didn't have her fake identity—Bonnie Bess—on them. They cited the Countess of Waterstone. If push came to shove, she could say she found the letter on the street and thought it was important. She was accomplished at spinning a good lie if she had to.

With a snarled curse at her indecisiveness, Lisbeth slowed and glanced over her shoulder. Three minutes and counting, and the fucking fuse appeared to have failed. Perhaps she should return? Try again? Every instinct in her body cautioned against it. Someone could have seen her near the hulls of the ships. Turning back would only draw attention. Her heartbeats hammered between her ears like the sound of crashing waves. No, she couldn't risk it.

Stick to your plan. Escape, recover, reconsider.

Upping her pace, Lisbeth frowned as she closed in on the *Syren*. Shit! The ship was already leaving the dock. It must be minutes after midnight. Those were her instructions after all, and her quartermaster was, if anything, compliant to a fault. At midnight, sail out of port, even if she wasn't onboard. Lisbeth huffed a dark laugh. The one time she hoped the strict, rule-following Estelle wouldn't listen.

There was no hope for it… Lisbeth would have to run and make the jump, or stay and risk whatever it was Captain Delaney was summoning her for. Every well-honed instinct in her brain said it wasn't good and this was her last chance to get out of here unscathed. The *only* chance.

And her gut had never failed her.

She hauled a breath into her lungs, increased her speed until she got to the very edge of the wharf, and then launched herself through the air. Time sped up and slowed down at the same time, her body careening across the widening divide while her brain processed in slow motion.

Black water churned beneath her. God above, she wasn't going to make it! She was going to plummet into the depths of the sea, and she well knew the kind of sea creatures that came out at night. The moray eels in the cove were particularly vicious. Sharks would be, too. It wasn't a huge gap, about five or six feet, but every half second meant that her ship was pulling further away and out of reach. Seven feet was stretching it, eight would be a miracle, and nine would be impossible.

"You'll make it!" she grunted, but braced for the embrace of cold, dark, dangerous waters.

Luck, it seemed, hadn't been on her side all night.

Two

Raphael squinted at the ship's grim quartermaster who kept looking back toward the wharf as if expecting trouble and wondered if he'd made yet another terrible mistake. The fact that the second under the ship's captain was a woman had made him falter, but in his unpopular opinion, female smugglers were more than capable of being just as merciless as their male counterparts. Perhaps even more so. This one had a cutlass and two pistols strapped to her hips, and eyes that were sharp and hard. It had made him worry just a bit. He'd have better odds with a man who could be more easily fooled. Women tended to be more discerning.

Fortuitously or not, she'd hired him—*thank you, charm and false confidence*—but only after making him sweat with pointed questions about his experience reading charts and navigational skills. He was proficient in seafaring but had his own sailing masters on his ships, which meant he was out of practice. Since the only way off this godforsaken island was to board a vessel exiting the harbor in short order, which meant *this* ship, he'd had no choice but to obfuscate. Raphael hadn't even looked at the name of the ship. Then again, that didn't matter.

The only thing that mattered was the fact that it was leaving.

It helped that he was familiar with this particular inlet as well as the surrounding seas, at least enough to be hired as a passably competent sailing artist, as the pirates of old called it. In truth, he did not like navigating in the dead of night—there were too many things that could go wrong in the darkness—but a storm was brewing in the winds. He could smell it. Besides, he'd rather be out on the open seas with a chance to outrun a squall than stuck here on a very small island with his uncle who wanted him dead.

Dubois was the only one who knew about Raphael's ties to Tobago and that from time to time, he dropped off money and supplies to his relatives who lived on the island. Unfortunately, he hadn't counted on a mutiny…or being thrown into irons the second they'd put into port. He let out a growl. When he got his hands on his treacherous uncle, Raphael was going to throttle the man and feed his body to the sharks!

He could have boarded either of the two ships at the far end of the harbor—both of which were part of his merchant fleet and belonged to him—but sailing required a capable, and clearly loyal, crew. And the truth was he did not have the time to gather up enough new sailors he could trust to get them safely to sea…at least not here. They were probably all Delaney's men, and by default, his uncle's. Raphael would rather not be tricked and incarcerated again, thank you very much.

Live to see another day and all that.

"Estelle!"

He frowned as the faint cry reached his ears. Was that a bellow from the dock or the rising wind? A storm was definitely brewing, which made him want to make haste even faster, despite the late hour. He did not want to be stranded because the ship could not leave the inlet due to a reef made more dangerous by the incoming tide and rougher seas.

"Damn it, Estelle, you soulless witch, ease up!"

He frowned. Dieu, that was a *voice,* not in fact the sound of the billowing wind, and it sounded much closer now. Wasn't the quartermaster called Estelle? He strode to the stern where the gangway had been pulled aside and peered into the darkness toward the docks. Though he could barely differentiate between the shadows, one of them seemed to be thicker than the others.

Thicker and getting bigger. And person-sized.

What the *devil*?

Raphael barely had time to think before what looked like a small boy launched himself from the end of the wharf in his direction over six feet of open space. His lips twitched in admiration at the lad's sheer ballocks. Jumping that distance in the dark was no mean feat of courage.

Well, it was either courage or madness.

Either way, even if the boy succeeded, Raphael was certain that the surly, hard-as-granite quartermaster didn't have time for stowaways or extra mouths to feed. She had made it abundantly and sternly clear that *he* was a last resort and that he'd have half rations because of his size. No doubt this new arrival would be disappointed to learn that he'd have to swim back to the dock since Raphael wasn't giving up his spot!

He had barely locked his stance when the small, airborne mass hurtled onto the deck, rolled, and crashed into him where he stood. A tight cap flew off in the collision, and coils of pale hair tumbled into a chaotic cloud as the unexpected scent of orange blossoms and honey flew into his nostrils. He blinked in shock while his hands automatically reached out for purchase and he found his fingers full of a pleasantly rounded bosom.

An infuriated, savage curse had his eyes widening. "Get your filthy hands off me, you bloody cretin!"

He did and stepped back, even as several crew members cheered and whooped at the newcomer's entrance. "Who the hell are you?"

"The bloody captain," the virago who was most definitely *not* a boy snarled. "Who the *hell* are *you*?"

Raphael blinked in delayed shock. *This* was the ship's captain? His eyes took in her petite stature, at least compared to him, and the bold jut of her chin. She looked like a wrathful Viking warrior. "I'm your new sailing master," he replied, though to his horror it sounded more like a question than a statement.

Lip curling into a sneer, she glared at him. "The fuck you are."

He smirked at the foul oath dropping from that pair of perfectly plump lips, with a Cupid's bow on the upper, the only feature he could see beneath the tangled mass of wheat-colored tresses. "Sorry to say but I am," he said genially. "I was hired this very evening by a cheerful quartermaster who assured me that I'd be in excellent company on this here ship for the fair exchange of my services."

"Cheerful, is she?" she muttered and then rolled her eyes. "Estelle, turn this goddamned ship around," she bellowed, but the statuesque brunette with the uncompromising mien who had interrogated him was nowhere to be found. She was no longer on the quarterdeck where Raphael had seen her last.

Still panting for breath from her death-defying leap, the woman claiming to be captain shoved the damp locks out of her brow, and Raphael's eyes went even wider. Streaked, icy-blond, half-braided hair surrounded a heart-shaped face with a pert chin, a down-turned but full mouth, and a pair of sharp light eyes that shone with equal parts grit, loathing, and irritation.

His heart gave a sudden thump. Not what he was expecting at all. This part of Tobago, a port known for its smugglers, thieves, and generally an unsavory sort, attracted rough people of all sexes, but certainly not anyone who looked like *her*. He would have remembered.

Fiery Valkyries with murder in their eyes would command notice.

His heart thumped again.

Despite that and the utterly unwanted tug of attraction in his gut, he shrugged it away. His reaction—a very normal biological reaction—could have been because he'd had his hands full with her very feminine charms a moment ago. Considering he'd been locked in jail for weeks with no one but Jimmy for company, it was no wonder certain parts of him had perked up.

That furious stare of hers churned with savagery and displeasure, but he held his ground and kept his nascent desires in check. His instincts warned that, unlike the quartermaster, this lady might not be so easily charmed or hoodwinked. She was mesmerizing in the way a wild hawk was…like something that soared and hunted, and could never be caged. Or tamed.

"So you're truly the captain," he repeated. "Of this vessel."

She tilted her head backward to meet his stare with hers. In the guttering lamplight, a pair of changeling, siren's eyes leaned toward the darkest green of the ocean. "Did I bloody stutter?"

He opened his mouth to say no and shake his head meekly—because why would he risk his means of escape—but blurted out instead, "What were you running from just now?"

"None of your business. Estelle, come out, you lily-livered coward, and explain the meaning of this before I have your wretched carcass lashed!"

"Promises, promises," a voice called back, and Raphael blinked. That didn't sound like distress at all. In fact, it sounded…flirtatious.

The captain scowled as she peered around, her top teeth sinking into her plush bottom lip, and he felt that sensual jolt again. He ignored both it and the urge to lean forward to sample that full red lip himself. She'd probably lash *him* into strips if he tried, and he was quite fond of being in one piece. Best not to tangle with an infuriated woman who had the power to kick him off her ship and right back into irons.

The tall, stoic quartermaster strolled out from the port deck. "Cap'n."

"Don't 'Cap'n' me. What the deuce is this, Estelle?"

Estelle grunted, her face giving away nothing. "We needed a sailing master. There was no one else, and you demanded to leave in short order, if you recall. I didn't have time to find anyone more suitable. In fact, I'd lost hope we'd have anyone at all until he showed up."

"Showed up?" she bit out. "That's coincidental."

"Kismet," Estelle countered, and the captain hissed a curse he didn't quite catch. "He claims to know the routes and the sea, and has enough navigational knowledge to steer us out of here in one piece."

Damn right he knew the sea! Raphael puffed his chest, not missing the captain's narrowed gaze on that part of his anatomy, considering she was standing an arm's length away. It was a rather nice chest, if he did say so himself. He couldn't help it—he gave a subtle stretch. Her mouth flattened even more when he noticed her sidelong observation. Maybe his first impression had been off, and he *could* turn on the charm to flick that frown upside down.

Or not, as a long fierce hiss eased from compressed lips.

"He doesn't belong here," the sullen captain growled,

stalking across the deck to get in her quartermaster's face. "We're a vessel full of women and we have no idea who he is. He's a lowlife and a bottom-feeding pirate! Look at him. He's a distraction, he smells like a distillery, and he'll eat everything onboard."

Rude! Raphael blinked. He'd only eat his share, and surely he didn't smell that bad. He'd bathed! With soap! Then again, a bucket of water thrown at him once a week for two months didn't actually constitute bathing.

But what was that about a ship full of women? Now that he looked around at the faces and bodies crowding the deck, he saw that it was indeed true. More than half of the hard-faced sailors were female. Why did that seem unnervingly familiar...like something he should know? A strange feeling of foreboding slunk through his bones.

"Women who can fight as well as any men," the quartermaster replied, undeterred by the mortal threat in her captain's voice. "We need a sailing master, Bess. Unless you want to take our chances and guess our way out of here with that reef in the middle of the night. He knows the inlet."

That deep-water glower just about incinerated him. He could see the captain thinking and considering the alternative of taking her chances without him, and then fuming when she realized she couldn't. She glared at him. "You better not be lying about what you know, Pirate."

"I'm not, Valkyrie." And then he sucked in a breath as her eyes flared with renewed fury at the moniker, the foreboding he'd felt earlier spearing its claws into his gut as the name Estelle had called her echoed through him like a gong. “Wait, *Bess*?”

Dieu, was this ship the goddamned *Syren*? Of all the vessels he could have stumbled upon, he’d chosen this one! They’d gut him inside a week!

The captain’s grin was near feral, the corner of her mouth kicking up in a way that made his ballocks shrivel with apprehension. “Aye, Bonnie Bess. Perhaps you’ve heard of me?”

Raphael felt his jaw drop. *Everyone* with a pulse knew the name of the dreaded female captain taking the seafaring world by storm who made other captains look like bumbling, inept infants. Her ship was fast, she was deviously smart, and her crew—a disproportionately female crew that was uncommon in their walk of life—was unerringly steadfast. And, by all accounts, vicious.

Rumor had it she had an inflexible code of conduct on her ship. Assault of female crew or prisoners was punishable by beheading, and defectors had their ears removed. The island locals had even made up a sea shanty about Bonnie Bess. If he recalled correctly, there was a part about her skill with bullets and blades, and a razor-sharp tongue that enjoyed inflicting pain instead of pleasure—not that he was interested in validating any part of that.

He’d rather take his chances with the eels in the bay.

“Well, this has been—” The reply was ripped from his mouth by an explosion that lit up the darkness and made part of the dock crash into the ocean and a wave of debris flood toward them. He planted his feet to keep his balance even as shouts from the wharf in the distance followed when red and orange flames barreled upward into the night sky. "What the hell was that?" he shouted.

"Looks like a ship or half of the harbor!" one of the deckhands yelled as everyone scattered back to their posts. Raphael stared toward the south end of the wharves.

Merde. Were those *his* ships?

The quartermaster sprinted to the top deck and squinted through a narrow looking glass, but it was too far to tell and they were already nearly out of the cove. "I heard rumors of the revenue cutters sniffing around, Cap'n," one of the boatswains hollered. "The customs house has been clamping down on smugglers, following ships and seizing their cargo. Could be them."

Raphael clenched his jaw. No, not the cutters. His fucking uncle. Rage filled him, slow and savage. That sniveling, cowardly bastard would pay.

The dragon of a captain didn't reply, her lips tight as she peered toward the fire. Something like satisfaction burned in her eyes, fists clenching at her sides, but she didn't react to the billow of flames in the distance. "Get those boilers lit," she ordered, and the remaining crew scurried to do her bidding. "Sails up. Loosen the braces. If there's trouble, the faster we're out of here, the better." She turned to him, a wide grin on her face that was completely at odds with the violence in her stare. That broad, guileless smile should have been his first warning that he was in deep shit. "Time to show me what you can do."

Raphael had a decision to make. One that did not lead

him to jumping ship, not if that would put him back in irons. But it was obvious this captain did not want him here and he would be fish food if he didn't play his cards right. He glanced down at her, frowning at her ferocious expression. He could always predict a storm on the horizon, and this woman made a roaring hurricane look like light rain.

He raked a hand through his loose hair and cursed under his breath. He could do this.

Honestly, how bad could it be?

Lisbeth wanted to shove the annoyance of a brute off the side, but she had no choice now. She *needed* him to navigate the waters and this particular reef, especially now at night, and as fast as possible. This southwestern coast of Tobago and this specific part of the inlet were treacherous. She'd seen more than one ship torn up on the lethal five reef flats that lay beneath the seemingly placid waters of the cove.

She could take her chances, Lisbeth supposed, but she wouldn't risk the lives of her crew because her instincts about the man were firing. She could already tell that he had an ego on him, just by the smirk on his face, the slight growl of command in his voice, and that overconfident stance. This was a man used to being obeyed, not one who took orders. He was amiable and deferential because he wanted to be, not because that was his nature. He was going to be trouble; she could feel it in her bones.

And he reeked like a dockside tavern, which brought its own problems.

"Lift the aft sail, hard-a-starboard into the wind for a spell," the smelly pirate commanded Estelle, and Lisbeth watched as her quartermaster didn't hesitate to obey the directive from her position at the helm. Estelle wasn't one to trust easily, but for the moment it seemed like their new crewmate knew what he was doing. Time would tell. Something that they were in short supply of.

Faint shouts from the shore reached her ears. The fires had died down after the initial explosions. It would be a while before either of those ships were seaworthy, if they didn't sink outright. She didn't have any regrets. Well, other than not meeting the elusive Captain Prince, but that was a goal for another day. Lisbeth climbed to the quarterdeck of the stern and didn't relax until they'd successfully cleared the reefs and were out to sea.

"Did I convince you of my skills, Captain?" a deep voice said from behind her.

"Well enough, I suppose," she conceded. "We're not aground on a reef or at the bottom of the bay."

"So hard to please," he replied, that maddening lopsided smile still in place. "I see I have my work cut out for me."

Lisbeth whirled. "I beg your pardon?"

That smile faltered, curiosity glinting in his eyes at her choice of words, and she wanted to kick herself for sounding so missish and proper. A lowbrow sea captain would never speak thus, but something about him had her rattled. He was no one! A dock rat that Estelle had taken pity on, who'd been scheming for a ride out of Tobago.

"You *beg* my pardon? Somehow, I can't fathom you begging for anything," he remarked. "Rather the reverse—voicing your orders and expecting them to be obeyed."

God damn her eyes, why did everything he said sound like it held a double meaning? Lisbeth shoved the instant vision of him on his knees in wanton supplication from her mind. Bloody hell, she was nonsensical. It was his mouth, she decided. Even closed and silent, its wicked curve and perpetually quirked corner edges conveyed indecent promises of pleasure.

Her brow arched. "It's an expression, nothing more. Or perhaps you intend to be the grammar master instead of the sailing master?"

A pair of thick eyelashes dipped, though that aggravating smirk seemed to deepen. "I can be anything you wish, Captain."

Staring out to sea, Lisbeth scowled and ignored the way that rumbling baritone crept over her senses like a balmy ocean wind. It had been a long time since she felt attraction to a man. Not even her old retired spymaster partner and former husband of convenience, the Duke of Thornbury, had held her interest for long. Their past, very brief interactions had been of mutual accord as opposed to any true, grand passion, and he was happily remarried now.

The new Duchess of Thornbury was a spectacular woman. In fact, Lisbeth had joked to Thornbury that she could have easily been smitten with her, given half a chance. Alas, the duchess was as madly in love with her husband as he was with her, and Lisbeth could only hope to find such happiness for herself one day with a partner she could tolerate long enough. She exhaled a huff of amusement. One day when Charles Dubois was behind bars, at least, which at this rate might be never.

Two years ago, she'd met Estelle in a fancy dress shop in New York. She'd never tell the woman, who'd gone from dressmaker to shipmate to lover to trusted friend, but Lisbeth had pursued her on purpose. Per her information from the Treasury Department, Estelle had sailed to Europe on several ships, both as a sailor and dressmaker, and had a wealth of empirical knowledge. *And* she was a suspected smuggler of ladies' fabrics. Given Lisbeth's latest assignment to capture the Prince of Smugglers, she'd needed a crew, a person with knowledge of the customs houses, and a dependable quartermaster.

Estelle had instantly agreed. They had warmed each other's beds for the better part of a year, and then that, too, had lost its luster. Lisbeth had found over the years that her lovers had to catch her interest, and not just at a surface level. While she appreciated looks as much as anyone, compassion, intelligence, humor, and insight held more of a draw for her. Most of her romantic relationships seemed to have no legs to go the distance—not that she needed that sort of distraction in her profession. Lovers took *effort.*

And the truth was, her job left little space for affairs of the heart.

Lisbeth glanced over her shoulder at the sailing master, who stood there like a silent, obedient, pretty statue. His stark cheekbones stood out, with the gauntness of a half-starved creature. Her eyes narrowed. What kind of feral cur had Estelle welcomed onboard? He was tall, at least a half-a-foot taller than her, and rangy in build. Long inky hair fell in a thick windswept skein from his crown to his shoulders, framing that angular, sculpted face, the bottom half of a square jaw covered in a thick layer of dark scruff. Two gold hoops hung from his right ear, one at the top through his cartilage and one in his lobe.

He certainly had the look of a long-ago pirate. Dashing. Roguish. Definitely dodgy.

His eyes were an unusual gray color with a tawny starburst at the center, made even more striking by his rich brown skin, and his longish nose had a bump in it as though it'd been broken by a fist. Or a shovel. A girl could dream. But it was that mouth—curved into a crooked, ingratiating smile—that made her hackles rise. Everything seemed to be of perpetual amusement to him, those irises alight with something puckish that provoked and irritated. A staunch scoundrel through and through.

Lisbeth had to hand some credit to him, however. He'd passed muster to get them out of port safely, even if he did smell like he'd bathed in a vat of rum. Her crew drank like any other sailors on the sea, but liquor had its place, just like everything else. Drunk mariners made mistakes. Took liberties. Were too loose with their pride and their tongues.

Were *dangerous*.

She fastened her gaze to him. "Who are you? Who are your people?"

As if waiting for the inquiry, he stepped up beside her at the railing. The pungent smell of rum curled around her, but it was underscored by the salt of the sea and something that hinted of cedar and spice. "What do you wish to know, Captain?"

"All of it. Are you Caribbean? English? European? What brought you here?"

His lips quirked. "Once upon a time, there was a boy, now a man. A strapping, charming man, beloved by all. Especially bloodthirsty Vikings." She let out a low growl, brows slamming together, and the rotter threw up his hands in surrender with a chuckle that shouldn't have made her want to smile despite herself. "Very well, the boring version, then. I'm French by birth. My grandfather was one of the initial French settlers in Tobago and my grandmother was a free French Creole woman from Martinique. They had one child—my father—who in turn met and married a free islander from the neighboring island of Trinidad, one descended from East Indian and Amerindian parents. So the first and the last, I suppose."

That explained his singular looks, Lisbeth thought, and the sun-kissed brown hue of his complexion. She filed away the information he'd offered and let out a tiny mocking huff of laughter. "A sailing master without a ship is like a hermit crab without a shell. Whose ship were you on before? What brought you to Tobago, and why did you need to leave so suddenly?"

A muscle leaped to life in his jaw. The fact that he had to think about his answer made her pause, but Lisbeth waited. Everyone had secrets… She just had to make sure that his were no threat to her or her crew. The last thing she needed to have on her plate was a man with a complicated past bringing his tribulations to her ship. She was in enough of the stew because of Davy.

"A bit of business that went bad, I'm afraid," he replied. "Trusted the wrong sort and ended up stranded and shipless."

That sounded reasonable and plausible, but Lisbeth trusted no one she hadn't thoroughly investigated herself. "Where are you trying to get to?"

"Bermuda or Nassau, the second preferably."

She frowned, her brain sparking. What were the odds that a sailing master of his skill would choose either of those islands? Both places were strongholds of smuggling activity, ports she'd planned to infiltrate herself. Just like the upper-crust echelons of the British *ton*, the smuggling world had rules and hierarchy. Lisbeth would have worked her way in there earlier, but the inner circles were tight and one had to be someone of enough repute to be granted entry.

Could this marauder be her way back in? The hope was a stretch at best, or perhaps she was grasping at straws. Then again, Lisbeth was nearly out of options. It was either that or head back to New York empty-handed with her tail between her legs…and she did not like to fail.

No, when a door closed, a window could be pried open.

And this was a window. A very, very, *very* small window, but one nonetheless. What was the harm in seeing him to his destination? And if she discovered that he could be useful, well then that would be a boon.

"Nassau it is," she said. "And Pirate?"

Those mercurial gray eyes flashed. "Yes, Captain?"

"Keep your head down or you'll find yourself tossed out with the rest of the slop."

The corner of his mouth kicked up as he moistened the lower of the two sensuous curves, the drag of the tip of his tongue unmistakable. The bloody knave had the audacity to wink. "Aye, aye. I've been told I do my best work with my head down. You won't regret it."

Lisbeth's cheeks heated—in instant irritation, of course—but he was gone before she could reply and cut him down to size, the lewd images she'd shoved away earlier returning in full salacious force. She let out a growl of a laugh.

Blast her floundering luck, she was bloody regretting it already.

Three

From his vantage point in the foremast crow's nest, Raphael peeled and bit into a juicy yellow mango, observing the crew milling about down below. On his own vessels, everyone had their assigned roles for the most part, but this ship was a tightly run machine. Each sailor and boatswain knew their place. A flutter of admiration crossed his brain. Maybe there was something to be said for a female leader.

Though, he'd been wrong about the crew being largely female. Roughly half of the gunners and deckhands were male, and the surgeon was an enormous pale Englishman ironically called Smalls who was never too far from his mistress's side. Case in point…Smalls lounged near the frigate's paddle wheel, a dark gaze fastened to Raphael's position in the crow's-nest.

He didn't begrudge the man his instincts; Raphael was new, not that he meant the ship or its truculent captain any harm. The woman was nothing like he'd imagined. In his head from the stories he'd heard over the past couple of years, Bonnie Bess was a loud, brazen giantess who wore the tokens of her enemies—ears, teeth, fingers—all strung together in a gruesome necklace about her person to remind herself of those who had wronged her.

Her reputation for cunning, ruthlessness, and violence preceded her by a mile, and most sailors with half a brain knew to steer clear of the *Syren*, which was a ship that fired cannons first and asked questions later.

He was probably lucky. No one built a name like that without *some* grain of truth to it. Then again, most people underestimated him as well. They thought him a bumbling, sotted fool. While the act worked well to get him into places he wanted or helped him go unnoticed when he needed to be, it wasn't him in the least. He had *plans*… ones he meant to see through no matter the cost.

Raphael took a huge bite of his mango, wiping the sweet juice from his chin with one sleeve. All he had to do was survive the rest of the way.

Five fucking days.

That would get him to Nassau at their current speed. He'd successfully charted a path for the *Syren* to the Port of Bridgetown in Barbados, where they would ensure they had extra provisions and armament for the remaining four-day journey to Nassau. Strangely, the lethal captain had not argued with his suggestion, which made him wonder if she was evading something—or *someone*—as well. It would not do to find them in the middle of the Atlantic on the way to the island without some form of defense.

Raphael had taken a look at the *Syren* once the sun had started to rise on the horizon. Much like some of his own, it was a ship built for invisibility and speed with its slate-gray color, side-wheel steamer, two steam engines, and low hull. The forward deck right below him was built like a turtle's back to combat rough seas, and if he wasn't mistaken, the ship itself was constructed from a much lighter-gauged but reinforced steel. Right now, her engines used normal coal as fuel, the plumes of dark smoke rising from its funnels visible as the sun rose.

The *Syren* was a beauty. Svelte, sharp, and most definitely deadly for a frigate. Much like her captain. His gaze drifted back to the woman in question, who was standing on the quarterdeck and looking nothing like he'd been led to expect. Stories had a way of doing that, he supposed.

In the light of the budding dawn, tangled sun-streaked hair blew in the wind, a sennit hat tarred with black fabric to make it waterproof keeping the longer tendrils out of her face. She was deep in conversation with her quartermaster, her boots planted wide on the deck and one palm flicking over the pommel of a cutlass at her hip. An open, worn frock coat and loose trousers hid her female form, but tactile memory was a devil of a thing. His palm warmed and balled.

Bonnie Bess might have delightful curves, but the risk was much worse than any fleeting reward. Raphael huffed a low laugh. That knowledge had gone a long way toward stifling the bolt of desire he'd felt at first. Though he still thought she was striking, now that his brain had caught up with his senses, she was definitely the kind of beauty one might admire from afar. Like something that would snatch up a prey when it got too close and devour it with relish.

Raphael had no doubt she'd be a woman of her word

and toss him overboard if she thought for one second that he was a threat to her ship or her crew. And he was, which was why he'd climbed to the crow's nest to get out of the way and avoid extra attention. He'd felt the press of her guarded gaze on him over much of the night as if he were a dangerous wolf in drunken sheep's clothing.

If sheep drank rum and sang off-key sea shanties.

He chuckled to himself, the sound drifting down on the wind. A pair of eyes snagged his as Bonnie Bess looked up, directly to where he was. Of course she would know his exact position. Nothing escaped her notice. Raphael kicked up his lips in his practiced, flirtatious smile and waved. A scowl overtook her face as she turned back to Estelle, dismissing him though it was clear she had eyes in the back of her head. If he moved, she'd undoubtedly know it.

Who *was* this Valkyrie really? How had she become involved in the smuggling world? Not that there weren't women smugglers… They just didn't have dreadful reputations like hers. Or captain ships with such a noticeable number of fierce female crew as she did. He'd only ever cared enough about other ships to know who his enemies were inside his uncle's circle, of which Bonnie Bess wasn't a part. *Not yet.* She was the kind of sea captain Dubois would have his eye upon.

Not just for her looks. Her reputation was formidable.

For some reason, the idea of his uncle getting his claws into her rankled.

A prickly sensation warmed between his shoulder

blades. Taking her to Nassau might be a mistake. He could disembark and melt away in Barbados. He had contacts there, but that may not be the best solution either. Dubois would certainly know of his escape by now, and Raphael needed to get back to men who were loyal to him as soon as he could. She was heading to Nassau anyway. Her reasons had nothing to do with him.

"Land, ho!" one of the boatswains called out.

Raphael glanced over his shoulder as the speed of the frigate reduced. Sure enough, the darkened coastline of the island came into view. He took a moment to appreciate the beauty of the golden sun rising over the rocky shoreline, naturally curved inlets, and green-tipped crests of Barbados. Maybe it *would* be better to slip away here. Wash his hands of Bonnie Bess and her shrewd, too-discerning eyes.

Raphael finished his mango in two messy bites and tossed the seed over the side before taking a sip from the rancid bottle of rum he'd procured from the galley. He swished the bitter liquid in his mouth and splashed some on his clothing for good measure. It never hurt to bolster the sotted face he showed to the world.

For now, he had a part to play.

As a longtime spy working for the British Crown and now on special assignment to the American government, Lisbeth had long learned to trust her gut. Without it, she would have been compromised or killed several times over. She was usually a good judge of character, but as she watched her new sailing master deftly climb down from the crow's nest and saunter—no, nearly stagger—across the foredeck, her steadfast instincts guttered.

Was the man bloody drunk?

Raphael Saint appeared to be unthreatening, but everything about how that long, lean body moved conflicted with the way the man smiled or smelled. He acted like a house cat but prowled like a hunting tiger. Until he'd made it down to the deck, his body had descended the mast with an ease that belied his current unsteady, rolling gait. So which was the act? The grinning buffoon or the powerful, skulking brigand in their midst? No amount of staggering or stumbling could hide the fact that he wasn't weak, and that in itself felt like a deception.

And yet...Lisbeth had allowed him to stay.

She should cast him off in Bridgetown. Take her chances with Nassau on her own.

Lisbeth composed her features into a blank mask as he approached. The stench of sour rum preceded him. Bloody hell, the man *was* fucking foxed! "I have a person here who can get us ammunition and weapons," he said, his face the soul of amiability.

Her brow vaulted. "Why should I trust you?"

"Not expecting you to, just making an offer," he said easily, that mouth quirking upward. Hell if it didn't make her want to punch it off that too-affable countenance. She clenched her fist around the hilt of her blade instead.

Eyes tracking the movement, he cocked his head, something astute glimmering for a second in that hooded gaze before it was blinked away by a fringe of sooty lashes. "But he's fast and cheap, which means we can be on our way once we refuel the coal and supplies. I gather you want to leave soon."

Grimacing, she snagged her upper lip between her teeth. The rogue had a point. Faster was better, considering she had no idea who would be coming after her following the stunt in the harbor. It'd been seven or eight hours since their sly flight from Tobago, and no one had been on their tail through the sea. Other ships had been spotted, but never one on the same route as the *Syren*. Lisbeth would never let her guard down, however. Out of sight did not mean out of mind. Being vigilant and on her toes had kept her crew safe for years.

"I don't need your help," she said.

He shrugged. "Suit yourself."

"Stay with the ship."

"Whatever you say, Captain."

If he was bothered by the curt command, he showed no sign of it...apart from that unctuous smile that dug under her skin like a relentless thorn. There was something infuriatingly *off* about him that she couldn't quite identify. As she hurried down to her cabin for a pouch of money, she shook her head. She'd tell Estelle to look for a new sailing master while in town. If they found someone capable that *wasn't* him, then all the better.

Lisbeth changed out of her clothes into fresh trousers

and a clean high-collared linen shirt. A jet-black, tightly fitted corset went on above that, pushing her breasts to the heavens. She tucked her hair up under a wrap, and then darkened her eyes with kohl and painted a scarlet stain on her lips. A bold beauty mark went above the corner of her left upper lip.

Reaching into her trunks for the bold burgundy frock coat with gold buttons and lace-trimmed cuffs, she slid into the garment and donned a straw hat with inventive wine-colored plumes. It was ostentatiously gaudy...but people remembered flashy. Finally, she buckled the thick belt with her weapons holstered and sheathed in place, including a curved ax strapped to her back, and drew in a breath at the image in the mirror.

Bonnie Bess stared back at her.

Ruthless. Forbidding. Everything she needed to be.

By now, Bess was known in most ports. The reputation she'd cultivated across the Caribbean and the United States had been vicious and hard-won. Oh, Lisbeth knew of the bloody stories told about her, each one more terrible than the last. She made no attempt to correct any of them. A delicate woman would drown in this world, and she had no intention of disappearing under treacherous seas. She *was* the fucking storm.

"Are you certain about this?" Estelle asked, meeting her in the corridor, voice low.

Lisbeth blinked. "Going to Nassau?"

"If Davy says you were near the ships and they catch you, your fate will not be kind."

Lisbeth rolled the sudden cold from her shoulders. "No one besides Davy heard me down on those docks." Brow wrinkling, she pursed her lips and brushed imaginary lint off her coat sleeves. "It will be my word against his. Look for a new sailing master if you can," she added. "I cannot abide having that man on my ship."

Estelle's brows flew high. "It's been seven hours, and he got us here in one piece in the dark of night. Those flats in Tobago have wrecked dozens of ships manned by sailors stupid enough to sail without line of sight. He's more than competent, if not the best we've had."

"He's lying about something," Lisbeth replied.

"Aren't we all, Cap'n?"

Her quartermaster wasn't wrong, but Lisbeth refused to ignore her intuition. "If you cannot hire someone, find out what you can from the locals about Raphael Saint. I'd rather be prepared than blindsided by a pretty face hiding ill intent."

She turned to climb the stairs to the deck when Estelle stopped her with a palm to her elbow. Dark eyes glittered down at her, fondness and care swirling in her gaze. In the past, Bonnie Bess and her quartermaster would disembark in the various ports and leave gold coins and chaos in their wake at the local taverns. The owners loved and loathed them in equal measure. Bess's generosity went in hand with her bloody reputation—blood was just as expected to be shed as money. It accomplished two things: fortified her status and made sure that she was remembered. Conjecture went a long way in building reputation.

The last time they'd kicked over the traces had been six months ago. She'd perched in Estelle's lap and their nights had been wild and pleasurable. The recollection of intertwined limbs and replete satisfaction flitted through her brain. Those memories were mirrored in her quartermaster's stare. Perhaps in her loneliest moments, Lisbeth regretted ending things.

They had been good together and Estelle had been an unselfish lover. But Lisbeth had needed her mind clear for her mission, and besides, Estelle wasn't one to settle down with one partner, whereas Lisbeth was a one-at-a-time kind of person. She'd never ask Estelle to change, but possessiveness ran deep in Lisbeth's blood. Being resentful of other paramours was not her style, and so they'd parted, but that didn't mean they didn't look out for each other.

A pair of flecked pewter eyes framed in dark lashes flicked through her vision, and Lisbeth very nearly changed her mind and took Estelle up on the silent offer that was always on the table. Perhaps a thorough bedding was exactly what she needed to get that rogue out of her head.

If not with Estelle, then any willing lover in port would do. Relationships were one thing, but from time to time, a rousing round in the sheets with no strings attached had its appeal.

"Be careful," the quartermaster said, her fingers flexing.

Lisbeth winked. "Always am."

"Just because we didn't see anyone doesn't mean no one is here. Word travels fast on the sea."

"All will be well, Estelle," Lisbeth said. "Smalls will stay close. And you know that I am more than capable of defending myself."

With that, they climbed to the foredeck where Smalls stood near the ladder and descended into the waiting rowboat that took them to the crowded harbor. Lisbeth glanced over her shoulder to her ship, noting the tall presence of the man she'd commanded to remain aboard. Even halfway across the bay, it felt like his gaze sought and imprisoned hers.

Her breath hitched, fingers clenching on the expensive fabric of her trousers as she wondered whether leaving a stranger on her ship had been the best idea. Half of her sailors remained aboard as well. What if he convinced them to leave? Lisbeth ground her teeth together. The *Syren* crew was loyal. And besides, no one would be daft enough to steal that particular ship. Its reputation was just as vicious as hers.

"So you think he's pretty?" Estelle said slyly as the crew rowed toward the shore. There was no need to clarify who the *he* was. Lisbeth clenched her teeth at her earlier slip about his pretty face.

"I'm not interested in a shipboard relationship, Estelle," she replied stiffly. "Especially with a man I know nothing about that *you* hired without my approval."

The quartermaster chuckled. "That doesn't answer the question."

"Just because something is pretty enough to be admired doesn't mean that it should be plucked. Sometimes it is best left to wither on the bush."

"Ah, so you have thought of...*plucking* him," Estelle said, glee in her voice and an infuriating emphasis on the second-to-last word. It was obvious she did not mean plucking, rather something that rhymed with it.

"You are not amusing." Lisbeth's gaze narrowed on the object of their discussion whose focus hadn't shifted from the rowboat since she'd left the ship. "I'm not blind when it comes to beauty, but that scoundrel is nothing but trouble."

"I seem to recall you like a bit of trouble."

Lisbeth shook her head hard. "Not that kind."

They reached the crowded wharf, secured the boat while Estelle distributed orders and funds, and quickly went their separate ways. The boatswains that had accompanied them had their own jobs to do. Eyes in the market drifted over her and quickly flitted away as she sauntered through the throng of fishermen, sailors, dock-workers, peddlers, and thieves. But that was also due to Smalls who stuck close like the colossal, looming, lethal shadow he was.

The smell of the briny seashore, the day's catch of the market, and dozens of spices filled the air. Lisbeth's stare coasted over the diverse group of locals, much the same as it had been in Tobago with only the occasional light-complexioned face peeking out from the sea of brown hues, from golden to russet to deepest mahogany. Most of the people here were not wealthy, trying to forge lives for themselves in the wake of enslavement and indentured labor, but as she'd learned from men like Rawley, the Duke of Ashvale's Antiguan cousin, it took a lot to defeat the tenacious spirits of Caribbean people.

"Cap'n Bess!" a lilting voice cried, and Lisbeth almost didn't recognize the girl who had called out. Her eyes widened with joy.

She hadn't seen Narina in over a year and a half—not since the start of her mission with the American Treasury. Cute as a child, she was even prettier now with a gorgeous tawny complexion and a cautious smile splitting her young face.

The then ten-year-old Narina had been running errands in her mama's tavern, and Lisbeth had always felt a kinship with the child. She had reminded her of herself when she was little. Bright, intelligent, and full of fire to learn. Though now, Lisbeth frowned, noting the worn clothing, her skinny frame, and the look of dull exhaustion in Narina's eyes.

Surely business hadn't been that bad?

"Nari," Lisbeth said, gathering the girl in her arms. "You've grown up!"

Narina smiled, though it did not meet her eyes, her young face looking much older for a second. "I'm twelve now," she said, puffing out her chest.

"How's your mama?"

Sadness made the girl's eyelids droop. "She died from yellow fever a year ago. It was quick, unlike others here. She didn't suffer, the doctor said."

"I am so sorry," Lisbeth said, her heart filling with sympathy. "She was a good woman."

"Aye."

"Who are you living with?" Lisbeth asked as she cast a look over the child's worn clothing. "Who took over the tavern?"

"My auntie but she's not really my auntie."

"What do you mean?" she asked.

Narina shrugged. "She was Mama's tenant."

Lisbeth was so focused on the troubling conversation that she hadn't immediately noticed that the crowd had thickened and also grown closer. Normally, Smalls was an efficient deterrent, if her own reputation didn't work, but more people had crowded around them while she'd been speaking with Narina. She put her hand on the pommel of her cutlass and reached for her pistol right as Smalls let out a roar. "Bess, to me!"

The sea of people shifted and a thin man with a sneering mouth and showy clothes got much too close for comfort. Lisbeth hadn't noticed him before, nor had she seen the handful of ruffians at his back. They did not seem to mean well. But Lisbeth wasn't the target—Narina was. A muscled arm slid around the child's shoulders, a knife held in idle fingers.

"What have we here?" he drawled. "Going to introduce us to your new friend, Daughter?"

Raphael watched from his vantage point in a nearby alleyway, one shoulder propped on the stone, a sliver of sweet sugarcane clamped between his teeth, although he made no move to interfere. Not yet.

One, the captain had expressly forbidden him to leave her ship. And two, knowing what Bonnie Bess was capable of from the sheer rage flattening her mouth to translucency, he wanted to see what she would do. She fascinated him to no end. In truth, he was a bit besotted by the Viking who even wore an ax on her back like the warriors of old.

Raphael canvassed the crowd. Smalls had been surrounded a few feet away by men with guns. They weren't locals as far as he could tell. Criminals of some sort, but maybe some who had gotten too comfortable with the easy life of preying on hardworking men and women. He knew the type. They claimed to charge a "fee for protection" when all they were doing was protecting the business owners from the lawlessness of their own men.

Call him a smuggler, but at least Raphael had a code: only steal from those who could afford the harm, because the cargo was insured by financial backers and they would not feel the loss, or lighten the pockets of worse criminals who operated by no code at all. Like Dubois.

In fact, Raphael had a sneaking suspicion that these might be Dubois's own men. He'd heard rumors that the ambitious arse was trying to establish strongholds in various islands by stationing his own thugs in place and collecting a tithe from those who could barely feed themselves.

"Come now. Don't you know who I am?" Bess said in a jovial voice that made the hairs rise on Raphael's arms. One of her hands remained on her cutlass while the other was propped loosely upon her hip, just above a gun and a narrow brace of daggers. In addition to the ax, she was armed to the teeth, and he had no doubt she knew how to use each and every weapon strapped to her form. He had the sudden urge to see her in action.

The man sneered. "I see a woman playing at a man's game."

Raphael blinked. Wrong answer, obviously. Bess's expression did not change though her lip twitched as violent storms brewed in her eyes. Even from where he stood hidden in the cramped alleyway, Raphael could see the muscles bunching in her slender body, readying for war. "Not a game, but you'll learn. Unhand the child."

"My daughter?" the man said with a leer that was decidedly *un*-fatherly. Raphael's eyes narrowed in disgust.

"I am not your bloody daughter, you ham-faced lout!" the girl growled and attempted, futilely, to escape his grasp.

"But of course you are. Your mama could not pay the tax, my sweet, and so we've made other arrangements. You'll work off her debt."

Raphael felt anger billow in his chest. Narina was fucking twelve years old, from what he'd overheard, and the girl clearly had not consented to any such arrangement. Still, he did not move, watching to see what Bess would do. And besides, he was supposed to be on the ship.

He did not have long to wait. The throng watched with avid interest, though some of them definitely had an inkling of who she was. Raphael noticed that the rest of the *Syren*'s crew had positioned themselves in the market square, weapons at the ready in case mayhem broke out. He almost wished it would. Since being in prison, he was itching for a rousing fight.

"Last chance. That's your answer, then?" the captain asked in a bored voice.

The girl's eyes widened in fear. "Bess, no! Those fucking flapdoodles killed Nestor and Lawrence." Raphael's lips twitched at the child's colorful vocabulary and the insult to her captor's masculinity.

"Flapdoodle," Lisbeth drawled. "That's a good one."

"My cock is working just fine if you want to take it for a turn," the foolish man boasted, licking his lips and cupping his crotch. "You're new to my harbor. There's a cost to dock on these here wharves."

Bess burst into laughter, the sound so unexpected and rich that Raphael sucked in a breath. "Last I looked, you weren't the governor of the Windward Islands." Her brows raised. "In fact, I'm certain you don't look like Sir James Walker at all. He's Scottish and a bit stout."

As if realizing that she wasn't afraid of him at all and, worse, might be toying with him just a bit, the man's eyes slitted. "One half of your ship's spoils and no trouble. That's the payment."

Her smile grew teeth. "But alas, you underestimate how much I love trouble."

That was all the notice the man had before all hell broke loose. In the half second it took for the bastard to blink, a small blade had lodged itself into his shoulder, launching the ruffian backward with a shrill howl. Raphael hadn't even seen Bess move, though her palm had flexed against her hip where the brace of daggers were. The girl ducked out of her captor's clutches and hurried to Bess's side as pandemonium erupted. Shots were fired into the crowd, making most of them scatter, except for the perpetrators.

Raphael's mouth fell open as he got his wish of seeing Bonnie Bess in action. Dieu, she was magnificent! She was a fluid artist in the midst of complete chaos, her body serpentine and vicious. Her fists flew in calculated blows...a soft throat here, a meaty torso there. Though she had blades and a pistol, she used none. She knew exactly where to hit, her fighting style nothing he'd ever seen before. A combination of strikes, lunges, spins, and jabs, it screamed of specialized military training, but had enough scrappy edges and movements to have been learned from the streets. Many, many kinds of streets.

Just who the *fuck* was Bonnie Bess?

Since he was observing her so intently, he was the only one to see the leader with the blade in his shoulder standing with a loaded gun pointed right at her. Raphael didn't hesitate. He took speedy aim with a gun he'd helped himself to from the captain's own chambers and fired.

Indubitably, she'd be furious at his defiance of her orders...but at least she'd be alive.

Raphael grinned. He might not be, however.

Worth it.

Four

Lisbeth finished off the man she'd been fighting with a solid foot to the jaw. Her knuckles and legs ached, but in the best way. This was what she'd needed—a physical outlet for all of the excess energy running through her body. Coitus was overrated. A good brawl always got her blood flowing and her heart pumping. An orgasm might do that as well…but the ones with a competent lover came with complications, more often than not.

The short hairs on her nape stood up, identifying danger in close quarters, and she barely had time to turn before heat singed her cheek and a ball of lead sped past her head, much too close for comfort. The shot had come from the brute who'd mouthed off while threatening Narina, but someone had felled him before she could duck or defend herself.

Lisbeth huffed a grateful breath that her crew always had her flanks covered. Her gaze spanned the space and locked on her rescuer holding the smoking weapon. A grinning, much-too-smug man. Gratitude faded and fury overtook her instead. That miserable, disobedient cur! She stalked toward him. "I told you to stay with the ship," she hissed. "I could have you lashed for such insubordination."

The insouciant prick smiled. "You could, but I just

saved your life, so perhaps save the lashes for later. Perhaps even in the privacy of your cabin. They can go quite well after a few drams of whiskey, I've heard."

His tone was teasing. Provocative. And the idea was... intriguing.

No, *no*.

It was terrible, rotten, idiotic. Out of the bloody question. Any punishments on her ship for misconduct—though she abhorred the brutal practice of lashings, preferring to toss culprits in the brig instead—were administered by Smalls or Estelle. Most of the crew agreed that Estelle was the harsher of the two, but the quartermaster only gave as much as she'd taken herself on far worse ships.

"I've shocked you speechless." Laughing pewter eyes caught and sparkled in the sunlight. Tipping her head back to stare up at him, she could see the bright tawny-brown starbursts around his pupils fringed by eyelashes so thick, it seemed as if he'd applied kohl to his lids. He'd tied his hair back into a queue with a bit of leather, though some bits escaped around his face. Her stare drifted to the spent weapon in his opposite hand—a walnut-carved antique revolver with gold edgings along the barrel that looked strangely familiar.

Her eyes narrowed. "Where did you get that?"

"Your cabin." He lifted it and pursed his lips. "Good design. A little too much recoil, but adequate to fell a man intent on my captain's demise, I suppose. Though in close quarters, I'm much better with an épée."

"You were in *my* cabin?" Good God, she didn't care about the deuced gun or his proficiency with fucking swords. She cared that he'd dared trespass in a place she considered very private. Lisbeth blinked, almost incapable of a response. Her quarters were her space. *Hers.*

"Where else was I supposed to find a weapon in short order?" he returned cheerfully and then canted his head when his gaze dipped to her hand flexing convulsively over the hilt of her cutlass. The corner of his mouth curled up in its usual crooked smirk. "Don't worry, I closed my eyes when I went near your sleeping area, though I must say those blue velvet curtains remind me of a much bawdier place than a ship. Classy taste, though."

Lisbeth's teeth ground together in sheer fury. Did the bloody man have a death wish? Not that she needed to explain things to anyone, but she enjoyed indulging in finer things here and there, and a lady's bedroom was one of the few places she was free to be herself. As a spy, she spent so much time living the lives of other people that it took effort to carve out space to remember who *she* was. The rich navy velvet brocade of the drapes on her custom-built bed was one such indulgence, hinting at the core of the woman who currently lived in the skin of a fierce, ruthless captain.

"Are you upset? It was really quite beautiful. A bordello fit for a queen."

Her fingers jolted. She really was going to skewer him and leave him for the pickpockets and crows. "No, I'm not upset. I'm trying not to teach you a bloody lesson in the middle of a public square and trounce you senseless," she snapped.

"Don't threaten me with a good time, Viking." The fool had the audacity to grin.

"Is everything a joke to you?"

"No, but life on the high seas is a lot easier with a sense of humor." His gaze tracked over her person. "You have blood on your cheek."

She swiped at it with her coat sleeve, but though she could feel wetness on her face, she had no idea where the splotch was. "That tends to happen in a brawl."

"Here, you missed it. Let me." Before Lisbeth could protest or move, a warm calloused thumb was sliding along her jaw from the corner of her lip to the base of her ear. Heat sparked under his touch. The contact was soft and much too tender, making her brows hit her hairline. She backed away and his hand hovered for a moment before dropping back to his side. For once, he had nothing clever or funny to say, only stood there staring at her with a pair of suddenly unreadable eyes.

"Who in the nine hells is this, then?" a young voice chirped as a gangly mix of arms and legs ran over to them, panting with exertion. "New crew?" Narina's curious eyes rounded as she glanced between them and then she gasped. "Oh, is he a lover? There's that look about the two of you like you're either going to stab or shag one another. Trust me, I see it in the tavern all the time. Let a girl know if you are going to fight or f—"

"Nari!" Lisbeth blinked out of her thrall at the

interruption, turning to glower at Narina, who thankfully was unharmed. At least, her loose lips seemed no worse for wear. Smalls had seen her to safety the minute Lisbeth's dagger had found its mark, though a part of her was wishing that he'd ferried the curious, too-observant menace far away.

"I was going to say 'flirt,' Bess," the girl said with a much-too-cheeky grin that suggested otherwise before turning to Saint. "Who're you?"

The sailing master sketched a jaunty bow. "Bonjour, mademoiselle, Raphael Saint at your service. My good friends know me as Saint." He glanced at Lisbeth and winked, voice lowering for Lisbeth's ears only. "Though my special friends call me Sinner."

Oh dear God, Lisbeth was going to vomit. *Who* said such ludicrous things? "And everyone else knows him as Jackass," she said loudly.

Narina collapsed into giggles. Studying him, she cocked her head. "Wait. I know you."

If Lisbeth wasn't looking at Saint—or wasn't well taught in the art of observation—she would have missed the way his brow wrinkled slightly and the way his spine snapped to attention as if suddenly aware of a possible hazard. Interesting.

She'd already suspected Saint had secrets, but it was clear that he wasn't as oblivious or as drunk as he seemed. A man in his cups would *never* have been able to finagle such a precise shot from such an awkward angle. She could barely see the square from the alley they occupied. In truth, it had been a miracle that she wasn't dead. Lisbeth supposed she should be grateful, but it irked her to offer him the satisfaction. Although, shame filled her, too. She was always generous with her praise when credit was due.

"Do you now?" he drawled to Narina, that obsequious expression back in force. A certain act, Lisbeth determined, to draw away from the fact that he was exceptionally alert.

Narina nodded and rubbed her nose. "When Mama was alive. You were meatier then. I remember you leaving extra coin for each of the servers in the tavern and paying what you owed with enough money to tide us over for months." Lisbeth blinked at that as Narina nodded enthusiastically. "Yes, yes. That's why I remember your face. You weren't stingy like most of the ratbags who passed through Bridgetown. Even Mama was smitten, and everyone in town knows that no one with a bad mind could get past her." She laughed and her brown cheeks went dusky. "The serving girls always talked about you."

"Generous, charming, *and* handsome make for a winning combination," he quipped with a warm smile that seemed astonishingly genuine, making his eyes crinkle at the corners. Lisbeth especially did not like the way that open smile hit her right in the chest, and she wasn't even the intended recipient.

"And full of self-adoration, clearly," she snapped and then focused on the matter at hand. She took Narina's arm, ignoring the presence of the infuriating rogue. "Don't even think about skirting the subject. Why was that cad saying you were his daughter? What's going on here?"

Narina's small shoulders lifted wearily, the bit of spark that had possessed her a minute ago fading. Strain weighed down on her slight frame. "There's trouble, Bess."

"What kind of trouble?"

"The worst kind."

Trouble wasn't uncommon in small fishing villages like these. Whether from hidden contraband, smuggled goods, or exploitation of the locals, danger and hardship were always present in the islands. Capitalists had embedded their greedy fingers into the core of the Caribbean, and the sense of entitlement was pervasive. People thought they could take with no consequence.

It was the main reason Lisbeth was so focused on catching Dubois. He wasn't some philanthropic smuggling king. He was a criminal who didn't care how many lives he snuffed out or stomped upon to make himself richer. In truth, he was a leech. A parasite, whose reach and power needed to be eradicated with minimal casualties before that became an impossible feat.

She nodded to Smalls, Estelle, and the rest of her crew who stood wary and vigilant with weapons at the ready, despite the fact that the market had already gone back to normal as if scuffles like this happened every day of the week. Flashmen and cutpurses were already snatching whatever they could take of value off the fallen assailants.

Lisbeth's eyes narrowed on the lowlife who'd come so

very close to ending her life and felt an uncomfortable ripple chase down her spine. She'd danced with Death before. Many times. In her line of work, it was inevitable. But this felt unnervingly real, like she'd escaped a shallow grave by the skin of her teeth. By the sheer luck—and it *had* to be luck—of the man who stood opposite her. No one could shoot around corners. Bloody hell, was she losing her edge?

Now she owed Saint. *Damn it!* She hated owing anyone anything.

Especially a pirate who appeared to hide behind a mask as elaborate as hers.

"Let's go back to the tavern," she said. She glanced over at the sailing master. She'd planned to ask around for a trustworthy arms dealer, but desperate times called for desperate measures, and she needed to figure out what was going on with Narina. "Is your man with the ammunitions reliable?" she asked him. Saint gave a short nod. Lisbeth beckoned to Smalls and thrust a pouch latched to her waist into his hands. "See what you can arrange for gunpowder, shells, and round shot. We leave once I make sure Narina's safe."

By the time they walked back to the tavern that Narina called home, Lisbeth's belly was churning with nerves. She did not have a good feeling about this...a feeling that became worse when she took in the unusual state of disrepair of the tavern. She'd remembered it being clean and bustling. Now it was dirty with cheap, broken furniture and a couple drunks holding down the fort and nursing mugs of stale liquor. It stank of old ale and piss. "What happened?"

Narina chewed on her lip and wrinkled her nose. "Porter—the feckless shitsack your shiny knight dispatched—and his men came, demanding protection fees."

"Not *shiny* at all," Lisbeth retorted before she could stop herself. It barely registered that she hadn't argued the "your" part or protested Narina's language. Heavens, she needed to put the dratted knave from her mind.

Narina rolled her eyes. "At first, Mama refused to pay the nackle-asses for security that we had never needed, but then bad things started to happen. Thieves would break in overnight. Brawls would start up for no reason at all, buggering all the furniture. The tavern started losing money, and then Mama got sick. One of the bloody ships putting into port brought the yellow fever." She blew out a breath, looking much too old for her tender years as she poured two glasses of water from a pitcher. "Hundreds in the village died. I got sick too, and I thought Mama was on the mend until she got a second infection, started vomiting dark blood, and was gone in days."

"I'm so sorry," Lisbeth said, reaching for the girl's hand and squeezing. There was nothing worse than yellow fever, especially that second deadly stage with internal hemorrhaging. Over the last decade, the virus had ravaged the lives of thousands of people in the islands. Bermuda had gone through four separate epidemics.

One of Lisbeth's colleagues in the American government had arrested a man called Dr. Blackburn, a Confederate agent who had paid his cronies to ship and distribute soiled, infected garments from Bermuda to President Lincoln and his allies in the Northern states. If Lisbeth recalled correctly, a month after the president's assassination three years ago, Blackburn was arrested in Nova Scotia and charged with conspiracy to commit murder. However, the man had been acquitted on a trifle—a violation of Canadian neutrality—since any alleged conspiracy was not toward a Canadian head of state. As far as Lisbeth knew, he'd been in New Orleans in the past year during another yellow fever epidemic.

Narina sniffed and ran a weary hand over her face. "It was bad luck that the fever didn't take Porter and his bloody meaters. They became rougher and bolder, and Mama's tenant had spent the last of our savings taking care of her. She had no bleeding choice but to pay the bastards with whatever coin came in..." She let her voice trail off, anxious fingers tugging at the frayed cuffs of her shirt. Lisbeth didn't have the heart to chastise her words. "And when that money ran out, Porter fancied himself a tavern owner as payment. He told Auntie she had to marry him or he would sell me."

Lisbeth felt her entire body tense with cold rage. "Why didn't your mama write to me at the address I gave her in New York? My people would have sent the correspondence to me."

Her shoulders lifted and fell. "She did. She mailed you dozens of letters."

Why hadn't she received any? Lisbeth had met with

her counterparts in the customs house in secret several times in New York under the guise of selling smuggled goods. She'd received letters from Bronwyn, the Duchess of Thornbury, who despite her retirement from clandestine operations liked to stay abreast of international politics, but none from Narina's mother.

There was only one reason Lisbeth's handlers would not have delivered them—if they felt her mission would have been compromised in some way. But still, Lisbeth felt guilt, followed by a swift rush of anger. Those letters were important, and she had a strong inkling that her handlers were more worried about her being *distracted* than compromised.

"I have money. Porter is dead and his men won't bother you anymore."

Narina lifted her eyes, a dark defiant stare meeting Lisbeth's that made her own gaze narrow. "Take me with you. On the *Syren*."

"The *Syren* is no room for children."

"I'm not a damned baby, Bess. I'm twelve!"

Lisbeth rolled her lips, frowning at the oath. She'd been barely a handful of years older than that when she'd been running with an unsavory crowd in London, to the despair of her father. However, given the fact that she was on the run in addition to the fact that Davy remained in possession of her private correspondence, the attention on her meant that Narina would be better off here than on her ship. Lisbeth would make sure that some of her crew stayed behind to ensure her protection.

"Where's your aunt?"

Narina's thin frame bristled. "She's not even my real aunt, Bess. She thinks she's lady of the goddamned manor. She doesn't even care about the tavern. Or me. She'll probably be looking for another protector now that Porter's dead."

Lisbeth shook her head decisively, noting the mutinous downturn of the girl's mouth. "Even so, Nari, it's safer for you here with her. I'll come back, I promise."

"Bess, please."

"I'm sorry, love, but the answer's no."

Arms purchase negotiated, paid, and delivered to the *Syren*, Raphael walked beside Smalls toward the wharves. The man barely said two words, other than grunts and curt jerks of his head in lieu of actual conversation. The whole interaction had almost been nipped in the bud when his contact, the clearly unforgiving and still livid Mr. Crawley, had pulled out a pistol and threated to shoot Raphael dead right then and there on his doorstep. Only the hefty promise of Bess's coin and the nearly too-late intervention of Smalls had saved his sorry hide.

It wasn't *Raphael's* fault that Crawley's daughter had taken a fancy to him a few years ago. The girl had been quite determined in her pursuit. Raphael had offered companionship and she had expected wedding bells. Crawley had worn much the same expression when he'd fired into the side of Raphael's ship and warned him never to set foot back in Bridgetown. And yet here he was... back in Bridgetown, without a ship, and a gun barrel in his face, facing down old foes to gain the trust of his new ship allies.

At least Raphael hoped they were allies. He was quite certain that Bonnie Bess vacillated between skewering him with her cutlass and feeding his remains to the hungry corbeaux that circled the wharves for carrion. Those vultures would eat anything! Raphael supposed he could stay in Barbados, work odd jobs, and eventually scrounge up passage to Nassau on his own. Despite Crawley's loathing, he was still owed favors by a few people.

But that would take time, and time he did not have.

No, passage on an exceptionally fast blockade-runner-turned-frigate that had been refitted with weaponry would get him there. He had no idea what business Bonnie Bess had in Nassau or Bermuda, nor did he care. She was a little fish in a very big sea. Raphael blinked. A little, *ferocious* fish. Like a baby barracuda. But even baby barracudas could rip a man to shreds. Maybe he should be using this time with Smalls to find out more about his temporary captain.

"Thanks for that back there, by the way," Raphael said to Smalls as they walked back toward town. "Women, right?"

A noncommittal grunt was the reply, or perhaps he'd only imagined that sound. Raphael glanced up to the side. He was a tall man, and Smalls still towered over him. His name was ironic in itself. Perhaps that was a moniker for what might be other less impressive parts of him. Raphael kept those uncharitable thoughts to himself, however.

Insulting a man's masculinity was a sure recipe for finding himself on the business end of Smalls's meaty fists. And those weren't small at all.

"Crawley's girl wanted wedlock," he went on in jovial tones as if Smalls had entered into the conversation. "I'm already married to the sea, and the sands are my occasional mistress. There's no tying this kind of bounty down. I told her this, but the deuced girl would not listen. How long have you been on the *Syren*?"

He waited, but there was no answer. If he hadn't heard the man growl a thank-you to Crawley, Raphael would have thought that he could not speak. Plenty of smugglers had their tongues cut out as punishment for insubordination on ships. Dubois had done something similar to his inner circle so they could not betray him. Barbaric in the extreme.

Then again, Raphael had been betrayed by his own crew. Admittedly, that had been his fault. Cholera had spread onboard, taking out half his men, and then a bout of yellow fever had near decimated the rest, and he'd had little choice but to employ replacements in Bermuda to get to Tobago. Looking back, it wouldn't surprise him if some of those men had been loyal to Dubois and had mutinied on his uncle's orders.

Not for the first time, he wanted to kick his own arse.

"Not a talker, eh?" he said to Smalls, sticking his hands in his pockets. "How long have you known the captain? From what I saw, the crew seems cheerful and content. Always a good sign of first-rate leadership, if you ask me."

"I didn't." The words were half-exhaled, half-growled, a big palm coming up to wipe the sweat from Smalls's brow. Short blond hair stood up in tufts as a pair of light-blue eyes found Raphael and glowered before flicking away in antipathy.

"Didn't what?"

"Ask," Smalls grunted.

Well, the man was talking, if three words could be called talking, which was better than the alternative. And he sounded irritated, which was even better. In Raphael's experience, people tended to give away a lot more when they were vexed than when they were calm. An emotional response meant words weren't considered as carefully in the heat of the moment.

"How did you get the name Smalls? Seems...a bit absurd for a man of your size. My friends have given me many names over the years, some of them I'm quite fond of. Saint is the most common and seems to have stuck." He thought for a moment and caught a telltale irritated intake of breath from the man at his side, as if hopeful that he would stop speaking. Raphael had long since learned to read people's reactions. "Then again, it *is* my last name, so that likely doesn't count as a nickname."

Smalls sighed loudly and Raphael could practically hear the man's molars grinding together. He opened his mouth to continue his monologue when Smalls let out a noise. "Two years. Long enough. It's my name. Deceive her and nothing on earth will save your wretched hide."

It took Raphael a second to realize the growled reply

provided answers to the three questions he'd asked. The last, obviously, was a not-so-subtle warning.

"I have no intention of harming a hair on the head of your magnificent captain. In fact, I think I might be in love with her. Or lust. They can be interchangeable, you know."

Smalls stopped so quickly that Raphael nearly crashed into him. "I don't like you."

"Tiens tiens!" Raphael gasped theatrically, a hand to his chest. "And here I thought we could be the best of friends. At least for the next four days."

"You're no sailing master," Smalls snapped through his teeth. "Aye, you've knowledge of the ocean and guided the *Syren* through the reef flats, but it's not your job. You're not fooling anyone."

After a solid minute of glaring on Smalls's part and wide-eyed innocence on his, they resumed walking back toward the ship. "And what do you think my job would be? Boatswain, gunner, cabin boy, perhaps? I am rather excellent at all three, particularly the last. Put in a good word with the captain for me, will you? Her cabin is…to die for."

That was one step too far as Raphael found himself slammed up against the nearest wall, an enormous fist wrapped in the collar of his shirt. Despite his situation, he wasn't too worried. Smalls was a big man, but size could be a disadvantage in certain spaces. Raphael had scuffled with bigger men and survived. But besides holding him in place with a savage glower on his face, Smalls didn't move.

"Dieu, you could snap me like a twig," Raphael said with his customary smirk that never failed to get a rise out of people. The fist at his throat tightened. He lifted his own hands on either side of Smalls's thick shoulders. "You're loyal and protective, I get that, but no need for the manhandling. All I want is safe passage to Nassau, mon frère. What you and your captain do after that is no business of mine. What kind of business is that, if you don't mind me asking for posterity's sake? Are you and she…?" Hell, he nearly bit off his own tongue that those words made it past his lips.

Smalls released him as quickly as he'd attacked, a look of horror crawling over his features. "I'm not your fucking brother, and I should thrash the living daylights out of you. She's like a daughter to me."

Raphael let out an inaudible sigh, his lungs compressing with…*something.* Was that relief flooding through him? Yes, definitely relief that he wouldn't have to fight off some overzealous, jealous lover while he plied the captain for information.

That was his new plan after all.

A ship outfitted like hers could come in handy, and despite her fearsome reputation, Bonnie Bess was no match for him. And besides, Raphael wasn't above a bit of commandeering.

Whether that was of the ship…or her vicious, sultry captain.

Five

Lisbeth's nape itched as her gaze prowled the gently rocking horizon from her position behind the *Syren*'s helm. The prickly sensation had warned her of peril more times than she could count, but now she was back on her ship that was filled with food and provisions, plenty of coal as well as anthracite, which made no smoke in case they ran into trouble, and more than enough ballast and powder for the ship's twelve cannons. They had departed port quickly, and two days into the journey at a steady seventeen knots, there was no other vessel in pursuit.

Not yet.

Still, something didn't feel right. Though the skies were clear and the seas calm, the hairs on her arms were standing at full attention. Was a storm in the winds? It was possible. The weather had been unpredictable in recent months, but the *Syren* was built to endure fierce squalls and her speed more often than not kept them out of oncoming perilous storms. No, it wasn't that. This was something different. Something aboard the ship.

Or someone.

Her gaze instantly flicked to her sailing master, who stood on the aft deck, his tall form hard to miss, legs planted wide on the deck and a thoughtful expression marring his starkly beautiful face as he, too, scanned the horizon. And despite her considerable dislike, *beautiful* was an apt word to describe him, especially now that he was clean-shaven.

Objectively, Saint was handsome—dark hair whipping into a broad brow, his features elegant yet boldly hewn. Prominent cheekbones and that square jaw should have been too angular a combination, but both were softened by a pair of plush lips and eyelashes any lady would envy. Though he was rangy, it was obvious he was strong, and his ease on the boat decks suggested he'd been sailing quite a long time.

Why, then, had he gone ashore, disobeying her direct order? A captain's word was law and the overt insubordination rubbed. Was it because she was female? Then again, if he hadn't defied her wishes, she would likely be dead or dying from a close-range gunshot wound. Her thoughts pulled her in two different directions. Lisbeth still didn't trust him, even if he had saved her life. Trust in this world had to be earned by blood and toil.

He isn't reliable.

No, it wasn't that. She was usually an excellent judge of character, and for all his inconsistencies, she sensed Raphael Saint lived by some internal code of honor. A dishonorable man would have let her die and then made a play for the vacant position of captain himself. He was no mere sailing master, of that she was now sure. Everything about him *commanded* as though he was well familiar with the position of leadership. A captain himself, perhaps.

Like recognized like.

Lisbeth frowned. It wasn't often that someone got under her skin so quickly or easily. Her frown deepened. But *why* was she allowing it? Coming to her defense was in itself an act of loyalty, but not one that invited blind faith or instant devotion. As a spymaster, she had met many people in her line of work who had exceptional skills. Some could blend in anywhere and make themselves practically invisible—or the opposite, if the situation warranted.

Others could feign any accent or change the entirety of their features with a simple expression. She'd also known masters of espionage who could infiltrate any society by virtue of affability and charm. They attracted fidelity—people desired to be near them and became desperate to have them in their lives. It was a personality trait that required incredible discipline. Her senses sharpened. Was Saint one of those? Dear God, was he a *spy*?

She almost balked at the thought. No. Of course he wasn't.

Then why hadn't she seen him take a sip of spirits despite smelling like a rum distillery? Why did that quick, ingratiating mockery of a smile make her instantly doubt his veracity? How had he known a reliable arms merchant in Barbados on short notice? And why did she sense he had confidences he would die to keep hidden? Everyone had secrets, but a man like him with such an affinity for deception undoubtedly had more.

Stop thinking about him, for pity's sake! You have worse

things to worry about than a man you probably won't see ever again after a few days.

Perhaps she was sinking too deep into her own worries and her fear of failure. It was possible that he was simply a sailor in need of a ride to Nassau. In her gut, however, she knew the assumption was false. There was nothing simple about Saint, although he pretended to be. But even if he was the most charismatic, charming person on the planet, Lisbeth had a job to do, and that meant reinfiltrating the tight ranks of the crème de la crème of smugglers. This was her last chance and she could not—*would not*—squander it.

Lisbeth tightened her hands on the wheel and sharpened her purpose. If Saint was a captain or had been a captain, she had to know what he knew about the port they were headed for. Drawing in a deep breath of the briny sea air, she nodded to Estelle and jerked her chin to her quarters. It was time for some interrogation.

"Saint," she called, descending the stairs with a glance up to him. "With me."

His face angled to hers, and for a moment what she saw there made her heart quicken, in light of her earlier thoughts. It was barely a blink, but again, if she hadn't been trained to observe, she would have missed it. A shrewd, tenacious look was swiftly exchanged for the blithe expression he was careful always to wear. The change in his facial appearance was staggering. The former made his square jaw hard, dominant, and unyielding, while the latter softened his entire face into compliance and an unthreatening demeanor.

Curious. She had to admit it; despite herself, she was impressed.

Lisbeth had always been drawn to complex people, usually those who were the wrong sort. Complex but *complicated*. People too much like herself—with the weight of enough baggage they could sink this very ship. The part of her that thrived on puzzles wanted to dissect and study him. Learn how that clever, cunning mind of his worked. Examine and appreciate the skills that came so naturally to him.

Half of her crew had already accepted him, and it was only a matter of time before the rest did. He respected the rules, he was witty and humorous, and he shouldered his share of the work. Even the stalwart Estelle had mellowed. That was probably because he had saved Lisbeth's life, but still. No one was that charming. Sadly, solving the fascinating mystery that was Saint wasn't the priority. Learning *who* and *what* he knew was.

Lisbeth flicked a hand at Smalls to follow, ever her faithful shadow, even though she was more than capable of taking care of herself with one man. She needed a witness in case she skewered the sailing master by accident. Interest seemed to be at constant war with irritation where he was concerned. How could one person fascinate and yet rile her so much?

That took talent.

Saint fell into step beside her, and she was acutely aware of his presence. Her nostrils flared, preparing herself for the stench of rum, but for once, he did not stink of sour liquor. Instead, the clean masculine scent of something citrusy and crisp wafted off of him. It was not unpleasant. Had he availed himself of a bath in Bridgetown in addition to shaving? She had certainly taken advantage of a good soak, but she hadn't expected him to. Sailors and hygiene did not always go hand in hand.

Another incongruity.

Speckled gray-brown eyes captured hers, mischief dancing in them, his voice pitched low and raspy. "You summoned me, Captain, my captain? Is it time for that tongue-lashing you promised? Or was that a regular lashing? Either way, I am your willing servant."

Heat filled her cheeks. Heavens, why was everything that came out of his mouth so suggestive? She had met many flirtatious people, but he was truly outrageous. "What is wrong with you?"

"Nothing, chérie, I only want to please you."

Oh, for fuck's sake. That was a French endearment, wasn't it? He'd said he had been born in France. The hairs on her arms lifted, not warning of danger...but something else. Something much more startling that she hadn't felt in a long time. With her occasional dockside trysts, and even with Estelle, she always kept her mind and body separate. And yet, the tug in her center was recognizable.

Lisbeth squashed down the sudden, inconvenient warmth that swirled through her veins, that made her nipples bead and tighten. Now was *not* the time for arousal. She was intrigued by the puzzle that was the sailing master, nothing more. Certainly not attracted to him because that would be absurd. The heat in her belly billowed and she ruthlessly tamped it down. She was a master of her body, not the reverse.

"Just Captain or Bess will do."

"Bess." He rolled her name over his tongue like a treat to savor, and suddenly, she regretted giving him leave to call her anything so personal. It wasn't even her real name and she felt like he was whispering it between tangled sheets.

Lisbeth reached her quarters and opened the door, canting her head for him to enter. "We need to talk."

A full lip and dark brow quirked in tandem. "Talk? In your bedchamber? How downright wicked of you." He clutched a hand to his chest like a born thespian. "I do declare, Bess, I don't know what you've heard, but I am not that kind of man."

Jolting again at the sinful caress of her name, Lisbeth rolled her eyes. "Nor am I that kind of woman. And you very well know it's an antechamber, not my *bedchamber,* since you've trespassed in here before without my permission."

"I needed a pistol," he pointed out. "To save your life."

As if she needed the reminder. Lisbeth gestured to the armchair on one side of the enormous desk that was covered with nautical maps and instruments. "Sit."

Lisbeth closed the door, catching Smalls's glare that she was shutting the door at all. She felt a long-forgotten whisper of propriety. It had been quite some time since she'd bothered with the tenets of female modesty. In London, an unmarried woman could not be in a room alone with a man—she would be ruined and shunned—and a married woman could not entertain a man in her private chambers who wasn't her husband.

Not that she was still the latter. However, as the Countess of Waterstone, even with a marriage that had been wrought and subsequently dissolved for the sake of duty by the queen, she'd had to toe the lines of decorum. Out here on the seas, however, the only lines to follow were the ones of her own making.

She obeyed no one. She spoke her mind. She made the laws.

Lisbeth cleared her throat and propped one hip on the side of the desk, staring down at her quarry who had sprawled in the chair like an indolent king upon his throne. "On that subject, why did you feel the need to defy my express command? The truth this time."

To her shock, he complied without fuss or mockery. "I kept watch and saw a man following you from the docks. He was armed and meant you harm."

She shot him a dry look. "And you were certain of that intent from so far away?"

Saint shrugged. "He was careful to keep the same distance between you from the minute the rowboat docked. Far enough to be unnoticeable and close enough to attack. I've faced enough mercenaries to know how they move."

"Why would you care about saving my life?" Lisbeth waved her arm. "You could have let me die and taken over my ship."

That grin of his flashed, though it wasn't as irritating

as it normally was. "Oui, I could have. But where's the fun in that? All work and no pleasure makes Jacques a very dull boy."

She ignored the not-so-subtle change in the adage and its resulting innuendo with effort, though her fingers brushed the hilt of her cutlass. His widening, knowing smile made her want to brandish it in his face. "Who are you? We both know you're no ordinary sailing master, if that is what you are at all. What do you want in Nassau?"

"I told you. My crew on my last ship mutinied, and I seek an eye for an eye from the man who paid them to do so."

Well, Lisbeth could understand vengeance. Swift and often brutal retaliation was part of their world after all. One did not cower when one's territory was trampled upon. Power had to be seized and retained. Of course, the other smugglers had no idea that the men she cut down were murderers and rapists. Gossip was ruinous, but beyond proper London drawing rooms, it was also an excellent tool. It made the idea of Bonnie Bess much worse than the reality, and right now, she had to hold to that.

"Who is the man?" she demanded in a harsh tone.

The bastard had the audacity to chuckle. "That's my business, Bess."

Her molars ground together. "If you're on my ship, it's *my* business." Eyes hard, she drew the curved blade from its sheath with no small amount of relish and pointed it at his chest. "Who?"

Saint didn't flinch, even though the sharp tip cut through the fabric of his shirt with little effort. As the material gaped, the tips of a pair of shadowed wings on the right side of his chest snagged her attention. The tattoo didn't surprise her. Most sailors had them. What did surprise her was the sudden desire to see more of it…to slice that shirt open from pectorals to navel and lay that art bare.

Focusing, she gritted her jaw. "I won't ask again, Saint. Who?"

In a move she didn't expect, he straightened, the tip of her blade going from fabric to skin with as much ease. A drop of scarlet blood welled and bloomed over the white linen like a poppy as metallic pewter eyes bored into her greens. Neither of them moved, the silent standoff between them only punctuated by the growing red stain on his shirt.

"Charles Dubois."

Raphael saw the shine of shock followed by what looked too much like a strange burst of exhilaration in her eyes before she hid it. *Interesting.* What could she want with a cur like Dubois? If he asked, he knew she would not tell him, so he sat back with a loud sigh. He plucked at his ruined shirt and formed a pronounced pout. "I just bought this, you know, with the last of my coin. It's not as though I have spares."

"Get one from Smalls." Bess wiped the blade on the edge of her sleeve and stuck it back into the sheath at her side.

"Have you seen the size of him? I'll swim in his clothing." Raphael's eyes canvassed the lean female body that was snugly garbed in a buttoned vest, high-collared shirt, and fitted trousers. He'd seen many a woman on the seas in similar attire, and yet, none of them had ever looked like her. Like pure sin wrapped in deceptively soft wool. "I reckon yours would be a much better fit."

"You wish to wear a woman's shirt?"

He smirked. "No, you misheard me. I wish to wear *your* shirt."

Bess glared at him. "Honestly, did you fall on your head as a child?"

"Of course not, my sweet-tongued Viking." A growl escaped her lips at the nickname as he knew it would. "Besides, you seem fond of gentlemen's clothing. Why should you or anyone judge me for my preferences, if indeed I had a predilection for female attire?"

If her lips tightened any further, they would disappear. "No one is judging you, you daft man. I don't care what you choose to wear. And I've changed my mind, it's 'Captain.'" Red spots formed on her cheeks, the fingers of her right hand twisting into the fabric of her trousers as she bolstered her fraying patience.

"It was quite fashionable and fetching, wouldn't you agree?" He pouted again and scrubbed at the crimson rosette on his shirt. "Before you ruined it."

"You ruined your shirt by leaning into a sharp blade like a simpleton."

"You cut it first," he countered. She pressed the heel of her hand to her forehead and clenched her jaw, her lips forming words—numbers, it appeared—as she counted herself back to equanimity. Raphael squashed the urge to grin, and lamented the loss a bit more, throwing all his acting ability into it. "I *loved* this shirt, you know."

"It's a bloody shirt. I'll get you ten others. Just stop talking, for mercy's sake."

Hiding his mirth, he lounged back in his seat, crossed one booted ankle over the other as if he didn't have a care in the world, and obediently mimed locking his lips shut with a key. She pinched the bridge of her nose with her thumb and forefinger. Raphael knew she had to see right through his game. She was much too astute not to, but he enjoyed playing the part of the oblivious scamp more than he'd expected, if only to see her so deliciously riled.

"Good," she ground out through translucent lips when she'd calmed enough to speak without skewering him. "*Dubois*."

"Is that a question?" he asked innocently. "Am I allowed to speak now?"

"Yes, speak." She leveled a cool look in his direction that meant business. "Tell me about him."

Caution slicked through him even as his own interest in her motives perked up, but he feigned indolence. "Surely you must know about the so-called Prince of Smugglers? Much like yours, Bonnie Bess, his reputation precedes him." He lifted his left hand and started with his index finger since she seemed partial to counting. "A man coveted by the customs houses. Rumored to be for smuggling countless shipments of lace, velvet, and silk into New York, avoiding millions in duties. Known to be callous and powerful. Fancies himself the leader of Smugglers Cove near Nassau. Will betray others without a qualm, including his own blood." When he ran out of fingers, he paused. "What more do you wish to know, Captain?"

"Smugglers Cove," she said, unable to quench her eagerness. "Where is that exactly?"

Ah. Raphael kept his expression blank. Bonnie Bess wanted what most other smugglers wanted…a way into the so-called smuggling elite. Smugglers Cove was an actual place, but it was also more of a community than a location. A select society of thieves, where Dubois longed to be the only sovereign…a feat he could only accomplish by getting rid of his biggest competition. Raphael. And he'd very nearly succeeded.

"Near Nassau," Raphael said, cataloging her reaction.

Her brows flew together in frustration. "Can you be more specific?"

"Why would you want to go there?" he asked curiously. "Do you wish to be part of Dubois's fleet?"

A narrowed green stare met his in challenge. "And if I did?"

"Then I would warn you to guard your back." His lips quirked. "And other parts of you that might not be on offer."

"I've gelded men for less," she replied and moved around to the other side of her desk, propping her hands on the surface. The excitement she had shown was throttled now as she considered him. Raphael guessed that she was working through scenarios in her head and the likelihood of whether he would lead her there. Or rather how to convince him to. "I'll pay you to take me."

Dieu, she made taunting her much too easy. He lifted a brow and smirked. "I'd take you any way you wanted for free, chérie."

"To take me to the cove, you concupiscent deviant!" she snapped, but a blush crested her cheeks as if she wasn't quite unaffected.

"My mistake." He grinned. "Alas, I am no ferryman and I have enough coin."

"You barely have a shirt and you've lost your ship," she said. Something like desperation flew across her eyes before it was buried. "Surely you are in need of money."

"I will have plenty once I get where I'm going."

A frown marred her brow. "Then what do you want in exchange?"

Raphael stalled, observing her carefully, waiting to see just *how* eager she was. And she had to be—he hadn't misread the excitement that he'd glimpsed earlier or the subsequent fear of having something she desired slip from her fingers. He'd spent enough years watching the clues and changes in demeanor of people to know she wanted in badly. But *how* badly? He licked his lips and saw her eyes flick there, a shadow of ferocity limning her features.

"No," she snapped, hand hovering over that bloodthirsty, razor-sharp cutlass of hers.

His brows shot up with mock innocence. "I haven't said a word."

"You didn't have to," she said. "You're not my type."

"And if I were interested in what you think I am about to propose, mistakenly might I add, what *is* your type, Captain Bess?"

"Not you."

He leaned forward with a grin. "I think you're lying to yourself. From the blush on your face, I wager I might pique your interest a little, my lady."

The slightest jerk passed over her shoulders at his insincere address, but Raphael caught that, too. Had she been a lady at one time? She certainly carried herself with the innate poise associated with the aristocracy, though he couldn't imagine any British peeress willingly becoming a criminal and captaining a frigate on the high seas.

Prison would be a cruel place for a woman, much less a highborn one. Still, he was a tarnished French duke and here he was. Little more than a modern pirate himself. He could not throw stones from his own glass house without damaging himself. And besides, what did it matter? Out here, titles held no value. Power, influence, and fearlessness did.

He shot her a circumspect look. "Tell me something true and I'll think about it."

"What does that even mean?" she replied with a scowl. "No more of these games. What do you want, Saint?"

"What if I told you I wanted the *Syren* for my troubles?"

Her jaw unhinged with incredulity. "My ship?"

"Yes."

"No," she bit out.

"That's my price, Your Ladyship. Take it or leave it." Raphael had no idea where the mocking moniker came from. Perhaps it was on the heels of thinking of her as nobility.

"It's Captain," she snarled. "I could kill you with no one the wiser."

"But then you still wouldn't be any closer to Smugglers Cove." He winked and shot a smug smile that he knew would infuriate her to no end. "And I am the only one who knows the exact coordinates...and the *only* one with the status not to have you shot and sunk before you dared to breach the bay."

She glared at him through suspicious eyes. "Just who the hell are you?"

"Your guide, should you so choose. It will only cost you one little ship."

Raphael didn't actually need her ship. He planned to use one of his own once he got to Nassau. He would have one or two vessels in port there, but he wanted to see how far she would go. And then he wanted to find out why. Greed drove most smugglers, but somehow, he didn't think that was her motivation. No, this went deeper. He remembered her intense expression when he'd mentioned Dubois, like the focus of a spider catching sight of a fly nearing its web.

Had the man wronged her in some way? Raphael

wouldn't put it past him. His uncle had a trail of enemies as wide as the Atlantic.

"Fine." It was a growl, but the admission shocked him. "But you must promise to take care of the crew."

"You have my word." Her fingers clenched and Raphael was sure she was imagining them around his neck. "Lovely doing business with you."

"Fuck you, Saint." She seethed as he stood and walked toward the door.

Raphael grinned and blew her a kiss just as a compass from the desk came flying in his direction. He ducked with a chuckle as it thumped into the wall. "I'm not your type, remember. And keep that instrument handy. You're going to need it."

Six

"Cap'n, we have a stowaway."

Lisbeth stared at Estelle, not taking in her quartermaster's words. Her mind was much too consumed with thoughts of murder. How excruciatingly painful could she make it? Could she torture Saint for the information? Perhaps she could truss him up with rope and drag him behind the ship for an hour or two. Bind him to the mast to roast in the hot sun without clothing. She blinked that idea away rapidly.

That festering rotter. How dare he demand her ship as payment? Lisbeth hissed through her teeth and tugged on the snarls of her hair. The rat's nest was thanks to an utterly sleepless night because of the contemptible deal she'd made with an equally contemptible man. Surely such a steep price was not worth the information—or his unguaranteed boast of protection—that he'd offered in exchange? She hissed again, clenching her fingers on the railing.

God damn her eyes. It was. She'd pay *any* price if she had to.

After so many months, Smugglers Cove had always been just out of her reach. Infiltrating Dubois's circle and bringing the slippery criminal to justice was the point of her entire mission...the whole reason behind her undercover role as a smuggler for the past two years. The bloody ship wasn't even hers. The *Syren* was a captured blockade runner belonging to the American government that had been outfitted and loaned to her specifically for the purposes of the mission. Lisbeth had no idea why she was so upset. Her crew would be fine. But Estelle and Smalls were her family. She blinked and scrubbed at her temples.

"Bess."

Whirling around, Lisbeth glowered at her looming quartermaster. "What the bloody hell is it?"

Estelle's stoic face was carved from stone. "We have a stowaway."

Why on earth was Estelle bothering her with something so trivial? Lisbeth's irritation grew as her head pounded. Couldn't her second-in-command handle simple matters? It was a common enough occurrence whenever they made port, with people looking to escape their lives. She scowled. "It's not the first time this has happened, is it? Put them in the brig until we get to Nassau."

"Not this one, we can't."

Estelle jerked her chin over her left shoulder and Lisbeth followed her stare to where two people stood on the lower deck—one huge and the other half his size, attempting to hide behind his much bulkier frame. Oh, the fates had to be playing tricks on her...because that couldn't be a shamefaced, cowering Narina being held by Smalls. Lisbeth placed a balled fist against her forehead, her vision misting slightly as she fought to control her cascading emotions.

They were already four hundred nautical miles away

from Bridgetown. Turning the ship around when they were a day away from Nassau would be senseless, but Narina's presence onboard changed everything. Soon, the *Syren* wouldn't even be hers to command anyway. It would be *his*. The man watching her from the stern, casually peeling an orange without a care in the world.

Lisbeth's temper boiled over and she leaped over the rail, her boots making an ominous thumping sound on the deck as she landed like a cat. Furious, she stomped toward Narina and Smalls as Estelle followed down the stairs. "What the devil are you doing here, Nari? I told you it was safer for you to stay in Bridgetown!"

"Bess," the girl pleaded. "Let me explain."

"Explain what?" she snapped through her teeth. "That you defied me and went behind my back to hide on my ship when I told you that this journey could be dangerous!" Narina's lower lip wobbled and eyes welled with tears, but Lisbeth was much too irate to notice. "Now you've put me in an impossible situation!"

"Bess," Estelle chided softly.

"Don't you 'Bess' me," she ground out, cursing under her breath. "You should be manning the wheel, and I bloody well told her to stay put."

Estelle's brows rose. "When you were a child, did you always do everything you were told?"

"That's not the same. It isn't safe. I left men there for her protection."

"She's safer with you than in that shitty tavern on her own with no next of kin to care for her, and she's here now.

Nothing we can do about that, unless you wish to swing about and set course for Barbados?"

Lisbeth scowled. Turning around wasn't an option. "No."

"Well, work it out. Without making a spectacle of it." Her quartermaster rolled her eyes and strode back the way she'd come. "And control your goddamned temper."

Narina sniffled. "I had no one left."

"I'm not your mother." Lisbeth regretted the words as soon as they were out of her mouth, the stricken look on the girl's face making her heart clench. *Fuck!* This was why she did not get involved with people. Relationships, even ones with children, meant expectations, and shouldering the emotional toll when she invariably failed at giving them what they wanted.

The life of a spy was lonely work. Lonely work that Lisbeth loved because she did not seek out companionship. People were simply means to ends. Thornbury had been a convenient partner in arms. Estelle had been an opportune lover. Narina and her mother had been a useful connection for a bath and a hearty meal. Lisbeth rubbed at a spot in the center of her chest that felt like an elephant was sitting upon it. Christ, she had no time to be the hero. Especially not now...when she was on the cusp of ending this accursed assignment.

The pounding in Lisbeth's head grew. "Take her to my cabin," she finally said to Smalls, who stood like a silent shadow, while she willed the flames of her temper to cool. "She'll be secure there until I can figure out what to do."

"I'm sorry, Bess," Narina said with a dismal sniff. "I didn't mean to."

"It's a little too late now, isn't it?" Lisbeth barked.

A throat cleared from behind them. "Don't take your resentment out on her, Bessie love. The girl didn't mean it and she already apologized. Calm down."

What in the actual hell? Bessie-fucking-*love*? Calm-fucking-*down*? The furious embers she'd tried to quench billowed into an inferno at that deep, ever amused, loathsome baritone. "You!"

Fists balling, she spun to face her nemesis—finally, a target she could unleash her rotten mood upon. One who deserved it, simply for putting her—one of the Crown's best spymasters no less—into an intolerable, *unspeakable* situation. In fact, the moment he'd set foot on her ship, she'd regretted it. He was clearly the *something* her senses had been warning her about.

An arrogant eyebrow rose. "Moi?"

Oh, the bastard knew how to push her buttons. "Oui, toi," she replied in a mocking tone. A slow grin curled his lips at her response in scornful French. "Let's settle this once and for all."

"Settle what?" he countered. "We already have an agreement."

Resentment at being backed into a corner fueled the words on her tongue as she rolled her neck, signaling to Smalls who stared at her with surprise written all over his usually impassive face. "Since you boasted about your love for swords in close quarters, I challenge you to a fencing duel. First to draw blood wins. If I win, my forfeit is null. You'll give me the information I require in exchange for safe passage on *my* ship."

"Bess," Smalls cautioned, but she waved him off.

"Fetch the épées from my cabin."

Murmurs from the eavesdropping crew filled the air. The promise of a fight was always good entertainment at least. More abandoned their duties to get a better view, and she could already see coin and wagers changing hands.

"Why would I do that?" Saint drawled, crossing his arms. "And besides, you've already drawn my blood. I do not wish to have my trousers sliced to ribbons next." He waggled his brows. "Unless, of course, that is your diabolic intent, you sneaky Valkyrie, you."

Oh, for the love of God and his entire legion of avenging angels! Lisbeth closed her eyes and counted to ten. "Best me and you get my cut of the cargo in the hold. Salt, liquor, diamonds, and cigars bound for Florida, take your pick." Most of the items were confiscated goods from the customs houses to shore up the pretense, but no one needed to know that.

"I told you I am not in need of money."

What smuggler worth his salt refused the promise of more wealth? Her gaze narrowed on him anew. Who *was* this man? And again, why would he turn his back on such a lucrative deal? Men in their profession would salivate at getting their hands on any part of Bonnie Bess's hold.

"Then do it for honor's sake," she snarled, nearly

snatching the rapiers from a grimacing Smalls and tossing one of them toward the sailing master.

"Honor?" Saint asked, pointedly ignoring the thin-bladed sword that skidded to a stop at his feet. "Among *smugglers*? Surely you jest."

She swung the blade in a slow, wide circle, a twisted, vicious grin on her face. "Then tell me, Pirate, is it that you're afraid to fight a tiny little woman?"

Fuck if Raphael didn't want to toss the vicious sharp-tongued Viking over his shoulder and show her a much more enjoyable, *pleasurable* way to settle things. He also did not want an ax in his back or a sword through his ballocks, both of which were possible in the murderous mood she was in. He should have known his audacious price would have come back to haunt him.

Every captain had a special relationship with his or her ship, especially ones that had ferried them through countless hells on the open seas, and the *Syren* was synonymous with Bonnie Bess. He couldn't say he hadn't known exactly what he was doing, however.

Provoking her had become his favorite pastime.

"Afraid of you?" he scoffed with a laugh.

A blond brow arched. "Prove it."

Slowly, while keeping his eyes on her, he removed his coat and placed it over a nearby barrel. He didn't miss the way her eyes rounded when he untucked the hem of his shirt from his trousers. "Why the hell are you undressing?" she demanded, even as the rest of the crew hooted and hollered in bawdy appreciation.

He launched an injured stare in her direction. "God's teeth woman, this is my *only* shirt. I'd rather it not be in tatters at the end of this."

"Forfeit, then," she said. "Save yourself the trouble."

"And miss the chance to forage through your tightly guarded hold?" Those hot green eyes attempting to incinerate him by the power of her will alone darkened at the rather obvious intimation. "I think not, Viking."

"It's Captain, you cockish slouch!"

Even while her eyes flung daggers at him, Raphael tugged the tail end of his bloodied shirt up over his head and threw it onto his coat while flicking at the sword on the deck in front of him with the tip of his boot. He caught the rapier in his hand and sketched a courtly bow. Satisfaction flooded him as her eyes fastened on the ink on bold display over his sternum and right pectoral, a small gasp escaping her lips at sight of the tattoo of *Prometheus Bound* by Rubens.

An eagle descended, wings spread and claws extended over a man's body, the slightest hint of vermillion over his half-consumed liver: an eternal punishment for defying the gods. But that wasn't all. A curved gold ring was pierced through Raphael's right nipple, as though connecting to the inked chains that held the Titan in place. He felt her shock—and interest—as her eyes flicked to the metal, a violent blush painting her cheeks scarlet.

"Something catch your eye, Bess?" he asked.

Tossing her head and forcing her features into ruthless submission, his beautiful foe eyed the jewelry and the expansive tattoo that covered most of his upper chest. Both had been intense lessons in pain. She cleared her throat. "That's different."

He canted his head. "Reminds me of what's at stake and the consequences that await each of us."

Green eyes narrowed with renewed purpose as she circled him, weapon at the ready. "Prometheus also symbolizes the trickster. Is that what you are, Pirate? A man in disguise, hoping to deceive us all?"

"Or perhaps simply a man trying to do the right thing."

She struck out and he lifted his own blade to block her strike, the sound of clashing steel a harsh chime between them. "For whom? Himself?"

"You wound me," he said, darting out of the way of a practiced lunge that came much too close to carving a stripe down his exposed torso.

Raphael throttled his focus, the practiced skill of his opponent immediately apparent. He'd seen her in the market square in Bridgetown and the gracefully efficient way she'd pared down her enemies. *Without* weapons. There was no doubt in his mind that Bonnie Bess was as proficient in bladed weapons as she was with bare fists. She wouldn't have made such a wager if she wasn't convinced that she would win.

He lunged and she parried, the whine of metal whistling through the air. Three more slashes saw sparks flying as they danced together and flew apart. Every parry she made, he countered with a riposte. Until she thrust and he spun instead, forcing her off-balance. In a flash, he erased the distance between them. Raphael did not strike, instead going for an arm wrapped around her throat and drawing her supple body back against his, sword arm trapped at her side beneath his. She cursed, spine going rigid.

"Do you submit?" he whispered in her ear, the honeyed orange-blossom scent of her wafting into his nostrils.

In response, an elbow slammed into his gut as she let her body drop with her full weight and wrenched out of his hold. "You wish."

"I *do* wish," he said with a grin. He hadn't meant to keep her there; he'd only wanted to goad her.

"You are insufferable," she hissed.

"Careful, Viking," he taunted and slapped the tip of her blade in a downward arc. "Or I might start to think you're obsessed with me."

"In your dreams, you arrogant ass!"

He parried a brutal but elegant sequences of strikes, ones he recognized as if they'd been imparted by a European fencing master. When she performed a slight jump backward, Raphael knew the move because he'd learned the same. His suspicions were correct: Bonnie Bess had spent time in an aristocratic court or at least a family with enough wealth to spend on fencing lessons. He would bet his entire fleet upon it. "You fence well," he told her. "Pierre Prévost?"

"Yes," she said, eyes narrowing. "Do you know his style?"

He gave an exhilarated laugh. "I do. My father enjoyed

fencing and I essentially memorized *Theorie pratique de l'escrime.*"

Without warning, she sprang forward, nearly catching him in his arm before he spun away in the opposite direction, narrowly missing the edge of her blade. "Where did you learn?"

"Paris," he said. "You?"

"London."

Dimly, Raphael became aware of their audience, the whistles and cheers nearly deafening, especially when the captain continued her flashy moves. He'd been so caught up in her that he'd forgotten the crew that surrounded them. However stunning and capable she was, or whether they had fencing styles in common, Raphael still had a wager to win. He had no intention of losing, though the odds of winning lessened as time passed. Clearly, they'd honed the same skills.

Time to change up the game.

Watching her hips—as shapely as they were in those formfitting trousers, which gave away her movements—Raphael sucked in a tense breath. When she shunted left, he ducked and swiped out with his legs, taking hers out from under her. His adversary slammed to her back on the deck with a gasp, her sword flying from her hands a handful of feet away. As expected, she was not one for defeat and vaulted to her feet, fists at the ready.

"That was disgraceful," she snarled. "But then I shouldn't be surprised."

Raphael couldn't help the taunt that rose to his lips.

"Will you use your talons to source first blood, Viking, or should I expect more of that caustic tongue of yours?"

She bared her teeth at him. "Are you going to fight like a gentleman or keep scampering around like a rabid squirrel?"

"I do not scamper," he said, grinning.

"And I do not require a blade to make you bleed, Pirate."

Without warning, she shuttled in, one fist punching out to catch him in the jaw and a second jab into his ribs. A spinning kick caught him in the side while a second neatly clipped the sword from his grip. He wheezed as he fought for air to fill his lungs and staggered back out of her reach. "That was sneaky," he panted, putting some distance between them.

"All is fair in love and war."

He feinted right as she launched an attack to his left, barely evading the kick that came toward his thigh. "And here I was thinking we could only ever be war and war. There is hope for this poor, lovesick soul after all! Thank you, oh divine Goddess of the Sea!"

Bess stared at him, her lips twitching at his over-the-top dramatics. "You are the most absurd man I have ever met."

"Flirt!" he shot back and snatched up his fallen weapon.

"Trust me, Pirate, you'd know if I were flirting with you. Right now, I only mean to right a grievous wrong." With that, she closed the distance between them, crouching to the deck and ducking below the end of the blade that whistled past her head. A tuft of blond hair fluttered to the deck, but she paid it no mind and crashed into his belly with the full force of her shoulder.

The air blasted from him as they both toppled back. Without thinking, Raphael moved to cradle her from harm, releasing his weapon and taking the brunt of the fall on himself. They tumbled down in a tangle of limbs and crashed into the mast pole. Blinking the stars out of his vision, he reached up to his sore temple, his fingers coming away stained red.

Dieu, was he bleeding?

The virago of a captain straddled his waist with an impish grin that made those sea-green eyes light up with victory. "I win."

Raphael would forfeit the match a thousand times over if the decadent weight of her body and the heat of her thighs upon him was the penalty for the loss. The roar of her crew's cheers filled the air. "I call foul," he protested.

A full-blown smile formed, nearly made him dizzy as she leaned forward, the heat of her center pressing intimately down on his abdomen. "Are you being a sore loser?"

She propped her elbows on his sweaty chest, like the very eagle inked onto his skin, sent by Zeus himself to torture the Titan who'd stolen from him. The irony wasn't lost, the symbolism almost poetic in its beauty. Oblivious to their onlookers, a fingernail traced the top of one feathered wing. Raphael shuttled back a sharp exhale, the slight touch almost too exquisite to bear. He couldn't help noticing her gaze flick to his piercing. Would she dare to touch him there?

"Ride him good, Bess!" someone shouted, and the crew broke out into raucous laughter, breaking the charged silence between them. She snatched her hand away, a look of mortification brewing on her face as if she'd been caught doing something she hadn't intended to.

"I did not lose," he said. "You did not inflict first blood, the *Syren* did."

"Good thing she and I are one and the same." She sat up straight and scooted back, eyes ablaze.

Raphael couldn't help it, his body reacted at the precipitous jerk of her hips upon him...his cock swelling beneath the titillating press of her plump arse as his brain conjured images of fantasies he did not need with such an eager audience. Of his beautiful Valkyrie with her head thrown back in ecstasy, hands on her naked breasts, and riding him to her pleasure without mercy.

Blood rushed south in a flood as he fought futilely against his body's natural reaction. Her eyes widened, undoubtedly feeling the stiffening of his cock beneath her buttocks, and she moved to scramble off, but his hands came up to capture her thighs in place. "Pour l'amour du ciel. Do. Not. Move," he gritted out.

Plush lips parted, eyes going wide and cheeks crimson. "You're...hard."

"I am well aware. Give me a minute and my pride, Viking."

Her slender throat worked, that flush spreading down that pale column as if she, too, could not control her own reaction. A rousing fight tended to bring all those primitive humors to the surface. Would she be drenched in the seam of those trousers? Eyes fluttering shut, Raphael groaned and cursed himself for swelling even more. The hips above his trembled and his eyes snapped open, wondering if she was in similar physical torment.

But no. Of course not, because the bloody chit was laughing. Fighting her amusement, Bess pressed her lips together.

He scowled. “This isn’t remotely funny.”

“It’s enormously funny.”

“I wouldn’t poke fun at you if you were in such a condition, would I?” he whispered, the comment meant only for her ears, but a few raucous whistles followed.

“I’m not.” But her face flamed with the lie. Her eyes flew up to her crew. “Back to work, you lot. I’m not paying you to stand around and gawk! Show’s over.”

She moved to dismount, but Raphael’s fingers pressed down into the muscled meat of her thighs and his hips canted upward in a faint thrust. “*Oh.*” Her eyes flew wide, the sensual movement chasing the laughter from her lips as she attempted once more to rise, but his hands tightened to keep her firmly in place.

“Isn’t so funny now, is it, when the shoe is on the other foot?” he asked, sitting up and banding one arm across her back to hold her flush against him. The erotic shift in position made them both gasp. His lips grazed her ear. “If I slipped my fingers past the waistband of your trousers, what would I find, Viking?”

“Nothing,” she said.

"Don't lie to me."

Her eyes flashed fire at the command. "Then don't ask stupid questions."

Between them, her chest rose and fell in unsteady gasps, belying that hard gaze, the bloom of unwelcome pleasure evident in those deadly ocean eyes, until the fraught spell was broken by a shout from the quartermaster that had the rest of the lagging crew scrambling to their posts. "Squall on the horizon!"

Better than the one in his pants, Raphael supposed.

Seven

The late evening sky, normally a deep-blue twilight on a clear night, was completely dark, with thick clouds obscuring nearly all light. Sheets of rain lashed mercilessly into Lisbeth's face, a screaming wind whipped at her hair and tore at her sodden clothing. Luckily, the extra twenty-five pounds of cork in the bulky canvas vest she'd tied around herself helped keep her feet well grounded. It was heavy, but would keep her alive if she were swept overboard. And with this kind of squall, there was no telling how bad it would get—the warmer the sea, the stronger the storm.

Despite Estelle's hasty warning, the gale had closed the distance between them too fast, leaving them no choice but to sail directly into it. The best option would have been to steer around it, but with the fast-moving winds, that window had rapidly closed. They'd weathered worse and been fine. Thunder crashed when a bolt of cracked lightning forked the sky into blue-white sections as if to laugh at her foolish thoughts. It had already been hours and the storm showed no signs of lessening.

The ocean roiled, huge waves pitching the frigate as her hull plowed through the seething crests and descended the choppy back sides into the trough. The

Syren was designed to withstand a siege of this magnitude. The steam engines were working to get them through the storm as fast as possible, but the weather only seemed to be getting worse. This wasn't a normal summer storm that hit fast and hard. This was much worse. Hurricanes were common in this part of the world, and many ships did not survive the sea's wrath.

"Hard starboard," Saint roared to her left, his arms straining as he tightened loose rigging. "If she's into the wind, she'll capsize!" Lisbeth obeyed, trusting the sailing master's bellowed instructions implicitly. A second's hesitation on a good day could mean the difference between life and death. In a thunderstorm, the odds were much worse.

"You there," he yelled to a nearby deckhand. "Make sure those rowboats are battened down and that sail is secured with the lines." Anchored with ropes that had enough slack, the boatswain rushed to do his bidding.

Eyes tracking the men, Lisbeth saw that one of the rowboats had come loose from its deck mooring and hung drunkenly to the side, nearly listing overboard. She was grateful for Saint's warning. If the ship went down, God forbid, those rowboats would be their only hope of survival. Then again, if the *Syren* gave up the ghost to this storm, their chances in those flimsy boats were slim.

"Captain, need an extra hand?" Saint shouted, making his way to her, his voice almost lost to the deafening winds.

Lisbeth wanted to say no so badly, but that was her pride speaking. Her fingers were numb from cold and her muscles ached from keeping the helm tight for hours on end.

Her shoulders ached from the weight of the buoyant survival vest. Each crashing wave made the ship groan and the wheel yank off course. Estelle was busy in the engine room, making sure that they had enough coal to get them through the brunt of it. They'd be sitting ducks in an angry sea if they ran out of fuel, left to the violent whims of the ocean gods.

"Bess, let me take her for a turn." Saint braced behind her, feet planted wide against the violent pitching of the ship. "Get something in your belly. Keep your strength up. This storm isn't going anywhere."

"I'm fine," she said, gritting her teeth and wincing as a ferocious pitch knocked her off her feet right into him.

"I know you are, but you're no good weak. Take a break. Let me help."

Her first instinct was to argue that she *wasn't* weak, but her exhausted sailor's brain also understood Saint's words. She needed to be strong to make it through. If she was faint with hunger, her crew would suffer. Nobody's pride was worth that cost.

"Do you want the vest?" she asked.

"No, I'll be fine without it," he said.

With a grateful nod, she untied the rope keeping her secured to the railing and reached for another that would allow her to make it belowdecks without being washed overboard by a wild wave. Lord knew that had happened before. She'd lost crew that way, good men and women swept out to sea. Over her shoulder, she wiped the water out of her eyes as she watched Saint take the rope she'd untied and knot it around his waist.

She could see him bellowing orders to the crewmen around him, making sure that everything was locked down tight, but his words were lost to the winds. She had to trust that the *Syren* was in seemingly capable hands for the moment. Ducking down the stairs, she untied the rope and hung it on a peg. She made her way to the engine room and cranked open the door.

"Estelle," she shouted as the muffled sounds of the storm reverberated in the narrow corridor. "Report on fuel."

Her quartermaster's soot-stained face popped up at the bottom of the staircase while Lisbeth braced herself against one wall when the ship listed left. Her stomach swooped. "We have enough for a few more hours," Estelle yelled back. "How bad is it up there? Feels like we're in a cyclone down here."

"It's dreadful and going to get worse. Saint's at the wheel for a bit."

"Good," Estelle said. "Shout if you need me."

"Where is Narina?" she asked.

Estelle wiped sweat out of her eyes. "Your cabin with Smalls."

That was a relief. Smalls would ensure the girl's safety, before his own if he had to. She couldn't let herself fixate on the extra soul onboard, though nervous energy swirled through her at the defeatist thought that this might be the storm that triumphed over the *Syren*.

"Not on my bloody watch," Lisbeth muttered as she made her way to the galley. She'd attempt to fill her belly with the hope that the sustenance would stay down, and warm up before going back where she belonged. She loathed leaving the sailing master in her place, but this was a much-needed reprieve.

"Shirley, you in here?" she asked, water dripping off her in sheets.

"Aye, Cap'n," a voice yelled back.

"Where are you? I need some food. And a drink."

The cook had secured most of the sharp instruments and cooking pans, though some broken dishes and random foods littered the floor. A head of cabbage rolled past Lisbeth's feet, followed by an orange and some beets. The cook emerged from where she'd wedged herself in between two barrels, her weathered face green. Water sloshed around the floorboards.

With a groan as the ship hurtled down another wave and barreled up the other side, Shirley offered her a thick strip of salted meat and a flask. Chewing the jerky, Lisbeth tipped back some of the liquor. Bitter rum burned a warm path down her throat to her stomach. Forcing herself to finish the meat to get some nourishment into her body, she drank another mouthful of rum and wiped her face with the back of her hand. The spirits warmed her extremities, but too much would cloud her senses. She snagged the orange floating by her feet and nodded her thanks to the cook.

"See you on the other side, Shirley," she told the cook with a forced, cheery grin. "We'll get through this. The *Syren* can take it."

"But I don't know if I can," Shirley moaned, rushing for a pot near the barrels.

She wasn't alone. Lisbeth wasn't far off from casting up her accounts herself. She crawled her way out of the galley to her quarters, poking her head around the doorframe to where Smalls stood guard, a concerned gaze fastened to the porthole that was obscured by sheets of water. Narina's small body was huddled behind the drapes on her bed.

"You both all right?" Lisbeth asked over the pounding of the rain and the crashing of waves on all sides of the ship.

"Bess!" Narina shrieked. "Blow me down, you're bloody alive!"

"As well as can be, Cap'n," Smalls replied, his eyes tracking her from head to toe, relief in his gaze at seeing her in one piece. "Some squall."

"A moody bitch of a squall." She shot the girl a tired grin, reassured to see that Narina didn't seem too much the worse for wear. If anything, her young face was alight with excitement. "Stay with Smalls," Lisbeth told her. "I need to get back up top. Saint's at the helm and we need all the help we can get."

"We can help," Narina said. "I've been practicing being a pirate."

"You can help by staying put. I mean it, Nari." The girl pouted but nodded.

A sudden sharp lurch had the ship nearly listing sideways, and Lisbeth lost her balance, crashing hard into the doorframe as she struggled to stay upright. Narina went tumbling off the bed, but luckily, Smalls caught her in his strong grip before she could get hurt. Through the window, the barest sliver of moonlight that wasn't from lightning broke through the clouds.

"Keep her safe," she ordered Smalls. "This isn't over."

He nodded. "Aye, Cap'n."

"Bess, wait," Narina said, but Lisbeth had already shut the door and turned back toward the deck.

Wind and rain pelted her face, the howling storm much worse than when she'd left it barely thirty minutes before. Securing the rope around her waist, she bellowed her gratitude to the drenched boatswains who manned the lines tied to the masts, making sure that none of the beams swung loose. She glanced up, only able to see the tall mast when flashes of lightning drew jagged streaks across the angry sky.

She was right that the clouds gave way to one or two soft moonlit patches on the port side of the ship, while the starboard side remained dark, which meant that Saint must have been hoping to steer them out of the storm's path. The mast creaked as the *Syren* sped toward the bottom of another trough, her hull groaning at the steep descent. If the main mast snapped, the damage it could cause would be terrible.

"Stay steadfast, girl," she whispered. "Don't give up on me now."

Her gaze flicked to the figure on the quarterdeck, a burst of reluctant admiration spiraling through her at the sight of Saint. If she'd had any doubt that he was a captain in his own right, it was forever erased. Hands firm on the wheel, his muscles straining through his soaked transparent shirt, he stared down the punishing storm without a single iota of fear on his face. His mouth was a slash, his brow drawn with resolve.

Lisbeth exhaled a breath. If she had to give up control of the *Syren* to anyone, even for a short while, she was grateful it was him. His gaze caught hers as if summoned, and her lungs squeezed in her chest. For a moment, the sounds of the rain and wind stilled, and they were in perfect accord—two minds with one purpose—getting them out of this alive.

Lisbeth blinked rain out of her eyes when she caught his lips moving and frowned. She couldn't hear him, the wind snatching his words away. His gaze was no longer on her, she realized.

"Bess!" That shout wasn't his. It was high-pitched and came from behind her.

She whirled, eyes going wide with terror as she saw Narina's small frame chased by a horrified Smalls. "What are you doing? Get down below!"

"I'm fine," Narina shouted. "I wanted to give you this for luck. It's Saint Christopher." In her hand she held out a tarnished necklace. "Don't worry, I tied myself to a rope, too!"

The crest of another immense wave, one Lisbeth could see the curling lip of in the dimly lit sky, rose high and plowed into the stern. Water crashed over the deck in a powerful frenzy. The ocean would not relinquish any prize so easily. That realization was all too evident in Narina's terrified eyes as her feet swooshed out from under her and she went careening across the slick deck.

"Smalls!" Lisbeth screamed, hurrying to untie her own rope that wouldn't let her move another inch toward the girl. "Get her!"

But it was much too late.

In dizzying, chilling slow motion, Lisbeth watched as the childish loop Narina had fashioned unraveled from the power of the wave, her small hands scrabbling for purchase on the slippery boards. A wild scream tore from her throat as she was tossed against the rowboat and washed over the side.

The knot at Lisbeth's waist finally came loose and she didn't hesitate. She ran and dove over the railing, straight into the inky depths of hell.

Raphael watched the scene unroll as if from a great distance—the wave crashing, the girl being swept off her feet, and Bess, that brave irrational fool, hurtling over the side in the middle of a hurricane. The child was certainly lost; she had no hope of surviving the rough seas. But Bess...at least she had a chance with that vest she had on. It would keep her afloat.

"Fuck! Smalls," he bellowed. "Grab the wheel. Keep her on the port side. We're almost out of the path. Storm's moving right, stay on this course." He pointed to one of the nearby boatswains. "Get Estelle at once!"

When the man obeyed and an ashen Smalls had taken his place, Raphael leaped over to where the loose rowboat hung drunkenly to one side. "Help me get this loose and down!" he ordered, jerking the paralyzed deckhands into action. The clouds lessened as Smalls steered the *Syren* further away on the path Raphael had indicated and moonlight flickered on the wave crests. With the wind and the wild currents, Bess could be anywhere, but he had no time to lose.

Estelle clambered on deck, fear all over her face. "What the hell happened?" she demanded. "Where are you going?"

"Your fool captain decided to go for a swim."

Her eyes popped. "She fucking what?"

"The girl fell over and she went in," he explained brusquely. "Sail west and then head for Nassau," he added, watching as the rowboat descended via the pulleys into the thrashing waves. Without waiting for a reply, he grabbed hold of a rope and swung himself down. "We're hours away from the mainland, if that. With luck, we will make it there, too."

"Saint." He peered up into the quartermaster's pinched face, her fingers flexing on the rail. It was the most emotion he'd ever seen from her. "I'll go with you."

He shook his head. "You're the only one who can get the *Syren* out of this."

Estelle's throat worked as she swallowed, tears indistinguishable from the rain. "Please…"

"I'll find her, don't worry."

It was an impossible promise, but he made it nonetheless. Raphael grabbed the oars and braced against the churn of the waves. The lifeboat was sturdy enough, bobbing up and down over the choppy water as it was designed to do. Within minutes, the shadow of the *Syren* grew smaller as the distance between them widened, lost to a fog that seemed to thicken on the tail end of the storm.

Wasting no time, he pulled out the F. Barker & Son compass that he'd taken from Bess's desk. He'd been attempting to steer the *Syren* west, and he estimated that Narina and Bess had gone off in a northwesterly direction. After he consulted the compass in the meager light, he situated the boat and got to work, pulling hard on the oars. The currents could have dragged her anywhere, but it was somewhere to start. By his guess, it hadn't been more than a handful of minutes since she'd gone over.

"Bess!" he shouted with each stroke. More patchy moonlight lit the seas as the storm veered east, and while the seas churned in its wake, he could see that the rainfall was lessening.

"Bess! God damn you, Bess, answer!"

Raphael rowed until his arms ached and his muscles burned with strain. He stood, holding on to the sides as he scanned the ocean. Dawn was on the horizon, the wisps of light a welcome respite. The waves ebbed and flowed, nowhere near as wild as they had been. Just when despair nearly crashed over him, he spotted a bobbing shadow. It could be anything...a barrel, a piece of some other unfortunate ship, or *someone*. Grabbing the oars, he turned the boat and rowed toward it.

A fucking barrel. His heart sank.

Distraught, he stood again and shouted, his voice hoarse. "Bess! You stubborn witch of a woman, I know you're alive! You're a fucking Valkyrie! No paltry ocean can conquer you. Answer me!"

When no reply came, he cursed and searched the waves again. Exhaustion and defeat slumped his shoulders. It had been a shot in the dark. The sea did not give up its conquests so easily, and he'd been a bloody fool to even try…to make such an arrogant, preposterous promise. Finding anyone who'd gone overboard would be like searching for a needle in a haystack. He should know. Over years of sailing, he'd lost dozens of men to the sea in storms. Death by drowning, not to mention the predators that hunted beneath the waves.

I'm sorry.

"Going my way, Pirate?" His eyes snapped open, certain he'd imagined that thready, airless voice. The brain loved to play tricks when it was weary.

"Bess?" He stood up so quickly, he nearly toppled into the ocean himself, only to see the impossible. Bess floated in the water, held buoyant by the cork vest she wore. Blond hair was plastered to her skull and her reddened eyes looked like she'd faced down death and survived, but it was the limp body held in the crook of one arm that made him release a breath of astonishment. "You got her? She alive?"

"Barely," she said as he hauled the girl in first, feeling the faintest of pulses in her wrist. "How did you find us?"

"I don't even know," he said and lifted her into the boat.

Bess licked crusted lips. "Put the cork vest on Narina

just in case," she whispered, panting with probably the first full breaths she'd taken since she went overboard. She untied the straps and passed him the heavy garment. Raphael did as she requested, gently situating the bulky jacket around the unresponsive girl. If they made it to safety, she would need a doctor.

"There should be a tarpaulin near the bow," Bess rasped. "Use it to cover Narina so she can get warm. Should be water there, too." At his look, she gave him a weak smile. "I like to be prepared." He dug under the tarpaulin near the bow and passed her one of the bottles before pulling the covering over Narina, making sure she had room to breathe. Bess took a long draught and moved to trickle a few drops into the girl's mouth before offering the rest to Raphael.

He shook his head. "You drink. You need it more."

"Where's the *Syren*?" Bess asked.

"Estelle is sailing her to Nassau. I told her we'd meet her there."

Rubbing her arms, even as a cool mist still drizzled from the sky, Bess blinked and stared doubtfully at the oars. "We're going to row there? Do you know where we are?"

Raphael pulled out the compass from his pocket and watched the mica dial settle halfway between the triangular north marker and the circular south marker. "Our last position on the *Syren* was heading west to outrun the storm, and then I rowed north to track where you went in after the girl. If I'm right, we might be near the southern end of the archipelago. If we keep heading northeast, we'll hit land."

"Are you certain?"

He grinned with a wink, working one of the oars to point the boat in the direction of travel. "What kind of sailing master would I be if I wasn't?"

"Aren't most of those coral islands uninhabited?"

The grin on his face widened. "Some are and some are not. You'll see." Bess frowned, her pert nose wrinkling at his much-too-cryptic reply. He took pity on her after a beat, given her ordeal. "You wanted to go to Smugglers Cove, didn't you? Well, sit tight because here's your chance."

Her mouth fell open and then snapped shut.

For once, he'd struck her speechless.

Eight

Lisbeth's eyelids cracked painfully apart, filtered sunlight guttering through her lashes. Wincing, she blinked through the salty grit crusted on her irises. Her brain belatedly registered that she was warm and lying cocooned beneath soft sheets. On a bed. Alive. Or maybe she was dead and none of this was real.

She blinked rapidly, staring up at the wooden beams crossing the length of the room and the scent of fresh sea air that wafted through the curtains. She could hear the sound of waves breaking on a shore in the distance and the soft murmur of voices. Perhaps she was only dreaming and she simply needed to awaken.

Get up!

Lisbeth tried to obey the voice in her head, but was prevented from sitting up by the weight slung across her abdomen. Distractedly, she glanced down and froze at the vision of a bronzed, thick forearm that was dusted in dark hair. Lisbeth's eyes traveled across it. The arm that made her dry mouth even drier was connected to a very shirtless, very male body. Bloody hell, she was definitely dead because as a rule of thumb, she never let anyone sleep in her bed.

Her head was pounding, a painful thump echoing

between her temples. Dear God, had they put into port somewhere and she got so senselessly cup-shot that she'd climbed into bed with a stranger and spent the entire night without realizing it? Worse things had happened, she supposed. And it had to have been quite a night because every single muscle in her body was sore. And not the pleasant kind either. She felt like she'd been chewed up and spit out by a tornado.

Her eyes flew wide as she remembered, and she shoved the arm off. "Narina!"

The owner of the arm groused. "She's fine. Looked over by a doctor and resting. Go back to sleep for the sake of soft, sweet beds everywhere."

Saint? Lisbeth's eyes bulged so forcefully she worried they'd fall from her skull. Suddenly, she was acutely aware of her body that seemed clad only in a thin night rail beneath the sheets. She clutched the bedclothes to her breast, and he groaned, shifting from his side to his back and flinging an arm over his eyes.

Lisbeth was treated to an unobstructed view of a broad chest, the striking ink that rippled along his right pectoral, and that damned nipple ring that made the breath squeeze in her lungs. She had no idea why that small piece of jewelry seemed so attractive on him. So sultry. She'd known several women in Paris who'd gotten them, and most sailors had all manner of body parts inked or pierced. Her gaze panned to the abdominal muscles stacked like paired bricks and the trail of dark hair that led to a low-slung waistband and...a substantial bulge.

Lisbeth gulped while her tongue glued itself to the roof of her mouth. "Bloody hell, did we—?"

"No, Viking. Trust me, you'd know it." Saint sighed. "And I like to have my bed partners awake and able to consent for that kind of thing." His mouth split into a yawn, his lean body undulating and making the eagle on his chest seem like it was done with its meal of Prometheus's body and about to take flight.

"Then why are we in bed together?"

He peered at her from beneath his arm with an audible grumble. "Are we doing this? Are we done sleeping? Because God knows I could use a few more hours after all that rowing and not getting us shot on sight. Honestly, why don't all the novels say that being a hero is exhausting? Being a villain is so much easier. No damsels, no demands, no precious virtue to be ruined, no waking up at ungodly hours and being plied with incessant questions."

She rolled her eyes at his dramatics as snatches of the past few hours came back to her. Saint finding them. Setting course for the archipelago in a rowboat. Being picked up by a friendly Captain Boisie. Smugglers Cove. She'd attempted to stay awake so that she could memorize the route for future reference, but sheer weariness had won out. Lisbeth didn't even remember arriving on land, much less being undressed and put to bed.

"Saint, why are we in the same bed?" she demanded again, peering over at him. His mouth was downturned in an extremely disgruntled expression at being awake. "Did you undress me?"

"You begged me to stay. And one of the women lent you her clothes."

Lisbeth cringed. She'd never do that, would she? Beg *him*, of all people, to stay? No, that was Saint embellishing as usual. "I don't beg."

"Ah, chérie, that you do. Quite prettily, might I add."

"You're an ass and it's still 'Captain' to you." She didn't dwell on why the tender endearment chafed or why she'd stopped chastising him for calling her Viking. That was neither here nor there. "Did you say that Narina saw a doctor? How is she? Did she wake?"

Gray-brown eyes met hers as his arm slid away. "Dieu, we really are doing this. Yes, fine, and yes. She woke briefly to eat some broth and went back to sleep. She has a bump on her head from hitting the railing, which the physician said would have caused her to be unconscious."

"But she's alive," Lisbeth whispered, eyes stinging with something other than salt.

His voice softened. "Yes, she's alive."

Lisbeth shoved down the fear that had risen into her throat. She couldn't have borne it if anything had happened to the girl, especially not after the exchange when Lisbeth discovered she was a stowaway. The thought of Narina feeling like she was unwanted with no one in the world left Lisbeth cold. Emotions were complicated things. Her ability to compartmentalize them was what made her so good at her job. She wouldn't make excuses for that, but she felt…regret.

Her gaze flicked to the man at her side once more,

instantly noting that the large bulge at his crotch had gone from rest to unrest. "Oh for heaven's sake, put that away, will you?"

"Put your prudishness away," he replied easily. "It's a perfectly natural response for most men in the morning."

"Well, I'm not a man, am I? So how would I know?"

Saint shifted to prop himself on his elbow, making his tattoo—and the muscles beneath it—flex and ripple. Not that she was noticing. "You've never woken up with someone?"

"Not that it's any of your business, but I don't stay long enough to chitchat." Lisbeth looked away, feeling her cheeks uncharacteristically heat. That was another thing—she never used to blush this much. A benefit of having a choke hold on one's emotions was not giving in to emotional reactions. But here she was...bloody *reacting*. Shoving off the sheets, she stood up and nearly fell over. Her legs felt like jelly as she collapsed back onto the mattress. "What the hell?"

"Take it easy," Saint drawled. "The doctor said you need rest, too."

Her gaze flicked to him. Thankfully, he'd drawn one leg up as a barrier to his distended groin and there was no chance of her accidentally falling over onto his prick. A giggle built in her throat, but she thanked the heavens that her stupid thoughts were private. She hadn't fucked a man in ages, and even that rare coupling had been fast and unremarkable. Intercourse had always been a rarity, not a frequent indulgence.

Christ, why was she thinking about intercourse at all? Or intercourse with *Saint*?

The man was a menace.

One who rescued you from a watery grave.

She was being uncharitable, wasn't she? Perhaps that was why her wretched feelings were all over the place. She was *grateful*, and she was confusing gratitude with desire. How could she even be attracted to someone like him? A man for whom life was a constant source of amusement and nothing but a perpetual joke. Then again, someone who took nothing seriously did not risk their own neck... did not stay when people asked them to stay...and did not look at her with eyes that saw through to her very soul.

"I can feel your mind churning like Charybdis from here," Saint said with a deep groan. "What is it now?"

She hesitated and then blurted out the question that was bothering her. "Why did you really come after Narina and me?"

"Do I have to have a reason? It was the right thing to do."

But before she could reply, they were interrupted by the thump of boots and a hard knock on the door. A person entered without waiting for an invitation, and Lisbeth's stomach hurtled to the floor when she came face-to-face with a very well-heeled, good-looking older man. Neat, short golden-brown hair peeked out from beneath a straw hat and framed the kind of face that would make an artist salivate to get him on canvas. She did not find mustaches or side-whiskers particularly attractive, and yet, this man wore both with debonair flair.

Lisbeth's jaw went slack. "Who are you?"

The man smiled as if well accustomed to the effect of his face. "Charles Dubois, at your service."

"Holy hell, can't a man get some peace in this godforsaken shithole?" Raphael moaned as he straightened to prop his back against the headboard. He noticed Bess's stunned expression as her fingers flexed convulsively at her hip for the hilt of a cutlass and a brace of weapons that weren't on her person. Strange. Why would she have such a visceral, *furious* reaction to Dubois?

Normally, women sighed and swooned, but if he wasn't mistaken, the cold purpose brewing in those eyes had nothing to do with appreciation. Her body bracing for action, his fierce little Viking looked like she was about to surge forward and declare war. Before she could move, he wrapped a long arm around her body and drew her back to him. She stiffened, jaw going rigid when he drew his nose down the column of her throat just below her ear.

"Play along," he whispered.

It was a toss-up as to whether she would yield or punch him in the throat, but after a moment, she relaxed slightly against his hold, one hand going to his bent knee that was encased in thin linen. Raphael exhaled, the erection between his legs showing no sign of disappearing now that the press of her fingers lightly stroked over his leg. He'd slept in a near-constant state of arousal as she'd sighed in her sleep, her rounded bottom nestled against him any chance she'd gotten. Which had been often and pure fucking torture. Hence the iron bar he was sporting.

All of her hard edges had been softened in slumber, her trust in him absolute. It had floored him. When had *that* happened? Or better yet, how? Bonnie Bess would have slept with one eye open and a hand on her blade, and yet, she'd asked him to stay with her and slept comfortably all night wrapped in his arms. She must have been drained from her ordeal…and it stood to reason that a man who'd jumped into an ocean to rescue her would not do anything to cause her harm. It had to have been intuitive and involuntary.

Nimble fingers danced down his thigh, and he swallowed a gulp. "Turnabout is fair play, Pirate," she murmured. Perhaps Raphael hadn't quite thought this through. Then again, maybe it would help convince his nemesis and others here that she was *his*. It was the only way she would be safe in this haven of reprobates.

"What the devil do you want, Dubois?"

"Nephew, you're like a cat with nine lives," the man said, removing his hat and perching his body at the edge of a chair. Raphael sensed Bess's glance on him for a scant second.

"Said the man who tried to have me captured and executed."

Dubois's blue eyes widened with false innocence as he clasped a hand to his chest and gasped in outrage. "But I would never. We are family, you and I. You must know that I spent days and many men searching the seas for you, my boy. I heard about what happened in Tobago with your cargo. How tragic!"

Raphael's eyes narrowed at the false words, rage coursing through him. They were only related by blood considering Dubois was his father's half brother—a fact he resented with all his being. "And I wager you have no idea what happened to my ships in that harbor or why they exploded."

Dubois sniffed, his long nose tilting with haughty disdain. "Why would I do such an ill-advised thing? I would have emptied the holds of valuables first, but then what a waste of two perfectly good ships. We might have our trivial rivalries and diversions, Saint, but credit me with a little more frugality."

A slight tremor ran through the woman in his arms, but Raphael was too busy searching Dubois's face for truth. To his surprise, he found it. They had known each other much too long for him not to know when his uncle was lying. On the subject of the explosions, he seemed to be sincere. So then, who had had the audacity to blow up his ships? That was a mystery for later. Now, however, he needed to put Dubois in his place.

"*Nephew,* you say? Would any true blood relation of mine conspire to have my crew mutiny and lock me in a jailhouse?" He waved an arm. "Yes, yes, we both know what you're capable of. But as you can see, I am quite healthy and hale, and back home with a well-sated beauty in my arms."

Dubois's eyes lit with interest, not for any other reason than coveting what Raphael had. "And who is she, might I ask? My men informed me that you arrived before breakfast with not one but two females. Ever the overachiever, are you not, Monsieur le Duc?" He said the last part with no small amount of mockery and malice. "Those days of courting and frippery are well behind you, wouldn't you say?"

"We both know my title is barely worth a fart in the wind."

Thanks to *him*, not that Dubois would ever admit it.

Raphael felt Bess's surprise, but she let nothing show of it on her face. Instead, she turned her chin up to feather her lips over his jaw, making him freeze at the light contact.

"I'm Lisbeth," she said in the sweetest voice Raphael had ever heard come out of her mouth, then turned back to his fascinated relative. "And the girl is my much younger sister. We met Saint in Barbados. Sadly, the ship we were on ran into a dreadful storm, but somehow, my wonderful hero here managed to get us to safety."

"Your ship sank?" Dubois asked.

Bess—no—Lisbeth sighed. "I expect so. That storm was truly a monster." Her eyes went wide. "You haven't seen any other survivors, have you?"

"No, and if there were, trust me, they would not run aground on this island alive," he said and then slapped his leg with a derisive laugh. "Saint here, however, has the luck of the devil. By God, man, barely a week ago you were in irons, and now you've managed to rescue a woman—and a beautiful one at that. And then you're rescued by Boisie from a strange rowboat without the proper flag and aren't shot on sight. Your good fortune continually astounds me."

Raphael hid his smile. More like *confounded* him. Dubois, despite his pleasant countenance, was positively seething with frustration. With a nod, Raphael nuzzled his nose into Lisbeth's hair, his teeth nibbling the side of her ear. Christ, she tasted like salt and honey. "You know what they say about passion—it strikes when one least expects it." Her fingers, hidden by the crook of his knee, dug mercilessly into the meat of his thigh at his liberties, making him wince. There she was—the cruel Viking who would only allow the pretense to go so far.

"Welcome to Exuma, Miss Lisbeth," Dubois said, gathering his hat. "I'm sure Saint will see to your comforts, but do let me know if there's anything"—he paused with a sly grin—"anything at all to make your visit more…pleasurable." The bastard sounded like a deuced aristocrat hosting a country house party instead of the stone-cold killer he was.

Lashes dipping demurely, she offered up a shy smile in response, and fuck if he didn't feel jealousy boil in his gut. "I will, thank you. Mr. Dubois."

"Do call me Charles," he said.

After his uncle took his leave, Bess-turned-Lisbeth spared no time in bolting from the bed and stood glaring at him. Her eyes flashed, vacillating between disbelief, vexation, and fury. "*That's* Charles Dubois?" When Raphael nodded, she paced back and forth. "He looks nothing like I expected."

"What did you expect?" he asked.

"Not some dratted dandy! Who's your bloody family?"

Raphael shrugged. "I suppose it's similar to you and Bonnie Bess. Reputations are more exaggerated than the reality. And we might share blood, but that man is *not* my family." He cocked his head at her. "Who is Lisbeth? Quick thinking on that, by the way. Bess is much too recognizable a name in our circles."

For a moment, she stalled as if belatedly remembering the name she'd supplied earlier. "Someone I used to be a long time ago."

"Another thing we have in common."

"On that subject, since when are you a duke?" she asked, curious. "And how does a duke end up as a smuggler in the Caribbean? Shouldn't you be doing ducal things on a ducal estate in Europe somewhere?"

"Alas, I'm little more than a discredited duke without a dukedom, in fact."

Green eyes lifted to his. "That sounds like a story."

"Not right now, Bess."

She pinned her lips between her teeth and then released them in a pucker to exhale a slow, thoughtful breath. That mind of hers was ticking like busy clockwork as she paced at the side of the bed, barely taking notice of him. "I suppose you should practice calling me Lisbeth, if we're going to continue this farce that I'm not sure I'm happy about. Playing the damsel in distress is not my favorite, as you can imagine."

He cast his eyes down her form, appreciating the backlit

view from the sunlight through her near-transparent night rail. Raphael hid his grin since he knew she wasn't aware of the tantalizing vision she presented, and the truth was he wanted to enjoy the sight a little bit more. He pressed a palm on his throbbing groin, willing the stiffness to dissipate, and barely managed to suppress his groan at the contact. Could a man faint from prolonged stimulation?

For such a shrew of a captain, she had the body of a siren—high, firm breasts, slender waist, thick legs honed with muscle, and a lush, full arse that made him want to sink his teeth into it. He could worship at the altar of that voluptuous body for hours. He recalled the way her rounded buttocks had felt against him, and bit his knuckles with a groan. How could such a tiny thing have so many curves?

"Saint, are you well?" she demanded, scowling at him. "You're moaning like you're in pain."

"Tease a starving man with a banquet he cannot have, Viking, and his only state will be one of pure survival."

Her brows crashed together, a wrinkle forming between them. "Whatever do you mean? I'm sure there's breakfast around here. Speak plainly, or are you only predisposed to grandiose statements?"

Chuckling at her irritation, Raphael gestured at her silhouette. "Your nipples are erect."

With a wild gasp, she glanced down at herself, realizing what he was ogling before snatching a handful of the bedsheets. "You bloody pervert! You could have told me I was on such vulgar display."

"And deny myself the pleasure? No, thank you. I may

be honorable when it comes to the fastidious rules you've set between us, but I am not a monk."

Her cheeks grew crimson as his words sank in. "You are a scapegrace. Fine, I'll put on a front for as long as we need to with Dubois and his men to see Narina safe, but for the record, I am not interested in a relationship." She paused. "Or coitus, for that matter."

Raphael found it interesting that she would not meet his eyes, and the fingers of her right hand twisted into the sheets at her waist. He suspected that the attraction between them had become more than mutual, but he would always respect the lines she'd drawn. There were plenty of women on the island with whom he could slake his lust, if it came to that.

"That works for me," he said and rolled off the bed with a languid stretch, feeling his skin pull over his sore muscles.

"Fine. Agreed. I want to see Narina."

He glanced over his shoulder and caught her stare on his bare back before her lashes dropped over her eyes. A pink tongue snaked out to wet her lips, a soft tremor leaving her body. Raphael stood and turned, giving her enough time to look away, but she did not. Lisbeth's perusal was bold as it slowly swept from his nape to his tented groin to his feet and back up. His cock jumped, body warming under her thorough scrutiny.

"Change your mind?" he purred.

"No. Just returning the favor. See how you feel being ogled like a piece of meat."

He flexed his pectorals. "Captain, my *captain,* I'll happily be your personal banquet anytime you wish. Just say the word and all the tenderest cuts of me are yours."

Lisbeth shook her head before letting out an incredulous snicker. "You are truly the most insufferably obnoxious man I've ever met."

Raphael winked and sketched a bow. "Good thing I'm your hero, and you secretly hope to marry me and have seven of my babies."

"Never mind," she said with a snort as she headed for the privy. "You are definitely the most delusional man I've ever met."

"Doesn't stop you from wanting me, admit it!"

She laughed, the deep, rich sound taking him by complete surprise. "Never going to happen, Pirate."

Nine

Raphael stared at his uncle, marveling at the sheer ballocks on the cocky bastard. The fact that he coveted Lisbeth came as no surprise. The fact, however, that he was demanding a *turn* as though she were a thing to be passed around the men on the island made him see fucking red.

If Dubois only knew who she really was, Raphael was certain that he'd be running far away and girding his tiny loins from the wrath of Bonnie Bess. But keeping her identity under wraps was safer for both of them…at least until Raphael knew what he was dealing with, and who his allies were in this den of serpents.

The governance of Smugglers Cove shifted over time as fortunes did, though he and Dubois had been its unofficial leadership for several years now. Captains had come and gone, mostly those who had the wealth and power to be influential. Right now, Raphael was partaking of a brandy and cigars with three other men besides Dubois, two of whom he did not know very well. The last was Boisie, a West Indian man who had made a fortune in the silk trade, and was the closest thing to a friend Raphael had here.

While Exuma operated as a safe zone of sorts—no

killing, no stealing, no cheating, and all disputes were to be settled by words instead of blood—it was no secret that any peace hinged on the whim of criminals. And the worst of them seemed to want him gone by any means necessary. Even provoking him to violence by soliciting Lisbeth's favors.

Though Raphael had no real claim to her, his blood ran hot with rage.

"She's not a communal object, Dubois," he said, draining the rest of his excellent French brandy to keep his fingers busy and not around the rotter's throat. "Perhaps you should invest the time yourself and do the work to actually make a woman interested in you. Looks won't last forever, Uncle."

The other men guffawed as Dubois's face turned white with anger. He sneered. "And what of the sister?"

Raphael leaned forward, violence in every taut line of his body as he speared the odious man with a look that promised nothing but pain. "She's fucking twelve. Touch one hair on her head and I'll kill you."

Dubois tutted, his oily smile returning. "Is that a threat? *Here?* You know the rules, Saint. We conduct ourselves like gentlemen, not animals, and threats are not to be taken lightly." The man was goading him, clearly, but Raphael just shrugged.

"However you take my cautionary advice is up to you, Dubois. But I can assure you as a gentleman myself, that *no* peer would ever conduct himself with such dishonor to besmirch a *child's* virtue." That was all horseshit, of course.

Peers with privilege did whatever they wanted, even when it crossed legal and moral lines, and aristocrats across Europe courted girls who were barely older than Narina. And in their world, out on the sea, criminals took whatever could be considered part of the spoils. Even bartering women and children.

But Dubois had always fancied himself a blue blood and had carried a chip on his shoulder since he'd felt slighted by Napoléon himself in the matter of being awarded a duchy...hence his infamous moniker of the Prince of Smugglers, his own self-aggrandizing creation. And he hated Raphael with a passion because *Raphael's* father, Dubois's own half brother, had earned the victory title he'd so fancied.

Dieu, Raphael had to find a way to get ahold of one of his ships. At least two of them should have been en route from France, and their crews had been loyal to him for years. At the moment, he was a sitting duck...a captain without a ship. And who knew what angles Dubois had been working behind his back for the last months to turn the tide of power. He seemed rather friendly with these two captains who'd been brought into the inner circle. Normally those things happened with an informal vote, but Raphael hadn't been back to Exuma in months, attempting to bring his own plans to fruition by buying up his uncle's debt wherever he could.

An oversight, clearly, because things had changed in his absence.

"Where did you say you were from?" he asked the

stout man with a mustache that would require its own shipboard cabin. Calico Madge or some such. The name was as ridiculous as the man's facial hair.

"Florida. Liquor and cigars primarily." He lifted a thick Cuban cigar to his mouth with a smug smile. "I work for Mr. Dubois here."

Ah. There was one tie of loyalty that could not be ignored. Raphael glanced at the redheaded captain whose face reminded him of a fox. "And you? Delaney, right? We've met once or twice in passing."

The man nodded. "Miles Delaney. Born in London but made a name for myself across the Atlantic. Mostly smuggling fabrics from your native Paris." He grinned. "Everyone in America wants the latest fashions at a fraction of the cost. The taxes levied are bloody astronomical, but I am happy to oblige my New York clientele and line my pockets in the meantime."

"The U.S. Customs House there has been tightening their focus on levies for goods," Raphael said, tapping his fingers on his tumbler.

Delaney snorted. "They have agents stationed in Paris now, looking for spending patterns of American women, watching and waiting and reporting back to watch out for my ships. Smuggling is not as easy as it used to be, when it was like catching fish in a barrel. Now, they'll bankrupt me, if I'm not careful."

Raphael fought an eye roll as Madge nodded. "Florida, too. Jenks is a pain in my arse in Tampa Bay. Confiscated an entire cargo hold of gin and wine a week ago. The *Seadrift* and the *Margaret Ann* were seized too, and the customs agents kept the liquor for themselves. Bloody criminals."

The irony of it all: smugglers calling corrupt agents criminals.

Raphael wasn't by any means innocent, but a large portion of his wealth was redistributed to those who needed it in the islands.

"The women have the right of it," Delaney said. "This Bonnie Bess captain is making a name for herself with French goods and fabrics. Have you heard of her? My men said the *Syren* put into port in Nassau for a day or two before departing for Tampa."

Raphael froze though outwardly he kept his face calm. Relief that the ship had survived the storm filled him, but his skin went cold at the thought of Lisbeth being recognized as its notorious captain. Dubois might think of her as a mole in their midst, and even if he desired her, his usual strategy was to shoot first and ask questions later. He had no doubt that Bess could handle all of these men, including Dubois, with her eyes closed, but he could not risk it.

"*Is* she bonny?" Madge asked smacking his lips with a chuckle. "I like a bit of grit in my women."

Delaney made a nauseated face. "No, and rumor says she's likely to cut your ballocks off with her blade and feed them to you, if you take any such liberties with her person. No one knows where the bitch is from. Take your pick—Jamaica, the Middle West, Spain, India. Everyone has a different story. But she's smart, and bold, and rich."

"Weren't you with her in Tobago, Delaney?" Dubois asked, blue eyes flicking to Raphael for a second. "You wanted me to meet her, if I recall."

The man shrugged. "Yes, but for reasons unknown, she decided to put out to sea an hour or so before you arrived. That boy Davy who arrived on my ship seemed to be close with her. You can ask him."

"An hour before you say?"

"Aye."

For a tense moment, Raphael wondered if the man would put the two together, that his nephew had escaped with the captain of that very same ship, but Dubois shrugged. "Women who run their own ships are trouble. They can't be controlled. They don't understand the order of things." Hard blue eyes settled on him. "Women are only good for one thing."

Raphael nearly snorted. If the ignorant prick only knew.

Lisbeth let out the breath she'd been holding as she stared down at a sleeping Narina. Some color had returned to the girl's face, her tawny-brown skin no longer sallow and pale. And those harsh rattling breaths in the boat had evened out. She looked much younger than her scant decade of life. Lisbeth felt a twinge of pity at how much the girl had weathered in her life for one so young—loss, harassment, coercion.

She's not your burden...nor can you give her what she needs.

That logical inner voice was quick to remind her that she wasn't cut out to be anyone's guardian, much less Narina's. Her life was too unpredictable. Too dangerous. Case in point...barely a day after being on the *Syren,* the girl had nearly died. If that wasn't a sign, Lisbeth didn't know what was. And now, the windfall that was Charles Dubois had finally landed in her lap. After months of undercover toil in less than ideal circumstances, success was so close she could taste it. But as much as she wanted to arrest the man for an arm's-length list of crimes against the American treasury, she required reinforcements.

Slumping into a nearby chair at Narina's bedside, she put her head into her hands. She needed a ship to get to New York herself or get word to her contacts there. The *Syren* should have been in Nassau by now, but she was no longer Bonnie Bess. She was *Lisbeth*—the harmless, meek lover of one of the captains. It chafed, the switch from powerful woman in her own right to one who needed the protection of a man, but Lisbeth was no stranger to acting. She could play the role of Saint's woman without blinking an eye.

A shiver coursed through her at their interaction earlier that morning. Lisbeth couldn't recall the last time she'd slept a full night in *anyone's* arms. She never left herself that vulnerable. Apart from her annoying mounting attraction to him, she grudgingly *liked* the big blockhead. And even worse, she was beginning to trust him. Sure, fate had shoved them together into impossible circumstances, but he'd saved her life. Saved Narina's life. It did not escape notice that he could expose her at any moment. Tell Dubois who she really was.

Though would he?

Lisbeth had spent enough time observing him to know when that jovial mask appeared, it meant he was hiding something. And that morning with Dubois, the mask had been hammered into place. She suspected Saint mistrusted his uncle. Disliked him even. But blood wasn't something that could be ignored, not even bad blood.

"Bess?" Narina whispered.

She launched up when the girl's eyes flicked open. "Oh God, Nari. I was so worried. How are you feeling?"

"Like I swallowed the fucking sea." Narina gave a weak giggle that turned into a rasping cough. Lisbeth handed her the cup of water on the nearby table, not bothering to chastise her for the moment. "Where are we?"

"An island with Saint," Lisbeth replied.

"Sailing master Saint?" she asked with a soft, infatuated smile. Lisbeth wasn't sure she was that far behind infatuation at this point either. "He saved us?"

She nodded. "Yes."

"We should keep him," Narina whispered, her eyelashes drifting back down as she gave a small yawn.

Frowning, Lisbeth moved closer to the bed and leaned down close to the girl's ear. Who knew when she'd have the chance again and right now they were alone in the room, though she could hear someone bustling around in the adjacent chamber. "Nari, wait," she whispered. "You need more rest, but I don't know if we're safe here. For now, I'm Lisbeth, not Bess. If they ask you anything, we're sisters and friends of Saint."

"Sisters," Narina mumbled sleepily. "I like that… Lisbeth."

It's not real, Lisbeth wanted to say, but emotions clogged her throat at the sweet smile that settled on the girl's lips. *Don't break her heart. Don't make her into you. Jaded and cynical, and walled off from affection.*

Lisbeth waited until Narina's soft breaths fell into the even rhythm of sleep before slipping out. She could not afford to get attached. Attachments were weaknesses that could be exploited, and besides, she had to stay focused.

Her first—and only priority—was to catch the elusive Prince of Smugglers.

The bonfire on the beach blazed high, leaving long orange shadows on the sand. The sounds of fiddles and guitars filled the air. It was a Smugglers Cove tradition, when the spoils of victory and their successes were celebrated. Sailors, both men and women, drank and caroused and fucked, and it was usually a blazing good time to be had by all.

But Raphael was preoccupied. A muscle hammered in his jaw as he watched Lisbeth flirt with Dubois on the other side of the fire. What the hell was she doing? Didn't she know the man was a snake? That he was dangerous?

Earlier, she'd sauntered down to the beach, dressed in a loose blouse and a wrapped, frilled skirt in the local style. Her hair had been unbound, framing her striking face in white-gold wisps, and she'd looked like a barefoot sea sprite. Unlike Bonnie Bess who was made of blades and thorns, Lisbeth seemed to be made of melody and moonlight. Hell, when did his inner thoughts become so pathetic? Devil take it, he was a smuggler, not a poet!

He emptied his mug of ale and was instantly brought another by a pretty black-haired chit, whose midnight eyes were bright with invitation. Before he could think twice, he took it and pulled her squealing down into his lap. She was a beautiful girl and certainly someone he wouldn't hesitate to have warm his bed before a certain wild Viking stormed into his life. Had Lisbeth noticed that he was no longer sitting alone like a sullen boy? That a gorgeous woman who desired him lounged in his lap?

If she had, she gave no signal of it. Her cheeks were puffy with a wide smile instead of her usual scowl, and she appeared to be having the time of her life. She nursed the drink she held in her hand and listened intently to Dubois. Not once had her gaze flicked to Raphael's. The distance between her and Dubois on the log grew smaller as his uncle inched closer with a smarmy grin that Raphael wanted to beat off his face. Lisbeth let out an uninhibited laugh, delighted by whatever it was the bastard was saying.

"Saint?" she called out. His brows dipped at the merry tone of her voice but when he glanced up, the look in her eyes was pure ice. "Is it true that you fell off the poop deck the first time you sailed with Captain Dubois?"

"Charles, my dearest," Dubois corrected her, his gaze full of challenge.

Smiling agreeably, Lisbeth patted his knee, and Raphael's fingers balled. "Charles, of course."

Oh, she'd noticed Raphael's companion all right. Suddenly, he had the urge to plant the chit into the lap of the nearest sailor instead of his. He didn't play these games. He didn't get jealous, if that was what this feeling was. He went with however life rolled. If Lisbeth wanted Dubois, so be it. Her choices would always be her own. She wasn't some shrinking violet who needed to be rescued, and as much as he enjoyed the idea of being someone's hero, he wasn't a shining knight. It was too much work.

"It was a prank," he replied, taking a healthy swallow of his drink. "A terrible one." He'd nearly broken his neck in the fall, but his uncle had insisted it was a rite of passage and all in good fun. A little shit never hurt anyone, he'd said after hauling Raphael out of the water like a drowned fucking rat.

"I wish I could sail a ship," Lisbeth said dreamily and glanced up at Dubois with stars in her eyes. "Is it hard?"

Raphael choked on his mouthful of ale, and jerked so suddenly that he dislodged the woman perched on his knee. The boatswain to his right was quick to relocate the giggling chit, but Raphael only had eyes for the woman opposite. "It can be," Dubois purred. "And I have the biggest ship in the harbor."

"He wishes he had the biggest ship," Boisie joked, making the crowd laugh.

Madge guffawed from his place a few spaces down from them and patted his lap. "Why don't you come over and have a tour of mine, lassie?"

"I'm fine where I am, thank you, sir," Lisbeth replied primly, which earned her a satisfied leer from Dubois.

Raphael emptied his mug of ale with a grunt. He knew he shouldn't dull his senses, not with Dubois so close, but he couldn't help himself. He wanted to fucking break something. What was she *doing*? Bonnie Bess would have an edge with this kind of crowd, but Lisbeth was sweet and ripe for the plucking.

He gritted his teeth resentfully, wanting to shout his claim and demand she return to his side, but he knew that she would refuse. And Raphael would not allow himself to be rejected or ridiculed. So he feigned one of his signature lazy smiles and caught her eye.

"Having fun?" he asked her.

She must have seen something in his face because she blew him a kiss. "Don't be jealous, dear heart. I'm only getting to know your uncle a little better. He has such an interesting history."

"Worried I'll charm her away, Saint?" Dubois asked, lifting a jeweled hand to run his knuckles over her sleeve. "Who knows? She might decide that she prefers an older vintage."

Raphael laughed. "Not one sour enough to give a person indigestion, but don't quit on my account. If she's willing, she's free game."

He saw Lisbeth's lips tighten, and a pinch of disgust

rode the heels of the jealousy that had provoked him to be so crass. Lisbeth wasn't some temporary prize to be traded or won, and he *knew* that. Bloody hell, what was wrong with him? Fighting back the flood of shame, he ground his molars together and pretended he wasn't such a miserable jackass.

"Monsieur le Duc." Delaney interrupted his pity party, his voice slurring. "Tell us, how did a blue blood like you come into the business of seafaring?"

Those green eyes from across the way landed on him, frosty but inquisitive.

"One, I'm not a blue blood," he said, knowing the explanation was for her benefit. He could give two shits about what any of the rest of these sods knew about him or his personal past. "My father was landed gentry who fought in the Crimean War. He was awarded the victory title of a dukedom by Louis-Napoléon and became le Duc de Viel." He kept his voice calm, though he could feel heat simmering in his veins. "Unfortunately, my family fell from grace and my birthright was stripped from me on account of an alleged crime my father committed against the emperor. As I was unsuccessful in clearing his name, I turned to the sea to seek my fortunes." *Along with vengeance.*

"Alleged?" That was from Lisbeth.

"Accusations were made."

Dubois's expression was one of concern. "It baffles me as to who would do such a thing. My brother was a good man."

"It remains a mystery," Raphael said placidly, though his stomach churned.

Who indeed? The very culprit was sitting right there, looking him in the eye, his duplicitous face painted in sincerity. Raphael didn't even care about clearing his father's name. He wanted to bring the scheming, lying bastard down. Give Dubois the reckoning he deserved. And he would not rest until the man had nothing, until his empire was in ashes. He knew, deep down, that Dubois had had his own brother killed.

And one way or another, the devil would get his due.

He was so consumed by his thoughts that he didn't realize that Lisbeth had asked him a question. "Did you appeal to the French court?"

Raphael nodded. "Apparently, the evidence was convincing, especially to the empress."

"The empress?" Lisbeth frowned.

"Rumor is she had her husband's ear. And when my father died barely a year after the emperor denounced him, he took all his secrets to the grave, including who had discredited him. I suspect he knew." He let out a hissed sigh. "It had to be someone close to him, but I never had any proof."

"Let the past stay in the past, I say," Dubois pronounced, lifting his glass high, and the other men followed. "But never the memory of our loved ones. To my dear brother!"

"Hear, hear!" others yelled.

Raphael's jaw went hard, his fingers digging into his

thigh to keep him grounded and not vaulting over the fire to throttle his father's treacherous, silver-tongued sibling. He didn't bother to lift his mug in the toast, and when he caught Lisbeth staring at him with a strangely soft expression, his chest tightened. She had not lifted her glass either. That brief moment of solidarity—of tender, unconditional empathy—almost had him in its grip, before reality intruded. He did not need anyone's pity, much less hers.

They might be bound together in a performance of convenience, but Bonnie Bess clearly had her own agenda…and he'd do well to remember that.

Ten

"I NEED MY DEUCED SHIP," LISBETH SAID, PACING BACK and forth on the white-sand beach that was strewn with shells.

She hissed as one cut into the softness of her bare sole. The coastline was gorgeous to the eye, but untold dangers lay where one could not see them. Just like the turquoise water that hid the sharp, deadly coral reefs below the gently ebbing waves, a pretty shell could be an unforeseen danger. A ship would breach its hull upon those reefs before even getting close to this island. And the gunners hidden in the hills would finish anyone off who dared to enter.

It was a miracle that they had been picked up by an ally of Saint's and not blown out of the water, but as she was quickly learning, the Duc de Viel was a powerful ally on these shores. She didn't quite know how to feel about that or what she'd discovered about his past or the fact that their backgrounds were eerily similar.

He'd been granted a noble title, just as she'd been. They'd both received their elevations in station resulting from service to their respective crowns. His, via his father's efforts during wartime, and hers because of her undercover work with Thornbury who'd been the Earl of Waterstone when they'd been briefly married. That union had been little more than a facade for the sake of their partnership, but the title had been hers to keep after the marriage had been dissolved, by the queen's mandate. What were the odds that she and Saint would have something so unusual in common?

They were more alike than she'd expected.

And even if he wasn't a spy, it was more than obvious that he had an ax to grind…and all her well-honed instincts screamed that their target might be a commonality as well. *Dubois.* Were their goals aligned? Could she get Saint on her side? He obviously wanted vengeance against his uncle and she wanted justice. Those two weren't mutually exclusive.

Having someone watching her back in a place like this would have its advantages. Even while she was attempting to glean information from Dubois at the bonfire, she could sense the cunning and the brutality running through the man. There was a reason he'd evaded the authorities for so long, and it wasn't because he was lucky or gullible.

She frowned. She hadn't expected Dubois to be older either, but he was in his forties at least and old enough to be her father. And yet, the lascivious way he looked at her made her flesh crawl. She had no doubt that without her relationship to Saint, as vexing as the pretense was to her pride, she would not be off-limits to Dubois's whims. Even now, she was taking a risk walking alone with Narina on a deserted seashore, but the girl had needed some fresh air, and Lisbeth had wanted to clear her head.

She muttered a blue streak under her breath as another shell bit into her toe. "Blast these accursed things!"

"Here," Narina said with a giggle, taking Lisbeth's arm as she hobbled painfully on her heels and pulled her over to the trunk of a coconut palm that had grown sideways. "Sit and let me see."

"I should be taking care of you." Lisbeth winced as Narina picked out a tiny piece of cracked shell from between her toes, staring down at the girl's own bare feet. "How are you not impaled every ten seconds?"

"Been running around barefoot my whole life," she said. "You get thicker soles. These dainty princess feet you have are like sodding paper."

Lisbeth let out a playful growl and tugged on one of her braids. "Language! I'll have you know these princess feet have served me well."

Narina's nose wrinkled. "Why do you need to find your ship?"

"The crew needs to know I'm alive."

"You're Captain Bonnie Bess so of course they'll know you're alive," she said and then clapped a hand over her mouth, looking around with alarmed eyes. There was no one there to hear her slip so Lisbeth wasn't too worried. "Bloody hell, sorry, I mean Lisbeth." Narina's brows shot together, but before Lisbeth could chide the child, Narina went on. "Why did you change your name?"

"They can't know who I am," Lisbeth replied in soft tones, rubbing the sting out of her sore feet. The small cut had already stopped bleeding and she stood to walk gingerly to the water's edge, beckoning Narina to follow. She bent to roll up the cuffs of her loose trousers. A good dose of saltwater would help keep the tiny scratch clean. "As you can tell, the men on this island aren't very good men."

"But Saint's good, right?"

Lisbeth opened her mouth to reply yes and then hesitated. *Was* he? Would he betray them the first chance he got if it served his ends? It wasn't as though he owed them anything. In fact, the reverse was true. *They* owed him. But Lisbeth also hadn't kept herself alive this long by blindly trusting people. Everyone was an enemy…until her job was done. Loyalties and alliances were too capricious in the smuggling world.

"I suppose he is," she murmured, the balmy waves lapping at her ankles.

"He saved us," Narina said.

"True," she said. "But *why* did he? Motivations aren't always clear."

A low chuckle reached her ears making her swing around, hand at her waist for the dagger she'd snatched from one of the drawers in the cabin. But the readiness to inflict damage leached from her as the object of their conversation strolled down the sand. "After all this time, you still don't trust me?" Saint drawled, scrubbing at the layer of dark scruff on his jaw. "What do you need? A blood oath to convince you of my allegiance? The promise of my firstborn?"

"Don't take it personally. I don't trust anyone. And I

don't require blood or innocent children." Lisbeth eyed him. "Did you just awaken?"

Saint was garbed in a rumpled shirt that gaped open at the neckline as if he'd put it on in a hurry and tousled hair that tumbled over his shoulders in a wild, inky mass. The feathered wings of the eagle peeked out of the collar, the sight of the ink doing unwelcome, untoward things to her. It made her want to see the chains that led to that curved gold nipple ring again. Run her tongue over it.

Oh, stop.

His trousers were fastened at least, but his feet were bare and big like the rest of him, the intimate view of them making a strange heat unfurl in her abdomen. Lisbeth refused to admit how delicious he looked with the remnants of sleep still dampening his features.

Wait, were those his clothes from last evening?

Had he just rolled out of bed? Someone else's bed. The hour was early after all, and the festivities had gone late into the night. Lisbeth had retired early enough, but Saint had stayed. So had the gorgeous brunette with the legs for miles who couldn't stop eye-fucking him. The one he'd pulled onto his lap. It was obvious that they were familiar with each other in the way that lovers would be. Not that it was any of her business. Despite their fake arrangement, Lisbeth had no say in what he did. Or who he bedded. Or what he revealed about his past.

Clearly he hadn't wasted the opportunity, because he hadn't returned to the cabin the night before. She bit her lip hard and turned away, wiping any expression from her face despite her sour stomach. She wasn't a jealous person who was usually ruled by her humors, but she was quite inexplicably infuriated for no good reason at all. The hair and the shirt and the bare feet had her imagination roiling with images of him en déshabillé, locked in an impassioned embrace with the dark-haired beauty from the bonfire.

It was…beyond provoking.

Besides, if Saint was known and so beloved by the women in Smugglers Cove, and in tight with men like Dubois, he was one of them. A smuggler. A *criminal.* A man she might have to arrest if push came to shove, no matter her illogical feelings where he was concerned. The villain with the heart of gold was a myth. Villains were *villains,* and she needed to get that through her thick, confused skull. She was not being bitter; she was being practical. Saint wasn't some modern-day Robin Hood.

"You were gone," he said. "I looked inside the cabin."

"We woke early for a walk," she shot back. "Wanted to stretch our legs and take the air."

"It's not safe, Lisbeth."

She glared at him, her expression frigid. "I can take care of myself, or do I need to remind you who I am? Should I fall to my knees and thank all the stars in the night sky for you checking up on me this morning when you couldn't have cared less all night? So very charitable and *good* of you, Monsieur le Duc."

His mouth slackened, and the venomous sarcasm in her own voice took her by surprise.

Narina goggled between them, and then shook her head while backing away, hands waving in the air. "Oh good goddamn! There's a big fucking crab!"

Before Lisbeth could respond or discipline for the oath, the girl had already skipped a few feet away and crouched down to investigate what Lisbeth was certain was an imaginary crustacean. A part of her was relieved, however, that Narina had moved away. Her own histrionic reaction was unnerving enough without an audience.

Saint took a cautious step closer. "Lisbeth—"

"I don't care," she said quickly. "It's nothing to do with me where you spend your nights."

"I slept in a hammock," he said. "Alone."

Feigning indifference, she shrugged. "Good for you."

"If you don't believe me, ask anyone," he said. "And besides, why does it even matter where I spent the night? You seemed to be quite taken with Dubois. One could not wedge a sliver of bark between the two of you."

She glared at him in outrage, but he was oblivious to her ratcheting temper. A muscle flexed in his lean, stubbled cheek. "We were talking," she growled.

"Call it whatever you want, but based on what I saw, what was stopping *you* from getting restless during the night and doing some wandering of your own? Visiting Dubois's bed to further whatever your personal agenda is? The men were exchanging bets to see if you would abandon me for him."

The fury drained from her as she stared at him in surprise. Had she been so obvious in her methods to glean information? It didn't rankle that the sailors would think she was promiscuous—she'd been called much worse by lesser men intimidated by an assertive woman in her line of work—but it did bother her that *Saint* would assume she was so fickle. "It wasn't like that, and besides, he's a wanted criminal."

His shoulder jerked upward. "We're all criminals here. And who do you think you are? The secret judgment police? Your list of crimes are worse than half of the men on this island, so don't go casting stones, *Bess*."

She flinched at the snarled name as he blew out a breath, staring out at the horizon and the sunlight spreading its golden rays over the sea. With a grunt as though he was furious with himself, Saint moved to stand beside her and she had to crane her neck to look up at him. A breeze teased its way through his long hair, his sharp profile stark and unreadable. "My interest is purely…business, Saint," she said quietly.

His throat worked at the slight hesitation, though he did not look at her. "Do you want him?"

"Dubois?" she asked. "What do you mean?"

A harsh noise breaking from him, silvery-brown eyes crashed into hers. "Do you want to fuck him?"

"God, no!" she burst out before heat spun through her at the audacious question and its underlying possessive intent. Saint was an amiable, charming man, but the sudden dominance in his tone made her core clench. That was unusual. She was never submissive when it came to sexual encounters. Remaining in control made it easier to set the narrative, though control over her emotions was the last thing she felt at the moment. She felt…rudderless. Yanked into a roaring current of lust and need. Desperate to let go and let someone else take control.

For *him* to take control.

Her mind cleared enough from the fog of desire for her to spare Narina a glance. The girl had moved further down the beach, paying no attention to them. When Lisbeth turned back, her breathing stalled. Saint was so close, she could see the brilliant tawny starbursts around his irises, trace the whorls of dark hair spattering his jaw, and feel his warm breath gusting against her forehead.

"Saint."

"I… You… Dieu, you drive me to…" His lush lips parted again as if he had something more to say, but then he closed the remaining inches between their bodies, an arm sliding around her back. The sudden contact stole the air from her lungs as her core throbbed violently with lust. Her nipples went painfully tight. The last time she'd experienced arousal this sharply had been…

Hell, she couldn't recall when she'd last felt this way. This needy. This unhinged. This fucking *starved*.

A hairsbreadth away from her mouth, he paused and she nearly kicked him. "Stop me now, Viking, because I'm going to kiss you."

Breath shuddering, Lisbeth looped her arms around his neck and dragged her aching breasts over his chest. "Anyone ever tell you that you talk too much?"

It was a rhetorical question. She pushed up and crashed her mouth to his.

Fuck everything he'd ever said about staying away. She tasted exactly as he'd imagined. Sunlight and honey with a squeeze of bitter orange. Sweet and tart. Ripe but spicy, like mangoes doused in hothouse peppers. Raphael deepened the kiss, desperate for more of that delicious contradiction, wanting to lose himself in the taste and sensation that tore at his senses. His tongue delved hungrily, tangling and dueling with hers, as if she, too, could not get enough of him.

It was heady and intense, the force of the desire burning through him almost impossible to contain. Anyone could see them, and Raphael did not care. He groaned as those ruthless, purposeful hands wound into the loose fabric of his shirt and threaded through his hair, holding him in place like the siren she was. Lisbeth kissed like she fought—bold and powerful, giving up no quarter that she'd earned. Nails scoured at his back, the willing give of her soft lips at his front making him frantic. *Wild.*

She bit at his lip and the bite of pain served as a reminder of just who she was. No one to be underestimated. Savage. Vicious. A Valkyrie whose embrace meant death. A whimper broke free from her as he teased the upper ridges of her mouth and sucked on her soft bottom lip.

The kiss was brief, a handful of seconds at most, but

it felt as though it'd lasted forever, a strange permanence imprinting upon him like a tattoo only he could see. Kisses did not feel like agony and bliss all in one. But hers did. Her lips consumed and caressed, devoured and worshipped. They *branded*.

When they broke apart panting, his lips were tingling and swollen, the slight taste of copper pennies on his tongue. Had his bloodthirsty Viking drawn blood? Lisbeth's green eyes were molten, her pupils blown wide. Her mouth was full and reddened, and she lifted a finger to the full curve of her bottom lip. She looked as disordered as he felt...as though the embrace had taken her by surprise.

"Why did you want to kiss me?" she rasped, after checking that they did not have an unwanted audience, though Raphael was sure that Narina would have seen her share of taboo activities in the tavern in Bridgetown.

"You wanted to kiss me, too," he said.

The truth was Raphael didn't know what had possessed him. Oh, he knew *why*. He'd wanted to kiss her since the first time they'd met when she'd burned into his life like a beautiful comet. But normally he had more self-control, and Lisbeth had made it clear that she wasn't interested. One moment they'd been bickering, jealousy and resentment bubbling between them, and the next, they were locked at the lips, dueling for dominance in a different way.

Raphael was saved from having to answer when a whistle and a shout came from the other side of the rocky outcropping leading to the next bay. "Ship, ahoy!"

He put a hand to his brow, shading against the growing sunlight, and tried to see if the ship was one of his. The flags for entry flew in the proper sequence—black on top, red in the middle, and yellow at the bottom—and a bell tolled before they were hoisted down. The yellow jack was a recent addition, usually used to warn other ships of contagion via yellow fever. It kept the more curious ships, including ones belonging to the authorities, away.

Raphael did not recognize the dark-blue frigate as one of his, and his hopes fell. *Damn!* The longer they stayed here, the more danger Lisbeth and Narina were in, and he couldn't put them on a ship captained by someone he did not trust. Or worse, someone loyal to his uncle.

"Before I forget, the *Syren* is in Tampa," he said quietly. "They're safe."

She frowned. "Tampa? I thought you said Nassau."

"They were in Nassau briefly, and then they left for Florida." Raphael stared at her, seeing something like surprise and then understanding flash in her eyes, before her usual neutral look replaced the last. One day, he'd uncover some of the secrets she was hiding. "Any idea why they would go there?"

"No." It was an untruth. She was an excellent liar, but he was learning to read her. The nearly imperceptible twitch of her eyelid gave her away.

Raphael raked a hand over his hair. It wouldn't be long before someone on the island recognized Lisbeth. The smuggling world was small. Dubois would be unforgiving if he suspected that she was a spy in their midst, especially one with a reputation like hers. They might be a society of thieves, but there were rules in place. A captain had to *earn* his way to access the upper echelons and Bonnie Bess had not done that. She'd circumvented the system. Raphael had helped bring her in, but that would not save her, were her true identity to be discovered.

"Captain Saint," a young boatswain's voice yelled out from over the pier as he climbed into sight. "The Prince wants to see you." His gaze flicked to Lisbeth. "And he said to bring your woman. In the main house."

That could not be good, but refusing the summons would only increase suspicions. As much as he wanted to protect Lisbeth, they still had to play a part. It was the whole reason he hadn't cut off Dubois's fingers for daring to touch Lisbeth, while pretending that he didn't care if his uncle made a move or not. If he showed that he actually cared, it would be seen as weakness and used against him.

"Is it trouble?" Lisbeth asked in a low voice.

"I don't know. I don't recognize the ship that just entered the bay. Could be one of Dubois's or one of the other captains.'" His gaze roved over her, brows tightening with worry. "When we go in there, you need to draw as little attention to yourself as possible. Unbearable task, I know," he added with a wry grin.

"I can be unnoticeable," she said with a scowl.

"Can you?" He lifted a palm to cup her jaw, his thumb skating across the softness of her cheek, eyes tracing the pale-gold hair tumbling in loose waves down her back. She was dressed in a homespun jade cotton dress, embroidered with deep red flowers, but even in the simple clothing, she shone like a luminous pearl.

While she looked softer and younger without the guise and face paint of Bonnie Bess, she was hardly a woman that others did not notice. What they didn't realize was how deadly she was. She was like the blue-ringed octopus that hid in coral reefs and tide pools. Beautiful and alluring, its painless yet lethal bite had enough venom to kill twenty people. "You underestimate what people see when they look at you, Viking."

She lifted a blond brow. "A girl in a dress?"

"A *banshee* in a dress who can steal their weapons and gut them inside of a minute." His hand fell back to his side as he blew out a breath. "We cannot be sure that someone will not know your face. Someone could have seen you in Bridgetown or Tobago before that."

"What do you propose?" she asked.

"You need to let me do all of the talking. You and Narina need to remain as inconspicuous as possible." He shook his head as he glanced at the girl. "I was going to suggest letting her go back to the cabin or the doctor's house, but we can't take the chance that she will be safe. I prefer both of you to be close, if things take a bad turn."

"Do you suspect Dubois to have ill intentions?" she asked, her gaze scrutinizing his face as if digging for truth. But he had nothing to hide.

"Yes. The only thing that man craves more than wealth is power. I have been in his way for a very long time, and I suspect that he knows what I mean to do."

"Which is?" she asked softly, and Raphael hesitated.

"Get my pound of flesh."

"You hate him," she said.

It was not a question. "Yes."

"Why?" Her voice was a whisper. "You can tell me, Saint. I need to know what we're walking into here. You have to give me something to go on."

He stared at her. He didn't owe her a thing and they both knew that. Right now, she needed him more than he needed her. Raphael admired that about her. She was not in a position of power in her current circumstance and still she didn't cower. A lesser woman—or man—would not be so undaunted.

"Is Lisbeth your real name?" he asked instead, and he watched the shadows gather in her gaze. It was a small test, of course. Trust had to be earned before it was given.

Her lips tightened. "Yes."

"Last name?"

She huffed, but conceded. "Medford by marriage."

His own eyes widened in surprise. "You were married? Did you murder your poor unsuspecting husband in his sleep?"

"Yes, and then I cleaned my teeth with his bones." Reluctant humor glinted in her green eyes. "The union was brief. He is well and alive, and happily married to the love of his life. Are you satisfied?"

His gaze heated, a dozen answers flying to his lips that had no place being said. Dieu, her impudence fired his blood. "Yes, for now."

"Tell me something true, Saint," she whispered. They were his words, asked when he'd tricked her out of her ship and now served back to him. He closed his eyes and pinched the bridge of his nose between his fingers.

"You remember my story from the bonfire?" When she nodded, he stuck his hands in his pockets and turned back toward the ocean. He had no idea why he was being so obliging. So brutally *honest*. He'd told no one of his plans. But deep down, maybe he did trust her. Or maybe…he wanted her to trust *him*. "He's the reason my father is dead and the reason we lost everything."

"Dubois was?"

Raphael nodded. "After the Crimean War, he resented that my father, who had been his commander on the front lines, was the one to receive Napoléon's commendation. It festered that he, too, hadn't been elevated to duke or received lands."

"Did he deserve them?" Lisbeth asked.

Raphael released a guttural laugh. "No. Not when that piece of shit hung back like a lily-livered coward, and yet, when all was said and done, Dubois was there at my father's side, like a vainglorious hero. He was much more grandiloquent than my father was." Heat coasted over Raphael's back as the familiar bitterness coursed through him. His fingers balled into fists. "Eight years ago, Dubois saw his opportunity to unseat my father, who given his past military experience, had been acting as an advisor of sorts during the French intervention in Mexico, but Dubois informed the emperor that his beloved Duc de Viel was a traitor."

Her brows drew together, fury on his behalf flashing in that green stare. "How?"

"He claimed that my father sold secrets to President Juárez in Mexico about the movement of the French troops, allowing the Mexicans a clear advantage over the French. Napoléon was furious and my father's lands were seized." He swallowed. "He was vilified even though there was no actual proof, only cunning conjecture. His own brother, my treacherous serpent of an uncle, insisted he was unwell and had him committed to Salpêtrière Hospital in Paris. My father died shortly after, beaten to death." Raphael glanced at her, his voice gentling. "Is that something true enough for you?"

"Charles Dubois is fucking vile," she snapped fervently. "And he'll get what's coming to him."

Raphael glanced down at her glowering, fierce face and felt an odd tightening in his midsection. She looked like she was on the cusp of burning down the world for him. It felt...strangely heartwarming, if such a thing could be.

"Will he, Viking?" he murmured, wanting so desperately to kiss her again and not daring to.

"Yes. I can promise you that."

Eleven

Dubois clapped his hands as they entered the main building, though from the set of his face, Raphael knew that he was angry at having been kept waiting. But he didn't give a shit. After the beach, both he and Lisbeth needed to get dressed and settle into their respective personas. Showing any weakness to Dubois, especially when he already had his sights on Lisbeth, would be unwise.

"Good of you to join us, Nephew," he boomed, his voice carrying through the hall as if he were a king addressing his subjects.

Raphael smirked and tightened his arm around Lisbeth who walked beside him. Narina trailed a few steps behind. Dutifully, Lisbeth wrapped her fingers around his forearm and smiled up at him. The fight and fire in her eyes had been replaced with false obeisance. Taking in their interested audience, Raphael crudely adjusted his crotch.

"Apologies, lads. A warm bed with the accompaniment of a skilled bit of muslin is hard to leave."

The men around them broke into leers and laughter, mugs of ale already being lifted and lewd comments being shouted. He felt Lisbeth stiffen, but tapped his fingers over her torso. She'd changed into a pretty blue dress with a modest neckline and long skirts. Raphael knew that she would have blades strapped to her legs, and the thought of her armed while looking so deceptively harmless made his blood heat.

He liked the thought of that. She was a woman who could take care of herself.

A lethal force.

He'd never met anyone like her…so able to put on any face as though she'd done it many times before. Right now, she looked innocent and sweet, but she would cut her way through half the men in this hall before they could lay a finger on her or Narina. For her part, the girl was wide-eyed, taking in the great hall that had been designed like a medieval gallery, complete with sweeping tapestries and the heads of mounted game.

"Bugger my eyes," she whispered to herself, and Raphael smothered a laugh. The child's untoward tongue could rival those of some of the filthiest deckhands.

"Nari," came the swift whispered reprimand from Lisbeth.

He wished he and Lisbeth had had longer on the beach and hadn't been interrupted, and not just because the addictive taste of her was embedded in his senses. He had spilled his secrets, but she had yet to share hers. Raphael would bet his entire ill-gotten fortune that whatever she was hiding had to do with Dubois. But what? How had he wronged Bonnie Bess?

She hasn't always been Bonnie Bess.

The voice in his head was sharp. Who was Lisbeth Medford? He'd have to have his men look into who she was, once they arrived with his ships. He leaned down to press a kiss to her hair after he'd seated her and Narina in places at the first table near the dais. He wanted to be able to see them at all times. His lips grazed Lisbeth's ear. "I like you like this. Quiet and biddable."

Raphael had to bite back a laugh at the flash of ire in those green eyes before it was hidden by her lashes. Mouth flattened, her fingers clutched convulsively over her thigh as though they were on the cusp of reaching through the fabric for whatever weapon was concealed beneath. With a grin, he moved away before she could give in to the temptation of making him bleed.

He sprawled indolently in a chair at the main table and folded his arms over his chest before eyeing Dubois. "What the hell was so pressing that you had to call a meeting of every soul on the island?"

Dubois's expression slipped and his face soured at Raphael's tone. No one else had the audacity—or the power—to speak to him like that, and he resented it. "The ship that has just arrived in the harbor is one of mine. The captain received word that there were customs agents waiting at port so he pulled in here for a spell until things died down in a day or two. He was en route to Tampa."

"What does that have to do with me?" Raphael asked.

Dubois tutted. "So impatient, my dear boy. Patience is a virtue."

"So is pleasure," Raphael shot back and blew a noisy kiss at Lisbeth. Amid a new round of raucous cheering, she pretended to catch it midair, eyelashes fluttering, and clutch it to her breast. God, she was good. Narina made a gagging sound and rolled her eyes.

"Well, my boy, since you *lost* your own ships and cargo in Tobago, I thought you might be itching to get your sea legs wet again. My captain has taken ill, you see. And you're a captain without a ship at the moment." Dubois paused and steepled his fingers. "Some of the goods are perishable," he went on. "I'll give you a cut of twenty percent."

If Raphael hadn't been looking right at Lisbeth, he would have missed the sharp flare of interest in her gaze at the offer. No doubt it had to do with the destination of the ship. Was that a coincidence? That his uncle's ship was headed to Tampa...the same port as the *Syren*?

Or perhaps her interest was only out of concern for Narina and getting the girl off the island. He shared the sentiment. This was no place for a child. Exuma had a slim code of conduct, yes, and it was a neutral zone, but some of these men were hardened monsters who'd traded in flesh before. In the years leading up to the American Civil War, Dubois himself had supported the slave trade and supplied the Confederate Army with arms. The man hadn't cared where his fortune came from or whether it was steeped in blood.

Yet another reason to rid the world of his ilk.

Soon.

Raphael pretended to consider the offer. Like the unfortunate events that had led him to incarceration in Tobago, it was most certainly a trap. There was no way that Dubois would offer up twenty percent of the value of the goods in the cargo hold if he didn't have some ulterior motive. Would customs agents be waiting to take him into custody?

"Why can't you take the ship in?" he asked.

Dubois sighed as if the weight of the world was on his shoulders. "Alas, I have urgent business in Nassau that calls for my attention. One of my crews was decimated by yellow fever. And I'm scheduled for a delivery in New York by the end of the month."

"And no other captain here is capable or headed to Florida?" Raphael pushed. "Delaney? Madge?"

Both men shook their heads and stared into their cups as if they'd been instructed to refuse. "They are otherwise occupied with their own ships, and I need someone I can trust," Dubois said. "And you're the only one."

Raphael quirked his lips upward and canted his head as though appreciative of the praise. "Fifty percent, Uncle, and I inspect the hold and choose my crew."

Dubois's fleeting look of triumph solidified Raphael's suspicions. "Very well, dear boy. You drive a hard bargain, but I'm in your debt."

It was an easy promise for Dubois to make, considering his motives.

If Dubois had his way, there'd be no debt to repay… because Raphael would be dead.

Lisbeth paced a hole in the braided rugs strewn over the cabin floor. Once they'd set sail on the *Avalon*, a bulky steamship with a paddle wheel that had seen better days, she'd changed from the dress into a pair of trousers and boots, paired with a loose shirt, vest, and navy sack coat. She felt more like herself, but she still had a part to play and that was as Saint's shipboard lover. Which meant keeping her head down and acting like a lovesick goose. Deep down, she enjoyed the switch in roles, despite the perceived absence of power, and being an observer instead of a leader. Men acted differently around women they did not consider a threat.

Saint had chosen most of the sailors, so a good portion of them were people he trusted. Should any kind of mutiny occur, he would have the advantage. Together, they'd meticulously inspected the cargo, finding crates of tobacco, salt, coffee, and tea. The goods were hardly perishable, but it was obvious that the entire thing was a farce. Still, Saint had said that he wouldn't put it past his uncle to plant explosives like the ones he'd used to destroy his ships in Tobago.

Damn and blast. Lisbeth should confess that she'd planted the explosives.

But if she did that, she would have to explain why. And that would compromise her entire mission. As guilty as she felt, her loyalty to her employer came first. She left the cramped quarters she shared with Narina and walked down the narrow corridor to the stairs leading to the deck. At the mouth of it she was stalled by a glinting blade pointing right at her head.

"Ahoy there, wench! Show me your sodding treasure or face my bloodthirsty blade!"

Lisbeth peered up to see Narina, sporting a pair of boys' breeches, shirt, boots, and a pirate-style tricorn she'd fashioned from an old sailor's hat, and brandishing a cutlass that was much too large for her. An eye patch covered one eye, her mouth curled in a snarl. Lisbeth bit back a smile, despite her ire at the girl's unrepentant tongue. Years spent in a tavern full of drunk sailors would do that. Slowly with her palms raised, she edged her way onto the deck. "Language, and who might you be?"

Narina cocked her head. "Pirates always say the worst words. I'm Bonnie Bess, scourge of the Caribbean Sea."

Lisbeth folder her arms and lifted a brow. "I have it on excellent authority that Bonnie Bess is not a pirate. She's a smuggler."

The girl's small nose wrinkled as she snorted and lowered her voice. "That's 'cause you *are* her. What's the difference?"

"Pirates attack ships on the seas and plunder them," Lisbeth explained and then hesitated. "Smugglers help get goods to people who need them without paying astronomical duties."

"So smugglers are good?"

"No, they're not." She thought about Saint and his peculiar Robin Hood behavior. She also thought about herself and the crimes she'd committed undercover in the name of the Crown. Over the past few years, she'd smuggled goods into the United States, with and without clearance from the American treasury. If Bonnie Bess was caught and detained by a random customs agent, she would be arrested, no questions asked. Still, Lisbeth felt the need to defend the gray area of where she stood. "But some aren't bad either. Some have…reasons."

Narina thought about that for a moment and then shrugged with a growl as if she didn't care much either way. "Argh, shiver me timbers, ye bilge-sucking rat sore! I'm Anne Bonny and there's booty to be plundered on this here ship!"

"That's a good one," a deep voice said, tugging on one of Narina's braids visible under the homemade tricorn. "Bilge-sucking rat sore. Playing at being a pirate?"

Narina scowled. "Blow me down! I'm not playin', ye festering scabby sea bass of a cockswain." Lisbeth's eyebrows shot toward her hairline even as Saint fought not to laugh. "I'll rip and bugger yer Jolly Roger and then cleave you to the bloody brisket!"

"Nari!" Lisbeth said in shocked horror.

Saint crouched down to be on a level with the girl and tweaked her nose. "I think you mean captain, lassie. Sass me again, and you'll find yourself swinging from the yardarm with an appointment at Davy Jones's locker."

Narina's face brightened at the creative pirate threats. "Aye, aye, Cap'n!"

"I need you to be on the lookout, savvy?" he told her sternly, though his pretty gray eyes twinkled. "For other ships and the old salts. And all young pirates on my ships use better words."

"Better words?" she asked, scrunching up her face in confusion.

"We're gentlemen and lady pirates, lassie. On this ship, our words are our weapons. So no cussing."

"Bugg—" she started to say and then cut off. "Very well, Cap'n."

The girl nodded and raced off, threatening boatswains manning the rigging and the paddle as she screamed bloody murder and threats that she had her one working eye on them. There was nary an oath on her lips.

"You're good with her," Lisbeth said, watching her with a fond smile.

"She's a decent nut. A bit rough around the edges, but who wasn't at that age? She'll come around. Diamonds never start out as diamonds."

She glanced up at him, surprised by the poetic sentiment. "I suppose that's true. Do you have any siblings?"

"No. I'm an only child. You?"

Her lips curled. "Another thing we have in common, it seems." The scent of him—salt and citrus—curled into her nostrils. The stench of rum no longer soiled his person, and whenever he spoke to her, his speech had lost its customary slur. He was jocund with the crew, however, maintaining the amused mien he'd crafted to perfection.

"Any trouble so far?" she asked in a low voice.

"None since we left."

She eyed him. "You think he'll do something? Dubois?"

"Most definitely, but not now," Saint said, gripping the railing and looking out to the empty horizon. "He's too much of a coward for that. He will want to distance himself from any foul play. It's how he works, like a moray eel in the dead of night, waiting for the perfect time to strike with no one the wiser."

He ran a hand through his sea-blown hair, the inky strands tangling around his fingers. The fabric of his slightly damp shirt pulled tight over his biceps and shoulders as he gathered his hair into a tail, and Lisbeth stared. Since when was she calf-eyed for a few bulging muscles?

"Who's on the wheel?" she asked, her voice too throaty for comfort.

"Boisie." She'd met the stout, friendly, dark-skinned man when he'd brought them to Exuma. He was an old captain Saint trusted to watch his back, and he appeared to be respected by most of the crew, old and new. She could have helped man the helm, of course, but it would have revealed their ruse. Saint rubbed his stomach. "Need to eat and then I'll be back up there. Shouldn't be too long to Cedar Key."

She frowned. "Not Tampa?"

"Give me some credit, love. I might be a bumbling fool on a good day, but I am not so stupid as to sail right into a trap where a surprise inspection by corrupt customs agents might be on the books."

The rumbled endearment was part of their fake performance, but it still landed like an arrow right between her thighs. When had liking his company given way to feelings of desire? Without thinking, she reached up to tuck a wayward tendril that had blown loose from his queue behind his ear. Saint froze, that silvery-brown stare falling on her like a tangible caress that she felt drift over her skin, pebbling her nipples and making her core throb deliciously.

Heavens, it had been so long since she'd enjoyed the attentions of a lover.

Ever since that kiss on the beach, the tension between them had only heightened. Her fingers shook as she curled them into a ball and let them drop instead of winding in his collar and dragging him down to her. She wanted more of his hands on her and her mouth on his. She wanted him splayed down on a bed and her tongue tracing the edges of that beautiful tattoo on his chest…following that dark line of hair to his waistband and what lay beneath.

Oh, good God, what was *wrong* with her? Her cheeks flushed at her indecent thoughts.

"Stop looking at me like that, for the love of all things holy," Saint groaned in a low whisper, as though conscious of the deckhands milling past them.

Lisbeth exhaled. "Like what?"

"Like a ship you intend to commandeer and plunder," he muttered.

Well then. He wasn't wrong. "And if I do?"

Saint's eyes *burned* in response. She had no idea where the boldness came from, only that they were on a vessel that belonged to a devious man who had his own designs upon the voyage. There were no explosives that she'd seen, but the ship wasn't small. The tiniest hole in the hull could cause the largest of ships to sink. Or worse, what if there was another ship waiting on the open sea to blast them to pieces? Life out here was much too short to wonder about what ifs. She wanted him like she'd never wanted anything. She *ached*.

"Lisbeth." The low snap of his voice held a warning that the tether of his control was thin. That whatever game she was playing would come to swift fruition. That she'd better be certain of what she was offering.

"Yes, Saint?"

His pupils expanded at the husky rasp of his name, and her cheeks flared hotter, lashes dipping to hide her reaction. Lisbeth was rarely embarrassed, and she wasn't ever needy. She was a woman who went after what she wanted and made no excuses for it. The freedom from the expectations of her sex in the ballrooms of London did not exist here. There were no exclusionary drawing rooms, no gossip rags to write about scandalous behavior, and no dreadful social rules to obey.

Lisbeth lifted her eyes to his, letting him see the desire there. It was barely a heartbeat and then she was being swept off her feet as he swooped her into those strong arms she'd ogled earlier, to the lewd whistles and raunchy hollers of the surrounding crew. Core heating, Lisbeth buried her face into his neck, breathing in the unique smell that was Saint. Unable to help herself, she licked the sweet salt of his skin beneath his ear and felt him shudder, arms banding tight about her.

"Keep that up," he rasped. "And I'll have you right here, discretion be damned, and give the crew a show they won't soon forget."

That idea should not have been as titillating as it was—to be pleasured in front of an audience. The space between her legs went liquid at the scandalous, vulgar fantasy that overtook her imagination. Lisbeth was the furthest thing from a prude, but the notion of people watching them couple while in the throes of pleasure was both absurd and arousing.

They reached his quarters, which were adjacent to hers, and Saint kicked the door shut with his bootheel before sliding her down to her feet. On the way down, she felt every delicious hard inch of his body, including the breath-stealing extra ones at his groin Like the rest of him, he was big, no doubt of that. The thought was enough to send a frisson of nerves through her, but it didn't stop the desire that pulsed wantonly in her veins.

They stood there for an eternity, pressed together and panting, their breaths harsh in the silence of the empty cabin. "It's not too late to change your mind," Saint said.

That low-pitched baritone did unspeakable things to her. Lisbeth crept her hands up the front of his shirt, her fingertips ghosting over the piercing in his nipple. He sucked in a breath when she gave it a teasing flick of her nail. "Do you want to change *your* mind, Pirate?"

His answer was to cup his big hands under her arse and lift her to grind against him so that there wasn't any question of what he wanted. With a groan, she wrapped her legs around his waist as he walked them toward the anchored table in the middle of the space. The surface of it grazed the back of her thighs, and then she was sitting with her legs splayed wide to accommodate his size between them. One palm slid to her lower back, keeping her in place as he ground his pelvis into her, making them both moan.

"Does it feel like I'm going to change my mind, Viking?"

There was that silly nickname again. The one that never failed to aggravate and get a rise out of her. Only now, the playful notes of it only made her want him more. A quiet, wistful part of her wondered what it would sound like were he to call her *love* in this scenario, and she shoved that errant thought back right where it belonged. In the land of make-believe and never. She was much too cynical in the ways of the world to believe that lust was love in any form. This was about carnal pleasure, nothing more.

Keep telling yourself that.

It was a lie, she knew. The bane of her existence was the need to have an emotional connection with a partner before any physical entanglements. She didn't even have to love the person. Respect was enough. Admiration even better. Some measure of trust was essential. Fondness came occasionally, as it had with Estelle. Her feelings for Saint were complex, but they were definitely there. Fucking him might be the worst mistake she could make, but she'd never been a woman to wallow in regret.

She reached over to untuck the hem of his shirt before grazing her knuckles down the front of his trousers, causing him to hiss in pleasure. "No, it doesn't feel like that at all," she whispered throatily. "It feels like you're committed to staying the course."

Lisbeth rocked back to her elbows on the table, needing to take charge because it was what she did. With intercourse, she usually controlled the pace and the positions. She wasn't submissive by nature, and ordinarily, her lovers let her take the lead. Saint did not move and her eyes lifted to his. Clearly, he wasn't submissive either, and the thought made her core tighten. Who would yield in a show of dominance?

With a grin, Lisbeth arched a brow and unlocked her booted foot from behind his waist to plant it firmly against his chest. She shimmied backward for purchase on the table. "I'm the one doing the plundering, remember?" When his eyes dilated as her heel drifted south, her grin widened. "Now show me the bounty that's mine to claim."

The tendons in his neck corded with strain as Saint stepped back, eyes like slashes of icy moonlight with his burnished brown complexion, those full lips taut with tension. He licked them when he saw her looking and her center hummed as if it wanted his tongue *there*. Saint smiled like her vulgar thoughts were transparent, a wicked grin lighting up his countenance.

God, Lisbeth had never seen a more stunning specimen of a man. When he smiled like that, even more so. His cheekbones were stark in the graceful terrain of his face, strands of inky loosened hair falling into that broad brow. His fine-grained, masculine beauty and whiplike form reminded her of one of the fairy folk, fanciful fae warriors she'd read about in Irish and French folktales. Lovely but lethal. Elegant but inhumanly strong.

Her breath caught as he lifted his shirt over his head in one swift motion. The leather queue came loose as well, the waterfall of his raven curls tumbling over wide, sun-kissed shoulders. Lisbeth didn't know where to look—at the slope of his pectoral muscles, that gold ring winking through his brown nipple, or the tapered topology of his steel-cut abdominals. He was not a man to shy away from hard work on the sea, and it showed in every sculpted swell and hollowed dip.

"More," she whispered. "All of it."

With a gratified smirk at the way she squirmed fitfully on the table, knowing very well how the sight of his gorgeous body was affecting her, he bent to remove his boots and stockings, giving her a tantalizing glimpse of the ripped, winged muscles along his side. Then, his hands went to the fastenings of his fly and made deft work of removing the rest of his clothing.

Saint did not tease, did not delay, only gave her what she'd demanded, until he stood there in nude, spectacular glory. Lisbeth's mouth dried as her gaze fell on his engorged, jutting staff. Her core released an indecent gush of wetness even as her brain recoiled from the sheer size of him. But that wasn't even what made her dizzy with desire.

Because, devil take her breath, the crown of Saint's staff was *pierced*.

Twelve

"Cat got your tongue, Viking?" Raphael rasped.

Bloody hell, he'd never been so aroused in all his life, his cock so hard, it felt as though he was going to burst out of his skin at any moment. She had needed to take the lead, he realized, and while he was usually a dominant lover, he wanted her to feel safe with him. Even if it meant standing there like a clockwork toy, he'd do it. For her.

Those hungry siren's eyes on him were the best and worst kind of torture. With a silent groan, he fisted himself and remained in place a few feet away, watching her ocean-green eyes darken and dilate with lust when his fingers skated over the piercing at the end of his cock. He hissed at the contact when his thumb slid across it.

"Did that hurt?" she whispered, stare glued to the end of his staff where the gold running through his swollen crown peeked out on top and below.

"Some," he said, strolling toward her until he was back in the cradle of her thighs. His cock jutted up obscenely between them, her gaze locked on the studded ends of the gold jewelry. "But the pain was worth it. I got the nipple done in France and the apadravya piercing in India."

"Is that what it's called?" she asked softly, staring down. "That one?"

"Yes. It dates as far back as the Kama Sutra."

Curious eyes lifted to his nipple and the gold ring situated there. "Where did you go in France? I've heard of places there that offer intimate piercings."

"A small parlor on the rue de Rivoli in Paris, belonging to one Madame Beaumont."

Lisbeth licked her lips again, a faint shudder going through her. "God, I love when you speak French," she murmured and then smiled. "I have friends in London who swear that the…pleasure of such jewelry is unfathomably extraordinary, both for the owner of the piece and the recipient of the attentions."

"That is true."

Her lashes dipped. "But one of those…"

"Apadravya," he supplied helpfully.

"I've never heard of anything like it."

His fingers passed over her cheek. "Depending on the position, the metal can hit a spot inside that brings immeasurable pleasure to a woman."

"Oh." She swallowed. "And for you?"

"Every stroke can be intense. Pain and pleasure are a unique combination."

She gulped when Raphael's hands went to the lapels of her coat, helping her shrug out of it, and then to the laces on her shirt. She wasn't wearing a corset, only the thinnest of shifts that did little to hide the peaked nipples that yearned for his attention. Slowly, he traced the delicate bud of her right breast with one fingertip, enjoying her sharp inhale of breath. He pinched, relishing the flare in her irises, and she bit her lip with a soft cry.

"So fucking beautiful," he murmured before ducking his head to capture the peak in his mouth, soothing the hurt he'd created. His tongue dragged over the fabric, wetting it to translucency as her back arched, a whimper escaping her lips. He nipped and met her lust-drunk stare. "Like that, it's but a pinch, and then it's over, but the pleasure afterward is ten times more acute."

Eyes on his, she leaned forward and licked his nipple, lips passing right over the ring with the lightest of suction as she caught it between her teeth. A groan tore from him, the wet scrape of her tongue feeling as though it was connected to his throbbing cock. If it was even possible, he thickened more. "I can see that," she said.

"You are wicked, Viking," he ground out.

"And here as well?" That bright gaze dropped down between them to where a bead of moisture pooled crudely on the tip of his cock. She licked her lips as though she wanted to repeat the action she'd done on his nipple… only down *there,* and the vision of her bending to take him into her mouth was nearly his undoing.

"That, I'll leave for you to discover on your own."

She let out a hungry whimper.

"Fuck, Lisbeth." Raphael surged against the seam of her trousers, eyes rolling back into his head at the carnal sound she made.

"Undress me," she whispered, pushing to her feet. "I want to feel you bare against me."

He did not need to be told twice. The top layers went. Then her boots and trousers, her hips canting obligingly toward him so he could slide the fabric over her rump. Within seconds, she was as naked as he. Raphael took a moment to appreciate the shapely contours of her body and the stark contrasts between her lightly tanned skin and the darker brown of his. Freckles dusted her neck and torso like a constellation of stars he wanted to memorize with his tongue.

Her curves were the counterpoint to his harder angles, but Lisbeth wasn't soft. Her body was strong and sinewy with honed, well-used muscle, though her luscious breasts were full and perky, and her hips succulently rounded. Despite her mouthwateringly feminine assets, Raphael knew she could take him to the ground in one fell swoop if she desired. Her beauty, her inherent skills, her sharp intelligence, and her confidence all combined to make him nonsensical.

She let out a gasp when one palm cupped her nape and the other slid down her ribs to grasp a handful of her firm bottom, dragging her against his front as he took her lips in a deep, ravenous kiss. His mouth slanted over hers and she opened eagerly for him.

"Your taste," he groaned, his tongue licking deep into her heat. "I can't get enough."

He sucked on her lips, delved his tongue and rubbed it hungrily against hers. She met him stroke for stroke, as if the hunger was mutual, her nails scraping over the muscle of his back and the flesh of his buttocks. He enjoyed kissing as much as the next man, but generally, he was quick to move on to the main event. With Lisbeth, he could linger at her lips forever.

Lifting her back into position on the table, he left the haven of her mouth even as she protested the loss. Raphael smiled. "Patience, chérie." His fingers ghosted along her jaw where the scrape of his stubble had abraded her tender skin.

"Why did you stop?" she asked.

"Not stopping," he said. "Savoring."

"Savor later, Pirate."

He chuckled and tilted her face up to his, dropping a kiss to her pert nose. "Nice try, but I'm the captain now. This ship is mine to steer. You're here to enjoy the ride."

"Is that so?"

"Yes. If you do exactly as I say, you'll be rewarded." His thumb flicked over her bottom lip and pressed into her mouth. "Suck." When she obeyed without question, though her eyes flashed and her teeth grazed the sides of his thumb, he grinned. His vicious Valkyrie couldn't help herself—she'd submit but with conditions. She'd bend but only so far. He removed his thumb and cupped her chin. "Are you going to be good for me?"

Her eyes went molten at the gravelly rasp, mirroring the deep, dark green of a churning sea, her lips red and swollen, and her cheeks flushed with desire. He rolled her left nipple between two of his fingers when she didn't answer. "I need words, Lisbeth."

"Yes," she moaned. "God, yes."

"Good girl."

A tremor tracked through her body at the praise, and Raphael wanted nothing more than to see her come undone. He pressed heated kisses to her jaw and her neck, making his way down to her collarbones and the perfect breasts he couldn't get enough of. Full and palm-sized, they were tipped with rose-colored nipples that begged to be pleasured. He kneaded one as he closed his lips over the other and sucked hard. The ragged whimpers that left her lips were gratifying.

"Saint, please," she panted against him, spine bowing as he lavished the taut peak with attention, at times flicking it with his tongue, and others, pulling it deep. When he switched to its twin and repeated the process, it wasn't long before she was a writhing, moaning mess. She was so fucking responsive, he couldn't wait to explore the rest of her… one place in particular. His mouth watered at the thought.

"My name is Raphael," he said and kissed her stomach gently before sinking to his knees.

"What are you doing?" she asked, confused. "I thought…"

He pushed her knees apart, dragging his nose on the inside of her leg. Her skin was like velvet as he kissed and nuzzled his way to the crease. Inhaling deeply, he closed his teeth over the flesh of her inner thigh and bit down, eyes meeting hers when she stared down at him with a ragged gasp. "What did I say?" he asked.

She gulped when his hand cupped the heart of her. "You're…the captain."

"And?"

"I'll behave," she said but still rocked her hips up against his palm in search of friction to soothe the need building inside of her. He almost laughed at her impatience and the obvious lie in her reply, but the promise of the treasure that lay a breath away took up too much of his brain. He inhaled again. God, she smelled divine…like the ocean at daybreak after a storm. And the sight of her—the wispy thatch of silvery-blond curls above petal-pink lips that glistened with arousal—was nearly his undoing. She was *soaked*. For him.

"Look at you," he groaned. "Tell me what you need, chérie. Qu'est-ce que tu veux?"

The blush on her cheeks descended all the way down her chest. "That's not fair. For mercy's sake, cease the sultry French, you dreadful man. I don't know what I want."

"Don't you?" he teased. "Ask me properly and you'll get it."

Of course she knew what she wanted. Lisbeth swallowed. "You're really going to make me beg, Saint?"

"Raphael." He blew a stream of air against her sex that made her hiss and arch like a wanton. "And yes. Good girls get rewarded, remember?"

Stubborn to the end, she still didn't concede. "What about good dukes? You're not being very ducal or nice at the moment."

"You should know by now that I'm the last thing from nice."

The look he gave her was full of wicked intent. It was

her only warning before his mouth latched on to her sex, the first taste of her nearly making his eyes roll back in his head. Salty and sweet like the most delicate ambrosia. He lapped at the pearl crowning the top of her sex, nipping it gently, and then grinned as her thighs squeezed compulsively around him.

"*Raph—*" The second half of his name devolved into an indecipherable moan.

"Is this what you what?" he teased with a long, slow lick from bottom to top that had her whimpering and writhing into his face. "You want me to devour you?"

"Ngnh."

He smiled. "If this was all it took to get you to stop quarreling with me, I would have done it a lot sooner. I would have dined on you for… Every. Single. Meal."

Forget good girls because *good Lord*, she was going to die.

His last three words were punctuated with hot, flat-tongued lashes against her quivering sex that made her entire body turn to liquid before he set his mouth to her body to feast. And feast he did. The man was gorging on her like he'd been famished for weeks at sea.

Lisbeth glanced down. Other lovers had performed this act before, but the sight of those broad muscular shoulders wedging her thighs voluptuously wide did something to her. Made her feral with desire. When one thick finger slid into her tight passage, she felt the pleasure uncoiling within start to build in intensity, more so when he added a second, and she shivered sensuously from the delicious stretch.

"Oh, that's good," she whispered. "Faster."

"You'll get what you're given," he growled against her damp flesh, making her writhe from the rumbles of his lips. God, that voice! So gravelly and carnal.

Lisbeth trembled. She wanted to cry out as he pumped in and out of her in time with the punishing stripes of his tongue over the sensitive bundle of nerves at the top of her quim. But when he crooked his fingers inside of her and sucked, the whine that came out of her was ungodly. Her body seized as waves of intense pleasure crashed over her and her passage clamped down on him, drawing out each ounce of bliss.

"So fucking tight," he said, that fringe of dark lashes lifting to reveal molten-silver eyes that were full of pure satisfaction. "I can't wait to feel you clenching like this on my cock."

Lisbeth swallowed, apprehension dancing on the heels of his words and dousing the bright glow of her orgasm. His girth was much thicker than his two fingers...and that *piercing*. The thought of the drag of the metal inside of her made her shudder. From nerves or excitement? She wasn't sure if she could take it. Take him. Or worse, not be enough to accommodate or please him. Her brain took over, dampening the pleasure she felt.

He pulled up to his full height with a slight frown, reading her face and the slight stiffening of her body. "What's wrong?"

"I haven't..." Face burning, she trailed off. "It's been a while since I've been with a man," she confessed.

Saint's smile was warm, a soft genuine one she hadn't seen before. "We'll go as slow as you need, Lisbeth. Or we can stop right now, if that is your wish."

Her brow wrinkled in surprise. Given their state of undress, the act he'd just performed upon her, and his own unfulfilled state, would he truly? And he was definitely still erect. She could feel the hard brand of him against her thigh. In her limited experience, most men would expect or demand reciprocity of some sort. Then again, Raphael Saint didn't seem to be like most men, as she was continually discovering.

She offered him a small, wry grin. "I thought you were the captain?"

"I might be at the wheel, but you are the ship's rudder. You decide the course. I do not want to rush you or do anything that you're not comfortable with."

Was *that* it? The source of her trepidation? Was it about her comfort? Since when was she so worried about sexual performance? She couldn't begin to unravel the sudden tangle of knots in her chest, but maybe her fears were something deeper than surface level arousal. It wasn't about his piercing or his size.

More with Saint would complicate things. Complicate *who* she was, and for some reason, that didn't feel like something she was prepared for. Her stomach dipped. *Bloody hell.* Would her refusal disappoint him?

"And you?" Lisbeth glanced at the length between them.

"I've been that way before, and besides, it's nothing

that my own two hands can't handle." He gave her a soft kiss on the lips. "If you prefer to wait, I'll wait. And if you decide that this is not what you desire, that's fine, too. I want all of you to be present." He touched her temple and grazed her hip. "Here *and* down here."

Heavens, how did he know exactly what to say...how to articulate her own convoluted worries? But it was the sincerity and unguarded care in his voice that made her tension loosen. Coitus for her was never only physical. Things in her head had to be in alignment, and while the worry of not being good for him was real enough, she *wasn't* ready to go further. It felt bigger than she was ready to deal with...on all levels.

"I'm sorry," she whispered. "I didn't mean to lead you along."

He tipped her chin up, making sure their eyes met. Her gaze scoured his face. Nothing in his expression showed frustration, disappointment, or deception. "You did not lead me anywhere I didn't want to go, so put that nonsense out of your head, Viking, or so help me, you'll get another tongue-lashing that will keep you on the edge for hours."

Lisbeth couldn't help her smile before she pinned her lips. "I would not complain. The first was quite tolerable."

He lifted an outraged brow. "Just *tolerable*? That was the performance of a century, I'll have you know."

"Your hubris is showing, Pirate."

With a low laugh at her reply, Saint shook his head. "Were I a lesser man, I would be shredded by such an undeserved, harsh assessment, but I know my skills. And trust me, chérie, you would not have come so hard on my tongue and fingers if you hadn't enjoyed those abilities to the fullest."

Heat filled her anew as she clenched her trembling thighs together, recalling just how talented his tongue had been. He wasn't wrong. With a playful grin, he shifted to gather the clothing they'd strewn about, reaching for hers first. If it wasn't for the fact that they were both naked, and yes, that she'd just had the quickest orgasm in recent history, one could think they were having a chat on the upper decks. It was so easy to be with him, even the midst of whatever *this* awkwardness was.

"Raphael, wait."

He canted his head to the side. "What is it?"

Lisbeth let out a measured breath, her gaze dropping to the thick erection that wasn't quite as angry as it had been before, but was still swollen. She felt her cheeks heat, recollecting the way he'd praised her. *Good girl.* Why the hell did those two words have such a filthy effect on her? They made her want to roll over like a puppy, show him her belly, and beg him to scratch it. "I was good, wasn't I? I…behaved."

He stiffened, eyes narrowing on her and her husky tones, despite her balking on the last. With one brow arched, his lips tilted into a slight smirk, curling up one side of his mouth. "Yes, you did."

"So then…" Lisbeth faltered but pushed on. It was too late to change her mind now, and besides, she *wanted* to do this for him. She wanted to please him. She wasn't a woman who required praise to perform, but in this instance, his approval brought her pleasure, too. However, that did not mean she'd be meek. "I deserve my reward."

Raphael went so still she wasn't sure if he was breathing, but then a shallow intake of air slipped through his lips. "Which is?"

God, that voice was pure seduction, the deep notes pulsating through her. She might not be ready for the act, but the raw desire he made her feel could not be denied.

"I want to watch you. On this table in my place. Showing me what you like."

Air hissed out of him. "Viking."

Lisbeth slid off the table and walked around him, letting her fingertips drift over the tantalizing rise of his bare arse. "Show me how you handle that monster with your own two hands, or was that an empty, shallow boast?"

"Lisbeth…"

"It's *Captain* to you." She settled her naked body into the captain's chair on the other side of the table, propping one knee up and knowing exactly the lewd vision she presented when his eyes rounded and his mouth went slack. The tattoo on his chest flexed as his muscles clenched. "Now, be a good duke and obey my orders. Stroke yourself for me."

Those gray eyes flashed at the command, but he dropped the shirt in his hands and fisted his cock obediently instead. Pleasure unspooled like honey in her veins. Lisbeth had expected his large palm to dwarf his length, but if anything, it was proportionate in size. Big hands… big everything else.

A groan broke free from him as he worked from root to crown, but he kept his eyes fastened on hers as if every ounce of ecstasy he experienced belonged solely to her. Lisbeth bit her lip as he rubbed the moisture at his tip into the head, thumb flicking over the glimmering piercing and making his big body twitch.

"Again and slowly," she demanded and exhaled when he complied. "How does it feel?"

"Trop bon. Tu me rends fou." His reply was guttural. The switch to French told her how close to the edge he was and they'd barely started. *Good,* she wanted him unraveling as fast as she had. Tendons flexed and quivered with strain, her eyes drawn to the slow, precise movements of his hand. God, how could forearms be so bloody sinful? Thick, veined, bronzed, and covered in dark hair, they oozed raw sensuality.

"Grip yourself tighter," she told him. With a low snarl, he braced one palm on the edge of the table, veins popping and muscles bunching in his broad chest as he obeyed. Her eyes shifted to the fingers currently gripping his leaking cock in an unforgiving vise, admiring the bunch of his heavy thighs and the flex of his buttocks as he strained into his fist. Fuck if he wasn't the most erotic thing she'd ever seen...that lean body hunched with tension, his stomach muscles contracting with each thrust, and a molten stare *burning* into hers.

"What else does my captain command?" he rasped.

Holy hell, she could feel the moisture dripping between her legs. She'd wanted him to find completion;

she hadn't expected to feel so *involved*...so wrapped up in the pleasure he was wringing from himself. But each measured snap of his hips into his own palm made her core clench like a greedy fiend.

"Fuck your hand faster," she commanded, her own voice hoarse as she dropped her propped knee to press her throbbing thighs together...squirming in her seat to offset the mounting pressure between them. He obliged beautifully, working himself at a furious pace, and she was already on the brink of another orgasm just from watching him chase his release. Her hand slid down to her mound, his hot stare tracking the movement as she dragged a fingertip in her wetness.

"Bloody hell, Lisbeth, I'm going to spend."

"Don't."

His motions went jerky before halting, confusion twisting his lips into a grimace as he panted. "What?" he gritted out, tendons popping in his shoulders and chest glimmering with sweat as he fought for control...to bring himself back from the brink. "Why?"

Her eyes slipped to his tattoo—she was the eagle and he was Prometheus. "Did you think this would be easy? I thought you said you liked a little pain. You come when I say you can come."

A harsh bark of laughter left him. "I should have remembered how cruel you are, Viking."

Lisbeth stood slowly and walked around the table to where he stood shaking, as if it took every ounce of power within him not to come apart. He was gripping the base of his cock so hard that his knuckles were white. She glanced at the bulging head of his very swollen, very angry erection and bent at the waist to lick around the tip of his piercing before enclosing the entire crown into her mouth.

The growl that broke from him was savage. "Merde. I can't hold back…if you do that."

She released him with a soft pop, the salted tang of him bursting on her tongue. One day, she might have to indulge properly, but for now, the small taste would have to suffice. Lisbeth knelt, sitting back on her heels and presenting herself to him like an offering to the gods in the Greek temples of old. "Then don't. Now, come for your mistress."

Raphael's eyes widened, lust roaring through them, and a guttural sound flew from the depths of his chest as if all it took were her words for thick, hot ropes of his seed to splatter onto her bared breasts. It was feral, *primal* in the extreme, and she reveled in the carnality of it.

Lisbeth didn't have to touch herself to feel her own release break through her like a slow, undulating wave…a strange, complementary echo of his. She exhaled with stunned pleasure. Well, that was a first, though she'd been wound so tight that such a thing was entirely possible. She'd had orgasms in dreams before. This felt like that.

Panting, Raphael stared down at her, eyes on the mess he'd made and awe on his face. A spent, gorgeous Titan.

Lisbeth grinned up at him and winked. "Good boy."

Thirteen

The wharves at Cedar Key were extraordinarily busy, which meant that every hand on the *Avalon*'s decks was occupied in dropping anchor in the bay just off the coast. A good thing, considering whose ship they were on—a fact Raphael refused to forget. He wouldn't let his guard down so easily, no matter how normal things seemed.

Disaster struck when one least expected it. He should know.

The rest of the voyage around the southern coast of Florida had passed quietly enough, but that didn't mean the danger would not be in front of them. Changing ports at the last minute gave him some latitude, but staying one step ahead of Dubois required vigilance.

Not that Raphael was capable of rational, good sense at the moment.

He'd fucked all of his out onto his captain's gorgeous breasts. Even now, the thought of their frantic interlude had his ears going hot. They hadn't copulated, and yet, that had been one of the most erotic experiences of his adult life.

He'd meant it when he had told Lisbeth that the decision to continue was hers, and he'd been fully prepared to take himself in hand once he was alone. But what she'd made him *do*—the press of those siren's eyes observing every stroke, every groan, and every shudder before letting him indulge in a deliciously filthy fantasy he never knew he needed—had been astounding. And intensely arousing.

His body was still reeling from the aftershocks.

But that was Lisbeth...a woman-sized hurricane.

"Son of a biscuit eater! Land, ho, ye scurvy-ridden picaroons!" a childish voice hollered from the lower deck. "Get yer daddles working before I make ye walk the plank at the tip of me sword!"

Raphael stifled a laugh at Narina's antics. At least she was attempting to be more creative with her insults. He lifted a brow and whistled. "Who are you supposed to be, lass? Still Anne Bonny?"

She waved a stick she'd pilfered. "I'm Mary Read today, bucko!"

Raphael chuckled. She definitely wasn't lacking in energy or enthusiasm. "It's 'Captain' to you, you young scallywag." He glanced around for her minder, but Lisbeth was nowhere in sight. He frowned. "Where's your sister?"

"Who?" she shouted with a wrinkled nose before her eyes widened. She ran across the deck toward him and climbed the stairs to where he stood at the wheel. "Oh, ay. The sly wench went ashore with Ballsack and Gibbons to visit the sutler for supplies."

Raphael nearly choked on his own spit. "What did you say?"

"The sly wench went ashore—"

"No, no, that boatswain's name is Balzac, like the French novelist."

Her cute, too-innocent face scrunched up as she tugged on the handkerchief wrapped around her head. "Right. That's what I said. Ballsack."

If he hadn't seen the mischievous glint in her eye, Raphael would have been taken for a good long ride. The little brat knew *exactly* what she was saying. "When did Lisbeth leave?"

"Shiver me timbers, I don't recall." Narina picked up the spyglass on the ledge beside him and peered into it. She swung the glass to him, and he stared back with a pointed look until she sighed. "Not so long after we put into port, Cap'n."

His frustration was instant. God damn Lisbeth's impulsiveness! He shouldn't be angry that she had left without telling him, probably because he would not have allowed it. Blast her! She must have guessed that he would have pulled rank as the *Avalon*'s captain to forbid her from going to shore, or at least to insist he remain at her side.

At any rate, she hadn't gone alone. Ballsack—*damn it!*—Balzac and Gibbons were both capable men, and ones he trusted. That mollified him somewhat. Then again, Lisbeth was a fierce, proficient seafarer in her own right. She wasn't some damsel who needed defending. But sometimes, in his own head, it was hard to separate the two.

"I wanted to go with them," Narina muttered in a morose tone. "But she said she had important hornswaggling business to attend to."

Raphael blinked at the expression. He doubted it had anything to do with swindling people out of money, but with Lisbeth, one could not be sure. Bonnie Bess had her own contacts on the American mainland as well as in the wider West Indies. "Business?"

The child pouted. "People business, savvy?"

His hackles rose. What was the secretive harpy up to? "I beg your pardon," he said. "Did she say where she was going?"

"No." She made a swishing motion with the make-shift short stick that served as her sword. "You talk funny sometimes. All fancy-like. Like Bess does sometimes when she's well into her cups. 'Squiffy,' the pirates say. It means foxed." Narina scrunched up her face. "Most sod-heads mix up their words or slur. She just gets more and more proper. It's fucking funny. *I do beg your pardon, kind sir, may I have some more.*" She snorted laughter through her nose and stabbed her sword. "Now walk the sodding plank before I skewer yer insides with me blade!"

"What did we say about how we speak on this ship, lassie?" Raphael asked, turning his face to hide his grin. The child's language was truly atrocious, and hearing those words from such a cherubic face was rather diverting. Lisbeth, however, would be appalled.

Speaking of the petite pain in his arse, he frowned. Other than perhaps attempting to send word to the *Syren* in Tampa overland that she was alive, did she have any other reason to meet with someone in Cedar Key? He glanced down to where Narina was staring longingly at the wharves in the distance. Lisbeth was right to leave her behind. She was safer on the ship.

"Go fetch Boisie for me, will you?" He stooped down before she ran off and took the hat off his head and plopped it on hers. "Now, avast ye, lassie. I'm going to leave you in charge of the ship. It's a big job. Do you think you can handle being captain until I return?"

Her dark eyes went wide even as the brim of her faux tricorn nearly swallowed up her small head. "You want *me* to be the captain?"

"Only if you're up to the task," he said grimly. "It's a big responsibility. I can ask Boisie, if you can't do it."

Narina straightened her small spine, standing tall and letting out a growl worthy of Blackbeard himself. "Blow me down, Cap'n! Boisie's a scallywag! I'm your lass! If anyone comes close to the *Avalon*, I'll run a warning shot across their damned bow."

Raphael chuckled. "No firing cannons until I get back."

"Ay, Cap'n!" He watched as she ran off, shouting orders that men would get the cat-o'-nine and be scuppered if they didn't listen, and bit back a laugh. She was truly incorrigible.

He waited until Boisie, his acting quartermaster but also a capable captain in his own right, strolled down from the quarterdeck. He trusted the man with his life, considering Raphael had saved his several years ago, and Boisie hadn't batted an eye when Raphael had asked him to be part of the crew.

"Can you tell the lads to get the second rowboat

ready?" he asked. "And keep an eye on the lass, will you? She's slippery."

Boisie cracked an uncharacteristic smile, teeth white in his dark-brown face. "That she is."

"I'll take Peppers and Jim with me." Raphael lowered his voice. "Keep watch. I still don't know if we can trust everyone on this ship. If there's any sign of mutiny, you take the girl and go, you hear me? If all's well, get the ship ready to sail in an hour."

"Aye, Saint." Boisie frowned. "You expecting trouble?"

Raphael let out a breath. "Always."

Lisbeth knew it was a huge risk to bring the two men from the ship with her, but she couldn't take the chance to come ashore alone. Not to mention she was wearing a bloody *dress*! She missed having her weapons strapped around her hips, clearly visible to everyone that she was not a female to be toyed with. Lisbeth let out a low huff. She hadn't realized how dependent she'd become on the swagger of Bonnie Bess and the liberties it afforded her.

No one dared cross the ruthless captain. Petty thieves and cutpurses scattered when the *Syren* put into local ports. Lisbeth had always been a strong woman, but Bonnie Bess had a pair of balls bigger than most men in their walk of life. Even here on American shores, her name and reputation held weight.

Cedar Key was a notorious smuggling hub, perhaps

even worse than Tampa. The trade ties between Cuba and Florida meant that it was a convenient port for ships trafficking a little extra liquor and cigars, which would be sent inland for resale on the black market. In recent months, the Treasury Department had grown fixated on capturing smugglers and had sent undercover agents to assist the customs officers.

There'd been a slew of new hires, and Lisbeth did not care to be detained and interrogated by some greenhorn out to make a name for himself. She was certain that was what Dubois had had in mind—to have the *Avalon* detained and searched with contraband goods hidden somewhere in its hold and its captain and crew taken into custody. If Saint was arrested, she would not be able to help him without revealing her biggest secret. And that she could not do…not when her target was so close.

Not even for him.

Something ached in the vicinity of her chest and she rubbed it hard. She could not afford softness with Saint because they'd been intimate. Shipboard liaisons happened in close quarters from time to time, and such brief interludes did not mean anything. The scorching-hot memory of Saint crouched down between her legs with his tongue laying fire to her drenched core begged to differ, however.

Or worse, what had come after…

Lisbeth flushed at the recollection of what she'd done—what *he'd* done—feeling her neck heat under the already hot afternoon sun. What on earth had possessed her to kneel in front of him as she had? Inviting him to… mark her with his spend. It had been brazen and wickedly erotic, and nothing she'd ever done before.

Enough. Exasperated with herself, she pulled the brim of her bonnet down and adjusted her suddenly itchy collar. *Stop obsessing about him.* Hell, she had bigger fish to fry, like how to make contact with her handler in the American government without raising the suspicions of the two men with her. Problem was…her contact might be in New York and not in Florida. But how to get rid of Gibbons and Balzac was her first hurdle.

What would Bonnie Bess do?

She'd tell them to bugger off, but Lisbeth wasn't the captain of the *Syren* at the moment, so she had to be more diplomatic. More *ladylike.* Her eyes canvassed the busy city as she strolled toward the main street. "Oh, look, a milliner's!" She clapped her hands, feigning a giddy delight that seemed to convince the two men. "I must have a look."

"Be quick, miss," Gibbons said. "The Cap'n won't like it if we take too long."

Guilt flashed through her. The captain didn't even know she'd left and definitely wouldn't like that she had lied about having his permission to come ashore. The two men had taken her word for it, considering she had been rather haughty and demanding, hardly giving them a chance to question whether she had the authority or not.

Act as if had always served her well in her profession. Uncertainty always led to hesitation and questions, whereas if one behaved like they were supposed to be where they were, most people went along with it. Confidence with a dash of arrogance was the key to selling a facade. As such, she'd dangled the fat pouch of money in front of them and said that darling Captain Saint wanted her to buy a nice dress for something special he had planned. And did *they* want to disappoint Captain Saint if he didn't get what he wanted?

The answer had been a resounding no.

Lisbeth should have felt bad for manipulating them, but business was business. She might not have another chance like this, especially if they went back to Exuma.

She shot the men a beaming smile. "I'll be quick, I promise. I only need twenty minutes or so to have a look." She dug into the pouch and handed them some money. "There's a tavern just over there. Have a quick pint on me, and I'll be done before you know it. Don't worry, I won't tell, if you won't."

The two men exchanged a look before grudgingly taking the money from her outstretched hand. Lisbeth admired that they were at least thinking about it for more than a second. That kind of loyalty was rare, and it made her feel even worse for the trickery.

Gibbons frowned. "Twenty minutes, miss. And then we're coming in after you."

"I'd expect nothing less."

Strolling into the shop as if she didn't have a care in the world, Lisbeth ducked out of sight of the nearest window. To her dismay, Gibbons remained at his post near the entrance while Balzac ambled across the street to the tavern.

Damn and blast! She would have to leave via another exit. Swearing under her breath, she waited to see if Gibbons would join Balzac, but no such luck. She'd already wasted two valuable minutes! Lisbeth walked over to the salesperson who was folding bolts of fabric. "Excuse me, but is there by chance a back entrance to this shop?"

The girl eyed her with suspicion. Lisbeth's dress and bonnet were sturdy but not expensive, and from the amount of silk on the shelves, this shop catered to a much wealthier clientele. Lisbeth ducked her head and bit her lip, making her body smaller and more helpless. "May I be honest with you? There's a man outside who has been following me, and this seemed like a safe establishment." She suppressed a fake sob, clutching her knuckles to her mouth. "But I think he's still out there."

Lisbeth knew she'd convinced the girl when she walked over to the window and spotted Gibbons's hulking form. Her eyes widened. "Husband?"

"A stranger from the docks. My ship only just came in, you see. I fear if I go back outside, I might be in danger. They could be thieves!"

The seconds ticked by before the girl nodded. "The owner of the shop is out doing a fitting but she will return soon. You can stay here in the meantime. Or shall I send for help? The local constable office is just up the street."

"No, I can do that," Lisbeth said hurriedly. "That's where I'll go if you have a back exit."

"Very well," the girl said. "There's a small alley that leads to a mews. If you cut through there, you'll be able to come around to the top part of the street. But I warn you, it's disgusting."

"No matter!" Lisbeth said. "You probably will have saved my life or at least my purse." She rummaged in the pouch and withdrew some folded bills. "Please take this to show my gratitude for your assistance."

The girl blushed but accepted the money and then led her through a narrow corridor to the even smaller alley that stank of piss, shit, and rotting garbage in the back. "Sorry, I told you it was vile."

She wasn't wrong. It was more of a passage for sewage than anything. But Lisbeth didn't have much choice and she was running out of time. "This will do. Thank you, again. Us women have to stick together."

"Good luck to you, miss."

Holding her nose from the foul stench, Lisbeth bypassed the puddles of sludge as best she could and made her way to the end. Hopefully no one would toss out dirty bathwater or worse from the dwellings above. She'd have a hard time enough convincing the men at the customs house that she needed to see someone in charge without smelling like a sewage drain.

Luckily she made it to the end without mishap. Calculating the directions and distance in her head, she took off through the mews, breathing in the scent of hay and horse a lot more readily than she had the putrid alleyway. The soft nicker of horses came from the stalls on the side.

One of the grooms looked up. "Oy, miss. Can I help you?"

"Don't mind me," she called out in a cheery American accent. "I forgot my riding boots like a silly goose and must go back to retrieve them."

It didn't take her long to reach the next street—about five minutes—which left her about ten before her time was up and Gibbons went in after her. She winced as she thought of what the girl might say or do, and then shoved it down. This was more important, and she would make amends to Gibbons later, if it came down to that.

Crossing the intersection, she hurried to where she remembered the customs house offices were located on Second Street in the Parson and Hale's General Store building. With any luck, she'd be able to pass on a message and ask for reinforcements. And if she was really lucky, she'd be able to pass on a message to Estelle, Smalls, and the rest of the crew of the *Syren* if they were in Tampa.

Lady Luck seemed to have deserted her, however. Either of those things would take a miracle. She had no doubt that Saint would have already discovered her unannounced leave and would be hot on her heels. The man was relentless. She'd bet her last penny that he would come after her now with the sole intent of keeping her out of danger.

Something deep inside of her went warm at the thought, even though she didn't need rescuing by anyone. The pistols strapped to the inside of each thigh were more than enough to defend herself, thanks to the hastily cut slits in the pockets of her dress, and Lisbeth wasn't above using her fists, if she had to.

The slit in the pockets was a trick she'd learned from the Duchess of Thornbury's intrepid sister-in-law. Lisbeth had met Ravenna, the very interesting and outspoken Duchess of Ashvale, and had liked her quite well. She and her duke spent their time between London and Antigua, and Lisbeth had seen their fancy passenger liners in the Port of New York. One day, when Lisbeth stopped living a hundred lives, she'd enjoy having some female friendships that lasted longer than each job she took.

As she cut briskly down the street, she let out a short sigh. What would things look like if she had a normal life… with a normal marriage that wasn't tied into undercover work? Perhaps a family of her own one day? Thornbury had done it, and his last letter had said that he and Bronwyn had finally decided to start trying for a family. That had been over a year ago, and Lisbeth had been undercover in the Caribbean for most of that time. She wondered if they'd been successful. He'd make a good father.

Caught up in her musings, she almost missed the turn for Second Street and hurried to the building. Just outside the entrance, Lisbeth took a moment to calm herself with a few deep breaths. Half the battle was confidence, and that she had in spades. Lifting her chin, she smoothed her skirts and strolled inside Parson and Hale's with purpose as she made her way to the customs office.

"May I help you, miss?" a man with a thin mustache asked when she arrived.

"I'm Mrs. Medford from Boston," she said in a haughty voice. "Who is in charge here?"

He blinked and replied before he could think twice about it. "Mr. Jenks but he's—"

Lisbeth cut him off with a wave of her hand, nearly dizzy with relief. Jenks was one of the few men she trusted in Florida, and he was someone who knew the truth of her identity. Normally, as an agent assigned to the Gulf Coast and a hands-on kind of fellow, he was out working rather than in the office. Perhaps her luck was turning. "Can you fetch him, please? It's a matter of some urgency."

His mustache wobbled up and down, eyes narrowing on her in much the same way the girl at the milliner's had, as if trying to regain control of the situation that he'd never had control of in the first place. "Well now, wait a moment. Do you have an appointment?"

"No, but he will see me." She suppressed her irritation. The man was simply doing his job, but any minute now, she expected the form of a large pirate to come bursting through the doors, and then her window of opportunity would be lost. "Medford is the name."

The man frowned. "Mr. Jenks is a busy man. If you don't have an appointment, I'm going to have to ask you to make one."

Bloody hell, she was going to flip the man onto his stubborn arse if he didn't cooperate. "Now look here, I am at the end of my rope—"

A male throat cleared from behind them followed by a

low whistle. "Bloody hell, Medford, is that *you*? Everyone thought you were dead!"

Lisbeth whirled to the stout man standing at the end of the corridor near an open office and nearly slumped with gratitude. "Jenks, you're a sight for sore eyes. I'm not dead as you can see, and we need to talk." She lifted a brow. "Privately and swiftly."

With a nod to his man, he led her into the office marked J. Harry Jenks and closed the door. Lisbeth laid out the pertinent facts as quickly as she could, knowing that time was not on her side. She explained about the storm and the rowboat, and that she was saved by a sailor. His eyes widened to the size of saucers when she explained that the sailor had taken her to the notorious smugglers' stronghold, but she wasn't certain exactly which island it was.

Lisbeth wasn't sure what had possessed her to keep the information of Saint's identity hidden as well as the name of the island from Jenks. They were on the same side, after all. Jenks was responsible for seizing the *Southern Star*, the *Margaret Ann*, and *Seadrift*, all attempting to smuggle contraband goods with cattle, and he was a man with integrity as far as customs agents went. She had every reason to trust him, but of late, her instincts favored caution.

Jenks is need-to-know only.

The half-truth tasted like ash in her mouth. The real truth was that she didn't want to implicate Saint, not when she didn't know how deep he was in with Dubois. And Saint had already been dealt a raw hand with his father's decline and death. She didn't want to be the cause of another. Not that it absolved him of any crimes against the American Treasury, but she couldn't help feeling conflicted.

One thing at a time.

Set up the takedown for Dubois first and then she would untangle the knot that was Raphael Saint.

"That's not really my department anymore," Jenks was saying, and Lisbeth forced her attention to him with a frown.

"Since when?"

He shook his head. "Don't worry. I'm here to provide whatever support you need, but I have been tasked with looking for a specific man. A Mr. Madge who has been evading capture for months and smuggling a fortune in untaxed cigars from Havana."

She stilled. Lisbeth had heard that name. He was one of the captains who had been in the great hall and at the bonfire, one of Dubois's cohorts. The one who had crudely invited her to sit on his lap. "He was there," she said. "One of the men was called Madge."

Jenks shot forward in his seat. "Are you certain?"

"Yes."

Unbridled interest lit his face for the first time since they'd sat down. "If there's a way you can get on a ship with them somewhere close to this coast and signal to us with the code, we can have men ready." The code was a flashing optical sequence used by the British Navy that Lisbeth had employed in the past to communicate her movements to Jenks and others along the shoreline.

"Not here, but I did hear Dubois say he had to go to New York for a shipment at the end of this month," she said. "Though Madge has his own ship."

Eager now, Jenks waved his arm. "I can make New York happen. A fortnight or so from now, you think? Dubois will lead us to him, if they are working together. A trapped rat will do anything to save itself, even eat through its own family."

That was absolutely a visual she did not need. Speaking of family, she cleared her throat. "Jenks, do you know a man called Captain Saint?"

He nodded. "He's a protégé of Dubois's."

"Is he on the list from the Treasury Department?"

Jenks sent her a circumspect look. "Why does it matter? If we can get Saint, Dubois, and Madge in one fell swoop, we'll be promoted. Or even knighted by your British Crown. Wouldn't that be a lark! *Sir* Harry Jenks at your service."

Lisbeth's stomach fell, but she kept her face composed. "I suppose you're right."

"Of course I'm right." He laughed and then sobered. "In the meantime, I'll speak to the Treasury agents in New York and let your people know you're alive. I'll try to get word to you about plans, but that ship to New York will be our best chance to catch the bastards. I'll arrange to have men at Cape May Point keeping a lookout over the next few weeks. You know the signal. Anything else?"

"Can you get a message to the *Syren* in Tampa to set

course for New York? I need my ship close if anything goes wrong."

"Very well. Good work, Agent Medford."

But as Lisbeth left Parson and Hale's, the sinking feeling in her stomach didn't feel like a job well done at all. And it only became worse when she saw the unsmiling man on the other side of the street observing her with wariness and mistrust written all over him.

Devil truly take her luck.

Fourteen

Raphael glanced up at the name on the building with a narrowed stare: Parson and Hale's General Store. He hadn't gone in there for good reason, deciding to wait in a shadowed overhang on the other side of the street. Though the building in question was a store and housed the Cedar Key Post Office, from recollection, it was also the home of the local customs office. And no doubt, there was someone in there who would be happy to catch a wanted smuggler on their stoop. And even if there wasn't, no need to tempt fate by flaunting his presence.

He was just about to send Gibbons or Balzac in when Lisbeth emerged. The expression on her face was hard to decipher. She seemed equally disgruntled and worried, which struck him as odd emotions to have after being in a general store. What would have caused her to have such a reaction? When she saw him, her face froze and then fell back into its usual neutral mask as she walked unhurriedly toward him.

"Before you say anything, it was my fault," she said. "I wanted to be alone for a few minutes without two shadows on my back every infernal second. Then I saw the general store and popped in to have a look at the dry goods and naval stores." She let out a sound of pique. "They were out of quinine. I wanted to get some in case of infection."

A reasonable justification, and one that could explain both of the emotions on her face, but Raphael wasn't convinced. Something felt too smooth—too *polished*—in her delivery of her explanation. "We have more than enough quinine on Exuma."

"We're not on Exuma, are we, Saint?" she shot back.

It rubbed a little that she was back to calling him Saint as if she intended to put distance between them. He did not know how he felt about that… He was of two minds. On the one hand, getting involved with a woman—and another smuggler, at that—would distract him from his main focus, but on the other, he *liked* Lisbeth.

Despite her many idiosyncrasies, being with her made him feel…hopeful. An even odder sentiment, but so much of his recent years had been filled with despair, drive, and bitterness. All working toward one goal—the destruction of the man responsible for his father's death. Lisbeth was an unexpected beam of light in an all-too-dismal terrain, and just like a stupid fucking moth to a flame, he couldn't help veering toward her.

Even knowing she could be his ruin.

"No, we're not," Raphael agreed with a grunt and turned toward the docks, before signaling to Gibbons and Balzac to go on ahead of them. "And you know very well that the men are for your safety."

She rolled her eyes. "This is Florida, and it's broad daylight with shopkeepers and lots of people around. Even if I weren't *me*, how much danger am I really in?"

He glanced down at her, amusement seeping through

his ire at having to chase her through the town when a shame-faced Gibbons had confessed she'd given them the slip. He'd been hounded from the milliner's by a young woman with a sizable broom—a scene that Raphael had come upon and would not soon forget. If he hadn't been hard-pressed to find Lisbeth, he would have laughed until his sides ached. The comical sight of a chit half the men's size screaming at them to stop their thievery had had Lisbeth's influence all over it.

"I seem to recall that danger finds you quite often," he pointed out. "Explosions, public street brawls, tropical storms, shopkeepers with brooms. I'm beginning to think you should come with a warning label: Beware, death by association entirely possible."

Her eyes widened. "She went after them with a broom? Good for her." Lisbeth snorted and smacked him with her reticule. "Besides, you like that about me. Don't even pretend. I keep you on your toes."

That was the problem. He liked everything about her fiery personality far too much.

"You're right. I do," he conceded.

She glanced at him. "I don't intimidate you at all, do I?"

"On the contrary, I'd be a fool if you didn't, but suffice it to say you impress me more." Unexpected pleasure bloomed in her eyes before it was banked. He wanted to see more of that genuine emotion. "And infuriate me," he added, and she laughed.

Lisbeth lived without apology, but even with all that self-assurance, she seemed so solitary, keeping everyone at arm's length. With her own crew, he'd noticed that she held herself apart. Not enough that it would be obvious, but *just* enough that she wouldn't get too close.

Oh, they adored her and she them, but those bonds felt…*conditional,* as if she were afraid to lose herself too completely. He recognized it as a form of self-preservation, because he kept himself guarded, too.

Yet another similarity they shared.

Coming to a halt, he turned to face her and caught his breath. He stared at her face, memorizing the way the sunlight hit her gilt-tipped lashes and highlighted the spattering of strawberry freckles over her small nose. Her lightly tanned cheeks were rosy from the sun, lips curling up into a half smile, while sea-glass green eyes sparkling with challenge peered up at him. She was so lovely that he nearly forgot what he'd meant to say.

"Are you ever going to be honest with me?" he asked quietly.

Shadows fell over that green gaze, her face morphing into the impersonal mask he was beginning to loathe with every ounce of his being. "Honesty requires trust, Saint."

"Raphael," he countered.

Her mouth tightened stubbornly. "I prefer Saint."

He could have left it, he supposed. It was just a name, but it bothered him for reasons he'd rather not define. He needed that mask of hers to slip. "Calling me Saint while the sweet taste of you is seared into my senses seems rather formal, wouldn't you say?" Now *that* elicited a response. Her cheeks flushed with hot color, but he wasn't done.

She might want to pretend that what happened between them was unremarkable, fine, but he had no intention of doing the same. "Or with my release soaking into your glowing, pretty skin."

"Saint, we're in public!" she hissed.

"So?" he countered. "Are you ashamed, Lisbeth?"

Her mouth gaped. "What? No! That's not it." She blew out a breath and shot a quick glance over her shoulder in the direction of Parson and Hale's. "What happened between us was—"

"If you say 'a mistake,' I will personally toss you over my shoulder, dunk you in the bay, and leave you to find your own way back to Exuma." He was only half joking.

"If you'd let me finish, I was going to say spontaneous. But that doesn't change who we are to each other." She glowered at him and started a brisk walk down the street.

"And what is that?" he asked, following her swift steps with long ones of his own. "Friends? Enemies? Almost lovers?"

"Shipmates."

Raphael caught up to her, noting that the flush of deep rose had wound its way down to her décolletage. The very same part of her that was carved so compellingly into his memory—a lethal goddess on her knees. "I think we're a little more than that. Why do you insist on keeping everyone at a distance?"

"I do not," she replied.

"I see you, Lisbeth Medford," he said, making her stumble slightly before she righted herself. At the next intersection, she turned blindly, striding down a narrow street, but Raphael kept pace easily with her. She was trying to run and she didn't even know it. "I see the softer parts of yourself that you try to hide and the fact that you try to be an island without letting anyone get too close to your shores." He blew out a breath. "Like Narina. Like Estelle. Like me."

Now she whirled, pure fire in her gaze, lips thin with anger. "Then take the hint and stay away. Don't presume to think you know me, Saint, or understand any part of my past or my choices," she said, seething. "Just because I let you have power over me for one second on that ship doesn't give you any right to try to study me and pass judgment. You see nothing."

He didn't falter in the face of her fury, knowing exactly from where it stemmed: fear that he was treading too close. "On that ship, *you* held all the power. And the truth is you don't *want* me to see the real you. Because what do you do when that happens, Lisbeth? When someone breaches all your defenses? Do you run? Do you hide? Do you push them away? Cut them out of your life for *daring* to care?"

The flare in her eyes told him that he'd hit a sore spot. She spun and advanced upon him until they were nearly touching, fury frothing from her very pores. One finger jammed into his chest. "You're operating on the flawed assumption that I give a rat's shit about any opinion *you* might have about me. You're nothing but a passing distraction who has already worn out his welcome."

He kept his hands at his sides, even though every instinct roared for him to press her to his chest and punish that beautiful, deceitful mouth with his. "I think you're lying to yourself. I think you do care and that scares the spit out of you."

She huffed a mocking laugh. "Trust me, Saint. Your tongue wasn't that good. If it's honesty you desire, women do it better."

He let the cruel barb go, a slow smile spreading over his lips. "Ruthless to a fault, aren't you, Viking?" One palm slid slowly across her heaving ribs and around to the middle of her back, loosely enough for her to pull away if she so chose. "But I'm afraid, chérie, you're going to have to do much better than that to damage my pride and chase me away."

Her body trembled at the light touch but she remained stationary, the only movements the rise and fall of her chest with each shallow breath. Desire warred with resentment in her eyes, her usual fight-or-flight impulses hard to control when overpowered by another more carnal compulsion...the need to lose herself in desire. He felt it, too.

Raphael ghosted his mouth over her brow as his other hand slid up to the strings of her bonnet, untying them and removing it before cupping her nape. He looped his fingers into the rope of hair there and drew her head back, watching her pupils blow wide with passion. "I warned you before. Lie to whomever you please, but not to me." He licked his lips as hers parted in unconscious invitation. "I'm going to kiss you now. Stop me or slap me, that power is always yours, but you can't run from this, Lisbeth."

Both hands skimmed up to cradle her face as he bent over her. With a groan, she shoved upward at the same time. The almost violent connection of their lips could hardly be called a kiss. It was a concentrated battle of lust and domination. His Viking kissed like she fought—with spite and rage, her teeth nearly grinding into his, tongue spearing into his mouth like she owned it, the taste of her drowning all his senses. He nipped her bottom lip and she bit him harder.

Without warning, she spun and shoved them into the nearest wall, thrusting her pelvis into his thighs, his hard length jutting into her stomach. She twined her hands into his coat and mortared her body to his. Raphael let her. She had her own demons to slay before she'd submit.

But submit she would…eventually.

And he'd be there to hold her the instant that happened.

Damn this man.

Who did he think he was?

Her thoughts were chaotic, vengeful, and bitter, even as she devoured him like he was the last repast she'd ever have. His mouth was just as forceful, offering no mercy like the callous pirate he was. He took and she returned the favor. God, kissing him was like sailing the ocean in the midst of a lightning storm. Beautiful. Violent. Powerful.

The risk of immolation there with every strike. They consumed each other, this thing between them electric and raw...and everything she should be running from.

Because what he'd said was true.

He did see her. And she fucking hated it. Hated that her usual artifices didn't work, that he kept coming, that he wasn't deterred by her insults. That he was so bloody unyielding with his shrewd words and those penetrating eyes boring through to the fragile truth of her. She'd always been an island onto herself, and that strategy had worked to keep everyone else at bay.

Until him.

She felt like an exposed nerve, but oddly, there was no real fear.

You're safe with him.

The minute her mouth softened, Raphael groaned an approving sound low in his throat that made her skin tighten with longing to hear it again. He turned them so that her back was to the wall, lifted her by the waist and wrapped her legs over his hips. Hell, if that didn't make the hardest part of him prod deliciously through her petticoats, right to her needy core. The moan that left her mouth was indecent, but she did not care who heard her.

Lisbeth yanked her lips away. They tingled, feeling swollen and bruised, even as they mourned the loss of him. His weren't much better, red and puffy like a wild animal had savaged them. Their breaths were harsh in the silence. Her nipples were peaked against her bodice, sensitive and wanting, and the space between her thighs hummed its own throbbing heartbeat. "Perhaps what we need to do is fuck this out of our systems," she said.

He eyed her, pupils blown out with desire. "Have you ever done something like that before?"

"No," she answered before she could think twice. "I don't shag indiscriminately. My body doesn't work like that. I have to…" *Bloody hell.* She ground her teeth and slammed her mouth shut at the word that had been about to slip out.

"Care?" the lousy man finished with a smug curl to his lips. Of course he'd guess, she realized sourly. Apparently, he was the patron saint of esoteric women.

"Yes, like I care for my crew," she said. "Of which you are a part."

"Does everyone on your crew make you whimper and writhe?" he drawled, punctuated by a slow punch of his hips that made her gasp.

Unable to dignify that with an answer that wasn't a complete fib or throw another spiteful, reprehensible, and patently false jab about female lovers just to hinder him, Lisbeth closed her eyes. "You are unendurable."

He kissed her nose. "Good thing you *care* about me."

Groaning, she shook her head in defeat, opened her eyes, and looked around as the haze of passion cleared slightly. Where the hell were they? It was a narrow, seedy alley like the one at the back of the milliner's shop, though not as filthy or smelly, thank God. Belatedly, however, she took stock of the fact that they had an audience.

"Raphael."

At her urgent whisper, he glanced over his shoulder, his body going on instant alert at the sight of the group of men closing ranks around them from the other side of the street. She counted eight of them, but there could be more lurking behind.

If Gibbons and Balzac hadn't gone ahead, four on eight would have been a quick fight. Two versus eight was a different matter.

The arrivals were shoddily dressed, their faces mean and haggard. Petty ruffians from the look of it, but a group that large at once could cause trouble. Clearly, they meant to, since they were blocking any avenue of escape as if this was a net they'd cast before on unsuspecting victims. They were equipped with various weapons including a few sharp cutlasses. Lisbeth exhaled and rolled her neck.

Oh well...she had a lot of energy racing around her body with no outlet.

"Are you armed?" Raphael asked softly, peering at her.

"A knife in each boot, daggered hairpins, and a pistol strapped to my thigh."

His dark chuckle and look of frank admiration made her blood heat. "Why am I not surprised? Then again, I could hardly feel a thing through your petticoats. I have plans for those dastardly layers later, involving a knife and my bare hands."

An unholy shiver wound through her at the scintillating thought of him cutting away her undergarments. "Not the time, Pirate," she warned as the men cinched closer.

"We don't want any trouble," Raphael said, turning

around fully to face them and keeping her shielded with his back.

It was strange that a voice had whispered that she was safe with him when they were alone, and now, Lisbeth felt even more so…while on the cusp of mortal danger. She hadn't felt so secure with anyone at her back since Thornbury and they had trained for years together. Raphael was no slouch, but this felt like more. An intuitive knowledge that he'd never leave her open and exposed. That he had her…no matter what…whether they were kissing or fighting for their lives.

The biggest of the men stared them down, baring teeth to show missing spaces and the glint of gold. "Give us your money and the woman."

"I can do the first, but not the second," Raphael replied as though they were having a polite conversation over brandy and cigars. "Unfortunately, she's spoken for."

The man spat a wad of phlegm to the side. "I don't care if she's owned by the fuckin' president. Your purse and the woman, or you can die being a hero."

Lisbeth's tinkling laughter drew their attention. "Oh, that's cute that they think you're the hero in this story."

Raphael snorted as she giggled harder.

"What's so funny, bitch?" another man yelled.

"Neither of us are heroes," she replied, hand sliding through to the layered slits in her dress and petticoats behind Raphael's torso. "We're the fucking villains, *bitch*."

With that, she yanked the pistol out and took out the one who had spoken with a cracking shot to the stomach.

He might live if he got himself to a doctor. It was pandemonium as the men screamed and shouted, rushing them all at once. In a move that could rival the grace of a ballerina, Raphael swung the pistol from his coat pocket to take out the man closest to him before sinking to his feet in an elegant sideways crouch to snatch a knife from its sheath in her right boot. The flat of the blade kissed her stockinged calf and made her suck in a sharp breath before embedding itself into another assailant.

That cheeky wretch!

Grinning with exhilaration and arousal, Lisbeth whirled, plucking the four-inch-long hairpins shaped like thin swords from her coiffure. She dragged one end lightly over Raphael's groin, eliciting a groan and a smothered oath of vengeance. Turnabout was fair play. With a wink, she put the weapons to better use by kicking the man coming at her right in the gut and then stabbing him through the ribs with rapid jabs of her wrists. He screamed and fell onto his arse.

Four down. Four to go, including the leader. He had a bemused expression on his face—as if he wasn't quite sure how his upper hand had gone south—but it turned quickly to rage. Two of the men dropped their weapons and fled, so Lisbeth cleaned her hairpins off on her dress and tucked them back into her hair before retrieving one of the fallen cutlasses with a wild grin. She almost wished there were more enemies.

She saw Raphael shoot her a wry glance at the red streaks on her striped ivory and blue muslin skirts.

"What?" She wrinkled her nose. "It's just a little blood. Don't go squeamish on me now."

"You are one of a kind, woman," he said.

Lisbeth swung the cutlass in a slow circle, testing the weight and getting comfortable with the wooden hilt as she and Raphael squared off against the two remaining hooligans. They didn't look too worried, and the reason for that became clear when footsteps clapped on the cobblestones as four more ruffians sprinted toward them. The two men who had run had gone for reinforcements. One of the new thugs had a pitchfork.

Anticipation sluiced through her veins. She'd gotten her wish.

Lisbeth let out a whoop. "This is the best day ever. Trident is mine!"

The heated look in Raphael's eyes promised filthy things that made her go hot, but then she was too busy slashing and twisting, hacking and ducking. Her arms burned and her chest ached with the breaths sawing out of her lungs as she fought like a devil. She swept a man's legs out from under him and kicked another in the side of his calf with a quick snap. The cutlass went flying from her grip in a moment of distraction when she heard Raphael roar in pain. But she could barely find him in the mass of dirty bodies.

A thick arm rounded her neck, but not before she instinctively tucked her chin down to protect her throat. "Enough!" a man bellowed, his fetid breath making her gag.

When the last attackers froze at the command, Lisbeth

caught sight of Raphael and the red across his abdomen. Blood welled from a deep gash, spreading like a scarlet line, but he stood tall despite the sudden pallor of his brown skin. *Damn.*

"I'm going to have to strangle her right in front of you to teach you a lesson," the man grasping her said, and tightened his hold.

"You say that like it's a threat," Lisbeth taunted with a giggle. The trick was to keep the enemy unbalanced. He'd already seen her fight, so he was aware of her skills. Playing the damsel would not get her anywhere, so acting the glib scoundrel was the next obvious choice. The tongue could be as effective as a blade in the right circumstance. "Sometimes a girl likes it rough."

Raphael's eyes bulged with rage when the disgusting cretin rubbed his crotch against her and one of the men still standing burst into raucous laughter. "Do you now?" her captor crooned. "I knew you'd be a handful, but I'll bind you all the same before I show you what a real man is like."

"Such confidence," she wheezed with another breathless laugh. Lisbeth didn't have to pretend the breathless part—the man was squeezing the space in her throat to a sliver even with her chin blocking him from fully choking her. Black spots began to dance in her vision. She had to make a move before she fainted from the lack of oxygen.

Focusing, Lisbeth shunted her hips backward into his erection, but only when she felt the tension in his grip lessen marginally did she step to the side and grasp his arm with both hands, one at the wrist and the other at the elbow. With all the force she could muster, she slammed her left hand back to his groin, catching him squarely on the hard column of flesh. He screamed, his body curling forward, and she swung her elbow up into his nose, hearing bone crack before he released her and toppled back.

Lisbeth could have stopped there, but he'd rubbed his grimy cock on her. Men like him would always try to take advantage of defenseless women. And *she* wasn't defenseless in the least. Staring at him, Lisbeth reached down for the knife in her boot.

"Touch another woman without her consent and I'll come back and cut it off." Then she buried it to the hilt right in his shriveled, tiny ballocks.

"Fuck! Fuck! You gelded me, you fucking bunter!"

Lisbeth wrinkled her nose. "And now you're insulting jades making an honest living. Honestly, do you *want* to die today? And that's Bonnie Bess to you."

When the man's face blanched even in his agony, eyes rounding with dread, she grinned. Good, he knew who she was. A blade in the balls was a blessing from someone with a brutal reputation like hers. The Bonnie Bess from the sea shanty would have cut them off and taken them with her as a souvenir.

"They're mine next time," she crooned in a honeyed voice, and he started sobbing.

More footsteps raced toward them, but it was Gibbons and Balzac, who had their guns in hand. They were followed by two other crew from the *Avalon*—Peppers and

Jim. The thieves who could still move scattered at the new arrivals, abandoning their leader who was curled up on the ground crying and clutching his bleeding crotch.

"Bloody hell, Raphael!" Lisbeth shouted, dashing to him as he swayed unsteadily on his feet, his skin an unhealthy wan color. Gibbons pulled one arm over his shoulders, making him grunt in pain. "Get him back to the ship and find a fucking doctor!" she ordered.

Raphael shot her a weak smile. "Worried about me, Viking?"

"Promises were made," she told him before kissing him soundly on the lips, those vicious green eyes unable to hide her fear. "Don't you dare die on me."

Fifteen

Of all the times to suffer a blade to the belly!

Raphael moved slightly and winced at the pain shooting along his sides. He glanced down. Beneath the sheets he wore nothing but a pair of smallclothes. A clean linen bandage surrounded his mottled torso. Clearly, the wound had been cleaned and stitched, and he remembered being warned to remain abed, lest he rip open the laceration. The amount of blood he'd lost had caused him to fall into a deep sleep the moment they'd set foot on the ship.

The bits and pieces of the past handful of days were a bit fuzzy, but the doctor—a man with kind brown eyes—had come to tend to him at the beginning. Later, he'd felt the ship start to move and wondered if he'd been dreaming. He had no sense of time, everything blurring into hours of awful agony and blessed silence.

Gentle fingers had cooled his brow when the fever had set in, feeding him sips of water and broth. On the occasions when his eyelids had cracked open, he had seen his Viking pacing in the background, her anxious gaze fastened to him as he plummeted back into oblivion. Right now his beautiful caretaker was asleep in the chair beside his bed.

They were no longer on a ship, but in a room with

gauzy curtains. How on earth had he gotten here? Were they still in Florida? Raphael licked parched lips, but his eyes flicked back to the sleeping goddess. He couldn't help watching her quietly. In repose, with her lashes leaving shadows on her cheeks and her pink lips parted, she seemed much younger. Golden wisps of hair curled into her relaxed brow, the freckles on her nose even more prominent. A tiny snore left her mouth and he smiled. She would positively loathe the fact that he'd heard her snoring.

Raphael exhaled a tiny puff of laughter, and gilded lashes tipped up to reveal soft green eyes that sharpened into relief. "You're awake," she said, sitting upright. "How do you feel?"

"Like some brigand got in a lucky strike because I couldn't take my eyes off a beautiful woman making mash of her enemies." His voice was nothing but a croak, and she instantly plied him with a cup of water. Raphael sipped gratefully.

"Are you well?" she asked. "Does the wound pain you? The doctor used catgut for the stitches and he also used carbolic acid to sterilize the thread and his instruments. He said it was your best chance."

"It's not too bad." The sutures didn't pull as much, which hopefully meant that he was healing. He formed a confused frown, taking in the space around him again. "Where are we? And what day is it?"

"Exuma," she replied. "Boisie got us back here in one piece. We had to stay in Cedar Key for a few days so the doctor could drain your wound, stitch it, and make sure infection didn't set in. Then you caught a fever, and it was touch and go for a while there." She blew out a breath. "Everyone was afraid that it was yellow fever, but Narina insisted it wasn't what her mama had. Beyond the chills and the fever, you weren't vomiting, so that was a good sign. It broke in two days and we were able to leave. It's been nine days since you were injured."

Nine days! No wonder he felt like such shit. He stared at her, seeing the conflicted expression on her face, and narrowed his eyes. "What aren't you telling me?"

"Your instincts were sound about Tampa. When we rounded the coast, we were pursued by frigates owned by the customs house agents and only managed to escape by the skin of our teeth, as well the luck of a squall that reduced visibility."

He scowled, though he wasn't surprised. Dubois wouldn't be Dubois without some perverse plot in place. "Where *is* my uncle? I'm shocked he didn't sneak someone in here to finish me off."

Something else—frustration or disappointment, perhaps—flitted across her face. "He'd already sailed for New York by the time we returned. He left early."

"Well, that's one small mercy." Raphael frowned. "So why the long face?"

"I was hoping to get back to the *Syren* with him on that voyage," she said cagily and her voice trailed off. But there was something more, some agenda that she was hiding. He could see it in the set of her shoulders and the tight lines bracketing her mouth, and the fact that she wouldn't make eye contact was a dead giveaway that something more was afoot.

"How do you know the *Syren* is in New York?" he asked softly and she froze. They stared at each other in silence, her upper lip tucked between her teeth. His gaze dipped to where her thumb and forefinger worried the fabric of her skirt. As far as physical tells, she didn't have many, but that was one sign that her infamous control was being held by a thread. He cleared his dry throat and shadowed green eyes met his. "Tell me one true thing, Lisbeth."

The conflict was evident in her face and in her hand white-knuckling the pleats of her skirts. She knew what the question meant; she *had* to know. She swallowed convulsively and ground her jaw. "I…cannot."

"Cannot or will not?"

"Saint," she begged. "Please. I just need time to think."

Saint. He closed his eyes and leaned back against the pillows, a strange sense of heavy disillusionment filling him at her refusal and the address. He had hoped… He clenched his teeth and banished that errant, pitiful thought. Well, hope was an infernally stupid thing, wasn't it? "Keep your secrets, then," he whispered and turned to his side.

"Raphael."

Her voice was agonized, but they were both spared more awkward discomfort when Narina bounded into the room and climbed onto the other side of the bed. A homemade eye patch covered nearly half of her face. "About sodding time, Cap'n! You scared the good goddamn out of me, savvy?"

"Good to see you too, lassie," he said at the same time that Lisbeth chided, "Language, Nari."

"Nearly lost your ship. Boisie wouldn't listen, that giant bucket of fartleberries, and it was because of *me* that we were able to lose the frigates in the storm." She plopped her hands on her hips, even as Raphael's lips twitched at her creative name-calling. "Every seadog worth his bloody salt knows you sail around a storm or into it. Never wait for it to catch you." A self-righteous smirk formed on her small face. "I told him I would tell you that he fancies a bit o' the ol' Bess and you would cleave him to the brisket, if you found out."

Raphael pushed upward with a groan at the pull of his aching muscles, and Lisbeth was quick to prop a pillow behind him. Her sweet scent teased his nostrils, and he fought the natural urge to reach for her…to bury his nose in her hair. "Thank you," he grunted.

"You're not going to get blood everywhere, are you?" Narina's eyes rounded with unease as she observed him, no doubt taking in the weeks' worth of dark scruff on his face and the remnants of illness that made his skin feel dry and tight. Dark circles probably flourished under his eyes, and he was sure he looked like a horse's arse.

"I won't lie. You look like you were shat"—Narina glanced at Lisbeth's pinched face and adjusted her words—"surely pooped out by wild goats."

"That sounds about right." He grinned at the quick save. "Know a lot about goat droppings, do you?"

She nodded sagely. "The neighbor behind the tavern kept goats. They can have diarrhea. It's vile. Soft, watery, and smelly." She wrinkled her nose and then held the end with her fingers. "Speaking of, you need a bath, Cap'n."

That reminded him. "Who tended to me while I was ill?"

Lisbeth turned her head away, but Narina was quick to volunteer the information. "Bess. I mean, Lisbeth did it. She could have had one of the women here help once we got back to the island, but she only made *me* take away the soiled linens." Narina made a gagging noise. "Smelly and fuc—deuced foul."

He had to laugh at the child's brutal honesty. "Thanks."

"Narina!" Lisbeth scolded, going red.

Why should she be embarrassed that she'd cared for him? It was a considerate thing to do, and besides, it wasn't like Lisbeth hadn't seen him in the altogether already.

"At least she can be honest," he said, making that upper lip disappear between her teeth again as her slender throat worked. "A virtue to be valued, no matter its delivery."

Lisbeth turned away, guilt swamping her. She knew what Raphael wanted, but the cost for her truths was too much to pay. Her entire career was riding on her success at this. All her life, her job had been her only calling, and now, suddenly, she felt torn in multiple directions. Her usually infallible sense of judgment felt stretched thin.

Because of *him*.

The last few days had been harrowing. Watching Raphael on the verge of death had had an impact that she never could have foreseen. Lisbeth *did* care about him. It would have hurt irreparably if she'd lost him… and that knowledge had shifted something vital inside of her. Something that she hadn't wanted to acknowledge. Somewhere along the way, the rogue had burrowed his way under her skin and breached every single one of her defenses.

If she told him one honest thing…she would tell him everything.

And that she could not do.

She needed to get to New York, get her ship, find Jenks's people, and finish her job. All other diversions could wait.

He's not a diversion.

No. Raphael Saint was much worse—he was a hazard.

"Can I see the healing cut?" Narina was asking. "Your grouchy grouch of a caretaker wouldn't let me. Said it wasn't a sight for young girls, but I've seen plenty of worse wounds before. Oozing pus and blood. I bet yours is nothing."

"Nari," Lisbeth said, feeling mortified again. "It's not proper to ask such a thing."

"You wouldn't say no to a boy," she replied sourly and scowled. "What if I wanted to be a surgeon? My delicate sensibles wouldn't matter then, would they?"

"Sensibilities," Lisbeth said.

"That's what I bloody said!"

Raphael shifted to a sitting position with a wince.

"She is only curious, and I want to have a look for myself anyway before I do have a wash. I am fine with her seeing it, if you are."

Narina wasn't wrong, but Lisbeth hadn't felt comfortable letting her gawp without Raphael's permission. She nodded and watched as he gingerly scooted to the side of the bed. He lifted his hem and removed the linen wrapped around him until the jagged gash was revealed.

At first glance, the injury wasn't too bad, about five and a half inches long from his navel to his left hip, though the skin was puffy and purple around the neat sutures. Catgut would disappear on its own in time. Some yellowish bruising expanded along his torso, but that was to be expected. The doctor, a physician from Jamaica—thank God it hadn't been Boisie or one of the other crewmates—had done an excellent job.

"Bloody hell," Narina whispered. "That must have stung like a bit…er, bee." She shot a sheepish glance at Lisbeth.

"I didn't feel it at the time," Raphael murmured. "Too busy trying not to get skewered a second time."

"Blimey!" Narina gave an excited squeal as Lisbeth busied herself with sending for one of the maids to arrange a bath. The wound should be healed enough for him to bathe properly, though he might require assistance. Would he ask for someone else? The hot jolt in her gut took her by surprise. "I heard you fought off a dozen cutpurses!" Narina was chattering. "Gibbons and Ballsack said it was just the two of you."

Lisbeth paused. Did she hear that name right? Knowing

Narina's cheek, she'd butchered the man's name on purpose. Lisbeth would never admit it aloud, but that was deviously clever for a twelve-year-old. Narina was another thing that she would have to take care of in some fashion when all of this was said and done.

The girl could not stay with her, nor could she return to Bridgetown unless Lisbeth could arrange care and a safe home for her there. She needed a strong, loving influence in her life and proper instruction, not getting her education from drunks from a tavern. Again, that was another problem for later.

Half a dozen women arrived with a few men carrying buckets filled with water to the adjacent bathing room, twittering and curious to get a look at their favorite captain. Including the pretty brunette Lisbeth knew fancied Raphael. She'd kept them all away before so he could rest, but now that he was awake, he could make his own decisions. She clenched her jaw and swallowed down the spurt of irrational jealousy.

"Nari, come," she snapped, harsher than she'd meant to. "Time to go."

"But I want to know about the fight," she whined.

"Saint needs his privacy." Lisbeth caught Raphael's jaw tightening at the name, and it hurt her too, but she had to do what was necessary to put distance between them. She shepherded the girl outside and hesitated at the door, acid pooling in her chest when one of the women teasingly offered to wash his back after the bath was filled. Her fingers pulled convulsively at the seam on her skirts.

"Lisbeth." His voice was low, commanding, and made parts of her warm.

She turned. "Yes?"

"Stay," he said.

"It appears that you have more than enough willing volunteers."

He glanced at the women with his playful lopsided smirk and made them give a collective sigh. Lisbeth suppressed her own sigh with a silent snarl. No need to inflate his ego even further. But it was true that that stupid smile of his was maddeningly effective at demolishing one's good sense. "Thank you, kind friends, but we can manage from here."

We? Lisbeth gulped.

"Are you certain?" the brunette cooed and dragged a fingertip over his arm. "I make a good nurse and I don't mind sharing."

Gray eyes met Lisbeth's where she stood. "Alas, I don't share."

The possessive note in his tone shouldn't have felt as good as it did.

Pouting with disappointment, the women trailed out, darting looks in her direction and muttering petty insults. If they really knew who she was, they would not be so quick to get in her face. Lisbeth bristled at the nerve, especially when the brunette in question slowed with a sneer. Unable to help herself, she let a little of Bonnie Bess show through her eyes and in the feral grin that twisted her lips, and the other woman flinched before hurrying after the others.

Raphael chuckled. "Easy, Viking. No need to terrify the poor chit."

They observed each other in tenuous silence, before he hobbled to the bathing room. He stopped at the doorway, peering over his shoulder. "You can't have it both ways. Either you come help me or I get one of the other women to do it. Your choice."

She went mutinous at that. "You could get one of the men to assist you."

"And you think the outcome will be any different?" he said. "Given your own preferences, you should be the last to assume that I won't enjoy it."

"God, you are insufferable." Lisbeth glared at him and gestured for him to go into the bathing room with a growl. "One of these days, your enormous ego will be the death of you."

"Everything about me is proportional," he said with a slight flex of his hips.

Her gaze went automatically to his groin as the cheeky rotter had intended, though she had to admit, the light bickering was vastly preferable to the fraught tension from earlier. "Good God, you're at death's doorstep and you can't help yourself, can you? Is everything a sexual spectacle with you?"

He smirked. "I'm a red-blooded man about to get naked with a beautiful woman ready to do my bidding."

Lisbeth's cheeks warmed. What was it with him and praise, along with her absurd desire to receive it? With an aggravated sigh, she closed the door and walked toward him. The closer she got, the less air she took in. His hair was greasy and his skin sallow, and still, her pulse leaped like a silly puppy with a bone. "Come on, Casanova. Even with your considerable flirtation skills, no one fancies a malodorous man."

She had done her best to sponge bathe him, and while Boisie had helped tend to his basic needs, she knew how hard it was to feel clean without a proper bath. Life on the sea required adjustments, including being able to wash with minimal supplies and cold rainwater, not to mention handling her courses. On a ship with so many women, that was a trial in itself, though they managed. Lisbeth enjoyed being clean. A leisurely bath was the first thing she treated herself to whenever she put into port.

Raphael was able to shuck out of his smallclothes without her assistance, and Lisbeth averted her gaze. It was one thing to bathe an oblivious patient and another to do it while he was awake with all that manly virility on display. Raphael winced as he put one leg over the side.

"Easy, let me do the work," she said. "You don't want to injure yourself further."

She offered her arm and took some of his weight while he eased himself over. Raphael sank down into the warm water with a grunt. Only after he was fully submerged did she look, though the water hid nothing. The strong lines of his body and the glint of both his piercings drew the eye, and she couldn't help staring.

With a silent curse, Lisbeth schooled herself and moved behind him with a pitcher to wet his hair. Sitting on a nearby stool, she reached for the jar of soap. When she lathered his locks and dug her fingers into his scalp, his deep groan was enough to make her shiver in response. "That feels good."

"Your hair is so thick," she murmured. "The color is so dark it absorbs the light."

"I've been told I get that from my mother," he told her. "That, my nose, and my complexion. She died in childbirth so I never knew her."

"I'm so sorry."

"Merci," he murmured. "My eyes I get from my father, however, and his chin."

It was quite a good chin—strong and square. His nose was nice, too, and though it was bold and long, it suited the sweeping angles and planes of his face. Like his hair, his eyelashes were thick, jet-black, and long, and droplets of water clung to them when his eyes closed. She knew the sandblasted stormy color of them by heart, however. Those singular gray eyes with their speckled brown sunbursts were quite unforgettable.

She rinsed his hair and lathered it again, the strands slippery in her fingers. "Did you grow up in Paris?"

"Yes, though we visited my mother's homeland often. It was strange but I felt more…myself there. In Tobago."

"Truly?" she asked, curious.

"A child with my skin and hair color tended to stand out in the fancy drawing rooms in Paris. At times, despite my father's status with the emperor, I felt like a charming oddity on display. Look at the beautiful boy, they would all coo and carry on, like I didn't have feelings or a brain in my head. Like I was a pretty object to admire. They say beauty is a curse, and it only worsened when I got older." He sighed. "And prettier."

She smiled and tugged on his hair. "Such vanity, Monsieur le Duc."

His eyes flashed open. "It was the bane of my existence."

"I am only teasing," she said and stroked her fingertips across his temples. "I know what it's like to be judged on the basis of one thing. In my case, it's my sex. I have had to work harder for every scrap of the name I've made for myself in a world dominated by men."

"Bonnie Bess?"

She exhaled sharply at the near miss. She'd meant as a spy, but her current identity would serve well enough. Carving out a space for herself in the cutthroat smuggling trade had nearly broken her. She'd had to say things, *do* things, that she wasn't proud of, but all of it had been in the name of her mission. Her crimes would be absolved. Still, the past two years had left an indelible mark on her soul.

She shrugged. "Women are expected to be good for one purpose...marriage and babies, when we are so much more than the sum of our wombs."

His stare bored into hers. "I agree wholeheartedly."

Lisbeth didn't know what made her ask. Perhaps she wanted to feel that connection strengthen between them one more time. Or perhaps she didn't want to feel so alone on her stupid self-imposed island when he was the only one who had ever truly seen her.

Who *saw* her now.

Her voice shook. "Tell me something true, Pirate."

Neither of them moved for a long moment, and she resigned herself to the fact that he might not answer. She deserved that for her refusal earlier. But when he finally did speak, his voice was so soft, she could barely hear him. "You deserve to be happy with whomever you choose to be. Whether that's Bonnie Bess or not. We choose the paths we follow. We determine who we are."

Sixteen

A WEEK LATER, RAPHAEL WAS HEALED ENOUGH TO make the short journey to Nassau after he received word that one of his ships from France had arrived in port. Lisbeth wondered if he'd want to sail back to Europe. If so, she'd have to find a way to the United States on her own. A daunting prospect, considering the role she was playing as Saint's paramour, but surely there would be someone leaving Nassau who would accommodate her. This wasn't Exuma. There were lawful transports here. She only needed to be able to pay her way.

And money she did not have, at least at present.

Despite her best efforts to figure out a way to get word to Jenks or get herself to New York, she was a sitting duck at the moment. Raphael already knew based on her slipup that the *Syren* was in port there. He didn't know *how* she knew, however, but the man was astute enough to guess that she might have mailed correspondence at the Cedar Key post office or worse—her stomach dipped—spoken to the customs agents directly, which she had.

She was undercover; deception was the nature of her profession.

So why did she feel so *guilty*?

Lisbeth had never felt conflicted about her work

before, but her overwhelmingly complicated feelings for the man were confusing both her morals and her motivations. And the soft truth he'd given her that night of the bath had seeded and grown roots in her mind.

Could she be someone other than a spy?

Could she simply be *happy*?

Lisbeth had always thought that happiness was a construct. She prided herself on a job well done, on the validation that she received from the Home Office, on completing each assignment and moving on to the next. Those things were things within her control that gave her satisfaction and pleasure. She had never depended on other people for that. But Raphael made her want more, made her think she was *deserving* of more. The barricaded island that had served her so faithfully for years suddenly felt...sparse and lonely.

"Bess, did you hear?" Narina shrieked, jerking her from her bothersome thoughts. "We're going to New York once Saint's ship has been readied with fuel and provisions. It's huge, too! That's it out there. Do you see it? Behind the two smaller ones. They big gray one with the huge masts. Saint says I can be his junior quartermaster. Me!"

"That's wonderful, Nari," she said, her eyes finding the ship instantly. Her gaze flicked back to its tall captain, though Raphael wasn't looking in their direction. He was talking to a tall man with auburn hair and pale skin. Was he charting course to New York for her? Or was that a strange coincidence?

Narina did a little dance, hopping from one foot to the

other, and growled like a pirate. "One day I'll have my own ship like you and Saint, and I'll sail the oceans leaving pillage and carnage in my wake!"

Lisbeth held back a snort of laughter. The child was bloodthirsty for such a little thing. Lisbeth supposed she hadn't been the best example to her over the past two years in her guise as Bonnie Bess, and her exploits would have been extra juicy gossip in many a tavern in the Caribbean. "How about less carnage and more honest hard work? That way, you won't get arrested."

Narina turned up her button nose in scorn at that. "Hard work is…too hard. Arrghh! I'll scupper those gutless scallywags if they try to catch me!"

"Piracy is a crime," Lisbeth said calmly. "You'll go to jail."

"All the men on Exuma do it," she said in that direct way of hers that said she saw and understood more than she should. Lisbeth frowned. Narina was much too observant and smart for her own good. Then again, they were in haven full of criminals, so what did she expect? "They talk about hiding goods all the time and snatching cargo from other ships."

Lisbeth cleared her throat, searching for the right words. "Some of these men are bad men, Nari, who do bad things. Stealing is wrong."

"But you do it," she said, her small face scrunching. "And Saint, too."

Oh, bloody hell.

"That's complicated and I promise I will explain it

to you someday," she said. "But there are always consequences for improper actions."

Narina stared at her for a long time before letting out a loud bellow, stomping her boot, and singing in a singsong tone, "Ohhhh, there once was a lass called Bonnie Bess. She sailed the seas with all the rest, but no one could catch her as she flew. She'll laugh and shout and run you through, bold Bonnie Bess!" Lisbeth's eyes went wide at the off-key shanty. "She's as pretty as a picture like they say, but cold in the heart so best you pray. You won't come upon her on the sea, or she'll gut you good and make you pee, bold Bonnie Bess!" She gave another stomp and a spin. "Oh, hai, she'll make you fly, then cut your ears and make you cry. She'll take your gold, then peel your bones, bold Bonnie Bess!"

Lisbeth gaped, jaw slack. "Where did you hear that?"

"The old salts on the *Avalon* were singing it," Narina said and then lowered her voice with a puzzled look. "Are you ever going to be Bess again?"

"I'm still Bess, Nari. But you do know that people make most of that up. Bonnie Bess is…" *Not real.* But she couldn't say that.

"A formidable sea captain, and I can tell you from experience, lassie, that jail with the company of rats and lice is not fun." That was from Raphael who had approached on silent feet. Lisbeth caught her breath, that low baritone brushing over her senses like softly lapping waves on a sandy shore. He ruffled Narina's hair and crouched down, peering at the threadbare coat she'd no doubt filched from some poor boatswain and the red sash around her waist. "Which pirate are you today?"

"Captain Kidd," she replied excitedly. "Did you know he stashed buried treasure in the harbor back in Exuma and in New York, too? We should go on a hunt when we get there!" She wrinkled her brow and peered at Raphael. "Wait, why were you in jail?"

"I was betrayed by people I trusted," he said.

Narina's gaze goggled between the two of them, her eyes much too shrewd for her tender years. "Then you need better friends, Saint."

He laughed and stood. "That is probably true."

They both watched as she skipped across the dock to natter with the crew of the new ship who were loading fresh supplies into rowboats. She started talking animatedly to the young man Raphael had been conversing with.

"Who is he?" she asked. "He looks familiar."

Raphael's brows lifted. "You wouldn't know him. He's the disowned son of an English peer. Thorin Alford, a trusted friend."

"His father is the Duke of Remington," she murmured without thinking and then froze at what that tidbit implied—familiarity with the aristocracy. She bit the inside of her cheek hard and wanted to kick herself. "I read in the gossip rags that he disappeared years ago. It's a unique name."

"It is," he said, but to her relief, he didn't say anything further. Perhaps he'd accepted her frail reasoning. With him, she never knew. He let out a small noise of amusement. "Narina has charmed him already, it seems."

Sure enough, the girl had him bending down and letting her wear his hat. Lisbeth laughed. "I swear, after years on the sea in constant mortal danger, it's that child who will be the death of me."

"She's a handful, but she's got a good heart," he said.

Lisbeth nodded, a thick knot forming in her throat. "She needs to…not be here. To be somewhere safe and normal. To play with children her own age, not…be with people who do what we do. This is no life for a young girl."

"I have friends in New York," she heard him say. "They own a shelter house for women and children. She could have a place there."

Lisbeth swallowed hard. "Is that why we're going there?"

"One of the reasons, yes."

What were the others? She felt the weight of his stare, but for the life of her, Lisbeth couldn't look up to meet his eyes. She did not know what she was going to see reflected there…or what she would feel when she did.

"How is your wound?" she mumbled.

"Itches and pulls on occasion, but I'm alive, thanks to you."

With a rough exhale, she kept her gaze on Narina who'd been put to work by Thorin and was carrying a small crate of oranges. "It was because of me we were in that mess in the first place."

"And I was the one who got distracted."

"I shouldn't have gone off on my own," she insisted.

Raphael shifted, toe tapping lightly on the wooden

planks of the dock. "And I should have trusted in your skills in the first place, not treated you like a damsel in need of protection."

Unable to bear it, she whirled. Tousled dark hair fell over his shoulders, the corner of his lip kicking up in that half smirk of amusement. Her eyes collided with his, and there they were, pooling in that warm gaze that undid her…all those emotions she was so afraid of. Warmth, humor, tenderness, and blatant affection. All directed at her, like the first rays of sunlight on an overcast sea. Her lungs squeezed as she tore her gaze away, her heart doing tumultuous flips behind her ribs.

"Stop doing that," she gritted out. "Stop trying to absolve me."

"*Absolve* you?" he shot back. "No, Lisbeth, I'm simply saying that I'm responsible for my own choices, my own actions." He sat next to her on the bench, the smell of salt and brine and citrus surrounding her. "And besides, don't you know chits go wild for scars."

Rolling her eyes, she shot him a dry look. "Good to see your injury hasn't hampered that ego of yours."

He chuckled, deep and long, the low rumbles making her skin heat. "You should know by now, Viking, *nothing* hampers this magnificence."

Hiding her grin, Lisbeth shook her head, and they sat in silence for a moment before she took the plunge to air her thoughts. "I suppose then it will be goodbye in New York," she said. "The *Syren* is there, and well, you have your own plans."

"Is that what you want?"

"It's what it has to be," she said. The plain truth was that Lisbeth did not want him anywhere near Dubois when everything went down. As a master spy, she had power, but not enough to save Raphael from prosecution if he was caught. His crimes might be less than Dubois or Madge, but he was guilty of them all the same. A twinge of conscience rolled through her. What would he feel when she took his vengeance away from him? When she stole his retribution from under his nose?

When she betrayed him in the worst possible way...

Because, by God, he would never, ever forgive her.

"When do we leave?" she whispered, her stomach churning with nerves and guilt, meeting his eyes briefly and seeing a flash of something else there. Something that looked too much like regret. Too much like the feelings of need and despair buried deep in her own chest.

"Daybreak."

In the dark of the moonlit night, Raphael spotted the other ship hugging the coast near Charleston right in front of the lights glinting at Fort Sumter before it sighted him—a much smaller vessel with a side-wheel paddle and a low, narrow frame with two short lower masts. It had the look of one of the blockade runners from the American Civil War with its dark charcoal color, but something told him it was a smuggling ship.

Possibly one of Delaney's, which meant the cargo might be worth the pursuit. It would be fast, but not faster than the *Vauquelin*, the vessel ship in his fleet with its triple-screw steam engines. Besides, the full armament of this particular ship was something to behold.

Yes, she was unequivocally his pride and joy.

Raphael nodded to Thorin at his side, his longtime friend and business partner, and made the signal that they were going to shadow and then chase. The grin on Thorin's face was predacious as he jumped to the lower deck to inform the rest of the crew. In the old days when they only had one ship between them, chasing down the worst of the smugglers and divesting them of their cargo had been a lucrative game. Later on, when most of their ships ran legitimate trade, only two had been left to continue the charade with Dubois. Raphael had lost them both in Tobago.

His uncle didn't know how big Raphael's business had gotten. He made sure to keep the men who captained the three dozen ships he owned separate from his operations where Dubois was concerned. The less he suspected, the better. And when Raphael finally brought him down, he'd be sure to remind him just how insignificant he was in the grand scheme of things. That despite his father's ruined name and the loss of their holdings in the Loire Valley, Raphael was not destitute.

He was, in fact, obscenely wealthy…and he was putting every centime of that fortune toward clearing the de Viel name and destroying Dubois. With a secret penchant for gambling, Dubois was in debt up to his ears, taking more and more risks with his cargo runs just to make money. Raphael had bought up most of the debt, and when the man had nothing left, Raphael planned to offer him a trade for a confession of his treachery.

The game had been long, but it was very nearly at its end.

He sent the message to the engine rooms to slow the ship. "Ready the guns and target the paddle box once we get within range. They'll slow soon enough." Raphael nodded to Boisie who had joined the few hundred men manning the *Vauquelin* for the voyage. "If there's an uproar, make sure the girl stays down below and watch her! You know how she is." He thought for a moment. "Take Peppers and Balzac with you."

"Aye, Cap'n."

Based on the scraps of what he'd overheard in her conversation with Lisbeth, Narina was much too enamored with piracy, and what they were about to do was definitely illegal. Lisbeth would not approve of the girl being part of sacking and plundering another vessel. Normally Lisbeth would be above decks, but she'd gone below to make sure the tiny scallywag of a pirate went to bed—after that little imp had wheedled a promise out of Raphael to man the wheel on the morrow.

He couldn't help his grin. He'd miss the cheeky little sprite. He blew out an uneven breath. He'd miss *her*, too. But it would be safer for Lisbeth to be back on her own ship. As a consolation prize, he would make sure to present Bonnie Bess as an inclusion in their ranks once he started closing the net on Dubois. Whatever her reasons were for wanting to be part of the Exuma elite, he would not forestall her.

A slender figure with mussed blond hair in worn trousers, a shirt, and a hastily donned coat ran up the stairs to the quarterdeck. "Why are we slowing?"

Of course she would have noticed. "Opportunity," he said.

"What?"

Raphael handed her the spyglass. "Frigate up ahead, port side, heading toward us. We're going to take it nice and quick."

The frown was unexpected, as was her next question. "*Take* it? But why?"

"Why not is the better question. They will either have a lot of valuable cargo or money received for cargo already sold and delivered. It's much easier to divest them of it."

Handing him back the spyglass, Lisbeth stared at him with shock on her face. "Wait, you attack other ships?"

"Only bad ones," he said.

Her confusion was baffling, though the shock on her face was morphing into something sharp and accusatory. "I don't understand. Why?"

"What does it matter, Bess? They're bloody criminals, just like we are. You of all people know that out here on the sea, only the strongest of us survive and the weak do not." He shrugged. "It's better this way. In a ship like that this near to the coast, sooner or later, they will get intercepted and arrested, and all those goods or money will be confiscated, going to the pockets of corrupt agents."

She blanched, her face tightening, but Raphael didn't have more time to continue the conversation as the *Vauquelin* closed the distance even at its reduced speed to the other ship.

"Ahoy, there!" Thorin roared. "State your name, captain, and fleet."

"SS *Frolic* and we have no quarrel with you," a voice called back. "I'm Captain Briggs on way to Cedar Key. We're merchants for Delaney Trading."

"Even better," Thorin said. "Well, Mr. Briggs, I regret to inform you that your journey ends here. You will be boarded, your crew disbanded, and your post terminated, and if you refuse our rather generous offer, we will put a hole in your hull." He cackled, enjoying every second of this. "A few holes. Do you surrender?"

"Now wait a minute, who do you think you—"

He didn't have a chance to finish his protest before Thorin gave a hand signal and the ship's aft mast was struck by a well-aimed shell. Wooden fragments flew everywhere, the explosion loud in the night. "Sink or swim, Briggsy. Or we shoot your paddle box next and leave you to take on the Treasury ships and certain incarceration coming this way." Raphael wanted to laugh. Thorin certainly had a flair for the dramatic, but he wasn't wrong. Any nearby ships patrolling the coast would have heard the shot. They didn't have much time.

"Surrender," Briggs cried eventually.

"Good decision," Thorin replied, and signaled for his crew to board the other ship.

It wasn't long before a chest full of money was identified along with several crates of unsold coffee and cigars. Briggs and his men were given the option to make their way inland in the rowboats or become crew under a new captain. Three-fourths of the men stayed, while the others left with Briggs.

Lisbeth all the while was frowning as she watched the transaction play out. When Thorin reboarded the *Vauquelin* a short time later, minus a good number of the men who had gone with him, her frown deepened as the *Frolic* sailed past and put out to sea as if she'd never been stopped in the first place. The soft splash of the rowboat oars were the only indication that there'd been a crew change.

"You're letting her go?" she said.

"That money is bound for the islands for people who need it. Not soft-bellied crooked agents who fatten their own pockets." He gave a boatswain the order for the ship to go back to its original pace of twenty knots. If they made good time, they'd be in New York in a day.

When she stood still staring at him as if trying to work through the details of what had happened, Raphael exhaled. "We don't keep the money. Anything taken from any ships in the business of smuggling is reinvested in infrastructure, food, and shelter for the people whose lands were stolen. Trust me, Delaney of all people will not miss it. The *Frolic* will head to Tobago and will most likely be scrapped for sale while the spoils are distributed to those in need."

Her eyes rounded with understanding and her voice was soft when she finally spoke. "Not everyone is corrupt. And maybe they think that that money rightly belongs to the American Treasury. It's stealing no matter how you look at it, even if you give it away."

"Ironic coming from a woman who has divested the American Treasury of hundreds of thousands of dollars in contraband herself," he countered. "Bonnie Bess is hardly innocent."

Shadows dropped over her eyes, making her look vulnerable for an instant before her face hardened to its usual neutrality. "No, she's not."

They were interrupted by a shriek and the sound of pounding feet as a determined Narina came running across the deck, three men at her heels, one hobbling and holding his crotch. "Was that a cannon?" she shouted. "I felt it shake the ship and I heard yelling, but those three cock-flapping dunghills tried to stop me from coming up! I tricked the filthy swabs, though. Pretended I was choking, then I kicked Ballsack right in the fucking ball sack."

"Nari, language!" Lisbeth yelled.

The girl ignored her guardian and rushed to the side to peer over the railing, eyes huge with excitement. "What did we scuttle? Who was it? Where are they? For fuck's sake, why is it so fucking dark?"

"Narina." Lisbeth gritted her teeth.

"A cannon went off accidentally when one of the gunners was cleaning it," Thorin interjected just as Raphael opened his mouth to defuse the situation.

Narina turned to him with a suspicious glower. "And the shouting?"

"I was angry. *I* shouted."

Her eyes narrowed. "Are you lying to me, bucko?"

"I would never dream of it, miss."

They all stood there in a silent staring contest as a ferocious twelve-year-old on the verge of a temper tantrum held them hostage. Eventually she huffed when Lisbeth growled her displeasure, clearly having had enough for the evening.

"Fine," Narina conceded and turned that fiery glare on each of them. "But I take the helm tomorrow and you'll all address me as *Captain* Nari, savvy?"

Thorin winked. "Savvy."

Seventeen

He stole money only to give it away.

From. Other. Criminals.

Lisbeth couldn't reconcile the information in her head. She'd thought him a modern-day Robin Hood before, but seeing him in action sprouted a whole host of conflicting emotions. It was morally gray behavior, and to any agent worth her salt, still punishable to the full extent of the law. The American Treasury agents would argue that it was *their* property, and recompense along with a trial would be due.

In their eyes, there was no difference between men like Dubois or Delaney and one like Raphael. Even if the people he robbed were thieves and lowlives themselves. And he hadn't harmed them. He'd given those sailors a choice and let them live. None of that made it right. But the lines of right and wrong were becoming more and more muddied.

Was that because of her feelings for him? Or were real lines being crossed and she was simply refusing to see that because of her own bias? Now that they had arrived in New York, should *she* turn him in? No, he wasn't her mission. Dubois was. But then again, Jenks had salivated at catching three elite smugglers.

With a snarl of frustration, she scrubbed at her face. *Damn it!*

"Lisbeth!" The object of her muddled thoughts burst into her current very well-appointed quarters. The room was quite spacious and luxurious, even though she knew it wasn't the master cabin. Everything about this steamer screamed extravagance. Even the guns were well polished and the crew's quarters immaculate. Narina had reported back on that.

She lifted a brow at Raphael. "What is it?"

"We need your help."

"What's happened? Is it Nari?" She bolted to her feet, thankful that she was fully dressed in a canary-yellow gown she'd found in Thorin's quarters. He'd insisted it was new, but Lisbeth hadn't cared if it had been worn by someone before. She wasn't going to arrive in New York City in rags, especially if she hoped to maintain her cover, and the dress had been lovely enough, if a little tight.

"No, she's well." Raphael's eyes widened on said gown, his gaze sticking on the creamy expanse of décolletage exposed by the off-the-shoulder *en coeur* neckline and the tight boning below, and Lisbeth felt her blood heat. His nostrils flared, his eyes burning over her from the tips of her shoes to her cinched-in waist and back to her overflowing bosom. He looked like she'd just waved a red rag in front of a bull...and she was its prize. "Fucking hell," he whispered.

"Stop gawking, Saint. What is the emergency?"

"I can't help it. You're bloody stunning."

Pleasure bloomed though she ignored it. "You've seen me in a gown before."

"Nothing like *that*. You put the ladies at court in Paris to shame, Viking." He blinked and shook his head as if emerging from a trance. He took one last lingering sweep of her body as if committing it to memory before speaking. "We have trouble and need your help. Agents from the customs house are demanding to see the ship's passenger log and cargo."

Her stomach took a nosedive. *Which* agents? And would she be recognized or inadvertently exposed? "So? Didn't you say the cargo was cleared in Nassau? Give them what they want and let them check."

Groaning, Raphael ran a hand through his already disheveled hair. "Not all of it, apparently. Thorin, that fool of a libertine, left a few chests of Parisian gowns that he meant to off-load to one of his current lovers here. A well-known dressmaker."

Lisbeth almost laughed out loud. It was a common enough ruse for smugglers, especially women. Estelle had been known to smuggle a few gowns in her time and had told Lisbeth stories of dressmakers and milliners who pretended to be highborn ladies wearing the fashionable costumes. Others traveled back from Europe with frills and accessories stitched into their petticoats so they didn't have to pay the exorbitant tariffs. They would then, of course, recreate the fashions or sell coveted accessories to their clients.

The demand by New York upper-class women for Parisian fabric, buttons, feathers, ribbons, lace, flowers, and entire gowns was astronomical. And after the

American Civil War, prices had doubled, not to mention the stiff levies on imported goods. In fact, Lisbeth could recall whole exposés being written about the fashionable smuggling phenomenon in the *New York Times*. That racket had caused the New York customs house to hire a slew of female inspectors to avoid a spectacle of impropriety if a passenger claimed the property was hers and refused a search by a male inspector.

Despite Lisbeth's defense of her fellow agents, Raphael hadn't been wrong in his assertion that there was corruption in the ranks of the customs house. The moiety system meant that those employed there would enjoy a piece of the profits of all taxes and penalties levied. Bribery was also rife, with dishonest inspectors accepting money to look the other way. While Lisbeth could not condone Raphael's actions fully, she did understand where they stemmed from.

Not that her superiors would view it that way, however.

He'd be lucky to escape unscathed.

"Let me guess," she said eventually. "The duties on those gowns will be exorbitant."

"Correct. We need you to say they're your private belongings, or we are all going to be detained." He shot her a wry expression. "And I'd rather not draw too much attention, if I can help it."

"Very well."

"At least you look the part," he said, sending another heated gaze her way.

Lisbeth frowned as she reached for a pair of gloves. "Is

Thorin in any kind of trouble as well? Do I need to worry about him?"

"No, and the *Vauquelin* is a legitimate ship with no history of unlawful transport." He ground his teeth together. "He's young and being led around by his cock. Trust me, I will flog that idiot for this, especially on *this* particular ship."

"Is it his?"

His brows slammed down. "It's *mine*."

Well then. Now she understood why he was so worked up. If this beauty of a ship was confiscated because of who he was, it would be a tragedy…and a windfall for the Treasury. "Stay out of sight, if you can." She stopped at the cabin door and smiled at him so seductively over her shoulder that he halted in his tracks. "And do try to keep your temper under control."

"My temper? Why?"

But she didn't answer, sauntering down to the cargo hold without a qualm as if she had every right to be there. Her shoulders went back, her spine straightened. Every muscle in her face relaxed into a practiced mien. One of privilege and grace. A countess used to deference, esteem, and respect.

As she stepped into the hold, which was just as lavish as the rest of the ship, she counted three people—two men and one of the infamous inspectresses—in addition to Thorin. There was no sign of Raphael, though she suspected he would be close. None of them were agents she recognized, but that did not mean they would not recognize her.

Playing a dual role was always perilous, the risk of discovery doubled. She cracked open a fan and waved it irritably as she strolled inside.

"Good God, darling, what is all of this hullabaloo? One of my maids said there was some urgency that would delay our disembarking." She pouted prettily. "You know I cannot be late for my luncheon with my dearest Lina and I must get ready. Mrs. Astor is *quite* particular about punctuality." The casual mention of the matriarch of one of the most prominent New York families did not go unnoticed.

"Who might you be, ma'am?" the lead agent asked. He was thin-faced with a heavy mustache and had keen eyes.

"Lady," she corrected with a sniff and a toss of her head. "I am *Lady* Lisbeth Medford, the Countess of Waterstone."

"Apologies, my lady," he said.

Thorin's eyes widened with surprise as she walked right up to him and kissed his cheek, but he caught on quickly. "Uh, darling, these men and woman would like to search your trunks. They don't believe the gowns are yours and have reason to believe that they are contraband."

"My gowns?" she scoffed. "*Contraband*? Good God, the audacity! Heavens, darling, if your father, the Duke of Remington, even knew what horrid treatment we were being subjected to, he would be appalled." Thorin's huff of surprise was audible, but he covered that up with a cough.

Perhaps she was laying it on a little too thickly, given the look on the lead agent's face, but she had to sell the performance for it to be believable. The British peerage as a whole considered themselves superior to Americans, even those with ragged, declining estates, though they were quick to marry into American money if it meant shoring up those very estates. It was despicable, but Lisbeth wasn't here to make a point about titles and privilege. She was there to save Raphael's ship.

"This is an outrage!" she cried, fanning herself harder.

"Allow me to handle this, my dear," Thorin said and turned to the agent. "How can we be of service to you to clear up any misunderstandings? We are en route from Paris. Would you like my fiancée to try on any of these gowns? She is wearing one of them right now, and if I dare say, she is quite ravishing." He drew up her knuckles and pressed a loud kiss to them. Lisbeth ducked her head as though overcome by his ardor, but she kept a close eye on their unwelcome guests.

A heavy arm slid across her back and curled around her waist, and Lisbeth stiffened at the unexpected intimacy before she guessed that Thorin was trying to shore up their performance. Or not, as she followed his quick sidelong glance to an adjacent room, where she caught sight of Raphael's surly face.

Thorin might be more interested in provoking his friend. *Fiancée,* indeed. She wondered idly what Raphael would think of her title…one she hadn't used in years, though it was very much real. Or more importantly, whether he was, in fact, seething with jealousy at Thorin's words and proximity. Perhaps she should play along…to sell the thing.

She shot Thorin a sultry smile. "Darling, do not flirt. You know I do not wish to be late because of your mischief. And we cannot embarrass our guests. Do behave."

"But I do so love to misbehave." He tickled her side and then kissed her cheek as a savage growl emanated through the space.

"Is there a dog onboard?" the inspectress asked, which made Lisbeth burst into a spate of uncontrollable laughter. Oh, dear God, she couldn't breathe!

"Just our pet mastiff, Brutus," she said, nearly wheezing with mirth.

Oh, she really was terrible.

The lead agent nodded and scribbled something in a notebook he carried with him. "Very good, my lady, my lord. There will be no need for you to model these gowns. Is there anywhere we can escort you? A residence, perhaps."

Lisbeth blinked. She'd underestimated him. He was as sharp as a razor. She didn't give Thorin the chance to give a fake address. The agent was much too clever for that. This was a ploy to see if they were indeed who they claimed and not convincing pretenders. She gave the only address she knew—the New York residence of her former husband of convenience, the current Duke of Thornbury, on Fifth Avenue. With any luck, the duke and duchess would not be in residence and the staff would recognize her. She hoped.

"That's so kind of you, sir," she said. "Allow us to ready ourselves. We shall meet you on the docks posthaste."

The agents had barely left before Raphael came

barreling out of hiding and clocked poor Thorin right in the jaw. The young nob went down like a sack of bricks, groaning and clutching his chin.

"Raphael, what the devil has come over you?" Lisbeth cried.

"He touched you. Kissed you." Fury rolled off of Raphael in violent waves. He turned that burning glare on her, and she shivered, but it wasn't fear she felt at all.

"On the cheek, for the agents," she said slowly, placatingly. "They're gone now."

Without speaking, he prowled toward her, and Lisbeth felt her legs go weak. *Do* not *swoon, you weak-minded fool!* He shot a fulminating look at Thorin who staggered to his feet. "Get out!"

"Raphael, the agents are waiting," she said when Thorin took his leave after a concerned look in her direction. She waved him away. She wasn't in any danger.

At least not the mortal kind.

Anything else, however…

"Let them wait," Raphael rumbled, that possessive sound shooting right to her aching center. God, she was so wet already, it was indecent.

"I—" But the minute she opened her mouth, he pounced, his lips crashing to hers and his tongue sweeping in to snatch the speech that could only turn into helpless moans as she held on for dear life.

Damn and blast, he was going to put her over his knee. Show her exactly who she belonged to on this ship. Ruin her for any other who came after, man or woman. But first, he would kiss her until neither of them could breathe. Punish her for daring to put those lips on another man in his presence. God, she tasted like heaven and hell, spite and seduction, life and death. Everything in between.

"This fucking dress," he muttered against her mouth, tonguing her across the roof of her mouth, the rough swipe chasing shivers through her as she scrabbled for purchase on his coat. "You drive me to bloody distraction, Viking. Did you know I was there?"

"Yes," she admitted, arching as his mouth descended the column of her throat to tug on that tight bodice and free those tempting swells.

"Wicked woman. I shall have to punish you for that." He lifted her breasts from their confines and stared at the full teardrop shape of them, his mouth watering to taste. Berry-tipped and peaked, ready for his tongue. His *teeth*. But first he looked. He gorged himself on the luscious bounty before him. Christ, was there anyone lovelier than her?

"Raphael," she moaned as he rolled one furled tip between his fingers. "We don't have time for this."

"Do you want me to stop?"

"No," she whimpered.

"Good girl." He bent to take the second sweet peak into his mouth, his tongue curling around the taut little bud, and sucked hard.

"God, I hate you," she said, writhing and arching up against him as if daring him to take her entire breast into his mouth. He did just that, opening as wide as he could and filling his mouth with her succulent flesh before dragging his teeth along her tender skin. His tongue painted her flesh in hot, wet lashes, switching from breast to breast until her moans had reduced to half-garbled sounds of need. He was so hard it hurt, but this was for her. To remind her exactly who brought her pleasure.

"But you don't really hate me, do you, Viking?" he crooned, alternating tender laps with stinging nips, leaving the marks of his stubble on her pale, creamy skin. "In fact, when you donned this dress, you were thinking of me fucking you in it, weren't you? Lifting up these satin skirts and feeling how soaked you were."

She jolted at his filthy words and panted. "Oh God."

Raphael rucked up the hem of her gown torturously slow, wanting to feel her bare skin beneath his fingertips but also wanting to prolong the torture for as long as possible. He was dying to see if she was as drenched as he was hard, but he had every intention of ensuring that she was a sodden, needy mess by the time he gave in.

He'd meant every word when he said he planned to keep her on the edge for hours. He kissed a wet path up her neck and captured her lips again. She could barely function, her tongue chasing his in complete utter need, a mess of pleas and strangled whispers as he cupped her chin and feasted on her mouth. He alternated between soft, drugging kisses and hard, deep plunges, leaving no part of her mouth unexplored...marking every corner and crevice as his.

"Please, Raphael, I need..."

"I know what you need." He spun her so that she was facing the wall and grabbed handfuls of her skirts, gathering them roughly in his palm just below her navel. The curled knuckles of his hand pressed into her mound and she rocked up, instinctively seeking more friction.

"What are you doing?" she groused, attempting to turn back. "I need you to face me."

"Don't move," he growled. "You don't get to control everything, Viking."

"But—"

Raphael bent and bit into the meat of her shoulder, running the knuckles of his free hand down the length of her corseted spine. The noise that came from her mouth was inhuman when he sucked the spot he'd bitten and repeated the sequence at the base of her throat. Bite, *suck*.

Gentler this time, however. She would bruise easily, and while the thought excited him more than it should, he did not want to compromise her. She was no ingenue by her own admission, but if she was truly a countess as she'd claimed, he understood the rules of the aristocracy only too well. Gossip did not care about circumstances.

He licked up her throat to the sensitive space below her ear and worried her lobe with his teeth. Raphael twisted her chin up to take her lips in a hot, open-mouthed kiss. "Fuck, you've no idea how much I want to mark this pale, pretty skin."

"Then do it," she moaned insensibly.

He moved back to her shoulders, baring the elegant line and hollow beneath her scapula, just visible over the lace of her corset. Christ, every inch of her was elegance wrapped in strength. Every dip of bone, every taut muscle, every inch of downy skin was uncharted territory. He wanted to map her body, learn every ridge, trace every sinful curve.

Raphael kissed a short path down the upper knobs of her spine and shifted left ever so slightly before taking her flesh between his teeth and sucking hard. She cried out, writhing back against him, her body confused at the bite of pain in the midst of so much pleasure. And then he slipped his free hand through the damp slit in her drawers, his left arm banding her skirts in place, a finger dragging through the copious wetness he found there.

"I knew you'd be this wet."

"Yes," she said.

He groaned in satisfaction, rolling his impossibly hard cock against her bottom, tentatively at first in case she still wasn't ready, but when she shoved back against him with a guttural whimper, his legs nearly buckled. The friction against his apadravya piercing was almost enough to catapult him over the edge, but he refused to do so without her.

Raphael's middle finger slid inside her slick passage while he rocked into her arse. She moaned at the intrusion, though her hips didn't cease thrusting into his hand as she chased her release. He added a second finger, feeling her stretch deliciously around him. She was trapped between his pelvis and his palm, impaling herself onto his fingers while grinding her buttocks into his erection. Each rub of his piercing made his vision go white.

It was the most sublime torture he'd ever endured in his life.

"God, Raphael, I'm going to..."

So was he. His thumb swiped the bundle of nerves at the top of her sex, and she swallowed a scream as her body seized and curled onto itself, shuddering uncontrollably. Her orgasm ignited his own as he followed with a suffocated shout, his cock exploding into his trousers. Rhythmic pulses clamped around the fingers that were still buried inside her even as hot ropes of his seed jetted from his body in unending spurts. He hadn't ever come so hard.

"Bloody hell, Viking," he huffed into her hair. "You undo me."

Gently, he removed his hand from the clasp of her center, letting her gown fall back into place, and turned her in his arms. Her eyes were dazed from her release, her mouth swollen and parted. "Glad to know the feeling is mutual, Pirate." She sighed and adjusted her bodice, hiding those beautiful breasts away. "I hate the fact that practically everyone will know what we have been doing."

"And what was that?" With a wicked smile, he lifted his fingers that were still glistening with her arousal and slid them into his mouth. "Having dessert?"

"You are filthy," she said, eyes sparking with heat as he licked each finger clean.

“I make no apologies and neither should you.” He stared down at her. “You will not be going with Thorin. You will be going in a carriage with me.”

“Raphael, be reasonable. You know what the agents are capable of, should they realize who you are.” She flushed and glanced toward the closed door to the hold. “And besides, how do we explain you *and* my fiancé?”

His teeth smashed together so hard, they nearly cracked. “Duck *fucker*. When I see that pigeon-livered sack of pricks, I’m going to flatten him for that.”

She glowered. “Do *not* let Nari hear you say any of that or heaven help me, you’ll be flattened right next to Thorin.” She peered down at the enormous wet spot on his pants and then blushed like the dichotomy she was. “Now go get cleaned up, stop acting like an infant, get Narina, and meet us at 530 Fifth Avenue.”

Eighteen

Lisbeth sat in the carriage across from the lead male agent with Thorin ensconced at her side. The others were on horseback and, hopefully, Raphael was following somewhere behind with Narina in tow. All three of the customs house inspectors had been practically fuming by the time she emerged on the footbridge. It hadn't been *that* long; twenty frantic, well-spent minutes at the most.

Besides, a lady should never be rushed.

A lady shouldn't be fucking her lover in the cargo hold either, but there she was.

Lisbeth had barely had time to fix her hair, sponge herself hurriedly, and tend to her soiled undergarments. The satin overlayer of her dress was crumpled, thanks to its adventures in Raphael's big hands, but that could not be helped. Nor could her rosy cheeks, the sparkle in her eye, or that obvious post-orgasm glow. Taking a page from Raphael's book, she refused to make apologies for any of it.

Thorin couldn't stop sending her sly looks and she'd elbowed him in the ribs when they'd climbed into the waiting coach. Thankfully, he didn't make any attempt to be cozy or flirty in the carriage. She would not have been able to support that, not after what she and Raphael had done. Or with that mustached agent staring her down like he was attempting to dissect her into pieces. He kept goggling between her and Thorin, clearly noting her fiancé's youth, not that that was uncommon. Still, Thorin had to be about twenty.

She met his eyes directly, arching a haughty brow. "Is something amiss, Mr.—"

"Carr," he supplied. "And no. I'm simply fascinated by the British aristocracy, Lady Waterstone."

Lisbeth gave a dismissive sniff. "Well, I suppose we can be quite intriguing, but staring is impolite, sir."

"I apologize." His tone suggested the opposite.

Lisbeth directed her attention to the small square window as they drove through the bustling streets. The city had come a long way since the end of the Civil War, growing in both occupancy and wealth. Two years ago was the last time she'd been here and things had not been as prosperous, the city fighting through a depression with veterans returning from the war and a lack of jobs. Broadway was a busy street, however, bustling with carriages and crowded storefronts. Well-dressed pedestrians ambled the sidewalks as they passed through General Worth Square at Twenty-Fifth Street.

Briefly, she wondered if Thornbury had sold the residence he'd had constructed around the same time that William Astor had built his brownstone home on Thirty-Fourth Street. Before he'd become duke, Valentine had loved that place, which was why she was hoping beyond hope that he'd kept it, despite living in Scotland and London. She was taking a big gamble, considering

Valentine's marriage and the fact that his wife might impact his decisions. Otherwise, she would look quite the fool showing up at a stranger's house.

"It's just over there on the left, past dear Lina's," she said.

Carr's face twisted with ill-concealed rancor but he hid it quickly. Lisbeth huffed a small laugh. The way Caroline Astor flaunted both her money and her name would offend anyone with half a brain. She was by all accounts one of the biggest snobs Lisbeth had ever met and the self-appointed pinnacle of New York high society. Her servants wore court livery, she fed her guests on gold plates, and her elite parties were the subject of every newssheet in existence. And she adored Valentine, more so since he'd become duke.

When the coach stopped, Lisbeth descended gracefully. "Thank you, Mr. Carr, we are most obliged." The stone-faced man watched her carefully, but she ignored the awful feeling his attention provoked. "Come along, darling," she said to Thorin, taking his arm to ascend the steps.

The door opened before she could knock, and the familiar face of the butler made her stomach dip with sweet relief. "Barnaby, wonderful to see you!"

The older man, who had been employed by Valentine for years and knew quite a bit about their clandestine operations back in the day, did not miss a beat, eyes flicking to the stern-faced entourage on the street. "Lady Waterstone."

"Is the duke in residence?" she asked. "This is the Earl of Rennard."

"I don't use that name," Thorin whispered from the side of his mouth, but she glared him back into silence.

"Welcome to the club of defunct, disgraced, and discarded titles. Until the laws of primogeniture change, you can refuse your birthright all you want, but it will still be yours."

"Lord Rennard." Barnaby held the door open and welcomed them inside. "Will your other visitors be joining us?"

"Oh, no," she said with an airy wave to the agents, lifting her voice slightly so it would carry. "They insisted on delivering my fiancé and me here, you see. Quite generous though unnecessary of them."

When the door closed behind them, Lisbeth nearly collapsed against it with a loud groan. "Barnaby, you clever, clever man. How are you? It's been an age, but you look marvelous."

The butler gave her a doting grin. "Thank you, my lady, as do you. I have been perfectly well. May I offer you a glass of brandy while I alert the staff to ready the Rose Rooms?"

Between the debacle with the dresses, her interlude with Raphael, and the silent standoff with Agent Carr, she was absolutely ready for a glass of brandy. She nodded and then frowned at the rarely used suite of rooms on the third floor. "Rose Rooms?"

He canted his head. "With His Grace and the duchess in residence, your previous apartments are occupied."

Wait. Thornbury was here? And Bronwyn, too? What

were the chances? Not that she was looking a gift horse in the mouth, but she also did not want her cover to be compromised by an errant slip of the tongue. "Yes, of course," she said to Barnaby and then glanced up at the polished staircase. "Are either of them at home to callers?"

"They are not, right at the moment," Barnaby said in a tone that suggested the couple might be at home, but indisposed. Lisbeth hid a smirk at the thought of the very serious, very stern Duke of Thornbury, former fearsome spymaster, being put through his paces by his feisty, young wife. He deserved to have some fun in his life.

"We shall wait in the—"

But her words were interrupted when a well-familiar, all-too-mocking laugh greeted her. "Well, well, well. What have we here?"

"Val," she said, staring up at the man who had been her best friend for so many years, and the beautiful woman he'd married leaning over the balustrade.

They both looked as though they'd tumbled out of bed and thrown on the closest garments they could find. Valentine's waistcoat buttons were mismatched and Bronwyn's dark hair was practically a bird's nest. Lisbeth grinned. Good to see that they were still infatuated with each other. She'd heard scandalous rumors of their adventurous trysts before their marriage and had struggled to believe the straitlaced Valentine could be so brazen. Now, she revised that opinion.

He looked...happy.

"Causing trouble?" Valentine asked, as Bronwyn

bounded down the steps with no thought to propriety whatsoever and enveloped Lisbeth into an exuberant embrace.

Lisbeth laughed, hugging the woman back. "Always."

"How long has it been?" Bronwyn shrieked. "At least since the wedding. Where have you been anyway? You look well. Glowing, I would say." She frowned and looked over Lisbeth's shoulder. "Is that…? Are you? I beg your pardon, but did I overhear you say 'fiancé' before?" She released Lisbeth with a noise of surprise as she turned to Thorin. "Gracious, Lord Rennard, I nearly did not recognize you," she exclaimed as her husband joined them.

Thorin bowed. "It is, but I do not go by that address anymore. Just Thorin will do. I'd heard word of your nuptials during my travels, Your Graces. May I offer my belated congratulations."

Lisbeth winced. Reports of his estrangement with his father had been the talk of London several years ago, but Lisbeth hadn't realized that Thorin had cut off all contact. Or fully renounced his birthright. Now she felt badly for reminding him about the pillars of primogeniture.

"What brings you both to New York?" Valentine asked. "Are you traveling?"

The inflection on the last was subtle, but Lisbeth nodded. "Funny story actually," she replied with a weary laugh, wondering where on earth she could possibly start without unraveling the whole thing. "And one best told over a glass or several of the strongest, most expensive liquor you have."

"That can be arranged."

After being ushered into the adjacent salon, which Lisbeth noticed had been updated with plush furniture and soft, velvet drapes—Bronwyn's touch, of course—she took a long sip of the duke's excellent brandy and cleared her throat. "To start, Thorin is not really my fiancé. As to my whereabouts the last two years, well, that's a tad more complicated. I bought a ship and sailed for the open ocean."

"A liner?" Bronwyn asked, and Lisbeth shook her head. Bronwyn's brother was the Duke of Ashvale who owned several luxury liners. She'd been on one herself at the start of Valentine's and Bronwyn's unconventional courtship.

"A frigate. The *Syren*. She's small and fast. I dabbled in goods and trade."

Valentine sent her a sidelong glance. He would obviously know what dabbling meant, but he would also understand the need for discretion. He let out a low laugh. "Somehow, I can absolutely imagine you at the helm of a ship. Tell us more. How did you and Thorin cross paths?"

At their fascinated expressions, she opened her mouth to continue, but was forestalled by a very loud and equally obnoxious childish squeal that nearly made her ears ring.

"Blow me down, Cap'n, but this is the fanciest fucking house I've ever seen!"

Raphael gave his hat to the butler, taking in Narina's awed expression with a smile. No doubt everyone in the residence had heard her foulmouthed opinion, including the butler, but he did not even bat an eyelash. Raphael respected the man for that alone. "Le Duc de Viel, a friend of the countess," he said. "And Miss Narina."

"Your Grace, miss," the butler greeted them with the barest twitch of his lips at the girl's insufferable cheek, and Raphael blinked. *Your Grace* was the formal address for dukes in England, unlike *Monsieur le Duc* in France and French territories.

Narina frowned up at him. "Wait, you're an actual duke?"

"You knew that. Everyone calls me Monsieur le Duc."

She didn't look convinced. "I thought that was a sodding joke." She tugged on the lace collar of the pretty blue dress Raphael had sent Thorin's quartermaster to procure. "I hate this. It itches. Why couldn't I have worn my breeches? Pirates don't wear dresses."

"You're not a pirate," Raphael said. "And you stank. You needed a bath and clean clothes."

"You smelled worse," she replied in outrage and stuck out her tongue.

"Do allow me to announce you," the butler interjected quickly, though by then he was fighting to hide his amusement. "The duke and duchess are in with the countess and her fiancé."

Oh, for *fuck's* sake. Now he wanted to bellow a few choice profanities as the butler announced them.

"Blimey," Narina whispered as her eyes rounded, taking in the lavish salon. By most accounts, it was tasteful and modern, and certainly not ostentatious, but Raphael supposed that to her, it might seem impressive. When she noticed the people in the room, her jaw slackened and her normally confident mien wobbled. "Hullo," she said shyly.

Lisbeth rose, graceful and exquisite, to take the girl's hand. Seeing her in a drawing room was surreal...as if the woman he'd come to know was someone else entirely. Breeding was imbued in every line of her body, her face a study in refined elegance. "This is Narina. She's my ward for the moment. Nari, these are my very dear friends, the Duke and Duchess of Thornbury. You may address them as Your Graces. Mind your manners."

Narina gnawed her lips and clung to Lisbeth's arm after doing a half-hearted curtsy. "Your Graces," she mumbled.

Lastly, Lisbeth turned to him. "And this is de Viel, as Barnaby has said."

That was new. She'd never called him by his titled name before...and it felt peculiar. As if they were pretending to be strangers meeting for the very first time. He supposed they were—he as a duke, and she as a countess. They both wore the outer trappings of peers, while on the inside, they were anything but. He caught her subtle glance at him, taking in the polished boots, tailored trousers, fitted silver-trimmed waistcoat, and navy coat. A cravat and diamond stickpin finished the ensemble. He might be mistaken but the color in her cheeks had heightened.

A throat cleared and he tore his gaze away from a very intrigued audience. The duchess, especially, scrutinized them with a speculative look in her eyes. The Duke and Duchess of Thornbury made a handsome couple, though the duke appeared to be some years older than his effervescent wife. They sat uncharacteristically close though, so maybe it was a love match. Those were rare in aristocratic circles.

"Thornbury," he greeted. "Duchess, a pleasure to make your acquaintance." He moved over to where Lisbeth stood and raised her knuckles to his mouth. "Countess." It came out as a purr and he felt the slightest shiver roll through her. He deliberately ignored Thorin, knowing he'd be hard-pressed not to toss the smug cretin out the window.

The duke's eyes narrowed. "I believe we might have already been introduced, de Viel. At least you seem quite familiar to me. In Paris perhaps?"

Raphael lifted a brow, wondering how and when he might have crossed paths with someone like Thornbury. He'd heard whispers that the man used to be a spy for the Crown, but that had to be speculation at best. Most of the British peerage would hardly deign to be spies. Then again, most of them wouldn't be smugglers either, and there were two of those anomalies in the room. Three, if he counted Thorin, his shitsack of a best friend.

"I have not been back to France in years, I'm afraid." He canted his head at the duchess. "However, I have had the pleasure of meeting your wonderful aunt, Your Grace, la Comtesse de Valois. She's a firecracker."

"That she is," the duchess agreed. "But please, you must call me Bronwyn. The constant 'Your Gracing' is tedious." She let out a deprecating laugh. "And trust me, there will be enough of that in the days to come, if you're planning to stay awhile. Our more affluent neighbors are rather obsessive about titles and social status."

"Alas," Lisbeth said, "it will be a quick trip. I need to get back to the *Syren*—my crew should already be here—and those two have their own business to attend to."

Bronwyn pouted and then brightened as if she'd had a brilliant idea. "Then say you'll at least all be here tomorrow night? There's a masquerade ball, hosted by none other than Lina herself. We've accepted, but it would be so much more agreeable with you there."

"Can *I* go?" Narina piped up from where she sat, stuffing tea cake after tea cake into her mouth. Crumbs littered her dress that now had a tea stain on it. "I love dress up. I can be a pirate!"

"I doubt we would be welcomed at this juncture. She's very fastidious about her guest list," Lisbeth said and then shook her head at Narina. "No, love. You're much too young."

The duchess laughed. "You're a countess. He's a French duke, and Thorin, well..."

"Count me out," Thorin said jovially. "I have plans with a lovely modiste."

Raphael scowled. Ah yes, the modiste whose illegal gowns had nearly gotten them in hot water and attracted the attention of the most notorious customs house in the United States. His irritation spiked again.

"Speaking of," Thorin said, standing as if he could feel

the waves of malevolence directed his way. "I should be taking my leave. Lisbeth, Saint, Your Graces, a pleasure."

"What about me?" Narina demanded, her mouth full.

He stopped to ruffle her curls. "You too, Beastie. Keep out of trouble."

"Does a pirate shit in the sea?" she shot back, and Raphael caught Bronwyn struggling to hide a snort even as Lisbeth looked utterly mortified.

"Nari!" she muttered.

The girl had the wherewithal to blush. "Sorry, Bess. Er, I mean Lisbeth. Er, Countess Your Highness."

"Who's Bess?" Bronwyn asked, unable to hide her grin, and Raphael realized that Lisbeth's friends might not know about her secret identity. He kept his mouth sealed shut, but the cat was let out of the bag anyway.

"She's a smuggler," Narina said. "A good one, but also bad. Like Saint. Because they're stealing things. And stealing is wrong. Very bloody wrong." She said the last emphatically. It was obvious that she was trying to make up for the earlier embarrassment, unaware in her childish innocence that she was only making it worse.

Bronwyn's eyes rounded with delight. "Smuggling? Do tell."

Lisbeth sighed, but her spine snapped tight as though she was alarmed about something. "Too long a story for tonight. I'm quite tired, in need of a proper bath, and I have to get that one to bed before she gets it in her head to teach your staff pirate lexicon. The Rose Rooms will be perfect. Are you certain it's not an imposition?"

Raphael couldn't help noticing the meaningful, pleading gaze she sent to the duke and duchess as she spoke, almost as if they were privy to something that he was not a part of. Or perhaps he was inventing things because of all the territorial feelings that Thorin had elicited, and she was simply tired and did not want to get into her shenanigans as Bonnie Bess.

But something about the silent communication bothered him. What else was his beautiful Viking hiding?

"Of course not," Thornbury said smoothly. Raphael did not miss the warning glance he shot his wife as she opened her mouth to protest with a look of disappointment. "Barnaby, can you instruct Mrs. Barnaby to have the staff prepare the Vanguard Suite for Monsieur de Viel?"

The butler appeared in the doorway like a silent wraith. "At once, Your Grace."

"I thank you, but I have accommodation elsewhere," Raphael said.

Lisbeth whirled. "You do? Since when?"

"Nonsense," Thornbury said. "You will be on another floor if you are worried about propriety, and there are more than enough staff around to act as chaperones."

He blinked. For Narina? She was a child. At his baffled expression, Lisbeth cleared her throat, cheeks going pink.

Oh.

For him. And *her*. He almost smirked and pointed out that they had been sleeping within feet of each other for weeks. But decorum was a proclivity of haughty upper-class drawing rooms, not out on the sea where modesty propriety played second fiddle to power. However, right now, they were part of the very society he scorned and rules had to be minded.

"Thank you for your hospitality, Your Graces," he said. "I must respectfully decline."

The more distance from temptation the better.

"Have you brought trunks or clothes, Lisbeth?" Bronwyn asked brightly into the heavy silence and then frowned, considering there was no sign of any. "If not, you can always wear some of mine. We're about the same size except for our height, but I can have the maids alter any of the hemlines. And there's also a dressmaker here who should have some ready-made items for Narina. We can go tomorrow." Her face was earnest. "And don't worry about the ball. I have several unworn gowns that will suffice in a pinch."

Thornbury stood and finished his glass of brandy. "Would you join me for a cigar in the study before you leave, de Viel?"

Raphael stiffened. It did not sound like a request, and he couldn't very well deny their host. Lisbeth's panicked gaze flew to his, but he smiled reassuringly, letting her know that any of her secrets were hers to divulge. He was used to interrogations and treading the fine line between fact and fabrication.

"Of course."

"Good night, Saint!" Narina chirped, cheeks flushed and practically vibrating from all the sweets she had consumed. He did not envy Lisbeth the task of getting her to sleep with all that energy running through her bloodstream.

"Night, lassie."

The duke's study was handsomely and tastefully appointed, like the rest of the house. The dark paneling, enormous mahogany desk, and wooden bookcases seemed well suited to him. Raphael took a seat in one of the plush armchairs near the fireplace. Thornbury poured two fingers of whiskey and offered him a glass before reaching for a box of cigars. Raphael took the first but shook his head at the second. "I don't smoke, but please, feel free."

The duke's lip kicked up in a thin smile. "I don't either. I keep them for guests."

When Thornbury sat opposite him, Raphael crossed his booted foot over his knee and leaned back into his seat. "Then I suppose we should get right to it. What do you want to know?"

"You're direct," the duke said, but there was a grain of respect in his voice.

"I prefer not to waste time. Yours or mine." He sipped his drink. "If you're worried about my intentions toward Lisbeth, don't be. That woman has a head on her shoulders that could probably rival all of the men in your House of Lords."

"I know," Thornbury said. "I used to be married to her."

Raphael's eyes snapped up. How had he missed the connection? He'd been too busy worrying about Thorin that he hadn't thought about who Thornbury might be to her. A hot thread of jealousy twined through him, for no other reason than Lisbeth had said yes to this man.

"It was an arrangement," the duke said quietly. "That reached its end."

"Her past has nothing to do with me," Raphael said, only to receive a cool, calculating stare in return. "Besides, we part ways here in New York."

Thornbury frowned. "Will you?"

Something calculated moved through the duke's gaze, a confirmation of something he was working through in his head. Was it because he'd realized that Raphael meant so little to Lisbeth? That they were nothing more than friends with occasional diversions? Or something else? A shuttered amber gaze met his, and while Raphael did not feel threatened by the man, he had an idea that the duke could be lethal, should he so choose. It was in the way he held himself, as if consciously aware of everything around him—a skill earned from facing real danger on a consistent basis. Perhaps those rumors about him were true.

"Why did the child call you Saint? Is that a nickname?"

"A last name. Raphael Saint."

Thornbury frowned and then nodded to himself like information had suddenly clicked. "Now I know why you seem so familiar. I knew your father. Randolphe Saint. You have the look of him in the eyes." Raphael froze, his throat going tight. "I am sorry for your loss."

"How did you know him?" he croaked.

"We met in the emperor's court when the charges of treason were brought against him. I was there as a witness."

Raphael gritted his teeth. Why would *he* have been

there for such a purpose? And that long ago, he would have been an earl, not a duke. “They were slanderous lies.”

Thornbury nodded. “That does not surprise me.”

He did not like that the duke was watching him carefully, cataloging every tick, every subtle movement, and the coiled rage in every line of his body. Raphael clenched his fists and forced himself to inhale and exhale. This was neither the time nor the place.

And his target was Dubois, not this man.

“If that’s all, Your Grace, I’ll see myself out.”

Nineteen

"Why can't I go?" Narina whined, kicking her feet against the mattress with enough force to make the large bed shake.

Lisbeth fought for patience. "You're twelve years old, Nari. It's not a party for children."

"I am not a sodding child!" she shrieked, thumping harder.

"You're behaving like a child," Lisbeth responded evenly. Sometimes she forgot just how young Narina was. She behaved and spoke like an adult because of the environment in which she had been raised, but that did not change the fact that she was at a very tender age. "If you act nicely, I promise to take you to the ice cream parlor on Broadway for as much as you can eat tomorrow."

The kicking halted. "You promise? All I can have?"

"Without being sick, yes. But I cannot hear a single complaint from Mrs. Barnaby about your conduct *or* improper language tonight, or our agreement is off. Deal?"

Sufficiently bribed and all smiles, Narina nodded avidly. "You really do look pretty, Bess."

Lisbeth stared at herself in the mirrored glass in her borrowed ball gown, the silver threads and the glint of diamonds picking up the sun-lightened notes in her hair. It was on the simpler side for a ball gown and it still felt extravagant…with its layers of satin, chiffon, and tulle. It had been so long since she'd attended a ball, and while a part of her preferred to stay in bed, she wanted one night.

You want a perfect night with him.

Her inner voice wasn't wrong. The thought of leaving Raphael hurt more than she'd expected it to. They'd depended on each other, learned to trust each other, and cared for each other. In some of the worst times. She thought of her cabin on the *Syren* and the cargo hold on the *Vauquelin*. And some of the best times, too.

But he'd hate her…and she couldn't bear the thought of that more.

So leaving was a lesser ache.

One night. One night and then she'd let him go for good.

Besides, it would be a waste of a perfectly lovely gown. Bronwyn's local modiste had done a wonderful job with the length and also letting out some of the too-tight bodice. They'd spent part of the morning there, purchasing a few day dresses, chemises, and petticoats for Narina, which she loathed on sight, and tailored boys' knickerbockers that buttoned below the knees and loose blouses, which she loved. The dressmakers had been scandalized when she'd announced that she was half pirate.

Bronwyn had been in fits of laughter, and of course Narina had reveled in the attention. New shoes and a fetching new bonnet had been added to the purchases.

While Narina was getting fitted, Bronwyn had leaned in. "Where are her people?"

"Dead. She has no one. I was hoping to find her somewhere safe to live and have a proper education, but with all this business with the *Syren*, I'd rather not keep her on a ship for the next few weeks. Or worse, have her get hurt."

Bronwyn had not hesitated. "Valentine and I are here for the month, if that is helpful. She can stay with us until you return to the city."

"You would do that?"

"That's what friends are for, and she is delightful," Bronwyn had said. "A little rough around the edges, but nothing that some love and guidance won't polish."

Lisbeth was only waiting for the right time to break the news to the girl. Perhaps when she was drunk on ice cream might be a good time. Undeniably, she would not take being left behind well, but Lisbeth had to stand firm in her convictions. A ship like hers, or even Saint's, was no place for a child. Things were much too unpredictable, and now that she was going up against Dubois with the might of the Treasury at her back, she could not afford to be preoccupied with ensuring Narina's safety.

After the modiste, Bronwyn left her calling card at Mrs. Astor's address with a short note letting her know that she would be bringing guests. She made sure to list their titles, knowing the lady would hardly refuse. The more dukes at her affair, the better she appeared to the rest of New York society. Sure enough, a message had come shortly after with an enthusiastic reply in the affirmative.

"My lady, Her Grace has sent me to fetch you," the soft-spoken maid who had helped dress Lisbeth said. "She says your French duke is here."

"I'll be right down."

Her French duke. A shiver rolled through her as Lisbeth tied the ends of the silver spangled mask. He wasn't hers, but they deserved one night of magic, if a future of happiness was out of their reach. She spun once in front of the mirror, and Narina squealed at the flare of silver and ivory. "You look like the best damned princess this world ever did see!"

Lisbeth laughed at her enthusiasm, not even bothering to chide her for the slip. "Sleep well, love, and remember your promise."

"I shall." She narrowed dark eyes and pointed. "You remember *yours*. All I can eat and that will be the size of a ship."

And that was why Lisbeth had laughter on her lips as she stepped down the staircase. But when she reached the second-to-last step, her breath stalled in her lungs because the gentleman waiting for her was the most gorgeous man she had ever seen. She'd never seen him in fancy evening clothes, the pristine black coat and trousers, onyx waistcoat with a sheen of midnight blue, and a sparkling white shirt combining to make his otherworldly beauty seem ethereal. His features were sharper, his lips fuller. Glossy hair tumbled over his shoulders, those gray eyes shining like stars in his burnished face, his bearing impossibly regal.

He truly was her fairy prince come to life.

And he was staring at her the same way she was looking at him, mouth ajar with wonder and stark desire in his expression. "Mon Dieu…you…" He broke off, unable to speak in either language, and that was flattery enough.

"Do you like it?" she asked almost shyly.

"You shine brighter than the moon over the ocean, Countess."

Oh. Her knees wobbled at the hoarse rasp. Was she about to swoon?

Bronwyn sailed in from the study, eyes fever-bright and her lips looking suspiciously swollen, followed by her smirking husband whose hair was decidedly mussed. Clearly, those two were even more smitten with each other than they'd been the day before. The duchess was lovely in an ice-blue gown that made her light-blue eyes pop, and from the way Valentine was looking at her, it was obvious he wanted nothing more than to ferry them back to the study they'd just vacated. Despite her envy, Lisbeth was glad for them.

Was that what love would feel like? Like one's heart was so full, it was stretched to capacity. Like love was the air one needed to breathe. Like every smile and every touch made one feel like flying… Perhaps one day, she might be so lucky.

But for now she could be happy for one night.

With a slow inhale, she accepted Raphael's arm as they descended to the waiting coach with Valentine and Bronwyn. The carriage ride was short, but just long enough for her to gather herself. This, too, would be somewhat of a performance.

But it seemed like she blinked before they entered the residence at 350 Fifth Avenue, and were swallowed up by a crowd of satin and lace, feathered fans and jeweled tiaras, welcoming smiles and looks of envy. Lisbeth was quickly reminded of how much she disliked the upper classes, and this was much too similar to the life she'd left. Everyone vying to be the diamond. Everyone desperate to be seen, to be esteemed, to gain favor that might never come.

And the queen, Mrs. Astor, presided above it all on her red velvet couch. Lina had been pleased to see Lisbeth, happy to add more peers, even—*gasp*—divorced ones, to her grandiose party. True to form, the gold and silver plates were present. The silk-lined walls of the ballroom were so opulent, beautiful art decorating its backdrop. Everything else had been painted and draped in hues of her favorite color, *royal* purple. Feathered rugs dotted the space, and servants in formal livery trotted around to anticipate every possible need of the guests, even before they knew it themselves.

Lisbeth sipped her glass of champagne, wishing she had something stronger to take the edge off her shivering nerves. Why she was nervous, she had no idea. Though it likely had to do with the man who occupied all her thoughts. Her gaze slid to him. Raphael was dancing with Bronwyn, and the two of them made quite the picture.

"So," a low voice said behind her. "You're in deep."

"It's all under control," she told Valentine. He would

know. After all, she'd gotten some of her information from reports he'd compiled about Dubois while he'd been undercover in France years ago. "You know I like to play with my food before I eat it."

"I was talking about de Viel."

Her breathing stuttered. *Him, too,* the wicked voice in her head wanted to say. But the truth was, when it came to Raphael Saint, she was well beyond games. She had learned a thing or two from her time with Valentine, and she remained silent. Less was more in many cases, and with someone as astute as her former partner, a decorated, retired spymaster himself, it would be impossible to prevaricate.

"Does he know what you intend for Dubois?" Valentine asked when she did not speak.

She exhaled. "No."

"I suspect he has his own plans, and a man driven by personal vengeance can be impulsive." He shifted and she sensed him looking at her. "Do you know what you're doing, Lisbeth?"

"I am no novice, Val," she said coolly.

"I meant with him." He let out a breath. "When someone you…care about is involved, the mind can become muddled. Unclear. Leading to mistakes. I should know."

"I am not you," she said softly. "And we are not involved, don't worry."

Not after tonight, anyway.

The music ended—and, by default, their hushed conversation—as they were rejoined by their respective partners. It wasn't long before Bronwyn and Valentine disappeared out on the terrace, and Raphael asked Lisbeth to dance. It was a waltz and one of her favorite dances. Lisbeth should have been in her element. But the conversation with Valentine had rattled her. Was she unduly influenced and making different decisions because she *cared* about Raphael?

"Why the grim look?" Raphael said softly as they danced, the steps of the waltz coming back to her with each three-count of the music. "Tell me something true, Viking."

She closed her eyes, the words like bittersweet kisses on her skin. "I don't know who I am anymore," she whispered.

"But I do," he told her. "You're the fiercest, most compassionate, most loyal, most intelligent, most capable, and most decidedly deadly"—they both laughed at that—"woman I have ever had the honor of knowing. It doesn't matter what face you show to the world, Lisbeth. Those who love you see you as you are."

Love... He couldn't possibly mean what she thought it could be.

That he might love her.

But hope was a dangerous thing...the tiniest spark to dry, unlit tinder. Despite a thin thread of alarm, her feelings grew bright and buoyant. With each beat of the music, their intensity grew until she felt fit to burst, and surrounded by hundreds, only the two of them existed in that moment. Her eyes collided with his silvery brown-flecked irises, and she let out a shudder as his strong hand flexed at her waist. God, how she wanted him.

Raphael was consuming and forceful, a storm she could either sail around or sail into.

She wanted to brace and batten down the hatches.

She wanted to scream into his winds.

"Monsieur de Viel," she told him as the music came to a close. "I need some air."

With a faint smirk at the address, as if he knew she was holding on by a thread, he escorted her outside, the crisp evening breeze caressing her overheated cheeks. Lisbeth breathed in huge gulps of air, but nothing cooled the need brewing in the pit of her belly. They were standing much too close at the balustrade facing the gardens, her arm grazing his, the heat of his body fueling hers to greater heights. She had absolutely no intention of moving. The gossip would be hitting the rafters, but Lisbeth did not give a flying fuck who was watching.

"Pirate," she said.

Thick lashes lifted to reveal those eyes that branded her soul. "Yes, Viking?"

She leaned in closer, her arm pressing against the length of his. "Where have you been staying? On the *Vauquelin*?"

"No, the Fifth Avenue Hotel."

"Is it close?"

He blinked. "Not far, why?"

She smiled and lifted her arm to let the backs of her knuckles graze over the front of his trousers. Satisfaction filled her. He was rock-fucking-hard, the tip of his piercing beneath the fabric a jolt to her own spiking desire. "I am going to make a spectacle and drop to my knees in the next thirty seconds, if you don't get us out of here."

"Fuck, Lisbeth!" he hissed.

"Thirty, twenty-nine, twenty-eight..."

But even as she started the countdown, they were moving. Not through the ballroom, around it. Flying through the gardens and then she was practically being tossed into an empty barouche with a pair of prancing white horses. "Whose carriage is this?"

"Who cares? Hold on!"

She gasped as he grabbed the reins. "You can't steal this, you daft man!"

"Who says? I'm already doing it. You act like you never break the rules."

Lisbeth couldn't help it. She tipped back her head and laughed to the moonlit sky, exhilaration and fire filling her to the brim. When they arrived at the address of Raphael's hotel on Twenty-Third Street, the white marble of the massive building lit by moonlight, he paid the attendant a small fortune to return the barouche to Mrs. Astor's residence.

Her partner in crime grinned at her. "Only borrowing, darling."

Her heart skipped at the endearment that sounded very different coming from his lips than it had from Thorin's. The exchange with Thorin had been fake. This was...the opposite of fake, even though it might have started in much the same way. But suddenly she was unable to think as he made no bones about scooping her up into his arms, striding under the portico to the grand entrance hall lined with Corinthian columns, and ferrying her into the passenger elevator.

Lisbeth's eyes widened as the liftman closed the door of the car and up they went. A vertical railway, they called such things. There was even a bench for people to sit, but Raphael kept her firmly in his arms to the mortification of the elevator operator. "It's the first of its kind in the United States," he told her. "A marvel of modern engineering."

"Fascinating," she murmured, though she was much more interested in the man who held her like he'd never let her go. She trailed a gloved finger over his jaw as the car stopped and they hurried to his rooms. He fumbled with the key, but managed to get the door open as she breathed in his scent of sea and citrus. "Where did you come from, Raphael?"

"Dieu, I love when you say my name."

She feathered a finger over his lips. "I want to scream it."

Every muscle in his body locked before he slowly slid her down the length of him and cupped her face in his hands. He stared at her for an interminable moment, giving her room to change her mind or move away. But she wanted neither of those things. Lisbeth stepped back, his hands hovering in midair before they fell, his face sphinx-like. She knew he would let her leave if that was what she chose. But tonight was for them. For *her*.

The devil inside, however, made her walk toward the door as though she were changing her mind. At the jamb, she glanced over her shoulder with a sly look. She pressed a hand to the wall and arched her back.

"Unlace me."

Her duke was upon her before she could take another breath or step, hands everywhere, mouth on her neck, breath fanning into her hair. Fastenings and laces came frantically undone, chiffon and satin gaping as he fussed at her crinoline, a frustrated groan escaping him when he was faced with her undercorset. "Too many deuced layers!"

Lisbeth laughed, but he was determined and managed to get the corset sufficiently loosened until she stepped out of the mound of fabric, clad only in a filmy chemise, stockings, and dancing slippers. He stared at her for a prolonged moment, his throat working like a man starved, before he dropped to his knees to slip off her shoes. His fingers trembled on the curve of her ankle, but he did not linger, as though he could not trust himself.

"You are the most exquisite thing I've ever seen," he whispered, looking up at her from his position on the floor.

"Your turn," she told him, voice husky.

He was much quicker, boots going flying, coat and cravat stripped away, waistcoat, shirt, and smallclothes shorn off, until he stood in the altogether like a sultry, dark prince. Lisbeth gulped at the mesmerizing vision of him—all sculpted, lean bronzed muscle, his nipple ring glinting over the sprawling tattoo on his chest, the corrugated planes of his abdomen leading to the thick cock that jutted out from a nest of black curls, the gold of his apadravya making a surge of lust pour through her. How would *that* feel inside?

Raphael prowled toward her, that big body moving like liquid grace. Her mouth dried when he scooped her up again and ferried her to the bed, the feel of his hot bare skin a delightful shock. He shot her a wicked smile and leaned over her, his powerful muscles rippling. God, she could stare at him forever and never get bored.

You don't have forever.

Lisbeth closed her eyes, shutting out the painful reminder.

"Kiss me," she told him.

He complied, but the kiss was teasingly brief, just enough for her to enjoy the smallest taste of him before he was gone, pressing close-mouthed kisses down her lawn-covered body, fluttering over the peak of each breast and blowing streams of hot air. Just enough to torment, not enough to slake the need roaring inside. She wanted to scream in frustration. Those light butterfly kisses continued in a path to her stomach and lower still.

Lisbeth froze as he shifted on the bed between her thighs, her heart hammering behind her ribs, but he did not touch her where she craved it most. Instead he went to the tapes of her stockings. Gentle fingers untied and unrolled, lips following in their wake. She felt the scrape of his teeth on the inside of one knee and nearly came off the bed. Who knew she was so sensitive there? He repeated the process on the other side, and by the time he crawled back up her limbs, she could feel how shockingly wet she was.

When he paused at the junction of her legs and inhaled deeply through the linen, she writhed. "You smell like summer on the sea," he said, his voice a dark, delicious rumble. "Just like you taste."

She was so hot, her skin felt like it was coming apart at the seams. Usually, she was quite vocal with her lovers, but with Raphael, she felt tongue-tied. She could only feel and feel and *feel*. She was so worked up that when he unhurriedly dragged the hem of her chemise up over her hips, she felt every scrape of the linen on her sensitive flesh, on every rib, on the sides of her breasts. A moan clawed its way up her throat as the fabric dragged over her overstimulated nipples, and finally over her head. He hadn't even really touched her and she was so on edge, she wanted to sob with the intensity of it.

Most of him was still lodged in the cradle between her legs. "Tell me what you want, Viking."

She bit her lip, every inch of her on fire. "You know what I want."

The devious beast smirked at her before reaching down to bite her on the edge of her bare hip—a punishment and a promise. She wasn't sure which of those she craved more. "Do I? I'm not sure exactly."

He drew small circles around her navel.

"Stop teasing me, for fuck's sake," she cried, arching

toward him, angling her hips toward any part of him that might relieve the pressure.

He brushed his knuckles over her mound, and she nearly wept. "Then use your words like a good girl."

Twenty

God. Why, oh why did those words turn her into a mewling mess?

"Make me come," she panted, instinctively canting her hips up again in search of friction.

"How? With my fingers? With my cock? With my tongue?" A stream of his breath blew against her core and her spine bowed. "You want me to lick you here? Then say please."

"Please, you bastard," she gritted out.

He chuckled wickedly and then in the next moment had them flipped on the bed, with her hips straddling his chest. He was embarrassingly close to the neediest part of her. "W-what are you doing?"

Strong hands grasped her waist and shuttled her forward until she was hovering over him in the most scandalous position imaginable. "Giving you what you asked for so nicely, though we will need to work on your manners."

"Raphael…" But she couldn't even finish whatever it was she'd been about to say as he pulled her down onto his face, his open mouth covering her dripping center. "Guh!"

Her eyes rolled back into her head when he sucked, pleasure shooting through all her nerve endings as he stroked up into her with the firm length of his tongue and then licked from opening to apex with the flat of it. With a groan of pure need, he worried the bundle of nerves there with his teeth, scraping gently, and the keening sound that came from her was unearthly.

Shamelessly, she ground down on him, seeking more of everything he had to offer, uncaring that she was crushing him, but he wasn't complaining. Given her heightened state of arousal, it didn't take long before her body stilled and seized, the orgasm crashing through her as she rode it out with ruthless hunger. He took every drop of it until she was quivering and too sensitive to take anymore.

Shimmying backward to move her weight to the knees on either side of his chest, Lisbeth stared down at him as he licked his still glistening lips, his chin covered with evidence of her release. The sight of that made something dark and possessive come awake inside of her.

"Fuck, Viking, you taste like heaven."

"How do you know what heaven tastes like?" she asked and bent to kiss him deeply before licking her own lips. The taste of her mixed with him was sweet and tangy.

"I don't," he said. "But that's what I imagine it would be."

She laughed. "You say the sweetest things, Pirate."

"One of my many outstanding gifts," he said.

"There's that ego talking again. Should I shut him up?"

His hands went to her hips as if he meant to draw her back for another round of suffocate-the-pirate, but she shook her head and slid down the hard planes of his belly. "My turn to play." She licked at his nipple ring, gently tugging it between her teeth, and making his hands ball into the sheets. Her fingers wandered as she wriggled lower. She traced the raised and reddened scar left behind by the knife wound and traced her lips over it.

She peered up at him, eyes fusing with his. "You're right. Scars are attractive."

"Told you so."

"So arrogant." When she shifted down between his thick, muscled thighs, his swollen cock front and center, he sucked in a ragged breath. "You seemed to enjoy teasing," she purred. "Let's see if you like it when the shoe is on the other foot, hmm?"

She blew on the rounded crown as he had on her, watching his length jerk.

"Bloody hell!"

Lisbeth did it again, but lightly scratched her nails over the tight spheres at the base of him this time. He stiffened even more, a bead of translucent liquid forming at his tip. Eyes on him, she bowed and lapped gently, the salty taste making her want more. Her tongue flicked around the top of his piercing, forcing a deep groan from his chest. "Lisbeth."

"Does it feel good?"

"Yes."

When she took the thick head of him inside her mouth, careful with both ends of the apadravya, his hands fisted the bedsheets. She gripped the base of him with one hand and swirled her tongue. Raphael almost came off the bed, his hips thrusting jerkily toward her. Lisbeth took him as deep as she could, the metal dragging along the roof of her mouth and the flat of her tongue as he slowly withdrew. It was not unpleasant, but the idea of it stroking elsewhere made her empty passage clench on air. She moaned around his crown.

As if he'd read her mind, Raphael sat up and pulled her to him, capturing her lips.

"I wasn't finished," she protested.

"And I want to be inside you." With that, he settled her over his pelvis, the blunt head of him gliding over her entrance. Cool metal hit the needy bud at the top of her sex, making her shiver. "Guide me in, Viking."

The excruciatingly tight slide of her down his throbbing length was going to kill him.

Raphael had meant to torture her by keeping her on edge, but that kind of seduction was a double-edged sword. Copious amounts of fluid had leaked out of him, his cock so engorged that even breathing had made him ache...and when she had taken him into the warm depths of her mouth, he'd had to think of every possibly repulsive thing he could conceive just so he wouldn't be too rough or spend too soon. And that fucking piercing was the bane of his existence.

Already, he could feel his ballocks tightening and he wasn't even fully seated, but that was because every sense felt raw with desire. He was drunk on the glorious sight of her like a goddess perched atop him with skeins of silvery-blond hair tumbling over her shoulders, lips parted and green eyes glazed with passion. The scent of her like ocean and sunlight. The feel of the miles and miles of velvety skin and the warm clasp of her body urging him inside. The sounds of her breathy whimpers as she worked to take him. And the taste, Dieu, the fucking *taste* of her. Even now, his mouth still watered for more.

"Raphael," she gasped, writhing down, her face flushed with exertion. "It's too much."

"Slow, love," he said and brushed his fingers down the front of her flat belly, his thumb going to her clitoris, nudging it in small circles.

"Oh…" she breathed as she canted her hips, eyes widening at the combination of sensations—the rough friction of his finger and the girth of him inside. "That's… fucking good."

Hinging upward slightly, she shuttled south, gaining another inch as they both groaned at the intensity of the fit. "Again," he told her, and when she complied, he quickened the circles of his thumb. "Good girl." Her passage clamped down around him so hard that he grunted, and he gave a dark chuckle. "Does my pretty Valkyrie like to be praised?"

"I don't know why," she admitted, cheeks on fire. "It's nonsensical. I've never been this way with anyone."

"Which way?"

"So goddamned needy as if all I want is for you to look at me the way you are right now." She worked her hips down the final inch until she was seated to the hilt, the pleasure intense as she squeezed him like a vise.

"Fuck, you're tight," he growled.

She panted. "Raphael, I can feel you everywhere. I'm so full. I feel like I need to move."

"How good of an equestrian are you?" he said with a grin.

That green gaze darkened with desire at the erotic suggestion, but she quirked a brow as she planted her hands on his chest. "Est-ce que tu veux que je te monte comme un cheval, Monsieur le Duc?"

He blinked. "You're fluent in French?"

"I speak seven languages," she told him.

Yet another thing he had not known about her. Who *was* the Countess of Waterstone, really? That was a riddle for later. "Alors, chérie, chevauche-moi."

His eyes nearly rolled back in his head when she did just that, posting on a diagonal slant using her thighs and then cresting down. She found a rhythm easily, the breathy sounds falling from her lips as she chased her pleasure, music to his ears.

Ciel, she was so beautiful like this—full, uplifted, pink-tipped breasts, firm, quivering stomach, and curving thighs clamped over his hips—her graceful, strong body eager to please. Running his hands up her ribs, he cupped her breasts and plucked at her taut nipples. He needed them in his mouth so he sat up, one palm splaying against her spine as he held her to him. He drew one furled peak into his mouth, relishing the cry on her lips when her head fell back.

"Wrap your legs around me, love," he whispered. When she did, they both groaned at the deliciously snug shift in position and the way his piercing rubbed up against that perfect spot inside her.

"Oh!" Her head snapped up, eyes wide as ragged breaths sawed from her lips when he planted his hands firmly on her hips and rocked her back and forth against him. "You're so deep…and, *yes,* right there."

It only took two more shallow thrusts before she was undulating around him, her channel rippling greedily as she clenched down hard, nails scouring into his shoulders, begging for more. He found her mouth, kissing her and swallowing her cries as she tumbled into her release. He was so close, too. He could feel it, lightning gathering at the base of his spine.

Lisbeth protested irritably as he withdrew from her, but then gasped when he flipped her to her hands and knees, and plunged back in without warning. "Raphael!" she screamed, her chest slumping to the mattress as her body broke anew and quivered around him.

As he fucked her relentlessly she started to shake, squeezing his cock with her spasming inner muscles, and Raphael reached around to stroke the nerves at the top of her sex.

"Again," he ordered.

Her reply was garbled. "I can't."

"The fuck you can't. Take me like the good girl you are and *come*!" And then she was shivering, sobbing into the sheets as his fingers and hips moved faster, taking control and choreographing every whimper and every quake into a crescendo that matched and met his.

Only when he felt her body start to seize and shudder,

did he withdraw from the heat of her, pumping furiously into his hand. Vision going white, a wild roar broke from him as he emptied himself onto the sheets between them.

Holy hell. Coitus had never been like that, like a cataclysmic, earth-shattering event.

Raphael panted for breath, propping himself on one arm and running a slow hand along Lisbeth's damp spine and the rounded globes of her arse. He leaned over to kiss her shoulder where she lay spent on her stomach. "Are you well, chérie?"

"Mmm." Her voice was muffled in the sheets, but she rolled limply to her side to stare up at him with a languid, satiated gaze. "More than well."

"Good." He winked. "*Girl.*"

She rolled her eyes. "You are a devil."

With a laugh, Raphael bunched the soiled sheets up beneath him and collapsed beside her on the bed so that they were facing each other. He swiped a damp tendril of wispy blond hair from her brow. "You're so fucking perfect, Lisbeth."

Something flashed in her eyes before she lowered her lashes, hiding her expression from him. "I'm not. There are things you don't know about me."

"We all have our secrets," he said, leaning in to kiss each corner of her mouth.

"Raphael…" she began and then closed her eyes, lips going tight, the words she'd been about to speak sealed away. It hurt that she didn't trust him fully, but her walls needed to come down on their own and of her own volition. If someone tried to tear them down by force, they would only go back up twice as strong. *She* had to allow herself to trust him.

"Tell me something true, Viking," he whispered.

Those beautiful green eyes slid open, desire and despair and dread swirling in them, and for once, she let him see all the things she normally hid. "I don't want to say goodbye."

It was on the tip of his tongue to tell her she didn't have to, but that would be a lie. They both had things to do. He had to settle the score with Dubois, and he did not want her getting caught in the middle of that. He'd seen the way the other man had looked at her, and a snake like his uncle would hurt her without a qualm. And she had to go take care of her crew and the *Syren*. Their paths were meant to diverge, but that didn't mean that someday they couldn't meet again.

"It doesn't have to be goodbye forever," he said.

She smiled sadly at him and then sighed, her palm reaching for his. "Perhaps you're right. Maybe we'll see each other again." She intertwined their fingers and squeezed. "Your turn. Tell me something true, Pirate."

The words were out before he could recall them, "I'm falling in love with you."

Lisbeth stared at him in mute shock.

"You don't have to say anything back," he said softly.

By God, she wanted to. Was that what she'd been

feeling all along? *Love*? The breathlessness that teased her lungs every time he gave her one of his genuine smiles… the way her blockaded heart felt because of the way he saw her like no one else had. She'd never been in love with anyone before. Her whole life had been lived with the sparest of emotions, not because she didn't feel things, but because feeling things meant distraction.

But for the first time in her life, she wanted to be distracted. He'd never pushed her, never pressured her. She had always controlled the pace and the consent for anything between them. Raphael had always respected the lines she'd drawn in the sand between them, but now she wanted to cross them all. Every piece of her wanted to lean in close, accept what he was offering, and let herself be held. Let herself be safe, cherished, and loved in someone else's arms. *His* arms.

He's in love with a lie.

Because everything about you is a lie.

The burgeoning hope inside of her flickered. A part of her wanted to confess everything. Tell him who she honestly was and the truth of her mission. Lay her soul bare and take whatever judgment he'd pass upon her. See if he could still love her after all of it. But could she give up Dubois for him? Could she walk away from all that she had worked for…for a chance at love.

If this was even love. How should she know? God, she was so conflicted.

Love wasn't tangible. Or predictable. Or fair.

People took chances with love and failed every day. If

she made that choice, gave up everything that she'd built for this man, and it was the wrong one, what would she be left with but regret?

Not everyone fails.

That tiny inner voice was correct in that. Valentine hadn't. He'd fallen in love with his best friend's sister, a decade younger than him and still his perfect match. Ravenna, her friend and the Duchess of Ashvale, hadn't. She'd fallen in love with the only boy she'd ever loved from her childhood, whom she'd thought dead, then found him again years later. Even the estranged Duke of Embry, a man of the sea himself once upon a time, had found the love of his life in a Eurasian princess a continent away.

Love was certainly possible.

It just wasn't possible for *her*.

In a state of mild panic, Lisbeth reached deep for her usual well of indifference, but all she felt waiting there was a desperate sanguinity. It was frightening. She'd given her friendship and her body freely, but never anything more. And now he wanted her heart.

Damn, *she* had made the inexcusable mistake in allowing things to go this far.

The magical night she had yearned for now felt like a curse.

Lisbeth blew out a breath and released his hand. *She* was in control of her future, not him and not her silly heart that yearned for approval and affection. She was the Countess of Waterstone, espionage agent for the American Treasury. A woman with a history of commendations under her belt. A spy who had become countless versions of herself and overcome hundreds of obstacles.

She *loved* her *life*.

"I should be getting back," she said, sitting up, unable to look at him and bear the awful weight on her chest. "I don't want to worry Bronwyn or Narina."

There was a beat of silence before she felt the dip of the mattress as he moved to the other side. "Very well."

There was no rancor in his voice. No hurt. No surprise. No nothing. Just a calm, undisputed acceptance of what she wanted. Suddenly, an inexplicable anger stormed through her. Did he never fight for anything? Would he always concede to her wishes and desires, no matter how hurtful or outrageous? Lisbeth blinked, astonished at herself. Devil take it, was that what she wanted? For him to convince her otherwise?

No, of course she didn't want that. But if he was truly in love with her as he claimed, wouldn't he be trying harder to get her to stay? Bloody hell, her head was churning! No wonder people shied away from love or lost themselves because of it.

It was consuming and *confusing* in the extreme.

They each dressed in silence, and when it was time for her to lace up the back of her corset and her gown, Raphael did it with gentle fingers and without having to be awkwardly asked. His hands left embers everywhere they made contact with her skin, and Lisbeth had the greatest urge to turn and beg him to pretend the last half hour never happened.

"Thank you," she whispered instead, and the moment was lost.

"You are welcome," he replied.

When she was finished with her gloves and once more looked respectable, with all evidence of the sin and stupidity erased from her body, she walked to the door. But before she could open it, Raphael tugged her to face him, hands on her shoulders. That beautiful face was shuttered as he stared at her, but his eyes…those shards of gorgeous moonlight, they glimmered with a compassion and a tenderness she did not deserve.

"I'm sorry," she blurted out before he could speak.

The corner of his lip kicked up. "Don't be. I could never regret any of this or you," he said quietly. "I didn't tell you I'd fallen in love with you because I wanted you to say it back, Lisbeth. I meant it, but something that is true for me might not be true for you. Not yet." He shrugged. "Maybe not ever. But I didn't want you not to know how I felt or that tonight wasn't precious to me."

"And you think it wasn't for me?" she shot back, unreasonably hurt.

A muscle flexed in his jaw. "That's not what I said."

"So that's it?" She couldn't help asking, the earlier bitterness she'd felt still obviously present. "You'll just let me go?"

"Sometimes you have to set something free and let it choose to come back to you."

She swallowed hard. "And what if it doesn't?" *What if I don't?*

Lisbeth thought he wasn't going to answer her, but then he shoved his hands into the pockets of his trousers and gave her that lopsided grin of his with a playful wink. "A hundred dollars says it will."

Entirely confused, she stared at him for a full five seconds before speaking. "Are you actually making a wager right now?"

"I have excellent odds."

She couldn't help her puff of disbelief when he lifted his brows in amused challenge, as if they hadn't been discussing her complete lack of a functioning heart a moment ago. "You are truly impossible," she muttered as he escorted her to the elevator, though said unfeeling heart felt quite inexplicably warm.

"I believe, Countess, the word you are looking for is 'impressive.'"

Twenty-one

The thunderous banging against his door woke him out of a deep slumber. Raphael groaned and rubbed his eyes blearily, the thumps echoing dreadfully in time with the hammering inside his head. He threw an arm over his eyes and winced. He'd gotten completely foxed after he'd escorted Lisbeth back to the Duke of Thornbury's residence; sometimes a man could only find clemency at the bottom of a tumbler. Though a tumbler—or ten—of the worst ale in Manhattan probably hadn't been the best idea.

Nor had wanting to drown his sorrows. He had meant everything that he'd said to Lisbeth the night before, but articulating the right words and doing the *right* thing didn't always equate to how one felt inside. Sometimes, it fucking hurt. To say he'd been shattered by her reaction was an understatement. Not that he expected her to return the sentiment, but he hadn't expected her to turn tail and run.

He *knew* she had feelings for him; they had been in her eyes, in the way her body had welcomed his, and layered in between her words. From what he'd learned about Lisbeth, she wasn't the type to share any intimacy without some fundamental level of trust…and affection. It might not be love, but she *did* care.

So *why* had she run? She wasn't a coward.

Harsh voices punctuated the knocks and his thoughts, the former growing more forceful in intensity and volume, until Raphael was forced to get up. Those voices weren't in his head! He threw his legs over the side of the bed and fought against the instant wave of unsteadiness. *Bloody hell.* He hadn't gotten this sotted in a long time.

Cursing a blue streak under his breath, he stalked to the door. "Whoever this is better have a bloody good reason—" He broke off at the sight of the New York Metropolitan Police along with the customs house agents he recognized from the *Vauquelin,* including their mustached leader, Mr. Carr. His gaze narrowed at the smug, victorious expression on the man's face.

"Captain Saint?" he said. "You are under arrest for the crime of smuggling and avoidance of paying customs duties."

"Duc de Viel, actually." Raphael kept his expression blank, despite his delayed confusion, thanks to the slowness of his brain. "On the basis of what evidence?"

"Several undeclared crates of liquor and cigars were found in your cabin hold," he said. "If you come quietly and don't make a scene, that will be best for you."

"Best for me or best for you?"

Carr's brows rose. "Everyone, *Your Grace.*" The English version of his title was spat with no small amount of insolence.

"There was no such cargo onboard that ship," Raphael countered, unwilling to leave until the matter had been explained to his satisfaction. He showed none of the inner turmoil he was feeling, however. There had been no crates on the *Vauquelin* other than the gowns and accessories for Thorin's mistress. "You must be mistaken or have received wrong information."

"We received a tip and searched your ship." Carr consulted a small notebook. "The *Vauquelin,* no?"

Raphael tamped down his rage that his ship had been boarded without permission, but the New York customs house had unchecked power from the American Treasury when it came to catching smugglers, which he *was* guilty of, but not this time. "Who gave you this supposed tip?"

Some of the policemen shifted with discomfort as if they understood that the accusation was being made against a peer. It was no small thing, especially with unfounded proof. "It was anonymous, but that does not matter since the contraband was found." His face tightened with a sneer. "Now, will you accompany us, Captain Saint, or will we have to put you in irons?"

Reason warred with pride. Going with them of his own accord was a much better option than being dragged out of the hotel like a felon. Regardless of the inconsequential weight of his title, it was still his father's title and Raphael would not besmirch it further. "Very well," he said. "But you will allow me to get dressed and leave in a manner befitting my station."

"Now see here—" Carr began, but was cut off by one of the policemen, a captain by the look of his insignia.

"There's no harm in letting the duke get dressed. We

can't afford to have the *New York Times* writing more articles about the state of the metropolitan police. There are no windows that he can escape from at this height, and we have men stationed outside on all corners." He glanced at Raphael. "You're not going to try to escape, are you, Your Grace?"

"Of course not," he replied. Not right then anyway. It wasn't practical to climb out a four-story window and break a limb, or worse, fall to his death.

"I must insist on a man inside," Carr sputtered.

The police captain frowned. "He is a duke, not a common criminal. I will not allow my department to shoulder the burden of your incompetence."

"He is a smugg—"

"I hope you have irrefutable proof before waving that kind of slander around, Mr. Carr," Raphael interrupted in a cool voice. "Goods can easily be planted by anyone, especially since I was not aboard my ship, but have been here as can be verified by the hotel staff." He paused and pointed to the two other agents, one male and one female behind him. "Besides, those two checked my ship when we arrived and there were no such crates onboard, were there?"

The other two looked uncomfortable, their eyes shifting away in obvious guilt, but they did not speak, leaving the response up to their superior. "They were obviously missed," Carr said. He was clearly on the hunt for a scapegoat.

"Missed or planted?" Raphael replied.

"We know who you are, de Viel, and about your ties to the man most wanted by the American Treasury department."

With an inscrutable look at Carr, Raphael shut the door in the man's face.

Fuck, fuck, fuck!

He'd known that staying so close to Dubois would be a risk, but to be tied to the man as an accomplice wasn't something he'd predicted. He rarely shipped contraband for resale on the two ships he'd kept in the Caribbean for the purposes of tracking Dubois. Instead he'd looted the vessels of other criminals that would have been seized by the very unethical agents outside his door. The fact that Carr was willing to look the other way on his supposed *proof* and arrest him to make a name for himself confirmed as much.

A promotion in the ranks of the customs house meant even more moiety benefits.

Raphael took his time getting ready, performing his morning ablutions in the adjacent bathing room of the apartments. He got dressed slowly and took perverse pleasure in making the odious man wait for as long as he could. When he finally emerged from the apartments, only Mr. Carr and the police captain stood there, both wearing identical expressions as if they'd been arguing the entire time. They descended to the entrance hall in silence.

It was early enough in the morning for the hall not to be inordinately busy, though it was bustling with shopkeepers and people using the facilities of the various offices. Raphael paid them no mind as he made his way outside to the waiting conveyance. He was accompanied by the dour Carr, but pointedly ignored the man.

"You think you're better than me, don't you?" the agent asked.

Raphael lifted a glacial gaze to the other man. "No, but I don't accuse men of crimes without factual evidence."

"You're a criminal," he hissed. "Everyone knows about Charles Dubois's protégé, the mysterious Captain Saint."

"I think you must have me confused with someone else." Raphael waved a gloved hand with an idle flick. "Saint is a common name. And sorry to disappoint but I am not in league with anyone called Dubois."

Carr's eyes narrowed. "Perhaps a little time in a cell will loosen your tongue."

Raphael remained silent. He did not want to give the man any ammunition to use against him. This had become a personal vendetta now…the potential loss of any commendation from his superiors. Any arrests made in conjunction with the notorious Charles Dubois would be lauded by the Treasury.

When they arrived at the customs house on Wall Street, he ignored the looks sent his way by Carr's colleagues and was ushered into a holding room on the first floor of the building. A small barred window at eye level showed the street outside.

Compared to the jail cell in Tobago, it was a veritable palace. Raphael sat and blew out an aggravated breath. It had to have been Dubois who'd sent in the *anonymous* tip. But until actual charges were brought against him and he was advised of a trial, he could only wait.

Wait and plot a way to escape.

"Damn it!" Lisbeth gritted through her teeth, reading the missive that had arrived from her contact at the customs house. Alarm filled her with each hastily scribbled word she read.

Bronwyn looked up from her plate at the breakfast table with surprise at the muffled oath. "What is it?"

Lisbeth crumpled and flung the note into the nearby grate, getting rid of the evidence quickly. She would not make the same mistake of leaving incriminating documents around, no matter where she was. It was safe at Valentine's private residence, but small repeated mistakes became bad habits and she had grown careless before. The papers Davy had found in Tobago still irritated her. That seemed like a lifetime ago, but she had to imagine by now that the boy had discarded or forgotten them. He could not read, so they would not have been of any use to him.

In hindsight, she should have gone back to meet Davy and taken the papers off him then, or at least convinced him that she'd found them somewhere. The boy would have believed her. She could be quite convincing, and he'd been infatuated. Then she would not have had to run in the dead of night or crossed paths with Saint, and everything would have been on track for her to complete her mission.

But you would not have met him…

"Lisbeth?" Bronwyn asked again.

She startled. "My apologies, my mind is spinning. De Viel was arrested for conspiracy against the American Treasury."

Bronwyn blinked. "The Treasury? Why?" She half stood out of her seat. "Wait, do you mean conspiracy for *smuggling*?" Her eyes widened comically. "You said you bought a ship and Narina also said your name is Bess… Goodness, Lisbeth are you on a mission?"

Thankfully they were alone in the breakfasting room. Narina was outside playing in the garden, and Valentine was in his study. "You know I cannot talk about it, Bronwyn," she said in a hushed voice.

"I know," she whispered. "I miss it sometimes. The excitement and the illicit thrill of danger." Bronwyn had never been an official agent of the British Crown, but she had ferried some dangerous documents across the Atlantic, and for a brief stint, had been known as a cunning spy called the Kestrel. It was how she and Valentine had met—she'd been his quarry. In more ways than one.

Lisbeth huffed and glanced circumspectly at the woman. "Bronwyn, might I ask you an odd question?"

"Of course."

She eased out a sharp-edged breath. "When you and Val were together, how did you know…he was the one for you?"

Blue eyes lit with sly intrigue. "Are you talking about de Viel?"

"Never mind," Lisbeth muttered, ears heating. "No. Yes." Her mortified gaze fell to the floor as her face grew even hotter. She inhaled and shook her head, fighting for courage. Despite her embarrassment, it was only Bronwyn, and she might as well throw the entire lot in to get some answers. "How did you know that it was love?"

"Oh…*oh*." Bronwyn took a hasty sip of her tea. "I suppose it was the way he put me first." She gave a wry laugh. "I guess I did run roughshod over him, but I was always his priority, even when I wasn't because of his strict sense of duty."

Duty…the very thing that bound Lisbeth in chains.

Bronwyn cleared her throat, a hint of color rising on her cheeks. "I thought you preferred women?" She bit her lip. "I'm sorry if that was tactless."

"No, you weren't. I like people," Lisbeth explained, taking care to express herself as thoughtfully as she could. "Once I know them and…come to care for them, I might find myself wanting to deepen the intimacy when I didn't before. Whatever their sex may be. Estelle made me laugh and live life to the fullest, and we were happy together until our paths diverged."

"I've never heard of that before," Bronwyn said, though there was no judgment in her face, only interest.

"It's me," Lisbeth said simply. "And I've long since learned to make no apologies for who I am and who I want."

"So you shouldn't." Bronwyn nodded and then arched a brow. "Does that mean you've come to desire de Viel?"

"Desire isn't the problem." Lisbeth coughed, heat swamping her as visions of their last interlude flooded her mind. "He says he's in love."

Bronwyn made a soft exclamation of wonder. "And how do you feel about that?"

"I don't know. It scared me, I suppose. What if it *isn't* love? What if it's infatuation and his interest will wane?"

Refilling her tea, Bronwyn blew on the hot liquid, her face thoughtful. "Infatuation infers strong feelings of attraction and fixation to someone you might not know well. Love is a deeper experience. Do you believe he doesn't actually know you well enough for it to be something genuine? *Is* it lust at first sight?"

"It wasn't that way for me, and he has always respected my needs and comfort. Certainly, he's a beautiful man, but as I told you, it's not purely about the physical. I suppose I liked him slowly at first and then all at once."

"What do you like best about him?"

She considered the question honestly. "He's clever and considerate, even when he's being a buffoon. He makes me laugh, though sometimes I want to lock him in the cargo hold. He respects who I am and never makes me feel like I'm less than. In a way, he's *seen* me more clearly than anyone ever has." Lisbeth paused, so many things coming to her that she could hardly choose between them. "He's so kind with Narina, too."

A soft smile lit Bronwyn's face. "Sounds like a good man."

He is…and I am too stubborn to do anything about it.

"You know what I do," she said, lowering her voice to

a whisper. Bronwyn was family because of Valentine, and she was one of only a few who could understand Lisbeth's dilemma. "The truth is he's part of the group I was tasked to infiltrate, and while he isn't my actual target, now he's in custody because of me."

"Is he...a criminal?" Bronwyn asked.

Lisbeth exhaled and ran her palms over her face in frustration. "It's complicated. He's involved, but it's not the same as the others. His moral compass is sound, but his actions might be construed as less so."

The expression on Bronwyn's face was one of understanding. "You know, Lisbeth, you've been in this game a lot longer than I have, but I can tell you one thing I have learned—the definitions of right and wrong are not always black and white." She breathed out. "You'll do the right thing. You always do."

Lisbeth was certain that what Bronwyn had meant by the right thing did not necessarily mean blowing a hole in a government building and liberating a prisoner in the middle of the night. But she had tried the diplomatic way and that had not worked. Jenks was nowhere to be found to support her position, though he would hardly approve of her claim that Saint was an innocent bystander, and Carr steadfastly refused to relinquish the only real link he had to Dubois...and the key to making a name for himself.

As head of the customs house and empowered by

Treasury Secretary Hugh McCulloch to control seizures, penalties, forfeitures, and goods in transit, Carr held all the cards. And Lisbeth hadn't wanted to blow her cover to pull rank on Carr. Doing that at this juncture would lose her all the inroads she'd gained with no result. And she did not have time to use her station to contact her handlers in the British Home Office working with the American Treasury Department to authorize Raphael's release.

The only power she had as the Countess of Waterstone was to insist that de Viel was a peer and should not be treated like a common thief. But all of that was to no avail. Her pleas and subsequent threats of action by the British Crown had fallen on deaf ears. She had one last chance, and that was to blow Raphael out, and get back to Exuma. Only then would she be able to lure Dubois into the trap she'd concocted with Jenks. She only hoped it wasn't too late.

That would explain why she had in her possession the same explosive that had landed her on this path in the first place—nitroglycerin. Remembering the size of the explosions in Tobago, she'd used less this time. She only needed to blow a hole small enough at street level for a person to pass through. Hearing voices, she ducked into the shadows, but no one came close to where she hid. What she was doing was incredibly risky, not to mention highly illegal. If she were caught, explaining her motives would be an uphill battle.

Don't get caught, then…

Easier said than done. Stealthily, she inched along the wall and set in place the small vial of nitroglycerin that she'd managed to get from one of her old contacts for an arm and a leg. She then moved to the window and peered inside. Through the bars, as her eyes adjusted, she could barely make out the long form on the cot. Her connection inside the customs house had told her where Saint was being held. There was a slim chance that he could have been moved, but it wasn't likely.

Lisbeth tapped on the glass and then froze, her heart slamming against her ribs. The sound was unnaturally loud to her ears. The lump on the bed did not move. She tapped harder and winced, and the shape sat up. She knew he couldn't see her well in the darkness, and she was dressed head to toe in black.

"Pirate," she said, hoping he could hear her through the thick pane.

The shadow moved closer. "Viking?"

She could have cried at the faint rasp of his voice, and determination filled her. "Stand back, I'm going to get you out of here. Turn the cot on its side and get behind it."

"How?" he asked.

"Earning a spot on the Treasury Department Most Wanted list by blowing up their building. Now go."

She counted to thirty in her head and then lit the fuse, running as fast as she could to the nearby alleyway. The explosion rocked the ground, the smell pungent and acrid as debris flew. People were screaming and alarms were sounding, but she rushed back to the hole she'd made and gaped. *Holy hell.* Maybe even less nitroglycerin next time.

"Raphael?" There was no reply for a horrific moment

and then he emerged with blankets over his nose and mouth to keep out the dust clouds. Lisbeth's relief was instant, but she had no time to celebrate. The Metropolitan Police would be there quickly. "I have horses to get us to the seaport. The *Syren* is waiting."

Keeping to the shadows, they ignored the people rushing toward the scene of the explosion and made their way quickly to where she'd left the horses. A coach would have provided more coverage, but horses were quicker and more nimble for the short distance. They rode fast and hard down the road, cutting through smaller side streets. Lisbeth had sent word to Estelle to have the ship ready for sailing. She huffed a laugh at the irony—running for her life toward the *Syren* in the dead of night seemed to be the story of her life.

Abandoning the horses once they got to seaport, she patted them on their rumps. They would find their way back to the mews she'd borrowed them from. The *Syren*'s steam engines were running, and she could just see Estelle's face at the wheel. Smalls stood near the gangplank, his rugged face a sight for sore eyes. She gasped for breath, wheezing as she and Raphael sprinted onboard and Smalls pulled back the footbridge.

"Welcome back, Bess," Smalls said, gathering her into a bear hug. "The ship hasn't been the same without you."

"Missed you, too," she replied with a grin and then ran up to the quarterdeck. "Estelle, take her out."

Estelle nodded and gave her the once-over, eyebrows rising. "You look like you've been having a jolly good time, Cap'n."

Lisbeth laughed and enfolded her quartermaster in a tight hug. "If you mean nearly drowning in a hurricane, being marooned on a smuggler's island, and blowing a man out of prison, then yes. Time of my bloody life."

"I meant taking a sailor for a ride," she quipped. "You've that look about you."

"What look?"

Involuntarily, Lisbeth glanced over her shoulder at Raphael, who had taken up a position in the crow's nest on the foremast, spyglass to his eye, and was giving directions to the boatswains below. She never had to ask him to do anything. It was as though he knew exactly where she needed him to be.

Estelle's low laughter made her blush. "*That* look."

"You're wrong as usual. Now, if you're done blathering, kindly get us out the fuck out of here."

"Aye, Cap'n! Good to have you back."

Twenty-two

Dubois stared incredulously at them, the rage in his eyes palpable. Three times now he'd been thwarted in his efforts to either murder or incarcerate Raphael, and his frustration was showing. The older man smiled but it was barely lips pulling over his teeth. "It gladdens my heart to see you well and alive. I'd heard, to my great horror, Nephew, that you had been taken in by the New York customs house. How on earth did you manage to leave unscathed?"

"Apparently, I am a French duke," Raphael drawled and snorted as if it was the most hilarious revelation, watching as the man's lips thinned with resentment and no small amount of displeasure. "Americans adore the nobility."

It was almost comical how incensed Dubois was… and how much he coveted such an illustrious title for himself. Raphael had no doubt he intended to claim to the emperor that he was the rightful duke when Raphael was no longer in a position to keep the title—either because of death or imprisonment or declaration of lunacy, just as his father had been committed and then died in the Salpêtrière Hospital.

Murdered in the hospital on his own brother's orders.

Raphael was certain he would do the same to him.

Dubois had been foiled in his plans to get rid of his brother, thinking the title would come to him. But noble titles did not work like that. They passed down to heirs apparent unless there were none, and then they went to the next living male relative. Raphael was now an obstacle.

A disgusted frown drew Dubois's brows together. "And upon your release, no one followed you here?"

"You know me better than that, *Uncle*." He grinned drunkenly for the benefit of the men sitting in the hall and took a huge draught of his rum, being sure to let enough spill down his chest in the process. "You taught me well. I did learn from the best, after all."

He'd learned how to be a silent snake in the grass… how to wait until one's target was close enough to strike. How to bide his time and be patient.

Dubois's answering smile was thin, though something calculated flashed in his piercing stare. "And the *Syren*? How did you come to be on that? Isn't that a chit's ship? The lady captain? Bonnie Bess?"

"It was in port in New York."

"So industrious, aren't you. Did you get rid of the captain? Where is this notorious she-beast? I heard she's so foul you can't even look upon her face."

He and Lisbeth had agreed on the journey to stay as tight-lipped as possible about their escape. Upon entry to Exuma, the *Syren* had flown the flags in the requisite order and been granted permission to dock. While the rest of the crew had joined him on land, Lisbeth had stayed behind on the ship, though she'd been furious. But

Raphael could not predict what his uncle would do once he realized he had been deceived by the infamous Bonnie Bess. He'd shoot first and ask questions later and be well within his rights to do so.

"It's the safer choice," he'd told her. "Trust me."

She'd glared daggers at him in the privacy of her cabin. "Trust *you*? I will not be left behind when my own goddamn ship brought us here, Saint!" she'd hissed with so much venom he'd recoiled. "I am the bloody captain!"

Raphael hadn't been proud of what he'd done next. He'd pretended to agree, at least enough to distract her with a kiss, and then he'd tied her to the bed. Admittedly, the sight of her with ropes around those slender wrists and ankles had sent so much lust tearing through him that he'd nearly collapsed from all the blood rushing to his cock.

"It won't be for long, Viking, I promise. Just trust me on this."

"You fucking bastard," she'd spat. "Untie me or I will gut you from nose to navel."

He'd winked, the flash of unfettered rage in her eyes making him even harder. "You are stunning when you're mad."

"Fuck you! Estelle! Smalls!" she had yelled right before he put a gag over her mouth, narrowly missing his fingers being bitten off.

"They've already gone. Be good for me."

The feral look in her eyes at that while she struggled futilely against her bonds had promised bloody retribution. He had no doubt she would come through on her vicious promises, but she'd be safe and that was all that mattered.

Whether he'd be safe from *her* was a different story...

Raphael opened his mouth to answer his uncle with some tale that he'd commandeered her crew and left her on some other island, and then shut it at the wave of chatter hitting the rafters. His eyes peered down through the tables dotting the floor of the main hall to find the source of the disturbance, and his stomach dropped as the object of his every obsession sauntered in. *Fuck.*

Raphael blinked. How she'd escaped his knots, he'd never know. He'd left Boisie, Gibbons, and Balzac, along with two more of his own men from Exuma behind to make sure that she was safe and remained in her cabin. But here she was, Bonnie Bess in the gorgeous flesh—trousers, corset, maroon gold-buttoned frock coat, scarlet lips, and armed to the fucking teeth.

The men in question he'd left to guard her limped in behind her in various degrees of injury. Boisie was bleeding, Gibbons was limping, and Balzac was clutching his crotch. He bit back a snort. Narina would have appreciated the irony of that, if she'd been here. Though they were all still alive... *He* was the only person she truly wanted to kill.

"I hear you've been looking for me, Prince," she said loudly enough for her beautiful voice to carry as she prowled forward. "Bonnie Bess at your service."

The men around the tables stared slack-jawed, reacting much the same as he'd done the first time he'd seen her. That Bonnie Bess was, in fact, stunning. Green eyes slammed into his from beneath the brim of her flashy sennit hat, and he flinched at the wrath that boiled there. That glare alone should have incinerated him where he stood, and then she smiled…a savage grin that promised violence. Hell, why did the thought of that make him so hot?

Dubois still had not said a word, his gaze quiet and contemplative, and it made every hair on Raphael's body stand on end. He should have been outraged, but he was calm. Too calm.

"Bonnie Bess," he drawled. "You stood me up in Tobago, if I recall. My boy Davy informed me that your ship left."

If Raphael did not know her so well, he wouldn't have seen the two fingers of her right hand twitch against her trousers. His gaze jumped to the thin lad who had served as both Dubois's and Delaney's runner and cabin boy for years. Raphael had never liked the little weasel who was the worst kind of snitcher.

"Alas, business called," Lisbeth trilled, sauntering closer, and Raphael's heart stuttered. Her guise as Bonnie Bess might fool someone from a ways away, but it wouldn't fool his uncle. "You know how that is for sailors like us. We're all opportunists at heart."

His gaze slid to Raphael for a beat. "Lucrative?"

"The only kind, Prince." She propped her hands to her hips. "I would like to make you an offer."

Dubois leaned forward in his seat, propping his hands

to the table, and waved as if he were Louis-Napoléon himself. "Speak."

Her mouth tightened at the derisive command, but she kept up the charade. "I recently sailed with a hefty amount of cargo to New York. A hundred thousand dollars' worth when I return to collect from my men trading inland there. It's yours, for a place here."

Raphael didn't need to look at his uncle to see that he was interested. A hundred thousand dollars was nothing to sneer at. "What's stopping me from killing you and taking your bounty? You're here uninvited."

"I invited her," Raphael said quickly, leaning back in his chair with the most lascivious smile he could muster. He licked his lips. "You see what she looks like. I can't wait to discover what's underneath all those layers."

His uncle laughed. "If you tried to fuck her, she'd cut your cock off and feed it to you." The men roared with laughter, slamming their tankards down on the tables. "But you don't call the shots here, Nephew, I do."

Out of the corner of his eye, Raphael saw Smalls, Estelle, and the rest of her crew gathering to defend their captain, if it came to that. This was going to turn into a bloodbath if he didn't intervene.

"I'll tell you what, Uncle," he said with a loud burp and a jester's grin. "How about a friendly boxing match. For the spoils and the prize. First to five points and winner takes all."

Dubois sneered. "Why duel when I can just take? And you're drunk. It would be like snatching a rattle from a baby."

"Maybe." Raphael stood with a rowdy laugh and spread his hands. "But the men deserve a show, don't they?" At that, the cheering began anew. His uncle might think he held all the power, but he did not. Most of the men here were common-born and a raucous mob, and nothing pleased the mob more than the promise of entertainment and blood. As much as he pretended to rule his fake kingdom, Dubois kept himself apart from the men…and it rankled. Raphael would play to that discontent if he had to.

"I am not a prize!" Lisbeth bit out from where she stood.

"Ah, girl, but you are," Dubois drawled. "You've wandered into the lion's den and now you must pay the levies." Two burly men stood, barricading her between them, but her face showed no sign of alarm. "Don't worry, Bess. I promise I'll take good care of you."

"Perhaps I'll take good care of you, Prince," she drawled back, matching his tone and wandering her fingertips down to the hilt of the cutlass that hung at her side. "If I'm not pleasured well, I'm rather fond of taking body parts as mementos of my lovers."

That earned her a round of boisterous whistles and more laughter. Tipping up his mug, Raphael swayed and glanced at his uncle, wondering if he'd refuse the bait but knowing he wouldn't when all the men were watching and heckling. "Tell you what, old man," he said, fully intending to goad him. "Even if I'm drunk, it's probably not a fair fight."

To the sound of boos, Dubois turned, greed and rage

lighting his stare. "If I win, I get the *Syren* and its captain, your ships and all cargo."

"Fine."

"And what do you want, boy?" his uncle asked.

Raphael bared his teeth at the insult, though he punctuated it with a loud belch. It was a battle for the throne and it would be dirty. "Exactly the same."

Lisbeth clenched the fingers of her left hand into her skirts, dread perforating the hot shroud of her anger. One, she was no man's prize. And two, she might want to gut Raphael herself and drag him behind the *Syren* for a prolonged spell, but this was not what she'd planned when she'd tracked him here. She'd been so spitting mad when the arrogant rotter had tied her up in her cabin and left her behind that she'd seen red.

In hindsight, perhaps she'd underestimated the brutality of this crowd.

They'd welcomed her as Raphael's woman, but as Bonnie Bess, they would view her as a greater threat. Especially Dubois. If he saw through her guise that she—and Raphael—had deceived him, there was no telling how things would go. And fucking *Davy*! What the hell was he doing there, next to Dubois of all people? He hadn't been here the last time; then again, there'd been more ships in the bay. The boy's gaze hadn't left her since she'd walked in, but she couldn't let herself be sidetracked.

She'd let this play out, and if things took a turn for the worse, well, the several vials of her favorite explosive she'd stashed around the dock would create an exit strategy, if needed. She wasn't too worried about the two complacent brutes at her side who did not even have weapons out. The rest of the men were clearing a space in the middle of the hall, and she watched as Raphael and his uncle faced off just inside of a makeshift ring. She didn't know much about bare-knuckle boxing, but there were no scorers. How would they tally the points?

They had removed their upper garments, clad only in loose pants and boots, and circled each other. She refused to notice anything about Raphael's honed body or the fact that his recently healed wound was on puckered display. The tension between them was practically solid. Raphael wore his usual lackadaisical grin, while his uncle looked like he was going to murder his own blood.

She narrowed her eyes. The older man was fit and had fought in a war. Raphael seemed to be well into his cups, if his tottering steps were any signal, but she had seen this dance before. That gray gaze was too clear. Catching her stare, the bastard looked at her and winked. With a scowl, she thrust her middle finger up in a lewd gesture as the cheering men around her shouted, wagered, and exchanged money. Smalls and her crew had sidled closer, but for now all attention was on the two men.

Raphael went in clumsily for the first punch, staggering wildly as though trying to orient himself. Dubois danced out of the way and landed a series of blows to his opponent's ribs that would have made a lesser man fall. In fact, Raphael did stumble and fall flat on his arse, but if Lisbeth hadn't been watching so closely, she would not have seen that his reaction had been a second delayed. More bets changed hands. It'd been on purpose, she was sure of it. What was he doing? Did he *intend* to lose?

"One point to me," Dubois crowed, and Lisbeth caught on to the scoring system. The opponent had to be knocked to the ground for a hit to be counted. Raphael stumbled to his knees, but before he could stand fully and get his bearings, Dubois was there to release a savage kick to his nephew's stomach. He let out a grunt and keeled over. "Two! Had enough, pup?"

"Foul play," she shouted, but no one listened.

Madge, who was standing in front of her, looked over his shoulder. "It's French street-fighting called savate. Punches and kicks are allowed. It's brutal."

This time, Raphael vaulted to his feet as if anticipating another blow, but Dubois was too busy swaggering. The two men came together again in a violent display of flying fists and vicious kicks meant to break bones.

Raphael was barely covering his torso even as his uncle leveled consistent blows right at his injury. She saw him wince right before a punch came at his jaw and he staggered straight back. Once more, a full second passed before he seemed to stumble and behave like the hit had been harder than it was. Lisbeth blinked at the odd timing.

Surely she was not imagining that? Raphael swayed and spat a mouthful of blood to the floor.

"Too easy, you worthless drunk," Dubois shouted, confident in his impending victory, beating on his bare chest like a caveman. Though he dressed like a dandy, he was built like a boxer. Thick and strong. His nephew, by contrast, was taller and leaner. And clearly more incapacitated than she'd thought. She caught Estelle's eye and subtly touched her finger to her ear.

In the hours before docking, Lisbeth had sketched out the layout of the smugglers' hidden sanctuary after Raphael had explained how to navigate the reefs to the bay. Not wanting to involve him in those particular plans so that any blame fell squarely on her, she had waited until he returned to his post before showing Estelle and Smalls where she planned to plant the explosives. One spot was an abandoned building and the other was one of the main docks. If things went bad, they were to light the fuses and prepare to sail.

Catching Estelle's nod, her gaze panned back to the fight, only to see that Raphael's attention was on her, a slight frown marring his face. Hell, had he seen the signal? The bloody man missed nothing even when he was in the middle of a fight that he was losing. He delved back into the fray as his uncle lurched toward him. It was imperceptible, but his fighting style transformed, his movements tight as he sidestepped the attack, one boot shunting out to launch a back heel into Dubois's belly.

The man had barely stood before Raphael had him flat again, this time with a combination jab to the torso and a spin kick to the back of the knees. He didn't fight dirty like his uncle and waited for the man to rush him again before finally shifting the score to three-two in his favor with an acrobatic handstand and a double-mule kick to the face that sent the older man to the ground.

"What are you playing at, boy?" Dubois screamed, the three successive points too fast to be believed.

Raphael shrugged and rolled his neck. "Drink's wearing off, Uncle. Guess I'm lucky."

A calculated slyness settled over Dubois's face. "Your father thought he was lucky, too." Lisbeth was close enough to hear the taunt and see Raphael stiffen, a wave of pain crossing his expression. Of course the man was guileful enough to try to get to Raphael that way. "Until he wasn't...and was accused of treason and then got sent to that hospital."

"You orchestrated that," Raphael snarled, fist snapping in rage at his uncle's face.

Dubois weaved out of the way and grinned because his strategy was working. "I was just doing my civic duty to the French crown."

"You fucking bastard!" Raphael thundered, and the pain in his voice made Lisbeth's stomach drop. "You betrayed your own blood. Did you have him beaten to death, too?"

Dubois spread his arms wide, taunting. "He was in the way."

"You fuck!" With a guttural bellow, Raphael rushed blindly at him, but Dubois had anticipated that well and dove out of the way before spinning to plant a kick right in Raphael's back.

He used the momentum to thrust the other man to his knees and then kicked him hard in the belly, right where Raphael had been stabbed. "Just like you're in the fucking way! Give up now and I'll let you leave with your dignity intact."

"As if you know a single thing about dignity," Raphael sneered at him from where he lay on the floor and then snapped sideways to twist his legs around and hook in between his uncle's, but the man leaped out of the way at the last moment. Lisbeth gritted her teeth. Rage and pain were making him clumsy and his movements more predictable, and that was what Dubois was counting on.

That and cheating.

Lisbeth saw the glint of steel in his hand much too late, right before Dubois darted in and slammed the tiny blade into his nephew's thigh and twisted. The knife disappeared into the crowd with a quick flick of his wrist. Raphael roared, but his black trousers hid any evidence of a wound. He hopped back, watching his uncle. "Can't win a fight fair, Dubois?"

The man eyed him with hostility. "You really shouldn't fight with old injuries. They can reopen so easily."

Lisbeth felt a wave of pure fury. That was a *new* injury. She hadn't realized she'd shouted it aloud until Dubois's dark gaze slid in her direction and his smile widened. "Not to mention the pretty little sea-snake you invited into our midst," he said. "How many secrets is she keeping from you? About who Bonnie Bess really is."

Never one to bend to a bully, Lisbeth laughed mockingly from the sidelines and pulled off her hat, letting her hair tumble down. "Can't get anything past you, can I?"

Some of the sailors she'd met before gaped in shock—trying to reconcile what they knew about the fearsome captain with the woman who'd drank with them at the bonfire. Madge's mouth gaped.

"Why don't you tell him who you are, *Lisbeth*," Dubois goaded.

Clenching his fists, Raphael glared. "I already know she's a countess."

When Dubois's smile grew fangs, Lisbeth frowned. "Ah, but did you know she's a British spy working with the American government?"

All the air was sucked out of the room.

Raphael's gaze swung to her and Dubois pounced, smashing into his nephew from the side and kicking his good leg out from under him. With a cry of pain as his wounded leg took all his weight, Raphael went down hard. "That's four," Dubois shouted. "You can't beat me, boy."

But Raphael wasn't looking at him; he was looking at *her*.

As livid as she'd felt toward him about the ropes, nothing compared to the expression of utter betrayal spreading across his face. "You're a spy?"

Her mouth opened but Dubois cackled before she

could answer. "Davy found letters to her from the Treasury. I've known all along that Bonnie Bess was an agent and intended to use that information for my own benefit." He shook his head. "But you see, it was only *today* that I connected who she truly was…an English countess. Tricky, tricky little serpent."

"Wait…"

"There's more," Dubois crooned with malicious pleasure. "Did you know that it was Bonnie Bess who blew up your ships in Tobago?"

Lisbeth's stomach sank in a pool of guilt as Raphael's eyes widened in realization. Bloody hell, she should have stayed on the ship. God, the *look* of devastation on his face. She blinked. She hadn't known they were his back then. "I didn't know they were yours."

A muscle flexed in his jaw. "And would it have made any difference? You lied to me."

She flinched at the uncharacteristic vitriol in his tone. "And you didn't?"

"No, I never lied to you. I was a sailing master in my earlier years. Dubois is my father's half brother. I am a French duke with no lands to his name." He exhaled hard. "Do you know how many families that cargo was meant to help?"

"I'm sorry."

Dubois's laugh was cruel. "My nephew and his misplaced philanthropy. Little did he know that I was tithing the very people he was helping. He was paying me, and he didn't even know it."

It took a second before his words sank in. Dubois's men had destroyed Narina's mother. They had been one of the poorer families who'd had to pay impossible protection taxes. She saw the moment Raphael understood the same, but it didn't make him look at her any differently. His uncle might be the villain, but she had just proven she might be worse.

Dubois took that tense moment to attack again, but Raphael defended himself as if he hadn't even been trying before. Even with his bleeding leg—a line of red was visible below the hem of the trousers and dripping down onto his boot—he moved like music. His fists flew, one smashing into Dubois's chin and sending the man sprawling to the floor.

With a snarl, Dubois turned to where Madge stood. "Shoot him and I'll give you half."

Out of the corner of her eye, Lisbeth saw the captain obligingly lift his pistol and she didn't think, she just reacted. A knife was yanked from her sheath and embedded in the man's hand before he could even aim. "You fucking bitch!" Dubois screamed. "Hold her down," he said to the two big men still crowding her.

But then pandemonium erupted as the first of the explosions went off.

Thank you, Estelle!

When the second detonated, everyone scattered. Lisbeth took advantage of men scurrying for cover, ducked out of reach, and ran through the melee. Just as she reached the door, her gaze connected with a blistering gray one. He stared at her for an interminable moment before his jaw tightened and he looked away. It was clear.

He never wanted to see her again.

Twenty-three

She had *lied* to him.

Everything they had shared for weeks had been underscored by a goddamn lie.

Lisbeth—Bonnie Bess—was a fucking spy.

All of the things he had missed came back to him. Her caginess. Her skill with weapons. Being able to speak so many languages. The ease of the masks she wore. The stop at the customs house in Cedar Key. Had she passed on information there? The silent exchanges with the Duke and Duchess of Thornbury. *They* had known her secret while she'd been so careful to keep him in the dark. Had the crew of the *Syren* known?

Raphael glanced over at her giant shadow, who fought to keep the tide of men from crushing her, but the look of astonishment on Smalls's face hadn't been fake. So maybe none of them had had any inkling. That knowledge mollified him slightly, not enough to erase the anger and the hurt, but enough to make them less raw. The fact that she'd deceived them didn't stop Smalls and the others from forming a tight circle around her to defend her. They were clearly more forgiving than he was.

"Saint!" a voice called. It was Boisie, frantically beckoning to him from the rear door. "This way! We got them!"

Got who? His uncle? Dubois had fled at the first sign of commotion. Raphael blinked and limped his way toward the back entrance of the hall. His thigh ached from the deep puncture wound he'd sustained during the fight. The dirty, underhanded act hadn't surprised him in the least. He pushed his way through the sea of men, worried about what had exploded and whether the building would be next.

Goddamn explosives. The ones that had reduced his ships to timber at the bottom of the sea in Tobago had been fast-burning and meticulously set along the hulls to cause maximum damage. He recalled the one in New York that had blown through a solid wall. These explosions had to have been her, too, up to her favorite kind of parlor tricks. What had she destroyed this time? More ships? Other buildings?

Thank God the *Vauquelin* was still in New York. He was certain that Thorin would be able to get it to leave or at least make sure she wasn't stripped, considering the ship was listed in his name for exactly these kinds of reasons. Plausible deniability. Carr and his men had been more focused on arresting Raphael on false charges to be concerned with papers of ownership. And whoever the anonymous tip had been from had only mentioned the name Captain Saint.

"Where are the others?" he demanded when he caught up to Boisie, whose nose was still trickling blood. "Did she do that?"

He pulled a shamefaced look. "No, I tripped over

Gibbons when he crashed into Balzac, who she did kick in the balls. She was spitting mad, too. Tied us up good at gunpoint."

Damn it, he should have taken or hidden her weapons. Raphael still wanted to know how she'd undone his knots. "How did you get loose?" he asked.

"Gibbons had a knife in his boot." Boisie rubbed at his nose and winced. "Cut us free."

Raphael followed him to where he ran on the side of the building. An old-looking barn was on fire as well as one of the docks on the far side of the island. Neither of which were high traffic areas. So she wasn't completely heartless. He nearly crashed into Boisie, who had come to a stop near the east end of the building. "What the—"

Lisbeth and Smalls stood at gunpoint between four of his men.

Something inside of him roared at seeing anyone pointing a loaded weapon at her, but then the reminder of her betrayal—of her *dishonesty*—was like a gush of cold water, freezing him in his tracks.

She'd kissed him. Let him inside her. Pretended to care.

He'd told her he'd fallen in love with her, when everything he'd been falling for had been a lie. Bonnie Bess did not exist and Lisbeth was a subset of dozens of people. Hell, how could he have been so stupid? She was an espionage agent working for the American Treasury. A good one, too, because he never would have suspected in a million years.

Christ, he felt like a hundred times a fool.

"Let them go," he said.

Boisie grunted. "Cap'n?"

"You heard me," he growled, unable to look at her though he could feel her surprise. He didn't want anything from her, not her gratitude, not her relief, nothing. "Release them."

Bitterness swirled through him at the faint scent of orange blossoms and honey as she and Smalls hurried past for one of the docks on the east end after throwing an unreadable look at him. He had to force himself not to acknowledge her. But at the bend of the building, she paused for an infinitesimal moment, those green eyes crashing into his, the storm in them reminding him of when they'd been together.

Tell me something true, Viking.

I don't want to say goodbye.

She had tried to tell him after they'd been intimate and he'd been too love-drunk to heed her words: *There are things you don't know about me.* Clearly, he should have listened, but he was of the opinion that everyone had secrets. Hers, however, were monumental.

Indefensible.

"I'm sorry," her beautiful mouth shaped, and then she was gone.

He hated the way his heart clenched as if trying to hold on to something impossible.

As hard as he tried, Raphael couldn't get his head around the ruse. She'd been Bonnie Bess for years, making a name for herself and working undercover to infiltrate the smuggling world for what? Or better yet, to get close to whom?

The realization was fast and cold: *Dubois*. No wonder she'd been so interested in him. His uncle was the only one—him and Madge—who had avoided the customs agents for years, the only ones they would send an undercover agent in for.

The understanding felt like another blade to the gut.

She *knew* of his plans for his uncle, and she had never said a word that he was her target. And he'd fallen for her lies like an overeager, bumbling, trusting fool. No wonder she couldn't reciprocate his feelings. She had kept so much of herself in reserve because she wasn't who she claimed to be. How could she even care for someone when she herself was a lie?

Bonnie Bess was fucking fiction. And so was everything they'd had.

The *Syren* had barely cut out of the bay into the Caribbean Sea, clear blue skies and open seas on the horizon, when the sound of a cannon split the air. Estelle shouted an oath. "Damn it! That nearly took our foremast!"

"Ship starboard!" Smalls yelled.

It was one of the vessels from the harbor, a sleek black frigate that was cutting through the water at a speed the *Syren* could not match at present, not with only one of her engines lit to navigate the dangers of the reef at half speed. Which meant she was easy pickings for the ship that had just sent a warning shot across her bow. Who the hell was that? She stiffened as the frigate slowed to match their speed. Did they intend to board the *Syren*? "Smalls, tell the gunners to get the cannons ready! This could be a dogfight."

"Bess, there's no way—"

She glared at him with a snarl. "Just do it! We're not going to lie down and take it!" Lisbeth grabbed the two pistols at her hips and cocked them, heading to the starboard side of the *Syren*.

"Ahoy!" a voice shouted. "Slow there!"

Lisbeth recoiled. That voice sounded much too familiar. The sight of Charles Dubois had her blood running hot with rage. She could shoot him in the head right now, but with the cannons of his vessel ready and trained upon her ship, what would be the outcome? He would be dead, but so would all her crew. He could have sunk her to the bottom of the sea, but hadn't. She gave the command to slow the steam engines. "What do you want?"

He grinned as his ship came abreast of hers. "You, love."

"I already told you, *Prince*." Recoiling at the endearment, she spat the last and trained the pistols on him, even though she knew she could not risk shooting him, not with the lives of everyone at risk. "I am no man's prize."

"You have a choice, Agent Medford, and two seconds to make it. You for the lives of your crew." Lisbeth's hands shook on her pistols; it would be so easy. "You're no fool and you'll have their blood on your hands. People who trusted you. Who were loyal to you. Only you lied to them, too, didn't you, Bess?" he asked, and she flinched, the guilt hitting her hard.

She gritted her teeth and glanced over her shoulder, eyes casting over the silent crew observing the standoff, each and every face dear to her, and then to Estelle who shook her head with fire in her eyes. They would fight to the death for her if she ordered it…but she could never ask that of them. Dubois was her mess. He obviously didn't want her dead, so she had time to work out a plan. She exhaled and lowered her guns. "Very well, but I want your word that the *Syren* sails free."

"Bess, no!" That shout was from her quartermaster.

"It will be all right, Estelle," she said as grappling hooks came over the side of the railing and a footbridge was lowered between the two ships. She released her belt before climbing on it. Her weapons would be taken, but at least she still had knives in her boot and her corset.

"Cap'n!" Smalls roared, running across the deck as if to stop her, only to catch a bullet in the leg and crash to the boards.

"No!" Lisbeth yelled, whirling to the shooter.

"The next will be to his head or to anyone who does something stupid," Dubois said, and Lisbeth's eyes flicked to the men behind him lined up with loaded weapons.

Face hard, she turned toward the *Syren*. "Do as he says. That's an order."

The two burly sailors who had stood next to her in the hall on Exuma crowded her as soon as her feet dropped to the deck of Dubois's ship, only now they had learned their lesson and grabbed her roughly by each arm. The *Syren* was released and the other ship gathered speed.

"Take her to the brig and don't let her out of your sight," Dubois commanded. "And fire!"

On his command, four cannons fired in rapid succession, the sound of exploding cannon-fire and steel being torn cleaved through the air. No! What had he done? Lisbeth tried to turn, but the men holding her were too strong. "Let me go, you bastards! You fucking gave your bloody word, Dubois!"

His grin was oily. "I did. Now she's free."

Her enraged shouts were muffled as she was dragged down and thrown into a smelly, dank room with a single cot in one corner. The door slammed behind her. She should have known he was a blasted liar. Damn him to hell! A frustrated tear ran down her cheek. They had to have survived! The crew of the *Syren* was hardy. They'd lived through much worse, and the frigate's steel hull had been reinforced to withstand a lot.

As the seconds and minutes passed, she resisted the urge to pound on the door as that would not do any good but bruise her hands. The porthole was much too small to squeeze through and the door was locked. She spent the time pacing instead with her knife in hand. And when her legs started to ache, she sat on the cot and slept. After what seemed like an entire day had passed, the door unlatched.

Startling awake and propelling herself at her jailer, she got in a few vicious slashes before a fist came at her face and the knife was bashed from her fingers. She saw stars and then felt the muzzle of a cold pistol under her chin.

"She cut my ear clean off!" a man screamed.

The second man holding the gun snorted, but she couldn't see his face. "She's Bonnie Bess, what did you think would happen?" She recognized the voice, though…Madge.

"I'm going to kill her!"

Lisbeth was roughly jostled forward, out of the way of the man she'd carved up. "She's the captain's," Madge said. "Now best go get that stitched up before you can't hear a word, you fucking twit."

She was manhandled down a narrow corridor and up more stairs before being hauled into a well-appointed, showy cabin that could only be the captain's quarters. Lisbeth remembered thinking that Dubois looked like a dandy and that was evident in his decor. The man she wanted to tear apart with her bare hands stood smugly behind a large desk in a smaller antechamber. Her fingers balled into fists.

"I don't want to have Madge shoot you in the leg, Agent Medford," he said, sipping from a glass filled with amber liquid. "But I am also not required to trade you back to your people in any specific condition besides being alive. So which will it be?"

She blinked. He was planning to ransom her off? The Treasury would not care, not when Charles Dubois, the Prince of Smugglers, was so close to being finally apprehended. And after the stunt she'd pulled in New York, she had to believe she was persona non grata. She remained silent and expressionless, her face automatically falling into the blank mask that gave nothing away.

"Check her for weapons, Madge," he said holding up a pistol, and the man did a thorough search, finding the thin blade tucked into the boning of her corset. "Clever, clever," Dubois said with a vulgar smirk. "But no need for that. Now that that's done, please sit." He pointed to a cup along with some bread, cheese, and salted meat on the desk. "Eat. Drink."

Lisbeth wanted to do neither, but she had to keep up her strength if she was going to survive this, and if he wanted to poison her, he would have done so already. Gritting her teeth at the discovery of her last blade, she did both, gulping down the water and soothing her parched throat. Her stomach growled as she chewed the bread. He stared at her the entire time, but she ignored him, concentrating on fueling her body.

He waved his pistol and dismissed the other man. "You can go, Madge."

Madge scowled, doing as ordered, though he didn't seem to like it.

"Bonnie Bess," Dubois said eventually. "I can see what my nephew sees in you." She couldn't help the raw bolt of pain that punched through her at the thought of Raphael, but throttled her reaction. "And here I thought you were no better than a warm Miss Laycock and not the tool of my exoneration."

She looked up, not reacting to the vile slur. "You're wrong if you think I'm worth anything to them."

"No, you're right about that, but the idea of a"—he spread his hands wide—"very public incident involving a peeress of England and a covert agreement between two governments is not a palatable one."

"Incident?" she asked.

"A detailed account of the execution of a very beautiful countess sent to the *New York Times* and the unwillingness of two callous governments to prevent such a tragedy from happening when they were the ones who sent you into danger."

She scoffed, nearly spitting out a mouthful of food. "That will never work."

"Public opinion is a powerful tool." He tipped his glass toward her. "Besides, I have proof. Good thing I kept those incriminating documents of yours, and I have already negotiated the terms of my pardon. One beautiful, wanted criminal for a free me."

Her chest squeezed. *Wanted criminal.* Was that what she had become?

"Now, since I am a gentleman, you may stay here or return to the brig. I wouldn't want your handlers to say I hadn't taken care of you." He canted his head as he rose. "The room has been cleared of all weapons, so don't go getting any ideas in that pretty little head of yours."

She scowled at him, but he only laughed and left. Lisbeth didn't wait to canvass the space. As Dubois had said, there was nothing but a lamp on the mantel, and the door was firmly locked. But she wasn't completely helpless. She reached up to the topknot of her half-braided coiffure and pulled her hairpins loose. Unlike the door to the brig that was built with a latch, this one was a keyhole and she could pick her way out of here.

The sealed porthole showed that it was still daylight, late afternoon from the sun's position and the just visible coastline. If she'd slept overnight and they were traveling at a shade under twenty knots—working on the assumption that this frigate was as fast as hers at top speed—they would be nearing the coastline of New Jersey in a few hours. The Cape May Point lighthouse might still be manned by Jenks's people. It was her only chance.

Waiting for the sun to go down was torture, but when the shadows lengthened and darkened the inside of the cabin, it was time to work. Lisbeth knelt and worked the hairpins into the lock until it clicked open. She cracked the door, but the captain's cabin was empty except for the light of a single lamp. Excellent—that meant she did not have to find a lamp. If worse came to worst, she could always burn down the ship and take her chances in the sea. Not wanting to be without a weapon, she grabbed a poker near the unlit grate.

Lisbeth blew out the lamp and tiptoed along the edge of the room to the outer open door. A thickset man she didn't recognize sat on a stool on one side, cleaning a knife. He was big, but she was fast. Putting the lamp down quietly, she inhaled and slipped out, slamming the blunted end of the poker into his temple before he could even react. When he slumped forward, she let out the breath she'd held.

Retrieving the lamp, she moved stealthily along the corridor to the upper deck. Lisbeth heard voices, but made sure to hide when any of them grew too loud or too close. The cool night sea air hit her as she climbed on deck, staying out of sight. The ship was dark enough to avoid notice. She made her way to the rear to a small overhang on the port side where the jutting ledge would be perfect. She would not have long before she was discovered so she lit the lamp and flashed the sequence, moving the flickering light behind and in front of the ledge.

There was no answering light from the coastline. Had she miscalculated the distance? Or were Jenks's men gone? No doubt he would have heard what she'd done by now. He would not put his career at risk by aiding and abetting. Panicked, she repeated the sequence and waited to no avail. No one was there…no one was coming.

"Found her, Cap'n!" someone shouted.

Lisbeth shoved the lamp at the man and ran, ducking around a corner and hiding behind a stack of crates. Her breath sawed in and out of her lungs. There was no telling what Dubois would do if she was caught. *Alive* could mean different things. Maybe it was time to swim for it, but right as she judged the distance to the railing and prepared to take her chances with the black, ominous ocean, calcium floodlights lit up the darkness in all directions. She hunched back down.

"Halt and surrender! By the order of Captain Webster of the *Mahoning* and the *Naugatuck*, you are surrounded!"

Those two gunboats belonged to the United States

Treasury Department! Lisbeth squinted against the brightness as shots rang out and men screamed, scrambling to escape. Her eyes caught on one figure at the bow of the closest cutter ship, his gaze scanning the deck of her frigate, and she blinked, unable to believe who she was seeing. *Smalls.*

It couldn't be him, her eyes had to be deceiving her, but when Estelle came up to stand behind him, Lisbeth almost sobbed. What were the odds? But when the last person she expected appeared, a tall, dark-haired man with a face that never failed to make her heart quicken, she knew it wasn't luck at all. She'd hurt him…and he'd still come.

Twenty-four

The flamboyant capture and arrest of the man most wanted by the Treasury Department was plastered all over the newssheets. Charles Dubois, the Prince of Smugglers, and Mr. Madge, scourge of the seas, were finally in custody.

As was Raphael Saint...who had turned himself in to the Revenue Marine and cooperated with them in exchange for Lisbeth's rescue. She couldn't get her mind around that, but Raphael had always surprised her. Even when he hated her, he was still there for her. Smalls and Estelle had explained that his frigate had reached them just in time, though the *Syren* could not be saved. The damage to her hull had been too great and she'd taken on too much water. Lisbeth had felt a twinge of sorrow at that, but she'd much prefer the ship be lost than any of her crew. The *Syren* could be replaced. Estelle, Smalls, and the others could not.

But now she had worse problems to deal with, including the release of a man who did not belong behind bars, no matter his past infractions with the law. There were countless historical instances of informants working with different organizations in return for reduced sentences or immunity from prosecution. She had used many of them in previous jobs.

"What do you mean, there's nothing you can do?" she demanded.

Customs agent Carr stared at her, and she wanted to punch him in his smug, supercilious face. "He's a criminal."

"He was working to help *me*," she said, gritting her teeth. "As part of *my* undercover investigation that I have been performing for years. And if we want to pull rank here, Mr. Carr, that can easily be arranged. This is *my* operation."

"Sitting on your arse playing pirate doesn't really count, does it?"

Oh no, he didn't! She nearly flew across the table in a wild rage, but was restrained at the last second by the light touch of the Duke of Thornbury on her right. "Don't give him the satisfaction," he whispered urgently. "He aims to discredit you. Easily done when you're female."

Fuming, Lisbeth stared at the man seated opposite them, ready to pull her hair out. Carr and his superiors were all congratulating themselves on a job well done, when she had been the one to put her safety and her life on the line for two goddamn years. Carr had it out for her, however. He was convinced she'd been behind Raphael's daring escape, and the press had dragged the customs agent over the coals for it.

Thankfully, he had no proof that she had broken Raphael out of the building, though he suspected it. He'd been particularly peeved that his only connection to Dubois had been rescued from prison, and while he had no evidence of Lisbeth's involvement, her disappearance on the *Syren* at the exact same time only increased his suspicions. Now he had a bone to pick and he was out to dishonor her by any means necessary, even sullying her character.

"At least I wasn't here sitting on *my* arse, waiting for someone else to do my work for me," she shot back calmly, though her insides roiled. "But isn't that how you prefer to do things? Have other people take the risk and you reap the reward?" She let out a breath and eyed the men in turn, including Carr's bosses. "If anyone deserves credit here besides me, it's Harry Jenks."

Sadly, she had learned that Jenks had been stabbed by unknown assailants at Cedar Key during a random raid. He was expected to live, but his injuries had been substantial. That had explained his absence in the last few weeks. As it was, support for her claims was abysmally thin. Jenks could have corroborated her story and their plan to bring Dubois and Madge in, which, for all intents and purposes, had succeeded. But he still hadn't awakened from the attack. Jenks deserved the credit, not this rat-faced, boot-licking rantallion!

Narina would be proud of her creative name-calling, though Lisbeth would hardly be the one to explain to a twelve-year-old that that particular designation referred to a man whose scrotum was longer than his cock.

Thornbury cleared his throat, drumming his fingers on the table, his face inscrutable as he directed his address to the most important man from the American government at the table—Secretary of the Treasury Hugh McCulloch.

"Mr. McCulloch, I understand that tempers are high with your...man"—Lisbeth nearly chuckled at the disdain conveyed in that single word, as if Carr's name was unworthy of even being in a duke's mouth—"but I do speak for the British Home Office, and the Crown is stating that Her Majesty does not want this to become a public hullabaloo." Lisbeth hid her smile. She'd mentioned Dubois's threat on his ship, and now the duke was employing the same strategy, using the power of the press to slam his point home. "Lady Waterstone is our agent and she has the full support of England."

"*Lady*? That's a fabrication," Carr sputtered, and Lisbeth sent him a cool stare.

"Oh, did someone neglect to mention that I am actually a peeress, Mr. Carr," she said in clipped tones. "And a decorated servant of Her Majesty, the Queen. Or did you forget to do your due diligence after escorting me to the Duke of Thornbury's residence a fortnight ago? I suggest next time you do a little research before slinging stones."

He opened his mouth to argue, but McCulloch cut him off with a sharp glare. "You say that Saint was working with you all along?"

Lisbeth nodded. "He was instrumental in my ability to infiltrate their group. Without him, I would not have gained access, and Dubois as well as Madge would still be at large." She lifted her chin. "After the hurricane, I nearly died. He rescued me, putting his own life at risk. That alone can tell you of the caliber of the man we're dealing with."

"It's obvious you're completely besotted!" Carr spat

out, earning himself another glare and a clenching of teeth, but he ignored the obvious warning. Lisbeth's heart hitched at his accusation, but her usual inner disavowals were astonishingly absent. All she felt was a warm kind of acceptance spreading inside. "The man is Dubois's nephew, for God's sake."

Lisbeth leaned forward. "Estranged nephew. Dubois arranged for the murder of Saint's father, his own brother. It was the sole reason Saint agreed to help me."

"I won't stand for these gross misrepresentations!" Carr growled at her. "You're desperate to save your lover. A fool could see it." Lisbeth bristled at the personal attack on her character, but before she could reply, the duke rose at her side.

"Carr." The single, growled word from Thornbury was enough to hush the man. "I would caution you to tread very carefully while insulting a British peeress in my presence."

"I won't stand for this," the customs agent repeated stubbornly.

"Then you can leave," McCulloch interjected. "I dislike threats, Mr. Carr."

"Sir!" he spluttered. "I am the lead customs agent on—"

The secretary scowled. "And I do not care. Please be silent or I suggest you remove yourself from this discussion before I have you forcibly removed."

At that, Carr very wisely shut his mouth, though his gaze pelted daggers at her.

McCulloch's stare shifted to the duke. "You can corroborate Lady Waterstone's account." It wasn't a question.

Thornbury gave a curt nod. “I can. The countess informed me of her plans and the Duc de Viel’s involvement when she visited New York a short time ago. I am willing to put that in writing for your report and pass my sworn testimony to the Home Office.”

A tense silence ensued, as the secretary weighed his options.

“Then I believe we’re done here,” McCulloch said, and Carr stormed off. “Your Grace, thank you. Lady Waterstone, well done. I will personally make sure that Mr. Jenks is commended for his contribution.” He gestured to the armed officer standing near the door. “Smith, give the order to have the Duc de Viel released at once.”

“Thank you, sir,” Lisbeth said, relief like an incoming tide.

Paris, France
One month later

Raphael frowned at the gold-engraved invitation that had been hand delivered to his residence a week ago for him to attend a ball at the Tuileries Palace. A handwritten note signed by the emperor himself and Empress Eugénie saying that no refusal would be tolerated since the ball was being held in his honor had been attached. Certainly out of character for the very serious emperor, but not something that could be ignored without consequence.

And so, here he was en route to the palace.

The thought of attending a ball, even one supposedly in his honor, left him cold…particularly since the last one had been with *her*. Raphael hadn't seen Lisbeth in the aftermath of his uncle's arrest, but he'd certainly read the *New York Times* and the scintillating account of the American Treasury's collaboration with the British Home Office to bring two criminals to justice. In a way, vengeance had been served, even though it had not been directly by his hand.

After his release, he'd visited Dubois in prison.

"I'll be out of here in no time," his uncle had said with a conceited grin. "Powerful people owe me favors."

Raphael had stared at him, the loathing in his heart nearly suffocating. "No one is coming to save you, Uncle."

"Delaney will come. He owes me."

"Delaney has been well compensated to look the other way," Raphael had told him with a dispassionate look. "The reign of Charles Dubois is finished. I've bought up all your debt, so I own you, down to the very clothes on your back."

"*How?*" his uncle sputtered. "I owed millions of dollars."

Raphael had cocked his head. "Did you think the loss of my father and all our lands would make me die of grief and wither away in poverty? It only strengthened my resolve to destroy you. So I built my fortune up with legitimate businesses. I stayed close with two small ships to convince you that I was under your thumb." He'd stared at the man who had ruined his life. "Goodbye, Uncle. May you face the same mercy my father did."

“We’re blood, Nephew!” Dubois had growled.

“Our ties vanished the day you murdered your brother in cold blood.”

“I’ll confess the truth to the emperor,” Dubois had shouted in desperation. “I’ll say it was my fault, that I made everything up. That he was innocent of any treason. I’ll confess to paying the orderlies at the hospital to hasten his death. Whatever you want, just don’t let me die here.”

Despite his internal agony, Raphael had smiled then, the first real smile since he’d entered that prison, as the grim-faced Duke of Thornbury emerged from the shadows. “I caught every word and am ready to testify to all that I heard here.”

Raphael said, in the coldest voice he could muster, “Thank you for your confession, Uncle. Rot in hell.”

And the two gentlemen left without turning back, to part when they reached the street with a nod of silent accord. Thornbury would ensure that Charles Dubois would face the highest sentencing for his crimes, and his uncle’s admission would finally clear Raphael’s family name. He turned his steps toward his home. It was a good day’s work. The thought of Lisbeth Medford, however, was unendurable.

Even now, wherever she was, she had his heart.

Not that he wanted it back. The useless organ could rot, too.

Back on Exuma, even though his brain had told him to cut his losses where she was concerned, when he’d heard the cannon blast echoing over the bay and a glance through a spyglass had confirmed that one of the two ships was the *Syren*, he hadn't hesitated to scramble for the closest vessel, which happened to be Boisie's.

He'd been too late to save Lisbeth, but just in time to rescue the crew of the sinking *Syren*. The decision to sail to Nassau, where Boisie's men had reported seeing one of the Treasury gunboats, had been spur of the moment... but all he could think about was saving her by any means necessary, even trading himself in return.

Yes, she'd lied to him.

Yes, she had let him believe she was someone else.

Yes, he'd fallen completely and irrevocably in love with her.

But he couldn't abandon her, not even then.

The past few weeks since he'd returned from the United States had been a blur as he got his affairs in order. Thorin had returned the *Vauquelin* in one piece, and Raphael had sailed it back to Paris. Thanks to the Duke of Thornbury's intervention, the French emperor received a confidential report from the British Crown detailing Dubois's confession regarding the former Duc de Viel, and all of his lands had been reinstated and his name cleared.

It had felt like an enormous weight had finally been lifted from Raphael's shoulders.

"Rest in peace, Papa," he'd whispered.

But since then, despite being busy tending to the needs of his estate just outside Paris and his tenants, unrest churned in his blood. He missed the sea. He missed sailing into the wind. He missed *her*.

She's gone, fool. Listen to your own bloody words and let her go.

Eventually, he'd move on. Perhaps even tonight at this wretched ball he'd meet someone and start to forget her. Even *that* thought ached.

As the carriage came to a stop in front of the gorgeous palace with its bold rooflines and prominent central dome, he exhaled and descended. He'd been to the palace with his father once when the former duc had been in favor with the emperor, but it had only been an informal gathering in the Salon d'Apollon before an intimate dinner in the Salon Louis XIV.

All magnificently and lavishly appointed, of course, but nothing compared to the grand Salle de Maréchaux where the ball was being held this evening. Gilded columns tied with beautiful floral arrangements, lush blue-and-gold-trimmed drapes embroidered with fleurs de lis, and sparkling gaslit sconces brightening the space. Enormous paintings dotted the walls and huge chandeliers hung from the domed ceilings, opulence evident in every single inch. The ballroom was filled with people dressed in their finery.

The emperor and empress sat at one end on red velvet thrones on a raised dais in front of four enormous floor-to-ceiling Greco-Roman statues.

"Monsieur de Viel," the majordomo intoned.

"Ah, our guest of honor has finally arrived," the emperor said, his blue eyes narrowed, when Raphael approached the dais and bowed low. Louis-Napoléon was not a handsome man, quite short and stocky, but his intelligence could not be underestimated. Empress Eugénie by contrast was a beautiful woman, born of Spanish nobility, and it was rumored that she influenced the emperor in many areas, especially the French intervention in Mexico that his father had been punished for. No wonder she'd been so willing to listen to Dubois's lies and turn the emperor's ear.

"You honor me, Majesté."

The emperor favored him with a benevolent smile, and the festivities continued. In truth, Raphael was bored and tired. Even after the emperor and empress took their leave, he remained out of obligation. Aware of the attention on him, he forced himself to dance with several young ladies, none of whom took his fancy. All he could envision were icy blond curls, full lips, and ocean-green eyes that could slay or seduce on a whim. He was just about to take a quiet turn on the terrace for some air when a feathery sensation ghosted over his senses.

A change in the air, in barometric pressure…that first hint of an incoming storm.

"La Comtesse de Waterstone," the majordomo announced.

He went still. No, it couldn't be. But unable to help himself, he turned in slow motion and there she was… the woman who had wrecked him so completely, standing like a goddess at the top of the stairs. His mouth dried. She was the only thing he could see: a shimmering silhouette in ivory and gold. God help him but her beauty outshone the sun. He stood stationary, unable to move a muscle as she descended the staircase and moved through the crowd, straight to him.

The scent of orange blossoms and honey invaded his senses.

"You're here," he rasped.

Lisbeth's smile was small, her heart in her eyes. She hid nothing from him, her face open and bright. "Someone very special to me told me once that sometimes you have to set something free and let it choose to come back to you." Her voice broke slightly on the last. "And there's nowhere else I'd rather be, if you can ever forgive me."

Raphael stared at her, emotion clogging his throat. "Tell me something true, Viking."

Green eyes brimmed. "I love you, Pirate."

The words were easier to say than Lisbeth imagined. Perhaps because she'd practiced them a hundred times before she'd arrived in Paris. A dozen times on the way to the palace. She had almost not gone inside, terrified of Raphael's reception and whether he would reject her out of hand. But if there was one thing she wasn't, it was a coward, and so here she was…with nothing but her heart on offer.

Lisbeth had seen him standing by the terrace doors as soon as she'd been announced, her gaze drawn to him in an instant, and her breath had all but disappeared in her lungs. So tall and dangerously attractive in his raven-black formal attire and snowy-white cravat, with his hair loosely tumbling over his shoulders the way she liked. Up close, those thickly lashed, cautious eyes held hers, his soft lips making her pulse trip.

"Why are you staring at me?" she whispered and bit her lip.

"You love me," he repeated.

"Yes, more than anything."

His pupils flared. "I can't believe you came. That you're real."

"I'm real." She hissed out a strangled breath, aware of all the curious eyes scrutinizing them, and the truths that she could barely rein in now that he was in front of her. "Raphael, I'm so sorry for not being fully honest with you. I'm sorry I didn't tell you that my target was your uncle, but I'd been working so long toward that objective that it was all I could see."

"I understand," he said, and then took her hand to lead her outside onto the terrace where they could have more privacy. His thoughtfulness, even in this very moment, undid her. "It was your job, Lisbeth. I cannot fault you for keeping those secrets, and once I got past feeling hurt, I accepted that you were bound by the oaths you'd taken."

She hated that she'd hurt him.

"You're the only person I've ever wanted to confess everything to. Suddenly, I didn't want to be Bonnie Bess anymore. For the first time in my life, my mission didn't matter. I wanted to be me, just Lisbeth. The *real* Lisbeth who I hadn't seen in decades. You made her feel like she could be happy, like she could be enough."

"You'll always be enough," he said softly.

"Raphael, you have to believe that it was me all along. I wasn't pretending when I was with you, and everything we shared came from somewhere true." She swallowed, the words rushing out like a waterfall. "You made me feel seen again, because somewhere along the way, I let all those other roles overtake who I was. It became safer to hide...to exist in those other personas."

"I know, chérie."

Lisbeth almost wept at the sweet endearment, having wondered for weeks if she'd ever hear it again. She sent him an earnest look, knowing he'd already forgiven her, but she owed him the full explanation. He deserved that and more. "Let me get it all out, please. I don't want to keep anything from you." She took a breath. "The truth is you were right about me. I was an island. I let nothing and no one in because that way I could never be hurt. I could never become *too* attached. Goodbye was always easy at the end of a job because no one was ever allowed to matter enough." She reached for his hands, lifting them and stepping toward him at the same time so their palms were cradled between their bodies. It was intimate in the extreme in the midst of the French emperor's ball, but she did not care. She would lay her soul bare before him in the middle of Paris if she had to. "I don't want to be like that anymore. I want to try to be different. With you."

"Even if it hurts?" he asked softly.

"As long as you're at my side, I'll take the good and the bad and everything in between."

Raphael stared down at her, his beloved face so beautiful that she could barely breathe. His fingers released hers to lift and stroke her cheek with the gentlest caress. Everything—the ballroom, the other guests, the entire world—fell away in that moment when he gathered her in his arms. They weren't dancing and yet it felt like they were, out there in the moonlight.

"So if I said I wanted to marry you, would you run?"

Her smile was tremulous. "Only to you."

"And what if I said I wanted to live a life on the sea?"

"You'd get no complaint from me." She paused, her heart so full that her rib cage felt a dozen sizes too small. Was this what happiness felt like? Like a person could float from sheer joy alone. "I'm thinking of retiring from my line of work, so I'll have a lot of time on my hands. I could be your sailing master, your deckhand, or your cabin girl."

That sultry, lopsided smirk of his appeared, taking all her good sense with it. "Cabin girl? I'm intrigued. Tell me more. What would her duties be?"

"To make her darling captain marvelously, stupidly, sublimely happy."

"I like the sound of that." Her gentle pirate ran a thumb over her bottom lip, eyes so bright they looked like stars in the night sky. "Then marry me, chérie. Marry me and make me the happiest man in the world."

Lisbeth pushed herself to her toes and kissed him. "I thought you'd never ask."

"Was that a yes?" he asked, pulling away.

Lisbeth grinned, taking a page from Narina's book. "Does a pirate shit in the sea?"

"That's still not a yes, you wicked tease. Don't make me toss you over my shoulder and cart you out of here to teach you some manners." He lowered his voice, his lips brushing her ear. "You're being a very bad girl and you know what happens to bad girls. They don't get to come."

That silky threat arrowed straight between her thighs, and from the dark look in those molten eyes, he'd meant it to. "What did you tell me when we first met?" she teased. "Don't threaten me with a good time. Yes, Pirate, the answer is yes. To everything."

Epilogue

"Get a move on, you piss-covered barnacles, before I scupper your stinking guts, savvy?"

The shrill voice of their daughter filtered down into the captain's quarters of the *Vauquelin,* and Lisbeth let out a snort of laughter. "At least Nari isn't using the really bad adult words," Raphael said. "She's gotten much better at that. So a victory for us?"

His beautiful wife agreed. Getting a fourteen-year-old who hadn't quite grown out of her pirate obsession not to curse was quite an achievement. "It's a good thing the crew adores her," she said.

"She has Smalls eating out of her hand," he scoffed. "And let's not even think about the clothes Estelle gets from Paris for her. She's spoiled rotten."

"Good thing we adore her, too."

He laughed. "That is true."

After their marriage a year and a half ago, they had officially adopted Narina. They had both asked her after their wedding whether she'd want to be their daughter, and she had screamed with delight. The Duke of Thornbury had some influence with a court in Massachusetts in the United States, which had been the first state to legalize modern adoption, to support their petition.

According to the law, the judge was the one who determined whether they were fit and proper with sufficient capability to raise the child, and luckily he had ruled in their favor. Since Narina was an only child with no next of kin, it had been a simple matter.

As a family, they spent their time mostly between Paris and Tobago, but also tried to make sure that Narina was able to visit her homeland of Barbados and learn about her birth mother's culture. They wanted her to know exactly where she came from and what made her so wonderfully unique. The differences between the various Caribbean islands were broad, and while there were many similarities, each island had its own unique history.

Narina was fascinated by Raphael's mixed origins, too, and the varied range of peoples on his island as well as his own French, Indian, and indigenous ancestry. While it was obvious in Paris that she was different, mostly because of her beautiful brown complexion, Raphael and Lisbeth both made every effort to let her know that she was perfect as she was and that she was loved. The rest of the crew on the *Vauquelin* worshipped the foulmouthed, cheeky little rascal.

Most of their shipping and trade investments were thriving under the watchful eye of Thorin, who had taken over the management of the company since Raphael spent most of his time taking care of his tenants on his estate in France. The twenty-two-year-old had come a long way since New York.

A large portion of their profits, however, was always

invested back into the island economy. Lisbeth, for her part, had completely left the service of the British Home Office and hadn't looked back. Raphael had once asked if she missed it, and her reply had been an emphatic no. Their life was adventure enough for her.

It was true. In the last two years, Lisbeth had blossomed. She was still highly skilled in weaponry and combat, and clever to a fault, but she laughed more and had a sly sense of humor that rivaled Narina's. Making his duchesse smile was one of Raphael's greatest pleasures.

He glanced down at where she was putting the finishing knots on the rope securing his right ankle to the bedpost. Thank God the bedroom door was securely locked. If anyone saw their captain in such a compromised position, he would lose all credibility.

Not that he was complaining.

Sultry green eyes lifted to his, and his cock leaped to attention at the purposeful look in his wife's eyes. With her lush figure and rounded belly, she was the most perfect thing he'd ever seen. Pregnancy had made her a thousand times more desirable, and her libido hadn't waned in the least. These playful little diversions of hers would be the death of him.

She crawled up the bed between his lewdly spread legs. "Did you think I'd forgotten, Monsieur le Duc?"

He groaned as she licked his bare inner thigh. "That was two *years* ago, Madame la Duchesse."

"Turnabout is fair play, wouldn't you say?" Lisbeth dragged her nails lightly over his ballocks, making him gasp her name, before grasping him firmly in hand and closing her mouth over the swollen head of him. "Now I have you right where I want you. Perhaps I should give you some lessons in knots."

When her teeth tugged on the piercing, his eyes nearly rolled back in his head. "How did you escape that day?" he gritted through clenched teeth. "You've never told me."

She propped herself up onto her elbows over his thighs as if his cock wasn't waving impudently in her face. "We learned it in training with the Home Office. If you're being restrained, you spread your fingers wide apart to make your muscles tense and your wrists as thick as possible. That allowed for a slight give in your knots. Then, I used a loose nail in the floorboards to release some of the tension by pushing and twisting. Child's play, really."

"Child's *play*?" He scowled, yanking at the expertly tied ropes on his wrists that had zero give. "I'll have you know I am excellent at knots. It's not my fault that my wife is a master of escape."

"A master of other things, too." She licked him from root to tip, eliciting a moan from the depths of his chest with a deep suck to the back of her throat before prowling up his body. His wife kissed him and then straddled his hips like the queen she was. "When it's my turn, you can practice on me. I shall be sure to judge your skills fairly."

When she took him inside her with a practiced downward thrust of her hips, Raphael felt like he'd discovered paradise. Then she began to move in earnest, levering her beautiful body up and down. He longed to wrap his arms around her, but in the position he was in, he was utterly helpless and at her mercy. All he could do was shallowly shunt his hips upward with a very limited range of motion.

"Bloody hell, Lisbeth, please, faster."

She stroked her breasts, knowing how much he enjoyed watching her, and rolled her hips at a torturously slow pace. "I love when you beg."

"You're a cruel woman." That was entirely the wrong thing to say as she leaned forward, the sudden slant of her pelvis providing enough friction to make him groan, and that was before she took his nipple ring between her lips and tugged on it. Hard. "Fuck!"

"Am I cruel now?" she taunted, raking her nails over his tattoo.

His muscles strained against the restraints. "Release me."

The growl of dominance made her shiver, but she reached up and tugged on one side of the rope, the knots instantly loosening. He yanked it free and then untied the second. He sat up and dislodged her gently to claim her mouth with his, swallowing her protests and gorging himself on her sweetness. His left hand grabbed her nape and the other her right hip as he pulled her back onto him.

"Raphael," she moaned as he drove deeply into her welcoming body. She was close, he could feel her starting to ripple around him. When she started to unravel, her sensitivity heightened from the pregnancy, he plucked at her nipples and she went right over the edge with a stifled scream. Staring at his wife lost to bliss was the most erotic sight of his life. Raphael couldn't help it as his orgasm crested on the heels of hers and he emptied himself inside of her.

"Je t'aime," he whispered.

His beautiful wife smiled. "Not as much as I love you."

Later on, after another round of passionate lovemaking when her virile husband took her on all fours and brought her to pleasure several more times, Lisbeth was as limp as a noodle and could no longer ignore the loud growls of her stomach. Her pregnant body was twice as sensitive during intercourse, but it was also twice as hungry. Forcing themselves out of bed, they washed and dressed, and wandered upstairs in search of breakfast.

The deck of the *Vauquelin* was empty, though a deserted table with remnants of crusty bread and jam and bowls of fresh oranges and mangoes greeted them.

"Where is everyone?" Lisbeth asked, peeling a mango and biting into the stringy yellow insides with a happy sigh. Though most of the sailors who manned the ship were ashore, they kept a skeleton crew onboard where they were anchored off the coast.

A trilling giggle reached them from the rear of the ship and Lisbeth headed to the stern. The sight of her daughter doing somersaults off of Smalls's enormous shoulders into the turquoise waters had her grinning and cheering.

"Look, Mama!" Narina squealed and did it again. Every time she heard the girl call her *Mama*, her heart swelled.

Lisbeth hadn't asked for her to call her that, but a few months ago, when Narina had shyly asked if she could, Lisbeth had been stunned. More so when Narina had told her that she knew she already had a mother and that she was simply lucky enough to have two.

"Well done, Nari!"

"Are you and Papa going to come in?" Narina asked, lying on her back and kicking her legs. "It's so warm."

Though the ship was anchored in a dark-blue stretch of water, indicating how deep it was, the area that Narina, Smalls, and the rest of the crew frolicked in was a light aquamarine with a bottom of soft coral white sand. It was quite an anomaly—like a sandbar in the middle of the ocean, partially surrounded by the reef. Raphael had told her that it was the only one of its kind in the whole world.

"Let me feed your baby brother or sister and then yes, I would love to join you."

Narina had been thrilled at the idea of being an older sibling and she was very excited for the baby to arrive. It would not be too long now, only two short months. After finishing her mango and some fresh pineapple, Lisbeth went down to their cabin to change into her bathing costume, narrowly evading her husband's wandering hands as she undressed.

"You are insatiable," she scolded him, darting out of reach.

He grinned. "That's because I have an irresistible wife. Don't blame me because I'm weak." Raphael glanced down as her hand drifted over her distended abdomen, barely fitting the loose tunic over it. "How are you feeling?"

"Good. She's been active lately. A lot of kicks."

His eyebrows shot up. "Do you think it's a girl?"

"No, I don't know." She eyed him. "Do you have a preference?"

Raphael gathered her in his arms and kissed her. "As long as they look like you, I have no strong feelings on the matter."

"I want them to look like you," she said. "And inherit this warm brown skin. I'm so pale I shine in the dark."

He grinned wider and popped a kiss on her nose. "Good thing I like to be able to find you in the middle of the night so I can have my wicked way with you."

"Your wicked way is what got us into this predicament in the first place," she quipped. "Come on, let's go swim before Narina launches a search party." She glanced at him. "Where's your shirt? You cannot possibly go swimming in your smallclothes."

Her husband smirked wickedly at her. "When I was a lad swimming in these waters, I didn't swim in *any* clothes."

Her cheeks flamed at the thought of her god of a husband swimming in the altogether. It was almost enough to convince her to stay onboard, but she did not want to disappoint their daughter. Raphael took her hand and led her back upstairs, and then down the ladder to the water. They swam together toward the sandbar that was only accessible by boat and joined the rest of their family.

"You're right, Nari. This is heavenly."

As she floated on her back, staring up at the clear blue skies, Lisbeth could only feel gratitude for the life she'd chosen. She hadn't lied to Raphael when he'd asked if she missed her life of being a spy. It had been exciting, but she was a different person now.

She had a husband who loved her, a smart, beautiful daughter, a circle of true friends, and a life she loved. When Raphael's arms wrapped around her and scooped her up to him, his salty lips finding hers to whistles and hoots from their avid audience, she grinned.

"Do you know, Viking," Raphael said softly, his lips caressing her lobe. "There's a legend that says if you kiss someone you love in this pool, your love will last a lifetime."

"Is that true?" she asked.

He nodded. "That's what the locals say."

Lisbeth wrapped her arms around him. Staring into his beautiful eyes, she smiled, perfectly at peace, perfectly happy. "Then we better not tempt Fate. Kiss me like you mean it, Pirate, and let's shoot for forever."

His lips met hers. "Forever it is, mon coeur."

BONNIE BESS SEA SHANTY

There once was a lass called Bonnie Bess.
She sailed the seas with all the rest,
but no one could catch her as she flew.
She'll laugh and shout and run you through.
Bold Bonnie Bess!

She's as pretty as a picture like they say,
but cold in the heart so best you pray
you won't come upon her on the sea,
or she'll gut you good and make you pee.
Bold Bonnie Bess!

Oh, hai, she'll make you fly,
then cut your ears and make you cry.
She'll take your gold, then peel your bones.
Bold Bonnie Bess!

Author's Note

This inclusive historical romance series has been such a pleasure to write, not only because I get to share my own multiracial culture and my beloved Caribbean, but also because I get to pen stories that encompass marginalized communities in historical eras. Everyone deserves to be seen, and I am so glad that I can celebrate joy and love in my stories for all. Thank you for being on this journey with me and helping me lift up happy ever after *for all*.

Whenever I am writing a historical romance novel, I love including real pieces of history, whether those are actual people, real places, or historical events. Research is one of my favorite things to do, and I make every effort to craft my fictional story with authentic historical elements.

For the main plot of *Any Duke in a Storm* (this title is a twist on a nautical phrase—any port in a storm—which I love) I focused on smuggling because, while piracy was rare in the Caribbean after the eighteenth century, smuggling spiked in the late 1860s in response to enormous taxes levied on imported goods to shore up the American economy. Duties were issued on silk, lace, velvet, liquor, cigars, tobacco, sugar, art, and diamonds, as well as any other imported merchandise or goods. Tariffs became the main source of income for the Treasury, which gave the customs houses immense power, not only to collect these taxes but also to enforce the law. The anti-smuggling act of 1866 allowed the Treasury to appoint agents to search any vessel, use any necessary force required, and sentence smugglers to fines and prison time. Smugglers from Bermuda, the Bahamas, Cuba, and other Caribbean islands entered the United States via Florida, New York, and other East Coast ports, and then the contraband was distributed internally and sold on illegal markets.

I chose Exuma as the hidden Smugglers Cove as these islands were a massive hub for piracy back in the 1600s, and some famous pirates like Captain Kidd were rumored to have buried treasure in Elizabeth Harbor. Others like Anne Bonny, Mary Read, and Blackbeard also landed on Exuma. During the American Civil War, the Bahamas was a convenient base for blockade running because of its proximity to the United States. Later on, Nassau and some of the smaller islands became busy ports for smuggling because of the many accessible shipping routes to the United States. Several of the ships mentioned in the story, including the *Syren* and the *Frolic,* were based on actual blockade runners during the 1860s. Some gunboats like the *Naugatuck* and the *Mahoning* were reassigned as revenue cutters by the American Treasury's Revenue Marine (later named Revenue Cutter Service in 1894) to catch smugglers. The *Mahoning* was renamed the *Levi Woodbury* in 1898.

My heroine's smuggling alias, Bonnie Bess, was based on a couple of different women. Chang I Sao was a Cantonese corsair who led her fleet of ships pillaging across Southeast Asia in the early nineteenth century. She had a very rigid code of conduct on her ships. Sexual assault was punished by beheading, and traitors had their ears cut off. She was known as one of the most successful pirates in history. The female pirate Anne Bonny was also inspiration for my heroine. She was said to have a "fierce and courageous temper," could fight with both pistol and cutlass, and could drink other pirates under the table.

After the war, "fashionable smuggling" became rife following the huge demand for French fashion. Dressmakers and milliners smuggled in fabrics and accessories to avoid paying high taxes on them and thereby decrease their manufacturing costs. The tax on silk imports alone was almost fifty percent higher than what it had been before the war. The fit of clothing was used to identify a possible smuggler. If the clothes looked bulky, were worn incorrectly, were ill-fitting or tight, or even if the travelers were nervous or overdressed, they were stopped and searched.

The first female inspectors were hired in 1861 (called inspectresses by 1867) for modesty with female passengers, who took to smuggling goods under their gowns. A French newspaper in the 1860s included an article where a woman tried to hide twelve partridges in her crinoline. Another woman was rumored to have fifteen pounds of tobacco and cigars, tea, gin, as well as tens of thousands of dollars in jewels stitched into her crinoline! In my story, when my heroine is interrogated by the customs agents in New York about the Parisian gowns on her ship, she is asked to prove they are hers since pretending to be an aristocrat was a known ruse.

My villain, Charles Dubois, was inspired by one of the most infamous smugglers and biggest perpetrators of customs fraud in U.S. history, Charles L. Lawrence. He was known as the Prince of Smugglers. He was captured in 1875 and was rumored to have smuggled nearly a hundred shipments of velvet, silk, and French lace through New York worth over three million dollars (about eighty-one million dollars in today's currency), avoiding over a million dollars in duties (about twenty-seven million dollars in today's currency). Between 1872 and 1873, the U.S. Customs House estimated that close to forty thousand travelers smuggled over a hundred and thirty million dollars of goods into the United States (worth over three billion dollars today).

One of the interesting historical figures mentioned in my story is J. Harry Jenks, who was an actual secret treasury agent. During his career, Jenks seized many ships suspected of alleged smuggling, but his main objective in 1868 was to capture the mysterious Mr. Madge, also a real historical person, who was suspected of smuggling large quantities of cigars. In my story Mr. Madge was arrested, but in real life, Jenks was never able to capture the elusive smuggler and his pursuit ended after he was stabbed in Cedar Key. Another historical figure who appears in my story is Treasury Secretary Hugh McCulloch, who on June 30, 1868, issued the memo stating that customs agents had the authority to conduct investigations, assess fines and forfeitures, and perform seizures.

In terms of setting, I was born in Trinidad and Tobago, so my hero, Raphael Saint, has some of his roots in Tobago. Most of the Caribbean is widely mixed in terms of race. My first cousins are a similar racial mix to Saint—Indian, French Creole, Black, and Amerindian (the indigenous peoples who lived in Trinidad and Tobago thousands of years before the arrival of Columbus). French settlers, some white and some free mixed people of African and European descent, settled in Tobago in 1783. While Trinidad became a British colony in 1802, Tobago wasn't annexed until 1889. Slavery was abolished in 1834 in the British Caribbean, and many of the freed people and indentured laborers went on to build lives for themselves as independent small farmers, artisans, and businessmen.

The Buccoo Reef and the Nylon Pool in Tobago, mentioned in the story, are both famous. The reef was visited by Jacques Cousteau and named one of the top three spectacular sights in the world. It became a marine park in 1973. The Nylon Pool, a gorgeous white coral-sand sandbar near the reef with clear, warm aquamarine waters, was named by Princess Margaret in 1962, who likened it to the transparency of nylon. It is one of Trinidad and Tobago's most popular attractions. The myth in the Epilogue about kissing in the Nylon Pool is a real one! I have snorkeled and swum in both the Buccoo Reef and the Nylon Pool, and they are incredible.

A note on the naughty stuff! Since my hero is pierced and inked, I did a lot of research on the history of tattoos and piercings. In different cultures around the world, both of these things have existed for centuries, if not thousands of years. In the latter half of the nineteenth century, pierced nipples and "bosom rings" became popular in Paris. The apadravya piercing is one of the oldest forms of genital piercing and goes as far back as the second century BC in India. It also appears in the Kama Sutra in 700 AD. Genital piercings in the Victorian era were mostly used by the nobility to demonstrate wealth and/or monogamy.

Tattoos have been around throughout human history as far back as 4000 BC. While the process was much longer, much more painful, and more prone to infection and disease than it is today, many people including aristocrats in the Victorian era had them. Early methods including using a wooden block to print the design on the skin and then using a single needle to puncture the ink into the skin. Sometimes, multiple needles were tied together, from three or four to dozens pushed through the end of a metal or wooden pole. Other tools included a tattooing comb with needles (ranging from five to fifty) made from bone or shells and fixed to a wooden handle that was then tapped with another stick into the skin. Some designs took years to complete because of their size. Queen Victoria's son Prince Albert got a cross in 1862, and his two sons got dragon tattoos in 1888 on a trip to Japan. In my own life, I have had a few piercings and I also have five tattoos.

A quick note on my heroine's title as a divorcée. Divorce was rare in the nineteenth century, but it did happen, especially after the Matrimonial Causes Act of 1857. While my heroine's marriage of convenience was undertaken to serve her job as a spy, the "life peerage" that was awarded to the Earl of Waterstone for service to the Crown was very real. As far as keeping her title after her divorce, I was inspired by a real case in the late 1800s. Lady Cowley and her husband, the third Earl Cowley, were divorced in the late nineteenth century, and he sought to legally stop her from using her title of countess. According to the case records, her lawyers argued that her life estate in the peerage was acquired in her husband's dignity, and the name of Countess Cowley was not dependent on the earl's death but would only end upon her marriage to a commoner. Therefore she was legally entitled the use of her name as a peeress.

Lastly, on the subject of sexual identity, LGBTQIA+ people were very present in historical times. Catherine Duleep Singh was a Sikh princess who was both a woman of color in Queen Victoria's court as well as a lesbian who lived with her governess and partner until she died. In modern terms, my heroine would identify as demiromantic (romantic feelings develop after an emotional connection) and pansexual (romantic, emotional, and sexual attraction to a person regardless of gender identity). While I try to be as respectful and as thoughtful as possible in my representation, not only for the BIPOC community but also the LGBTQIA+ community, my own collective identity and experience might not be reflective of others. We live in a beautifully diverse world where everyone's experience is valid, and I hope that many more stories are written to reflect that. Representation matters.

Thank you so much for reading *Any Duke in a Storm* and joining me on Lisbeth and Raphael's happy-*everyone*-after!

xo, Amalie

Acknowledgments

First, thank you to my awesome editor, Deb Werksman, who is always so enthusiastic about my projects. Four books in and I'm so grateful that I was able do this inclusive romance series with you. As a BIPOC writer, seeing myself on the page has been so incredibly meaningful to me. Thank you from the bottom of my heart for giving me the opportunity to do this.

To Thao Le, the absolute Jedi master of all agents, what can I say but you are truly one with the force. You might actually be the force. Thank you for being such a terrific advocate and for helping me grow my career doing what I love. You're always taking me to that next level and I am so here for it!

Big thanks to the production, design, sales, and publicity teams at Sourcebooks Casablanca for everything you do. Extra special thanks to Susie Benton, Jocelyn Travis, Pamela Jaffee, and Katie Stutz! Thank you being so passionate and exceptional at your jobs, and for giving my titles the best chance of success in a very competitive market. I appreciate you more than you know.

To the wonderful women in my life who are with me on this wild publishing adventure, thanks for calling, texting, reading my manuscript drafts, drooling over cover concepts, blurbing my books no matter how many times I ask, putting up with my grumbling, sending me funny TikToks, and generally making me feel appreciated, seen, and valued. I have nothing but love for all of you.

To all the readers, reviewers, influencers, booksellers, librarians, educators, and friends who support me and spread the word about my books, I am so grateful to have you in my corner. I wouldn't be here without you.

And finally, to my incredible family, Cameron, Connor, Noah, and Olivia, I love you all so much. Thanks for loving me back, even when I'm salty.

About the Author

Amalie Howard is a *USA Today* and *Publishers Weekly* bestselling author. *Rules For Heiresses* was an Apple Best Books selection and *The Beast of Beswick* was one of Oprah Daily's 24 Best Historical Romance Novels to Read. Her books have been featured in *The Hollywood Reporter, Entertainment Weekly, Cosmopolitan,* and *Seventeen*. She is also the author of several critically acclaimed, award-winning young adult novels, including her latest YA release, *Queen Bee*. When she's not writing, she can usually be found reading, being the president of her one-woman Harley Davidson motorcycle club, or power-napping. She lives in Colorado with her family.

Website: amaliehoward.com
Facebook: AmalieHowardAuthor
Instagram: @amaliehoward
Twitter: @AmalieHoward
TikTok: @amaliehowardauthor

ALSO BY AMALIE HOWARD

DARING DUKES

The Princess Stakes

Rules for Heiresses

The Duke in Question

THE DUKE IN QUESTION

James Bond meets *Bridgerton* in this steamy enemies-to-lovers historical romance by bestselling author Amalie Howard

Lady Bronwyn Chase will never be the delicate diamond her mother expects her to be. Which is why she's on her brother's passenger liner bound for America with a secret packet of letters that could get her into serious trouble—the kind the sister of a duke shouldn't be in.

Lord Valentine Medford, the Duke of Thornbury and retired agent of the Crown, cannot sit in quietude any longer. As he sniffs out the culprit who has stolen correspondence from the British Home Office, he crosses paths with the charming and off-limits Lady Bronwyn. It isn't long before the duke discovers that the thief who thwarted all his agents and the woman he can't stop thinking about are one and the same…

"[Howard's] prose is delightful, her writing masterful, her characters unforgettable."
—KERRIGAN BYRNE, *USA Today* bestselling author

IN THE EYES OF THE EARL

Kristin Vayden takes you straight to the heart of Regency England

Collin Morgan, Earl of Penderdale, has discovered that someone is committing crimes in his name, leaving him suspended from his work in the war office. Elizabeth Essex, the daughter of a well-respected professor at Cambridge University, longs to be recognized for her own scholarship—unheard of for a gently bred lady.

But with Elizabeth's secret threatened and Morgan's confrontation with his adversaries at a fever pitch, working together could be the only way to get to the truth they hope will set them free.

"Flawless storytelling! Vayden is a new Regency powerhouse."

—Rachel Van Dyken, #1 *New York Times* bestselling author

For more info about Sourcebooks's books and authors, visit: **sourcebooks.com**

LORDS OF THE ARMORY

Escape into the passion and adventure of the Lords of the Armory series from award-winning author Anna Harrington!

An Inconvenient Duke

Marcus Braddock, Duke of Hampton and former general, is back from war and faced with mourning the death of his beloved sister. He's sure Danielle Williams knows something about what happened, and the only option is to keep Danielle close…

An Unexpected Earl

Brandon Pearce, former brigadier and now the Earl West, is determined to help the girl he once loved save her property and the charity she's been struggling to build. But he'll have to deceive her first…

An Extraordinary Lord

Lord Merritt Rivers has dedicated his life to upholding the law, but when he meets a female thief-taker who takes his breath away, he'll have to decide what's worth saving—the life he's always known or the love that made him yearn for more…

"Harrington masterfully marries suspense and romance... Readers will be riveted."
—Publishers Weekly

For more info about Sourcebooks's books and authors, visit:
sourcebooks.com

THE CAPTIVE DUKE

A dazzling, sensuous Regency romance from *New York Times* bestselling author Grace Burrowes

Captured and tortured by the French, Christian Severn, Duke of Mercia, lost his wife, his son, and his will to live. He struggles to find a way back to the world he once knew until Gillian, Countess of Windmere, pointedly reminds him that he has a daughter who still needs him.

As Christian and Gilly spend time together trying to heal Margaret, who was traumatized by her mother's death, their attraction slowly begins to grow. But just as life seems to be getting back to normal, Gilly mysteriously refuses Christian's marriage proposal and Margaret's terrible secret threatens to tear them apart forever…

"Lush storytelling... Smart, compelling, and captivating."
—Kirkus Reviews

For more info about Sourcebooks's books and authors, visit:
sourcebooks.com